MOON DEEDS

STAR CHILDREN SAGA: BOOK ONE

By Palmer Pickering

Published by Mythology Press

MOON DEEDS: BOOK ONE OF THE STAR CHILDREN SAGA

ISBN 978-1-7325688-0-8 (Trade Paperback)

FIC009000	**FICTION** / Fantasy / General
FIC009100	**FICTION** / Fantasy / Action & Adventure
FIC009010	**FICTION** / Fantasy / Contemporary
FIC028000	**FICTION** / Science Fiction / General
FIC028030	**FICTION** / Science Fiction / Space Opera
FIC028010	**FICTION** / Science Fiction / Action & Adventure
FIC028090	**FICTION** / Science Fiction / Alien Contact
FIC028070	**FICTION** / Science Fiction / Apocalyptic & Post-Apocalyptic
FIC028050	**FICTION** / Science Fiction / Military

Cover art and design by J Caleb at jcalebdesign.com
Interior design and layout by Gretchen Dorris at www.inktobook.com

Published by Mythology Press

MYTHOLOGY
→ P R E S S ←

www.mythologypress.com
Follow Palmer at www.palmerpickering.com

10 9 8 7 6 5 4 3

In memory of my father, William Edmund Palmer, who advised me not to wait for perfection, and Jerry Ackerman, the first reader to love this story.

Thank you to my family, friends, editors, and many loyal readers who gave me their time, love, feedback, and support through this long journey. I couldn't have done it without you.

The path to power is cloaked in shadows, so if you avoid all the shadows, you'll never learn anything.

-Eridanus

TABLE OF CONTENTS

PREFACE I

———⟩———

H⊙ME

Planet Turya, Uttapta star system
Twenty-ninth Kalpa of the Tenth Age

Laris stood before Father-Heart-of-Sky, the great crystal globe perched atop a narrow ridge of the Ageless Mountains, as he had throughout the past twenty Fires. He was waiting for the day it would ignite and bring the twin Star Children home. Strains of singing floated across the mountaintop from the priestesses who maintained a constant chorus, calling out across the heavens to guide the Star Children to the pathways of light.

The globe towered at twice his height, its bottomless depths beckoning him. Laris placed his palm on the smooth surface, solid as ever, teasing him with a mystery that was recounted in great detail in the ancient scrolls but defied him in real life. Laris imagined what it would be like to walk into its shimmering depths and travel the pathways of light to another world.

He leaned forward, and his magnified eye peered back at him. It was all he had ever seen in the bottomless sphere: reflections of himself and the surrounding rocks tinged blood-red from the dying light of Uttapta.

PREFACE II

———————— ☽ ————————

THE CEPHEAN
INVASI⊙N ⊙F EARTH

Submitted by Cassidy Dagda

March 8, 2090, Assignment #3

History 201: Recent World History

Professor Cooper, San Jose State University, California

I t all started on January 2, 2038, when a strange-looking craft showed up on the landing field of Rothera Station Spaceport in Antarctica. The members of the landing party were humanoid, not so different from Earthlanders. They had a working knowledge of the Globalish language, and it had taken them some effort to prove they were from another planet—Thunder Walker, which orbits Errai in the Cepheus constellation.

At that time, Antarctica was a neutral zone. Representatives from each country were sent there to meet with the aliens, who turned out to be diplomats and scientists. Several more Cephean craft arrived in Antarctica over the course of two years. Earth delegations were invited to visit Thunder Walker. They came back impressed with the Cephs' advanced technology and orderly society and raved about faster-than-light travel.

The Cephs provided locations of several planets with humanoid populations, the primary three being Delos, Muria, and Iliad. The Cephs claimed that their race originated on Turya, a planet at the center of the galaxy, which orbits a star called Uttapta, the source of all life. However, the Cephs admitted that they were unable to locate Uttapta on any star maps, and no one had ever been to Turya.

A treaty was established in 2040: the Earth Alien Ceph Temporary Agreement for Limited Research and Knowledge Sharing (EACTA). This was followed by an influx of Cephean scientists and engineers who landed at various spaceports across the globe: Baikonur in Russia, Beersheba in the Holy Land, Jiuquan in China. The Cephs shared some of their technology, and soon Earthlanders were launching interstellar missions of their own using Cephean propulsion technology.

EACTA was extended in 2043 and offered thousands of new visas for Cephean scientists and engineers to come to Earth as temporary residents, with each country setting its own quota. Cephs began integrating into Earth communities—starting families and working in the technology, aerospace, and agricultural industries. The birth of children resulting from Earthlander-Ceph unions proved we were the same species, and supported the Cephs' claim that they had been visiting Earth since ancient times and interbreeding. Cephs are a bit taller than Earthlanders and have a heavy bone structure, black hair, and slate-gray eyes that produce sky-blue or emerald-green eyes in their half-breed offspring. Their minds are extremely sharp, testing higher than most Earthlanders on conventional intelligence tests.

In 2045, Djedefptah (Jed) Tegea was born in Athens, Greece. Tegea's father was a Ceph, and his mother was Greek, making him part of the new half-breed generation and a member of the early mixed-race communities that settled in Greece and Turkey.

During the decade of the 2050s, an American named Jared Metolius built a large mercenary army that operated in Eurasia and Africa. Metolius helped orchestrate military coups in several sub-Saharan African nations. His armies in Africa combined to impose military rule over all of sub-Saharan Africa, unifying the nations into a single trading block that could finally compete in the world economy. His other forces allied with Russia in their support for the president of Afghanistan and went on to win much of Eastern Europe for Russia.

In 2061 through 2063, a series of conflicts called the Early Wars erupted in Israel, Lebanon, and Egypt, where populations supportive of Ceph integration fought against those in the world opposed to giving the aliens equal status. The war ended in 2063 after the Jerusalem Massacre, in which hundreds of Cephs and Earthlander-Ceph half-breeds (many of them infants and children) were slaughtered.

Recoiling from the horror of the massacre, Greece offered safe haven for Cephs and full citizenship for half-breeds. Many young half-breed men, including Tegea, joined the Greek military as tensions were rising over Metolius's consolidation of power in Africa and Eurasia.

Tegea soon distinguished himself as a skilled fighter and charismatic leader, and was put in charge of a battalion of half-breeds. In 2066, his battalion successfully defended the government buildings in Athens from an attempted military coup backed by Metolius. In 2068, Tegea staged his own coup, taking control of Athens. Young men, including full-blooded Greeks, supported Tegea. They were downtrodden themselves—jobless, penniless, powerless—and rallied behind Tegea who had risen from less than nothing.

Tegea went on to lead gangs of half-breeds and disenfranchised young men in Turkey in an uprising, and took over the central government in Ankara in 2069. He maintained power in Greece and Turkey by giving administrative control back to the provinces and imposing a draft on all unemployed men aged 18–45 to serve in his army, which gave them jobs and quelled social unrest. The soldiers built dorms for unemployed women aged 18–30 to live in until they were married, and the communities gave the women jobs working in the fields and factories in exchange for housing. Young, unemployed men in Egypt, Syria, Iraq, and Iran flocked to Greece and Turkey to join Tegea's army. Over the next five years he led his swelling forces and toppled the governments of Egypt, Syria, Iraq, and Iran.

Everyone expected Metolius and Tegea to challenge each other and start World War III, but instead, they surprised the world by announcing they were joining forces. In 2077, they formed the Global Alliance, promising to unite the world under one government.

Metolius stepped into the role of President of the Global Alliance, influencing countries to join the Alliance through diplomacy. General Tegea took over Metolius's mercenary armies, combining them with his own forces and branding them the "Tegs." Not long thereafter, Tegea negotiated a weapons deal with the Cephs, the Technology Transfer Alliance Agreement (TTAA).

With the combined forces and the backing of the Cephs, the Tegs were unstoppable and over the next decade waged a multi-pronged campaign for global domination. Through a combination of military might, bribery, diplomacy, and economic treaties, they were quickly able to bring the rest of continental Europe and Asia into the Global Alliance. Oceania and South America followed. The most loyal national leaders earned seats on the Global Alliance Cabinet and were rewarded with development funds and promises of Cephean-designed interstellar spaceports.

Since the inception of the TTAA, Cephean influence has been seen far beyond their technology and weapons. When the Global Alliance gains control of a new region, they transform it into a Cephean-structured economy. Anyone who isn't in the military works the land or labors in factories and lives in gender-segregated work camps. The best goods and foodstuffs are shipped off to the Cephean Federation. It has become obvious that the Cephs are behind the Global Alliance and its Teg army, and are systematically turning Earth into a Cephean colony.

A couple of regions still remain free from Global Alliance control.

The Great Isles of England, Scotland, Wales, and Ireland teased the Global Alliance with several versions of a treaty, and then in 2084 suddenly raised a strange defensive shield, commonly called the Druid's Mist.

The Free States of North America had an isolationist government ever since the Early Wars, and refused to bargain with Metolius. The Tegs attacked Pensacola, Florida on March 8, 2085, with a Cephean bomb that appeared out of nowhere and turned the entire metropolitan area, the barrier islands, and the spaceport into a smoking, ash-filled crater that was consumed by the sea.

The Free States government surrendered one week later, but most states declared independence and fielded state militias, banding together to form Gaia United on July 4, 2085.

The Tegs waged an air and ground offensive against Gaia United, heading westward across the North American continent, defeating militias as they went. Denver put up a stubborn resistance, until the Tegs bombed the city on February 2, 2087.

Soon thereafter, the Shasta Shamans, a small Star Seeker sect in Northern California, erected the Shaman's Shield. This magical barrier protected the Western Free States from Teg aggression from land, sea, and sky, while cutting off all contact with the outside world and stopping all over-the-air communications inside the barrier.

It is not clear how long the people of the Western Free States can survive isolated inside the cloud barrier. But one thing has been proven by the Druid's Mist and Shaman's Shield: magic is an effective defense against the Tegs and their Cephean technology.

PART ONE

———————— ☽ ————————

EARTH

Map of California

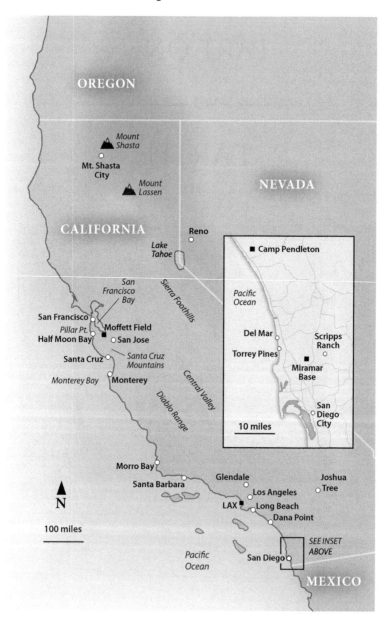

1

─────)─────

STAR S☉NG

West San Jose, California, Western Free States, Planet Earth
July 8, 2090

Cassidy stood in the backyard, staring up at the sky and listening to the music of the stars. The ash clouds of the Shaman's Shield loomed far overhead, enclosing the sky in a luminescent, vaulted ceiling, imbuing everything with an otherworldly glow. Ever since the Shaman's Shield had appeared three years ago, she had not seen the stars nor heard their music. But today the thin, ethereal strains wove through the neighborhood noise. The music was faint, but it was there.

It had been louder when she was a child, before Grandma Leann had shielded her. Cassidy had thought everyone could hear the music, a constant background noise of such poignant sweetness that sometimes it was painful to listen to. But she had realized over time that others did not hear it. Or perhaps they heard it subconsciously, or in their dreams, because sometimes she heard an echo of it when musicians played their instruments or choirs sang. Cassidy had tried to replicate the sound, studying violin as a child, then piano, but neither instrument captured the elusive tones.

The only one who understood was her twin brother, Torr. They had shared a room as children, and she used to sing to him.

"I recognize that song," he had said one time in the middle of the night. She had been sitting up in bed humming the tune that was streaming through her head. Torr had awoken from a deep sleep and sat upright, staring at her. "I heard it in my dream."

"You heard me humming," she corrected him.

"No," Torr said stubbornly. "The golden people were singing to me. Their song said you and I have to find them. We have to follow their voices." Torr closed his eyes and sang the melody more truly than she ever had, picking out parts of the multi-layered harmony she had never captured before. And he added something resembling words that she did not understand, but which made her cry.

In the morning he had remembered the dream, but he could not remember the song. For days afterwards he had tried to get her to sing it back to him, but she could not get the melody quite right, and she did not know the strange language. Then when Grandma Leann laid the blanket of silence over her, the song stopped. As time passed, Cassidy forgot the tune she had always hummed. She could only recall hints of it, like wisps of clouds that slipped away as she tried to grab them.

Now the sky was singing to her again. The melody came to her, carried on the wind as though from a distant mountaintop. She was filled with joy to hear it, though the song was more mournful than she recalled. She still could not understand the words, but she remembered what Torr had told her that night in their attic bedroom, that the two of them had to follow the golden people's voices and find them. She did not know who they were, or where they were, but they were still out there singing to her. Calling to her. Waiting.

2

MİRAMAR

San Diego California, Western Free States, Planet Earth
July 9, 2090

Something was not right with the air. There was a crackling that Torr could only sense when he stopped breathing. An intermittent wave of whispering, skin-tingling static. He lay on the platform inside the shadows of the cement bunker and stared through his rifle scope at the Shaman's Shield. For three years the cloud barrier had stood between the Western Free States and the Tegs. Torr had joined the Gaia United rebels at the southern border two years ago, facing the massive wall every day. It soared up into the sky as if it were a towering marble cliff or a plunging waterfall, five miles high, stretching east to west as far as the eye could see, shimmering like water but solid as stone. The most likely explanation was that it was a cumulonimbus cloud made of ash from the volcanic mountains, held together by an unknown shamanic magic. The scientists called it an electromagnetic force field, of a sort no one had ever seen before. At its peak, the wall curved overhead, sealing them in from above in a thick cloud cover. But today the southern wall had receded from its normal position, exposing flat desert scrubland and skeletal bushes coated in ash. Since dawn, dark, vertical shadows had appeared at the base of the wall, as though some giant creature had attacked it overnight with long, jagged claws.

Torr crawled forward and poked his head out through the open front of the bunker half-buried in the hillside, and peered up at the sky. The cloud barrier overhead still appeared intact; the sky was as gloomy as ever, though it smelled like a storm was brewing. He pulled himself back inside and settled down behind his gun, tightening its bipod and adjusting the sandbag under the butt of the rifle. He inhaled deeply, held in his breath for three seconds, then exhaled and held it out for three seconds, hoping the breathing exercise would stop his cheek from twitching. It hadn't bothered him in months—now his left cheek was spasming non-stop. He could not shoot with it jittering like that.

Inhale, one two three. Exhale, one two three.

He glanced over his right shoulder at Reina, propped up on her elbows on the plywood platform between him and the cement wall. She was staring through her spotting scope. Her TAFT stood on its bipod next to her, loaded and ready to mow down Tegs should they come streaming across the plain. Torr wanted to die before she did; he didn't think he could bear to watch her suffer, or see her dead eyes staring up at him. It was a selfish thing to wish, but he wished it anyway. And then there was Bobby, lying on the platform to his left—two hundred pounds of solid muscle. If he died before Bobby, Torr would lean into him as he died, and Bobby would tell him that everything was going to be all right—even though they both knew it wasn't.

The bunker was a cement box, a single room with a hip-high wall spanning the length of the open front, and one door at the side. Their ten shooting positions—the three-person platform, six benches, and a machine gun—were lined up next to each other against the front rampart, close enough that hot, spent brass would hit their neighbors if they ever ended up engaging the enemy. Torr figured at that point they'd have more to worry about than flying shells.

Five cots lined the back wall, which they used in shifts. Each person had a footlocker stuffed under the cots, overflowing with dirty clothes, books, and toiletries. Duffel bags and towels hung from hooks, and more belongings were stuffed into cubbies set against the side walls. A table and workout area took up the remaining floor space.

Bobby always joked that their bunker was a tomb, and now Torr saw the truth of it. They would die right here along with the rest of their company, dug into the hills of Scripps Ranch. Teg troops would come storming in from the south. His squad would shoot at wave after wave of enemy soldiers until he and each of his nine comrades-in-arms were killed. Torr hoped for a clean bullet to the head.

His left cheek finally grew still. He pressed his right cheek against the stock of his Dashiel, then set his eye to the rifle scope. The distance readout in the upper left field of view changed as he panned across the base of the cloud wall.

"It's pulled back another hundred yards," he said.

"Uh-huh," Reina said at his side. "It's at eleven-thirty-two yards now."

"The wind is crazy," he said.

"I can just barely pick up a mirage," Reina said. Her voice penetrated his earplugs as though she spoke to him through a thin metal pipe.

Torr dialed back his scope and examined the faint heat waves at five hundred yards. They were angling left to right. Five miles per hour. At seven hundred and fifty yards they went right to left, and at a thousand they were bubbling straight up. A few minutes ago he had smelled a sea breeze, then a couple minutes later it was a dry, desert breeze from the east, and now the stink of the bunker and ten sweating bodies overwhelmed his nostrils. A few of the leafless bushes on the newly exposed ground swayed back and forth, while others were completely still. It was going to be a trick to shoot in this.

"Rashon," Torr called across the bunker. "I know you've got your earplugs in." Rashon grumbled and shoved in his ear protection. "I'm gonna take a shot," Torr warned. Smiley and Bates fumbled for theirs. They were supposed to always wear them, but a whole lot of nothing had been going on for so long people had slid into bad habits.

He slowly let out his breath and aimed for a spot dead ahead, angling towards the ground just beyond the visible edge of the Shaman's Shield, and gently pulled back on the trigger. The rifle recoiled sharply against his shoulder with a loud report. The bullet did not skitter and hiss along the face of the wall as it should have, but instead pierced the cottony mass.

"Bates," Torr called to his buddy down the line as he threw back the bolt and the empty shell casing landed with a clink at his elbow. His heart was pounding in his ears. He was aware that he was shouting, but his voice sounded far away. "Go tell Lieutenant James the shield barrier is gone. We should send in some scouts." The lieutenant would yell at Torr for shooting without his command, but Torr didn't care.

Bates looked through his binoculars, and everyone else grabbed theirs. "Glad I'm not a scout," Bates muttered.

They had never sent in scouts before. Normally, nothing but filtered light could penetrate the Shaman's Shield. Torr stared into the ghostly magic, the last place he would willingly step into. Staying in the bunker was not much better. They should run for their lives. Torr sucked in his breath and tried to focus his attention on the air entering and leaving his lungs. *Inhale. Exhale. Inhale. Exhale.* The gun metal was warm in his hands. His pulse throbbed in his fingers. He would pull the trigger between heartbeats.

Bates left their position, and Torr tracked the sound of footsteps running towards Lieutenant James's bunker in the hillock behind them. Torr switched from his scope to his binoculars and scanned the base of the Shaman's Shield. The clouds shivered, and a new expanse of what looked like snow-covered ground became visible through a shroud of floating ashes.

His cheek resumed its twitching. "Damn it," he muttered, focusing on his pulse to quiet the nervous tic. The tic grew stronger, and he shifted his attention to a long, dark shadow. Something had moved. He held his breath to hold the image steady in his lenses. Masses of thick black tentacles crept from a crack in the wall and waved slowly through the air as though seeking prey.

He squeezed his eyes shut to clear the nightmarish image, and when he opened them the tentacles were gone. He stared into the dark fissure. Nothing was there, and his twitch calmed to a throbbing pulse.

His imagination was getting the better of him. It was bad enough that his dreams kept him awake at night, but now they were bleeding over into his waking life. He checked other rifts in the cloud wall. There were no signs of creeping tentacles. He swallowed down an upwelling of panic and concentrated on his breathing and pulse.

One of their Gaia United scout vehicles rumbled by, bouncing over the rough terrain. Torr counted his breaths until the armored jeep disappeared completely into the murky borderland. Another followed behind. Then a third. A hawk keened overhead. Torr got back on his rifle and focused in on the gap where the scouts had disappeared, wondering if they were riding on solid ground headed to face the enemy, or entering an unknown dimension, a gray netherworld they would never emerge from. He stared into the void. There was nothing to shoot at. *Breathe. Relax.*

"Torr, come here." It was Lieutenant James's deep voice.

Torr scrambled to the floor and stepped outside the bunker onto the dirt. "Yes, sir."

"Did I tell you to shoot?"

"No, sir."

The large black man towered a full head over Torr's six-foot stature. He glared down at him, and Torr stood tall, meeting his gaze. Lieutenant James cleared his throat and said, "The shield barrier is gone."

"I know, sir."

"We're going to need your sharp eyes," the lieutenant said sternly.

"Yes, sir."

"Back to your station."

"Yes, sir." Torr saluted and hurried inside, exhaling with relief that the lieutenant wasn't going to discipline him like he had the time Torr had taken his squad target shooting without his permission and used up all their ammunition. That time, Lieutenant James had made him crawl on his elbows and knees around the desert floor in his boxer shorts, looking for shell casings until his skin bled. Then he'd made Torr hand load every single intact shell. Torr had spent all his breaks in the armament shack, with the guys who normally reloaded ammo inspecting his work and being perfectionist pricks about it. It had taken him days.

He had gotten off easy this time, which did not really comfort him much—it just meant the shit was about to hit the fan. He wedged himself between Reina and Bobby, who gave him sidelong glances. Torr's lips quirked up as he adjusted his elbow pads and settled into his prone shooting position behind the Dashiel. His TAFT assault rifle rested at his side. He should switch out his bolt-action Dashiel for the semi-automatic so he could execute the hordes of enemies when they broke through the wall and charged across the valley. But TAFTs did not have the range or precision of the Dashiel. He was the Designated Marksman of the squad. His job was to take out long-range targets. That meant he would shoot first. Focus in on a man's chest. Or head. Pull the trigger and confirm the kill. Watch a man die. A man he killed.

"You okay?" Bobby asked.

"Yeah."

"Your buddies up in Shasta will fix the Shaman's Shield, right?" Bobby asked, trying to mask the desperation in his voice with a raspy chuckle.

Torr did not reply. His squad teased him mercilessly because he had grown up in Shasta, a fact he had let slip one drunken afternoon when a few of them had spent a rare day of leave at Del Mar beach, swimming in the ocean and drinking as much beer as they could haul out to the hot sand. He had made the even greater error of telling them his mother had been a Shasta Shaman when she was younger. They regarded him with awe and suspicion after that. Everyone thought the Shasta Shamans were crazy sorcerers. Dangerous saviors. They liked to ask him if he knew any magic. He didn't, but they never quite believed him. He thought they teased him just so they could keep asking him the same question, hoping that he really did.

Torr thought about how furious the Shaman's Shield must make General Tegea. He could picture the skinny, sour-faced leader of the Teg army pacing back and forth like a raving lunatic, screaming at his generals to do something about those pig-faced mountain wizards. He was probably trying to find magic for himself. But magic wasn't something you could buy or learn by studying books and following schematics. It required a calm mind and a connection to nature and spirit that someone like Tegea could never understand, much less master. Sure, he could hire shamans, but if they had bad intent, as Torr was sure they would, their power would eventually turn back on them. That's how it worked, his mother always said.

"They're gonna fix it, right?" Reina repeated.

He turned to her. She was staring at him with those great big brown eyes. "Yeah, I'm sure they will," he lied. Their hands found each other and he squeezed tight, trying to send her courage. They released their grip and turned back to their guns.

Reina reminded him of Cassidy. He tried not to worry about what would happen to his sister if the Shaman's Shield fell. She would be fine. She and their parents would retreat to Shasta and hide in the mountain caverns. He wanted to get online and contact his family, but Johnson was hogging the only wired connection, playing games on his laptop, as usual.

"Johnson, find out what's going on," Torr said.

"I'm trying. The WestWeb's crazy slow today. I can't even connect to the Gaia United portal."

Cell phones were useless inside the Shaman's Shield, which jammed all electromagnetic frequencies, making it impossible to call anyone over the cell network, or even to text. Torr's phone had died a while ago, and he hadn't bothered to replace it—he had his laptop for games and music. He had used the dead phone one time for target practice, taking a small delight in watching it explode.

He could run five miles to the base's communication center and call home to warn his family from their wired phones, but he was squad leader and couldn't abandon his post. Not now.

"Check the radio," he said to Johnson.

Radios hadn't worked the whole time they'd been here, for the same reason the cell network didn't function, but Johnson still checked occasionally, mostly because he was the Communications Tech and he was supposed to. Johnson put on his headset and started scanning frequencies for a signal. Without the Shaman's Shield, they would have access to the electromagnetic spectrum again, but so would the Tegs. Even worse, without the Shaman's Shield General Tegea would be free to bomb the shit out of them, or unleash some other alien Cephean weapon technology.

Reina got out her cell phone and tried to connect. Torr watched her screen over her shoulder. *No service.*

"Do you hear anything?" Reina asked Johnson.

He shook his head and continued scanning. "Wait. No."

Everyone's eyes turned to him.

"Static. Wait. Voices. No."

"Let me hear." Smiley was the closest and grabbed the headset off Johnson's head, receiving a shove in return.

Johnson unplugged the headset and tossed the wire at Smiley as the tinny speaker of the radio filled the bunker with a high-pitched whine.

Torr sat up. It was more noise than they'd ever gotten before; not the usual soft static of the Shaman's Shield. Johnson continued scanning the frequencies. Short snippets of voices and buzzing static phased in and out. There was nothing intelligible, but signals were reaching the radio. The Shaman's Shield was definitely losing its magic. Torr met Bobby's eyes, and they both turned to stare at the thinning barrier.

———————)———————

Morning turned to afternoon, and Torr watched the distance readout of his scope as the Shaman's Shield steadily receded. It now stood one mile from the bunker, and its half-mile retreat had exposed hills that rose up from the flat valley floor. The cloud wall itself was supposedly a mile thick. Best case, it was still a half-mile thick, or better yet, it was migrating south and would push the enemy back with it. Worst case, it was eroding from each side and would soon vanish completely.

The familiar squeak of a cleaning rod passing through a rifle barrel made Torr turn his head. Smiley was sitting at their make-shift table cleaning his TAFT again.

"You haven't shot that thing since you cleaned it this morning," Torr said.

"Shut the fuck up, Torr."

"That's squad leader to you," Torr said.

"Shut the fuck up, *squad leader,*" Smiley said as he pushed the rod through again.

Torr watched as Smiley pulled the rod back out and replaced the brush with a cleaning patch. "You're gonna use up all the solvent."

"Don't matter none," Smiley said, casting a dark look towards the Shaman's Shield.

Torr scanned the dim bunker. Donald was huddled on a cot in the back, scribbling furiously in his journal. Rashon was grunting as he did a set of pull-ups on the pipe they had stolen from the supply yard and mounted to the cement ceiling. At the far end of the rampart, Jessimar sat on a stool behind his belt-fed machine gun, running his fingers back and forth along the chain of bullets. Bates and Mike were seated at their benches holding their TAFTs, staring sullenly through their scopes towards Teg territory. Johnson was at the table, cursing at his laptop's screen.

The wind picked up, and the Shaman's Shield shook and rumbled as though a thunderstorm was approaching. Torr found himself praying, muttering under his breath, "Golden stars, shine down upon us. Let your golden light wash over us."

Johnson hopped to his feet and began pacing back and forth in the narrow floor space between the shooting benches and the table, fists clenched at his sides. His loud voice cut off Torr's prayer. "I'm gonna shoot those motherfucking Tegs all the way to Algol's hell. Those motherfuckers. I'll motherfucking fuck them all."

Rashon dropped to the floor and pulled his laptop out from under a cot. He sat at the table and disconnected the network cable from Johnson's rig and plugged it into his computer.

"WestWeb's down," Rashon announced.

"No shit, Einstein," Johnson said, and went to the table. He reached over Rashon's shoulder and unplugged and then reinserted the cable. He nudged Rashon aside and tapped loudly at the keyboard.

Torr and Bobby joined them. People took turns plugging the cable into their devices. Torr had been online just last night playing games. He got his laptop, plugged in the cable, and went to his browser. *Page not found.* He went into network settings. It showed that he was not connected.

"Let me check the cable," Johnson said, and ran outside.

Torr and Bobby went back to the shooting platform and got behind their guns.

Johnson returned a few minutes later. "Lieutenant James said the WestWeb's down. He sent somebody to the base to find out what's going on."

"It's the Tegs," Donald said, voicing what everyone was thinking. The bunker fell into a cavernous silence.

A loud sob from Jessimar broke the stillness. "My momma. I ain't said goodbye to my momma."

"Stop that bawling," Johnson snapped.

Another sob shook the big man's shoulders. "I told her I'd be back. I promised."

Torr looked away irritably. Reina lay motionless at his side, staring through her scope. Jessimar's sobbing grew louder.

"Stop it, I said." Johnson's voice was sharp.

Johnson pulled Jessimar from his stool, and they hit the ground with a thud, scrabbling on the cement floor. The pair rolled into the table leg, toppling Smiley's rifle off its stand. Smiley cursed and grabbed the rifle with one hand and the bottle of solvent with the other. Johnson pinned Jessimar with his knees and punched his face as Jessimar's big hands wrapped around Johnson's neck. Mike and Rashon pulled Johnson off, and he turned on them, the three of them falling to the ground in a tangle of arms and legs. Donald and Bates joined in the scuffle.

Torr let them fight. Anything to break the intolerable tension of watching the Shaman's Shield fade away to nothing. Soon the men were cursing and grumbling and stepping away from one another. Jessimar had a bloody nose and shoved a wad of toilet paper up his nostril, but at least he'd stopped crying.

A whistle sounded. Torr and the rest of them jumped; it was not a command whistle from Lieutenant James but an alert signal from a bunker down the line. Torr tensed and peered through his binoculars. A speck was approaching. Several specks. Teg vehicles. They were racing down the newly exposed hills.

"Tegs incoming," Reina shouted, and rattled off coordinates of the enemy vehicles. The bunker erupted in a chaotic flurry as Smiley assembled his gun and the others ran to their positions.

"Recon," Bobby said beside him.

Yes, they appeared to be scouts. Torr counted six Teg vehicles at two-hundred-yard intervals speeding towards the bunkers, trailed by clouds of ash. They had come to assess the Gaia United forces—their weak, strung out, meager forces. Taking footage that was no doubt trying to upload through the fading Shaman's Shield to the waiting satellites above, to download the Gaia United positions to a Teg command center somewhere in the world. To General Tegea himself.

Lieutenant James's whistle rang out. *At your stations. Prepare to attack.*

Torr's heart leapt into his throat. He wiped his sweaty palms on a rag and went back to his gun. A strange calm overtook him. His cheek was still, his hands had stopped shaking, and he realized with detachment that he no longer felt afraid. His muscles were relaxed. He slowed his breathing, pausing for a count of three between each inbreath and outbreath, feeling the heartbeat in his trigger finger. He found the closest vehicle in his scope. It was coming fast. He exhaled slowly. His nervous tension was replaced with cold calculation. The gun felt natural in his hands. He was good at this.

"The closest one is at eleven o'clock," Reina said. "Altitude three hundred feet ... two-ninety ... two-eighty. Fifty miles per hour. Distance fourteen hundred yards. Thirteen-fifty. Thirteen-ten. I can't get a good read on the wind, it keeps shifting."

Torr adjusted his scope to her data as she talked, getting a feel for the vehicle's speed and trajectory. The wind would be a crapshoot, so he left his crosshairs dead center. The Teg vehicle was a low-slung gray thing on wheels, bouncing over the uneven terrain. It had a thin slit for a windshield and a spinning camera globe the size of a soccer ball mounted on its roof. The vehicle's oncoming angle showed Torr a three-quarter view, the blood-red shield insignia of the Tegs visible on its door. It did not look like an assault vehicle. No guns or launchers poked from the windows or roof. The Teg recon unit would report that the Gaia United forces were pathetic—that without the Shaman's Shield their defenses were a joke.

"We have to take them out," Torr said.

Lieutenant James's whistle pierced through Torr's ear-plugs. *Fire.*

"Get 'em, get 'em, get 'em," Johnson yelled, his voice pitched high and sounding far away.

Gunfire went off around him. Curses bounced off the bunker walls between shuddering rounds. Torr dwelt in alert calmness, gauging the distance, speed, and angle of the oncoming vehicle as Reina reported its changing position.

"Eight hundred yards. Updraft. Strong gust," she said.

He dialed back his scope and up one click. The vehicle was on flat land now, and moving faster. "Right front tire, center," he said.

Torr pressed his cheek against the stock, aimed at the wide tire, and hit it. The vehicle did not slow.

"You hit the right edge," Reina said. "Half click right. He's at six hundred yards. No wind."

Torr smoothly cycled the action and adjusted his scope. "Center," he said, and then aimed and hit the tire. The vehicle kept coming.

"Center," Reina said, confirming his hit. "But no damage. The tires are made to be hit."

His squadmates continued firing, splattering the ground, sending up little chunks of dirt. Bullets hit the vehicle like rain on a tin roof, and did as little damage. Gun blasts resounded in the bunker, shaking Torr's bones. A blue line of light from

Bates's laser rifle sliced through the air, leaving a long scorch mark across the vehicle.

"Windshield, dead center," Torr said. He fired at the narrow windshield and hit it easily, but it sustained no damage.

"Spot on," Reina said.

"What the fuck is that thing made of?" Torr grumbled. His heart was pounding in a steady drumbeat.

Reina said, "He's accelerating. Seventy miles per hour. Four-fifty yards. Sea breeze five miles per hour. No. Desert breeze, eight to ten miles per hour. No, wait. Updraft. Damn it."

Torr went to adjust his scope, but the conditions were changing too fast. He had a feel for it. Fuck the scope. He always did better when he aimed with his heart instead of his head anyway. He reached out with his senses and felt the air. The wind was battering the open terrain from all sides. "Going for the camera," he said.

"It's two yards above the roof, dead center," Reina said.

Torr locked onto the target like he'd always done during shooting competitions as a boy, hooking his target as though with a grappling line, connecting to it with a strand of pulsating energy that spanned the space between. His gut senses dwelled in the energy thread, waiting for a lull in the wind, while his point of focus locked onto the camera. He stilled his breathing and pulled gently on the trigger. His blood sped and burned with the bullet. His chest contracted and expanded as the surveillance camera exploded in a starburst of flashing metal and sparks. Torr's body warped and shuddered, then grew still. Hollers of approval echoed from his squad as Torr ejected the spent shell and seated the next round.

"Torr, baby!" Rashon shouted, and fired his own weapon in jubilant bursts. But the vehicle kept coming.

Inhale, one two three. Exhale, one two three. Reina was talking but he didn't understand her words. The bunker shook as the field artillery section fired their weapons nearby. Torr widened the field of view of his scope and watched the scout vehicle barreling towards them. Shells exploded on the ground, leaving large craters that the vehicle swerved around. Suddenly it curved away. The Teg scouts had seen enough. They didn't need their spinning camera. The Gaia United positions were plain to see with the naked eye. The Tegs would escape to report in person what they'd observed. The vehicle sped off, ash billowing behind it.

"Five hundred yards," Reina said as the vehicle accelerated. "Six hundred. Seven."

Torr hit its bumper, reloaded, and shot again, peppering it with bullets, with no effect. It was made of hardened steel, or something more sinister—some Cephean material Torr was unfamiliar with. It started up the hillside, angling to the right.

An artillery round hit its mark and exploded under the fleeing vehicle, tossing the gray metal box into the air and flipping it. The vehicle landed on its roof, wheels spinning, the ground smoking. Torr snapped in a full magazine and got the vehicle in his sights. Rashon yelled out that a second vehicle was disabled, but Torr did not leave his target to look. Reina reported artillery shells exploding around his target vehicle and missing by several yards; automatic fire fanned the air but fell short.

Torr's eye focused on the door of the upside-down vehicle. The door slowly swung open.

"Target at nearside door," Reina said, her voice tight.

"I see it," Torr said.

"Sea breeze, eight miles per hour," Reina said.

A man's head and shoulders emerged from the wreck. Torr kept him in his crosshairs as the Teg wriggled from the vehicle and dropped to his feet. The man's eyes scanned Gaia United's defenses. He did not look afraid.

The Teg's hands came up together, aiming a large black handgun towards their bunker and obscuring his center mass. Torr locked his heart line onto the spot between the man's eyes, and pulled the trigger. The rifle recoiled against his shoulder, and a dark spot appeared on the man's forehead. Torr's forehead twinged, a spike of numbness passing through his brain. The scout fell, and a wave of dizziness took Torr with him. Torr held his breath and disconnected from the man—he was dead.

Torr steadied his breathing and relaxed his hands, ejecting the spent round and reseating the next in one swift motion.

"Man down," Reina said. "Target at the other door, far side." Everyone in the bunker was screaming at him, but Torr was dialed into Reina's voice, which was shaking but firm. "Head in sight," she said.

At the other side of the vehicle a man's eyes peeked over the wreck. The man glanced towards the bunkers, then took off at a run towards Teg territory. Torr's cheek was on the stock, his gaze locked on the enemy, his pulse throbbing in his fingers. The wind had died. Torr expelled his breath, drew a bead on the man's back between the shoulder blades, and in the space of a heartbeat squeezed the trigger. The man jerked and tripped, falling in a motionless heap. Torr's chest muscles seized for a moment, and he stopped breathing.

Torr's buddies shouted in victory.

"Man down," Reina said. "Is he dead?"

"Yes," Torr said, sucking in a mouthful of air as he pulled back on the bolt and pushed the next bullet into the chamber.

"Are you sure?"

Torr was floating in a haze. He blinked and focused on the limp body. It did not move. The man's face was visible, head tilted against the ash-covered ground. Torr found the man's eye and shot again. The head jerked, then was still. Torr felt nothing.

The man's face was young. His skin smooth. Fluid leaked from his eye socket. Torr loaded the next round and pulled the gunsight back to the vehicle as Reina looked for the next target.

Torr remained still and silent while his squad yelled reports of the other five vehicles: three were disabled and two escaped into the remnants of the Shaman's Shield. Two Gaia United jeeps took off in pursuit. Other skirmishes died down in the distance. The squad's chatter faded to muted background noise as Torr kept the upside-down vehicle in his sights. The vehicle felt cold and quiet. The wind kicked up, forming little spinning cyclones, man-sized dust devils that floated across Torr's field of view, disembodied spirits trying to distract him. Minutes passed, and no more scouts emerged.

"I'll watch," Reina said. "You can rest your eyes."

Torr lifted his head, and his hands started shaking. His cheek twitched. And he thought of his sister.

3

SWEET ALYSSUM

Cassidy held her hand to her chest and thought of Torr. Her heart felt strange, like a piece of it had been ripped away. "Mom," she called out. She heard her mother enter the kitchen. Cassidy turned away from the counter to face her. "Something's wrong with Torr."

Brianna looked sharply at Cassidy, then grew very still and closed her eyes as if she was listening. "He's not dead," Brianna said softly.

"No," Cassidy agreed. "But he's hurt. On the inside. Like he's got a broken heart or something. Not like a romantic broken heart, but like ..." She stopped, trying to put the sensation into words. "Like his spirit is torn, or something."

Brianna opened her eyes and gave a long sigh. "Yes," she said, as though it was inevitable. As though a broken spirit was a part of life, something her children would have to face eventually no matter what she did. Brianna joined her at the counter and stared out over the backyard, her face blank.

The normally still roof of clouds flowed and roiled overhead like a rushing river. "What's happening to the Shaman's Shield?" Cassidy asked.

Brianna's wild, curly black hair floated with static electricity, as it did whenever she was upset or excited. Her moss-green eyes gazed darkly at the clouds. "The connection has been broken," she said softly. "The energy is returning to the mountains."

The air left Cassidy's lungs. When she could speak again, she voiced what they both were thinking. "What about Torr?"

Brianna said nothing and looked down at the sink. Cassidy watched as her mother's hands sank into the hot, soapy water and began scouring a pot.

Cassidy left her mother and went to her bedroom, and logged onto her laptop to try and contact Torr. She opened her messaging app to see if Torr was online, which he rarely was—but it was worth a try. *Oops. Something went wrong! Try again later.* She tried again, then opened her email. *Page not found.* Same thing with video chat. She unplugged the cable and plugged it back in. It still didn't work.

She went back into the kitchen to look for her mother. "The WestWeb's down," Cassidy said.

Brianna looked up from the sink. Her eyes were penetrating. "The Tegs have broken through the Shaman's Shield." She turned back to the suds and stared out the window.

Cassidy stepped outside, her heart tripping frantically. It was happening. The Tegs were coming. She needed to reach Torr. Were they fighting the Tegs? Who was winning? Was Torr injured? She walked on trembling legs across the yard, weaving between the lush garden beds to the center, where a cement birdbath topped a pedestal. She gazed down into the still water, longing for an image of Torr to appear. But try as she might, none came. Despair overwhelmed her. Her grandmother had tried to teach her how to use water to see things, but all Cassidy ever saw were shadows and reflections.

She would beg her mother to look later, but most likely

Brianna would refuse. Except for working with her precious herbs, her mother shunned the old powers. She said they were dangerous. Easy to fall prey to, easy to get lost in their magic. She even regarded the Shaman's Shield with fear, even though it had protected them from the Tegs for so long. Still, Cassidy would ask her to look into the water to search for Torr.

Cassidy gazed impotently into the birdbath and cursed herself for being so useless. She breathed deeply, trying to cultivate the inner calm Grandma Leann had told her water scrying required. It could be water, could be a mirror. Crystal balls were best. Cassidy even had a small one, a gift from Great-Aunt Sophie, but it never revealed anything.

She blamed her grandmother for her blindness. Grandma Leann was dead now, but Cassidy remained bound by the shield her grandmother had placed on her that blocked her ability to see things from afar. Grandma Leann hadn't known how to remove it, even though she'd placed it there herself. Sometimes Cassidy thought Grandma Leann had been lying about that—that she did know how to remove it and could restore Cassidy's second sight, but had chosen not to. Now that her grandmother was dead, Cassidy was afraid she would be cut off from her vision forever.

At first the shield had been an enormous relief. It had felt like a giant, cool, dark blanket smothering a thundering, blinding inferno. She recalled clearly the night it had happened. It had been the winter before they'd moved from Shasta, when she and Torr were six. Cassidy had been sitting up in bed in their little garret bedroom, crying with loud, shaking sobs.

"What is it, darling?" her grandmother asked, turning on the light and rushing into the room. She sat on the bed and pulled Cassidy into her arms.

Cassidy talked through streaming tears as she buried her face in her grandmother's warm bosom. "Jasper's mother and father are screaming at each other again," she sobbed. "And Jasper is curled up in a ball under his blanket. He wants to come here. Can we go get him?"

"No, honey. Not now. It's the middle of the night."

"And, and," she sobbed, her world expanding, the pain increasing. "Men in gray jackets, in somebody's house, hitting the man with a stick, he's bleeding, the woman is crying and the bad men are dragging her into a room, and ..."

"Shhh," Grandma Leann said. "Quiet now, quiet. Everything will be fine."

The horrific images swirled and fought for her attention. The men tearing clothing off the shrieking woman. Uniformed men storming the street, dragging people from their homes, fires blazing in the distance, screeches and booms as blue and white fireballs exploded, blinding her. She was screaming, and her grandmother shook her by the shoulders and forced her to look into her eyes.

"BE STILL!" her grandmother commanded. And suddenly the blazing, screaming images stopped. A soft darkness settled over her mind's eye, muting everything to dull grays and muffled sounds, distant yells heard vaguely as though from underwater, shushed away by gentle, lapping waves.

She stopped crying abruptly and stared into her grandmother's eyes. The small room came sharply into focus. The small wooden dresser was piled high with teddy bears. The rug with a rocking horse design that Grandma Leann had hooked herself filled the small space between Cassidy's and Torr's single beds. Yellow gingham curtains that she had found so ugly seemed suddenly familiar and comforting.

Grandma Leann's lined face gazed at her with a mixture of concern and hope. "How do you feel now?" her grandmother asked gently, hesitantly, her arthritic hand smoothing Cassidy's mussed hair.

"Fine," she said.

And she had felt fine. And her life had gone on. Though ever since that night it felt like a piece of herself was missing. As though a world continued on, without her, behind a black curtain. As though someone very close to her had suddenly disappeared from her life. Someone she could not quite remember. She could recall the feelings she'd had when they had been together. She'd felt nourished. Alive. Filled with fire. But it was only a vague memory hovering at the edge of her consciousness. A fleeting shadow. A forgotten dream.

Cassidy's face stared up at her from the birdbath. She gave up and turned her gaze to the sky where the tattered clouds of the Shaman's Shield rushed by. Faint music teased her from beyond the cloud layer. She closed her eyes and listened.

———————————)———————————

Cassidy and her mother drifted around the house. They didn't look at one another or speak, as if ignoring the obvious would make it go away. The only breaks in the silence were when clients came for healing appointments with Brianna, who was an herbalist or, more precisely, a plant medicine woman. The clients' first anxious words were, "What's wrong with the Shaman's Shield?"

Brianna would smile comfortingly and lead them into her consultation room. Cassidy would slink away, ignoring her mother's gestures for her to join the session, where she wanted Cassidy to do the diagnosis and prescription as part of her training. Cassidy was particularly good at diagnosis because she could feel the pain in another person's body as if it were her own. Part of her mother's training efforts focused on teaching Cassidy how to manage this questionable gift, but Cassidy wasn't always very good at maintaining her boundaries, particularly with severe cases.

Brianna's herbal medicine had saved the lives of several people. When their family moved to the Bay Area, people at school had taunted Cassidy and Torr for having a witch mother from Shasta. But when someone was sick and modern medicine didn't cure them, they would show up at the Dagdas' door begging for Brianna's help. Her success rate was frighteningly high. Even the doctors knew of her, sending patients to her when they didn't know what else to do. When the war had made manufactured drugs harder to get and increasingly expensive, a steady stream of clients started coming to their home. Now since the Shaman's Shield had started acting so strangely, some clients with appointments were simply not showing up, while other people appeared at the door unexpectedly, in a rush to address some ailment before leaving home forever.

Cassidy heard a knock at the door and let in one such person. It was a neighbor who looked worried and in a hurry. Cassidy led him to Brianna's consultation room, then slipped away to the kitchen where she stared out the back window at the turbulent sky, fighting a deepening sense of unease.

She looked up as her father, Caden, let himself in through the side door from the garage, worn and tired and grumbling about traffic. He had left early that morning to deliver a load of produce to a convoy headed south towards the troops at the border. She followed him back out to the garage and watched as he arranged the supplies he'd gathered in case they had to leave quickly for Shasta. He avoided her eyes and sorted silently through the contents of several plastic crates. Her mother's old hovercraft sat like a relic from the past, dusty and abandoned since the Shaman's Shield had made the sensor-controlled craft non-functional.

"If the Shaman's Shield goes away, do you think Mom's hovercraft will work?" she asked.

Caden shrugged. "It can't hold all our stuff. Besides, the Tegs could track it."

Cassidy's heart was heavy. She left him and stepped out into the backyard, picking her way carefully between the vegetable rows and herb beds.

She stopped to look into the birdbath, but no visions broke the reflection of the stormy sky. She closed her eyes and listened for the star music. It was out there, weaving a faint, melancholy melody through her head. She let the distant sound fade from her awareness and looked around the yard where she had spent so many years. A yard she was afraid they would end up abandoning to the Tegs. The thought made her chest cave in. She took a deep breath and tried to feel her feet connected to the ground, willing her anxiety to drain into the solid earth.

The yard was a large, triangular-shaped plot that widened out to the back fence. In the center of the yard surrounding the birdbath were rows of sprawling plants heavy with tomatoes, cucumbers, and summer squash. A half-dozen small fruit trees lined the northern boundary. The northwest and southwest corners had small groves of tall redwoods and eucalyptus trees, one of which held a treehouse that Torr and their friend Jasper had built, hidden in its thick foliage.

Every other spare patch of earth was filled with medicinal herbs: clumps of flowers, trailing vines, plump bushes. Until the war had systematically shrunk their world, her mother had collected seeds and starts on herb-gathering trips across the globe. While some plants were not happy outside their native wilderness, Brianna had a talent for cultivating even the most temperamental plants.

Cassidy thought guiltily that she should be practicing her herbal studies, but she was too agitated. She would never be able to concentrate with the Shaman's Shield raging overhead like the American River during spring thaw, and with the sense of Torr's discomfort aching like a phantom limb. Instead, she lifted the broad, dark leaves of the squash plants and looked for zucchini hiding under them, trying to grow as fast as they could before being detected.

She found one the size of her forearm and pulled at it. It clung stubbornly to the stalk, then finally gave way to her insistent tugs. "You can't stay there forever," she said gently. "You'll get too big and tough. All you'll be good for is soup or bread." She rubbed at the green skin, wiping dirt from its fuzzy coat, then set it on the picnic table with a dozen of its cousins.

She uncoiled the hose and sent arcs of water over the garden beds. The parched earth soaked it up. The scent of mint and lavender filled the air as the water pattered on the leaves and flowers. Bees and butterflies buzzed and fluttered, dancing through the sudden mist.

Cassidy had spent most of the past few weeks out in this garden. She had taken the summer off from her history studies at the university to serve an apprenticeship under her mother. She had shown an early talent for understanding plants as though they were speaking to her, able to sense when a plant was good medicine and when it was bad.

She remembered one herb-gathering trip when she was eight.

Her mother had pointed to a field. "There are two kinds of plants out there. One soothes arthritis when pressed to the skin. The other is poisonous and will make you very ill if you eat it. Go fetch one of each for me."

Cassidy had gone out into the field and run her hands over the various plants. A tall bush with yellow flowers enveloped her hand in a soothing warmth. She felt, rather than heard, a gentle trilling sound that reminded her of a flute. That was the arthritis plant.

"Can I please take one of your flowers?" she asked the plant.

One of the blooms waved at her, the delicate stalk leaning towards Cassidy's hand as she went to pluck it. She did not tug very hard, but the entire plant pulled up from the ground, roots and all.

"Oh, I guess I need the roots. Thank you," she said to the plant. She shook the dirt off and tucked the plant in her bag.

When she went near another plant with dark green leaves and a cone of purple flowers, her hand jerked back. It was as though the plant were screeching at her to go away and at the same time luring her hand to touch it. When she brought her hand close, her skin prickled with sharp pain. She called her mother over.

"This is the bad one, but I don't want to touch it."

"Very good," her mother said. "It will give your skin a rash if you touch it and causes seizures if eaten. Very, very good." Her mother smiled her warm, beautiful smile, and gave Cassidy a hug.

Cassidy returned to the present and looked warily overhead. The sky rumbled angrily as dark clouds raced by. Goosebumps rose along her arms, and she returned her attention to the plants. Powerful allies, her mother called them. Cassidy supposed plant spirit medicine was a sort of shamanism. She wished she knew how to control the elements, like the real shamans up north at Mount Shasta. She would help hold the Shaman's Shield in place if she knew how. Cassidy wished her grandmother had never shielded her powers, that her mother had never left the shamans, and that they had never moved away from Shasta.

The familiar frustration surfaced again, making her angry at her dead grandmother, who had left her struggling to reach the vast field of awareness that used to be at her fingertips. All that was left to her was plants. What good would talking to plants do if she was captured by Tegs? Could plants help set her free? Could they help Torr? Maybe they could. They were the only tools she had, aside from praying to the stars.

She sighed and put the hose away, wondering if she would be able to focus on her homework. She needed to record the powers of every plant in her mother's herb garden. She had already transcribed their medicinal properties and made sketches of their roots, stems, leaves, flowers, fruits, and seeds. Now she was in the process of recording their spiritual, magical qualities.

She looked at the herb beds to see if any would signal to her, if any were strong enough to distract her from the pervading sense of doom that seemed to make even the plants droop. She slowly scanned the garden until dense bushes of tiny white Sweet Alyssum swayed in the stiff breeze, drawing her attention. When she relaxed and blurred her vision, the flowers appeared almost as if the ghost of a woman was kneeling and waving a scarf at her. But when Cassidy looked directly, they were simply clusters of blossoms rocking back and forth in the gusting wind. A shiver ran up the back of her neck. She fetched her canvas bag from the picnic table, then sat on a flagstone beside the clumps of white flowers and took her supplies from the bag. Placing her black notebook in her lap, she dipped the nib of her pen into the jar of Black Guya ink.

She closed her eyes for a moment and concentrated on her breathing and the beating of her heart. She waited for her mind to grow calm, dismissing her nagging worries as they tried to grab her attention like the reaching arms of blackberry brambles.

With a long, deep breath, Cassidy opened her eyes and focused on the Sweet Alyssum. Its delicate fragrance wafted through the air. A pair of small gray and yellow birds circled each other and landed on a bare patch of earth between clusters of blooms and began pecking at the dirt.

Cassidy ignored the birds and placed the pen tip onto a blank notebook page, emptied her mind, and reached with her senses towards the flowers. Holding the flowers in her awareness, she then reached out with her mind across the oceans to the Black Guya, the great father tree, which medicine men tapped for its magic ink. She conjured the image her mother had described of the massive trunk and powerful limbs, its bark slashed in many places to make it bleed the sap that would be made into ink. Cassidy held the Sweet Alyssum and the Black Guya tree in her consciousness together, connecting them to bring forth the magic needed to write down the plant spirit's message.

Cassidy drew back with a start, nearly breaking her concentration. The distinct form of an old woman squatted among the Sweet Alyssum. Cassidy kept her eyes blurred, not wanting to lose the vision. Yes, it was definitely a woman. Small and slight, with paper-thin brown skin hanging from bony arms.

The old woman wove sinew and bone together, her hands working like a spider building a web. White hair was pulled back tightly in a bun, stretching wrinkled skin away from her closed eyes. Layers of white gossamer draped her frail form in a flowing robe. A white scarf across her shoulders caught the wind and floated up around her bowed head, and a long, yellowed tooth hung from a leather cord around her neck. Her gnarled fingers flew—weaving, weaving.

The woman could only be the spirit of the plant, Sweet Alyssum. Cassidy's heart beat with excitement. Her mother had always said the plants contained spirits, but Cassidy had never taken her words literally. She'd thought the feelings plants aroused in her were what her mother had meant—intuitions that surfaced as a sort of knowing, forming almost words. Words that she could place on paper with the Black Guya ink, to read after she emerged from her trance. Her mother had insisted it was more than that, that the plants really were spirits who could become embodied to communicate with a true plant spirit medicine shaman. Cassidy had never drawn one out and seen for herself, so she'd doubted her mother's words. Now she gazed at the bone-spinning woman, enthralled. Her mother had been speaking the truth.

Cassidy held her breath as she sensed another figure standing at the edge of her vision. She slowly turned her head. The shadow took the form of a towering tree with a thick gray trunk, scarred with many rows of chevrons. Shivers ran up her spine and her hands shook, but she sat still. It must be the Black Guya tree. The tree shrank and morphed into a muscled warrior whose thick arms folded over a wide, bare chest, his dark skin scored and scarred from many bleedings. Sacrificing himself over and over so that others might gain knowledge. The old woman and the warrior looked at one another, then turned to Cassidy.

As the eyes of the Black Guya warrior bored into her, the pen moved in Cassidy's hand, laying its blood on the paper. The crone's crooked fingers pulled and twisted, tying knots to form a circular pattern from strands of sinew. Cassidy breathed deeply and the garden disappeared. Blackness filled her vision as she floated in the bottomless eyes of the Black Guya warrior, revealing a universe speckled with stars that glinted like eyes watching from ageless eternities. The stars were waiting for something. For some*one*.

An infinite length of translucent sinew pierced through Cassidy's belly from back to front, a filament of light that connected her to the heavens above and the heavens below, stretching back from the beginning of time to a future that awaited her.

Cassidy peered along the strand from her belly, trying to see where it led. It led to the moon and the stars. Bright pinpoints of light sang to her from the heavens. Behind her, pierced by the same strand that stretched from Cassidy's back, her mother floated and gazed at her with a love of such burning intensity it surprised her. Behind her mother, strung on the same strand, was Grandma Leann, dead these many years. Behind Grandma Leann was Great-Grandmother Corann, regarding Cassidy with the same look of love. The line of women stretched back like a golden thread strung with pearls, one after another. Tens. Hundreds. Thousands. A golden face glowed far off in the distance, like a gold bead holding all the others in place. Cassidy felt them all watching her. Pulling on her. Pushing. Hoping. Helping. Loving.

Cassidy floated, floated, and the birds in the garden fluttered around her head. And then the old crone Sweet Alyssum stood before her, snipping the sinew with yellowed teeth, showing Cassidy the circular web. Cassidy drew back in disgust as she realized it was decorated with the bones and small feathers of the gray and yellow birds, their remains hanging from fresh sinew still red with blood.

Suddenly the old woman was gone. Sweet Alyssum blossoms swayed in the wind. The patch of dirt was bare; there were no signs of the little birds. The shadow where the Black Guya had stood was bathed in light. The pen dropped from Cassidy's trembling hand.

She tried to imprint the faces of her forebears into her mind, but the images morphed and blended into the familiar visages of her mother and grandmother. She felt the thread of ancestral spirits pull into her belly as yarn coils onto itself to form a soft, solid ball.

Cassidy rubbed at her forehead, staving off dizziness, and peered down at the notebook. Her scrawled handwriting faded in and out, shifting forms and letters. First she deciphered the word *moon*. Then *spirit ... life ...* then the whole message:

Sweet Alyssum – Take two drops and the eye of the moon will awaken within you. Seek its wisdom, for it illumines the path of spirit. See through the eyes of your blood-kin as the threads of life weave your destiny.

The Black Guya ink finally resolved into flowing script that looked like a foreign language and was illegible to Cassidy. The ink was dry and the magic was set; the text would not make itself legible again until someone needed its medicine. The overwhelming intensity of the vision slowly lifted, and she was filled with excitement. She had drawn forth two plant spirits and recorded the Sweet Alyssum's medicine onto paper. Her mother would be proud.

The excitement quickly turned to unease. There was a stirring in the air she did not like. It felt like a swarm of bees buzzing just beyond the range of hearing. Her heart pounded in her chest, and prickles of dread crept up the back of her neck. The Shaman's Shield pulsed as though it was a living beast. The stars sang their mournful song.

She stoppered the ink well and placed it with the pen and notebook into the bag, then hopped to her feet. The warrior spirit of the Black Guya lingered like a subtle, musky scent, and the perfume of Sweet Alyssum floated to her on a gust of warm air. At her feet in the tangle of white blossoms rested a small dreamcatcher, no bigger than her palm. Cassidy froze as she stared at it. It was woven like a spider's web of translucent sinew within a hoop made of a thin, bent apple branch. Hanging from the bottom were strands of sinew strung with tiny bones and small gray and yellow feathers. A single, tiny gray bird with a bright yellow chest perched on a branch of the apple tree and sang down at her, then fluttered away.

Cassidy bent and pulled the dreamcatcher from the clutch of blossoms and cupped it in her palm. It was light and delicate—the feathers were little puffs of color, and the weaving was intricate. With her pocket knife she harvested several clumps of the Sweet Alyssum, then walked directly to the kitchen where she set the dreamcatcher and her bag on the counter. Brianna was at the kitchen table, talking quietly with Caden.

"Mom," she said, excitement and awe mingling in her heart. "I saw the spirit of Sweet Alyssum, and of the Black Guya warrior."

Her mother stopped talking mid-sentence and turned to stare at Cassidy. A flash of pride lit her face, followed by a smile. "Really? Both?"

Cassidy nodded happily.

"That is something," Brianna said. "The Black Guya rarely reveals himself. I myself have only seen him twice."

Cassidy beamed with pride. She had finally done it. She was finally a true plant spirit medicine woman. "What does it mean when he shows himself?"

Brianna turned thoughtful. "My teacher said it means there is an urgency behind the medicine. The Black Guya warrior appears to support the plant spirit whose essence will be needed. It means there is some profound purpose behind the prescription. You did record the prescription, didn't you?" she asked, her eyes suddenly anxious.

"Yes, I did. And I found this in the flower bed. Did you make it?" She held up the dreamcatcher.

Brianna eyed it. "No."

"I think the Sweet Alyssum plant spirit made it for me," Cassidy said quietly.

Brianna's eyes searched Cassidy's.

"Is that normal?" Cassidy asked.

Brianna's green eyes danced with flames. "Not unheard of. But not exactly normal." She exchanged a long glance with her husband.

Cassidy walked past her parents into her mother's workshop off the kitchen and hung the flowers from a line they used for drying herbs. Shelves were filled with dozens of dark brown glass bottles—distilled herbs she and her mother had made for their plant medicine. She looked through them and found several bottles with "Sweet Alyssum" written on the white labels in her mother's neat script.

"Mom," she said, stepping out of the workshop, holding up a bottle. "Is this from the Sweet Alyssum in the backyard? Is it the same plant?"

Brianna looked up and nodded. "Yes. They reseed themselves every year."

Cassidy placed two drops of the extract onto her tongue and swallowed. It was sweet and bitter at the same time. She shivered and placed the dreamcatcher into her bag, careful not to crush the feathers. The pungent taste of the Sweet Alyssum lingered on her tongue, and a wave of sadness washed over her. She saw an image of a dead man sprawled on a field of ash. She closed her eyes and blood rushed through her veins, sweeping away the unbidden image. The dead man was not Torr. At least it was not Torr.

4

DEATH WALKİNG

"Stop tormenting yourself," Reina told Torr softly. She was lying at his side on the shooting platform. She leaned her shoulder against his, knocking his focus away from the man he'd shot between the eyes.

"I'm not," he muttered, and found the waxen face again. He zoomed in on the man's eyes, which were open and staring at the sky.

A whole day had passed since Torr had killed the two Teg scouts. He had not slept except for dozing off a couple times with his cheek against the rifle stock. A sharp elbow from Bobby had pulled him out of gray nightmares crawling with dead men and monsters. Torr was continually drawn to the corpses sprawled in the field, consumed by a combination of morbid fascination and guilt; the same way he stared at roadkill, drawn and repulsed at the same time, wanting to see death. Maybe he was hoping the Tegs weren't really dead. That he hadn't actually killed a man—*two* men. Maybe they would stand up and limp away, and Torr would let them go.

Torr moved his scope to the second corpse, the one with the missing eye. Someone's son. Husband. Father? No, he was too young for that. He was a kid, like Torr. *He could be a father.* Torr pushed the thought from his mind and shifted his focus back to the man in front. He was older. He wore the sneer that had twisted his face as he'd lifted the black handgun.

Torr wanted that gun. It lay by the man's side. Torr thought it must be a Lectro, a Cephean weapon that shot little clamps they called snake jaws. They could dig in anywhere in the body, and when they met a nerve the victim was dead. Torr wondered what the range of a Lectro was. It must be far since the man had been aiming at them. He was tempted to go retrieve it, but they had been ordered to stay at their posts.

He moved his eye away from the scope and peered out over the landscape. The Shaman's Shield was in shreds, letting through shafts of sunlight that descended like pillars of light from the Star Seeker legends, ready to deliver the Star People who would bring peace on Earth. He tried to imagine golden beings floating down on outstretched wings, but all he saw were empty columns of light that pierced the sky like shining blades.

The flat scrubland below was completely exposed now, and the hills beyond rose in ridges, brown and gray, fading to smoky blue in the distance. Square buildings and white water towers crested the tops. Charcoal-gray swarms of Tegs covered the hill-sides like scars from a wildfire. Some were as close as a mile and a half away. They must have been sitting just beyond the exterior border of the Shaman's Shield this entire time.

There were foot soldiers organized in large companies of several hundred each. Legions of armored vehicles caught the sun, their narrow windshields flashing like eyes. Torr got back on his scope and found a cluster of troops, zooming in on faces. They were mostly young men, wearing the gray uniforms of the Tegs, many of them sitting on the ground with rifles at their sides. Talking. Laughing. Bored. Sipping from canteens. Gazing towards Gaia United territory.

"Torr. Look," Bobby said, pointing to the sky.

He switched to his binoculars and studied a formation of six strange aircraft heading northeast.

"I bet they're those Cephean craft," Bobby said. "Mantas."

Torr had heard the name but had never seen one. They were small craft, with wide, curved wings that undulated, like stingrays swimming through the ocean. He tried to figure out if they were mechanical or biological. They were unlike anything he'd ever seen.

Formations of large Teg craft had been flying overhead every hour or so, making Torr and his squadmates cower in the shadow of the bunker, but no bombs were dropped. They simply droned by and continued north.

A low, distant boom sent a tremor through the air, and his squadmates plastered their hands over their ears. The first sound of a spacecraft taking off from LAX had startled them during the night. If Torr had harbored any hope that the Shaman's Shield still provided protection, the fact that spacecraft could now launch dismissed that notion for good.

The distinctive sound was something Torr had grown up with, living ten miles from Moffett Field Spaceport. It was not a boom, really. It was more as though the atmosphere sucked in and sucked out, reminding Torr of the popping feeling of pulling his fingers out of his ears, only over his entire body. It only lasted a second, and Torr had grown accustomed to it, but it made a couple of his squadmates who had never lived near a spaceport uncomfortable.

Torr wondered if the launches were Gaia United craft heading to the moon colony and then on to other friendly planets, seeking aid. Or maybe the Global Alliance had taken over LAX already and opened traffic to the Cephean Federation.

Torr wished he and Cassidy had found a way to join Jasper on the moon, where they would be far removed from this whole crazy mess. Jasper's father, Kai, had sent him there—why hadn't their father done the same for them? The twins had even more reason to be on the moon than Jasper and Kai did—they had lunar land deeds passed down to them from Great-Aunt Sophie. His parents had expressed no interest in settling the land themselves, but that was no reason to keep Torr and Cassidy from their inheritance.

Developing lunar land was a huge undertaking. Still, Torr and Cassidy owned land there, and the moon was still free. Frustration and regret ate away at him as he scanned the feathery remnants of the Shaman's Shield. Taking possession of their land had seemed like an impossible dream when Torr and Cassidy were younger, but other people had figured out how to do it, so why hadn't they? They should be there right now. The stupidity of having left his moon deed to rot in a drawer made him want to drill bullets into the fading mist.

But it was too late. Everything was too late. He would die before he ever saw his land. Before he even discovered why he'd come into this world. Anger dissolved into hopeless despair, and he wished he were a small boy who could cry. Instead, all he could do was stare bleakly at the Teg army.

As terrifying as it was to see Teg troops amassed not two miles from Gaia United's front lines, it was the round, glinting eyes on the horizon that made Torr's blood chill. They could only be the silver eyes of Cephean Cyclops. He zoomed in on one. It looked like a tank, with a huge silver antenna dish mounted on the top, or rather, some sort of laser. They had large treads, but were able to fly. He'd seen footage of a fleet of flying Cyclops raze neighborhoods in China, leveling buildings and leaving behind fields of rubble. Another rank of Cyclops had followed, the invisible stare of the relentless machines churning up the ground until it turned to boiling mud. All that had remained after the Cyclops moved on were stretches of fine gray dirt that showed no sign of ever having been inhabited.

He wondered if the Cyclops had already turned San Diego City into dust. The Tegs would have evacuated the city and then methodically, "peacefully," transformed the land into a more "efficient configuration." The Cephean way.

The day stretched on. The WestWeb was still down, and Torr determined it was never coming back. The radio frequencies were jammed. None of the Scripps Ranch jeeps had returned, but no one talked about them. Their buddies were either dead or prisoners of war by now, a fate they might all share soon. Torr wanted to fight, meet the enemy head on. He would rather die fighting than sit in this rat trap. But their orders were to stand ready. It had been twenty-four hours of "standing ready," and nervous exhaustion wore at Torr.

"I need to sleep," he said to Reina. He put his hand over her forearm. "Wake me if anything changes."

She met his eyes with a tired smile, then rested her cheek against the stock of her TAFT, staring through her rifle scope towards the sea of Tegs. Torr went to the back of the dim bunker, unrolled his blankets on the cot in the corner, and let himself fall into the soft clutches of sleep.

—————————)—————————

Torr wandered in a dark dream and found the field of ash. He bent over the body, the dark hole in the forehead looking up at him like a third eye. The man lifted his hand and wiped at the blood crusted on one side of his face, then sat up, shaking his head as though bleary from sleep.

"Ow," he said to Torr, then gave him a little smirk. "Good shot. Couldn't have done better myself." The Teg lifted his hand and Torr pulled him to his feet. The back of the man's head had a larger, gaping hole clotted with dark red blood and pink pulp. Dried blood matted his hair. He didn't seem to notice. "Where's my buddy?"

Torr nodded to the body on the other side of the upturned vehicle. They stepped around the metal hulk, and Torr bent to the ground and shook the young Teg's shoulder. A bullet wound showed itself as a bloody stain between the shoulder blades. The back of his head had a clean exit wound, but his hair was bloody and matted like his buddy's. Torr pulled the body over, noting the hole in his chest and the gory mess where his eye used to be. The corpse opened his one eye and moaned, then raised himself onto an elbow and climbed painfully to his feet. "You didn't have to take out my eye," he said crossly, looking at Torr with the remaining one. "I was already dead."

"I wasn't sure," Torr said apologetically, and strode alongside the men as they walked together towards the Teg encampment. "Sorry."

The young Teg shrugged. "I would have done the same. You're pretty good with that thing." He nodded at the Dashiel hanging from Torr's shoulder.

Torr pursed his lips. "I was always a good shot. Now see what it brought me. I'm a killer."

The older Teg laughed wryly. "We're all killers. Don't worry about it. You were doing your job, you son of a bitch." He slapped Torr on the back. "We had it coming."

Torr breathed in the fresh air. There was a sea breeze blowing the ash and gloom away. He felt good. Alive. "What now?" Torr asked the men.

"You'll become a Teg," the older man said.

Torr stopped walking, and the Tegs halted, looking at him. "No, I won't."

"Sure you will. All Gaia United soldiers join the Tegs. The smart ones, that is." The Teg raised his eyebrows at Torr. "Why are you looking at me like that? Your other option is to become a slave. Is that what you want?" The man's eyes bulged with insistence.

Torr tried to dismiss the man's words, but his gaze became twisted in the other man's glare. "I don't want to be a Teg."

The older man laughed again, his red mouth gaping wide. His fat tongue was coated in white. "We're not so bad. If you can make it through the winnowing process, that is."

Torr was afraid to ask. He broke their gaze, and his eyes fell to the Tegs' red shield insignia on the man's left chest pocket. Sewn onto the right pocket was a name patch: EDGEMONT.

"All Tegs need to be killers," Edgemont went on. "The only way to make sure is to kill. Want to see?"

Torr shook his head but was unable to speak. They were suddenly standing in a flat field beyond the ranks of armored vehicles. A huge hole had been dug in the ground, and throngs of men lined the outside of the pit, taunting and jeering. The men Torr had killed elbowed their way through the crowd to get a better look. Torr did not want to follow, but found himself standing at the edge of the head-high fighting pit where two men circled each other, tight fists held up to their bare chests. Their muscled torsos were dirty and sweaty and glistened in the sun, their pants and boots muddy. The side of one man's face was swollen and bruised red, and his eye was a thin slit. The men were panting and dragging their feet, warily eyeing each other.

Edgemont gestured to the fight. "The recruits are pitted against each other. It might take a few face-offs, but eventually everyone either kills their opponent, or dies themselves. That's how we separate the killers from the others. It's quite efficient."

Torr swallowed and knotted his hands at his sides. "I'm already a killer," he said bitterly.

"Not a cold-blooded one. You killed an enemy on the battlefield in self-defense. That doesn't count." Edgemont smiled brightly. Torr felt dizzy. He did not like this man at all. "You see," Edgemont continued, "killing a brother is the only way to ensure a Teg is not afraid of death. And the absence of fear is the only thing that will turn you into a deadly weapon."

Torr's eyes were glued to the men circling each other. They looked just like men from his squad. They could almost be Smiley and Bates. He felt ill. "How does killing a friend make you not afraid?"

Edgemont barked a short, caustic laugh and slapped Torr on the shoulder. "Because after you kill a brother, you hate yourself so much you pray to the stars for death. That's why."

The men lunged at one another and staggered like rams fighting to the death. Torr turned and pushed his way out through the milling crowd as Edgemont laughed loudly after him.

Torr awoke to the pop of a spacecraft taking off. His blanket was twisted around his legs and he was soaked with sweat. He sat up, and Reina peered over her shoulder at him from the shooting platform.

"You okay?" she asked. "You were moaning."

Torr rubbed his eyes and swung his legs over the side of the cot. He crawled onto the platform next to her, got behind his rifle scope, and focused in on the dead bodies on the ground.

5

THE INHERİTANCE

Cassidy gazed out the kitchen window at the clear blue sky. Golden sun lit the backyard in a burst of green. The plants, accustomed to living under the shadow of the Shaman's Shield, stretched their leaves and petals towards the sun as though straining to embrace a long-lost love.

Her father had heard reports of a standoff at the southern border, where the Shaman's Shield no longer stood between Gaia United and the Teg army. Cassidy wondered how long it would be before hostilities commenced and Torr was either killed or captured. Pain stabbed at her side, making it difficult to breathe. She reached out to him, searching for hope. Maybe he would escape. Yes, he would escape. He had to.

She glanced down at her hands. She was clutching the bottle of Sweet Alyssum. The memory of the old woman and the stern warrior soothed her somehow. She placed two drops on her tongue, letting the bitter liquid slide down her throat.

She closed her eyes as the heat of the herb spread throughout her body, and tried to imagine where Torr was right now. An image came to her. She was looking out across a broad, flat expanse surrounded by a rim of low hills. Her mind zoomed in on the far hills where legions of Teg soldiers in their steely gray uniforms stood in clusters. Rows of armored vehicles sat in a field with soldiers leaning against them, talking and laughing. She inhaled sharply and opened her eyes.

Her heart raced in a quick, sharp staccato, and she struggled to breathe. She must calm herself. She was imagining her worst fears. Her mind had simply given her the pictures she expected. That was all. Her viewing was not real. She had no second sight left. Her grandmother had cured her of that.

She pushed the disquieting images from her mind and listened as her parents spoke in hushed tones from where they were sitting at the kitchen table with their hands clasped together.

"We'll go to Shasta. To my mother's house. Like we planned," her mother said.

Her father answered in muted words Cassidy could not decipher.

Grandma Leann had died six years before and passed the house down to Brianna. It stood empty most of the time, collecting dust and sheltering squirrels under its eaves. Cassidy missed her grandmother, with her ready smile, warm hugs, and tall tales. And she missed Shasta. The thick forests. The snowy peak. The unassuming people. Unassuming, that is, except for the shamans.

As far as Cassidy could tell, no one outside of Shasta had any magic. It seemed to be a localized phenomenon: normal in Shasta, but something people were afraid of everywhere else. Those who knew that Cassidy's family was from Shasta either asked them a lot of questions or avoided them with a wary eye. But no one had complained about being protected from the Tegs by the Shaman's Shield.

A loud rapping at the front door made them all jump.

Cassidy huddled behind the kitchen wall with her mom, and Caden crept to the front door as the rap-rap-rap came again.

"It's Bernie," a voice yelled through the door. "You guys still here?"

Cassidy and Brianna exhaled together and joined Caden in the living room.

Their neighbor stepped into the room with a gust of warm air. He pulled his ball cap off and twisted it in his hands. He was a tall man, and slouched to hide his height.

"How are things at Moffett?" Caden asked.

Bernie's brow furrowed together. "Spacecraft are taking off again. So that's good. But things are very tense there. I still have a job, far as I know. Lots of Gaia United officers about, though. That's a bit unnerving." Caden nodded, and Bernie said, "The Shaman's Shield is still holding north of here."

"It is? Where?" Brianna asked, grabbing Caden's arm.

"Just south of Mount Lassen and Mount Shasta, and it stretches all the way up to British Columbia."

Caden and Brianna exchanged relieved looks, and Cassidy felt a surge of elation. The Shaman's Shield still held. North of here, but it held.

Bernie and Caden shared information about the spaceport and the roadways, and Bernie rushed off.

Cassidy and her parents went into the kitchen and sat around the table. Brianna's frizzy hair was wild again. Caden's blue eyes were tired, and his short, gray hair was in total disarray.

Caden patted his wife's hand. "We won't be able to get through it," he said. "We'll be stuck outside the Shaman's Shield, instead of inside."

The gravity of his words sank in.

"I might be able to get through," Brianna said hesitantly.

"You haven't been practicing. And you don't know how they made it."

"I know enough," she said, her chin rising. "It's worth a shot. If we can get a message to Balor and Alissa, they can help get us inside."

"We can't get messages through the Shaman's Shield. You know that."

"There may be other ways." Her eyes grew distant.

"But then what about Torr?" Cassidy asked. "He won't be able to get through without you. He'll be stuck outside."

Her parents turned and stared at her. Grief etched their faces. Their plan had been for all of them to meet at Grandma Leann's house if things went to hell, and if necessary disappear into the caverns or the forests together.

"He's with the rebels, darling," her mother said. "Fighting. He's in the hands of Gaia United, with forces at his back. We are here, undefended. We need to go somewhere safer."

"The Tegs will come through the neighborhood eventually," Caden said, his eyes brimming with pain. "We need to get out before they come."

"But the war's not over yet. We haven't lost. The Shaman's Shield has just fallen, for star's sake." Cassidy realized her voice was shrill. She heard it as though someone else's pierced the air.

"You'd better pack your things," her father said gently. "You can pack a bag with Torr's things, if you'd like. Things he may want. In case he meets up with us later. In case we can't come back here."

Cassidy's throat hurt. How would Torr ever find them? Would he survive long enough to even try? Her vision of the Teg forces came back to her in a rush. She sniffed loudly, forcing herself not to cry. She wasn't the one facing death at the front lines. She needed to be brave.

"Mom. I gazed into the birdbath looking for Torr but didn't see him. Will you try?"

"I actually have been trying," her mother admitted. "I've been trying to contact Balor and Alissa. And I've looked for Torr." She shook her head. "Nothing."

Cassidy's heart fell. If her mother couldn't even water scry anymore, what chance did she have of crossing the Shaman's Shield? Cassidy left the table and went to her bedroom. She hadn't dared face the possibility that she might never see her brother again. She sat on her bed, trembling.

She slowly pulled herself together and took her large backpack down from the closet shelf. She rolled her sleeping bag tightly and strapped it to the bottom of the frame, then gathered a few changes of clothing and went into the bathroom for a towel and her toiletries. Grandma Leann's old, ornate copper brush and mirror sat on the shelf.

"Mom," she called. "Can I take Grandma's brush and mirror?"

A moment passed. "Yes," she heard back. She lifted the hand mirror, heavy with leaded glass and a green-tarnished metal backing with a pattern of an eight-sided star inside a circle. Of all the powers Cassidy had supposedly displayed as a child, she recalled only a few, apart from the visions her grandmother had put an end to. She remembered being able to bend metal spoons like they were hot wax, and slowing down balls as they flew through the air, simply by concentrating on them and willing them to change speed. And she remembered playing tricks on Torr and Jasper using this mirror. She forgot how it worked exactly, but she had been able to move things about by looking at them in the mirror, confounding her brother and Jasper to no end.

Cassidy took the brush and mirror and stepped into the hallway. Her father was carrying a plastic crate from their bedroom.

"When are we leaving?" she asked, feeling hollow inside.

"As soon as we're packed. Today."

"Today?" Her heart dropped. She quickly stepped back into her room and put the mirror, brush, and toiletries in her pack, then followed him out to the garage. "Today?" she repeated plaintively.

Caden plunked the crate heavily onto the floor, wearing that look he got when he was trying to be strong. Behind him on the workbench sat two rifles and a pistol, with a cleaning rod and rag lying next to them.

"You're taking the guns?" she asked. "For what? To shoot deer? Or Tegs?" Her mood darkened further.

He shrugged, his lips pulling down in a deep frown. His voice was thin but determined. "Just food, I hope. We might need to hunt if things go badly. You remember how to use these, right?" He took the old .22 rifle and handed it to her. "You were always pretty good with this one."

She made sure the safety was engaged and pulled the magazine from the bottom of the stock. It was empty. She set it on the workbench and drew back the bolt. The chamber was empty. She put the rifle to her shoulder and peered down the barrel at the open sights, found a spot on the floor, and lined up the little metal pin to the notch.

"I remember," she said, and glanced at the boxes of ammo stacked next to the guns. Her father went to the bench and started loading magazines. She didn't say anything, but gave her father a grim glare and placed the gun next to the green camouflage rifle Torr used for competitions. She left the garage, feeling worse than ever.

———————)———————

Cassidy had gotten so used to the Shaman's Shield, she'd almost forgotten it hadn't always been there. It had appeared three years ago, after the Tegs had blown up Denver and were charging westward. At first everyone had thought it was an unusually cloudy day. Then weather reporters claimed the clouds were not made from water, but from volcanic ash, though no eruptions had occurred. Rivers of ash had streamed through the atmosphere from all the volcanic peaks of the Cascade Range overnight. The morning news showed footage of massive plumes spreading in all directions. Then the media broadcast stopped.

Cassidy had stood in the living room with her brother and parents when the wall screen had gone black. At first they thought it was a power outage, but the lights were still on, and their solar roof was still pumping power through their inverter into their home and backup battery. When they tried to contact their friends, they found the entire wireless grid was down. They walked up and down the street and talked to their neighbors in person, something they almost never did except during the annual summer block party.

Caden tried to drive around to find out what was going on, but the roads were clogged, and he couldn't get past the main artery that intersected their street. They slowly gathered information from neighbors, who had walked home from their jobs at Moffett Field Spaceport and the various tech and aerospace companies in the valley. Groups of neighbors gathered in the streets and pieced together what had happened. Whatever this strange ash cloud was, it had stopped all satellite and wireless communications and grounded all hovercraft and spacecraft.

Everyone assumed it was a barrier of Cephean technology to place the whole west coast under siege. Then one elderly neighbor who still had an old-fashioned wired connection called them all over to his house. They crowded into his living room and gathered around an ancient television, where a Gaia United general announced that a Star Seeker sect, the Shasta

Shamans, had erected the shield as a defense against the oncoming Teg armies.

Cassidy's family stared at one another. The shamans had finally done it, just as their leader, Lawrence Remo, had promised. Cassidy remembered her parents and Grandma Leann, with their shaman friends Balor and Alissa, sitting around the table arguing over the magic that was brewing in the deep caverns of Mount Shasta. Grandma Leann had insisted it was possible to bend the elemental forces to one's will if they were skilled enough. Perhaps a group of them focusing their energy could form matter, or dissolve matter, as the need dictated. Or at least, move it. Alissa and Brianna exchanged concerned looks like they always did whenever Grandma started talking like that. Balor agreed with Grandma Leann, and told them about the time he had watched Remo make a sand castle without lifting a finger. Caden accused Balor of eating too many mushrooms and said people shouldn't mess with forces they didn't understand.

Then the Shaman's Shield proved it could hold back the Tegs. Suddenly the crazy Shasta Shamans were heroes. Cassidy still couldn't get over the fact that they had outwitted that bastard Tegea with magic. Who would have ever imagined that magic was the one weapon more powerful than the advanced alien technology of the Cephs?

Life changed after the Shaman's Shield appeared. Within a single day they lost a century of communication and transportation technology, and the normal rhythm of life ceased. The valley was resourceful, though, and everyone banded together, unearthing old technologies and connecting everything with wires. It was like a huge science project, and Cassidy had never seen the community so happy as when they were working together under the shelter of the Shaman's Shield to make a new life for themselves.

Cassidy had never realized how much of her life was dependent on the airwaves until it all stopped working: chat, phone, TV, radio, music, search, shopping, school assignments, computers, GPS ... everything. Her cell phone became no more than a glorified music player and camera that she had to connect to her wired computer to get anything new or share anything with anyone. The global Internet became the Western Free States Intranet, dubbed the WestWeb, isolated from the rest of the world and only connected by hard wires, like in the olden days. Within a few weeks people were back at work and school, and everyone was installing wired phones, computers, and wall screens. Old-fashioned wristwatches came back into fashion as the ubiquitous cell phones were less useful, and smart watches were suddenly dumb.

Rail trains had been decommissioned decades before, and the metal tracks had been torn up and replaced with high-speed hovercraft corridors. Hovercraft themselves never came back online, engineered as they were around complex satellite navigation systems. Vehicles with wheels became the only option. The roads were eventually cleared of grounded vehicles, and people dug out their bicycles and motorcycles, fixed up old wrecks of cars and trucks, and hooked up fuel cell charging pods. Caden had already been driving an old-fashioned truck, not trusting the frequent wartime satellite interference that paralyzed all transportation. The produce and other perishables he transported had to get to market whether or not the grid was functional.

Cassidy sat on her bed, breaking out of her reminiscing and wondering if the Cephs would allow universities to continue teaching. All she had heard about were work camps, farms, and factories. And breeding centers. She gathered her history textbooks, which were stacked on her desk collecting dust, and arranged them on her bookshelf. Her hands shook, but she finished her task anyway. If the Tegs came in here, the room would be neat and orderly. She made her bed and smoothed the comforter, then left the room, closing the door quietly behind her.

———————)———————

Cassidy opened the door to Torr's room. It was dim and the air was stale. Everything was as he'd left it during his last leave nearly a year ago. She pulled open the shades and cracked the window, then found his pack and gathered some clothing for him. She had folded his laundry often enough; she knew what he liked to wear.

Cassidy dug in his sock drawer looking for socks without holes, and pushed aside a scroll. The aged rubber band broke as she moved it, and the parchment unfurled in her hand. She knew what it was. She had one too. She took it out of the drawer and unrolled it. There were two pages. "Lunar Deed" was written in fancy calligraphy across the top of one. The second was a map of the moon. They were the deeds Great-Aunt Sophie had given them. Great-Aunt Sophie had no children and liked to bestow gifts on her only grand-niece and nephew. "One day you'll have everything of mine," she liked to say. "Might as well start handing it over bit by bit."

Cassidy's deed had been relegated to a drawer with all the other intriguing but useless gifts from Great-Aunt Sophie. Possessing a deed was one thing; developing land on a moon two hundred thousand miles away was quite another.

Cassidy scanned Torr's parchment. *"This deed grants the bearer sole rights to mining and settlement. Its bearer is granted citizenship on the Earth's moon, the independent republic, which is owned by none other than its inhabitants."*

Cassidy took Torr's deed to her room and found hers. She examined the inscriptions.

Transferred to Cassandra Cethlejan Dagda, year 2080.

Torr's read, *Transferred to Torrance Brenon Dagda, year 2080.*

Cassidy looked at the coordinates of their parcels, then plotted them on one of the maps. They were in the northwest quadrant of the near side of the moon. Together they encompassed a cluster of three large craters marked "Anaximenes." She slowly mouthed the syllables: *an-ax-IM-en-ees.*

She examined the deeds more closely. Signatures of transfer were at the bottom of the parchment, including her own signature in the careful script of a ten-year-old. A pair of fingerprints accompanied each signature, using the traditional index and middle fingers to identify each of the transferring and receiving parties. Above her own signature and fingerprints were those of Great-Aunt Sophie, *Sophie Airmid Cethlejan.* And above that, *Jared Michael Metolius.*

Cassidy examined the sloppy signature and large fingerprints of the President of the Global Alliance. His index finger's print was a perfect swirl, and his middle finger's was the shape of a raindrop with a small slash through the center. There was something oddly personal about having Metolius's fingerprints on the same page as hers. He had pressed his fingers on this very parchment.

It was a piece of exciting and equally disturbing family history. The man who was now dictator of nearly the entire planet had grown up in southern Oregon just north of Mount Shasta, and had attended Southern Oregon University in the same class as Great-Aunt Sophie. After university he had joined the military, then struck out on his own as a private military contractor. He had been the first owner of the deeds, purchased during the lunar land lottery in 2050. Cassidy knew from her history studies and family gossip that at that time Metolius had run a private mercenary company, contracting with governments to deploy small armies of professional soldiers and backing a series of military coups. He was so successful he eventually controlled the largest private army in the world. He combined forces with Tegea to form the Global Alliance, secured the backing of the Cephs, and became president, with the ambition of conquering the world.

Metolius had transferred the deeds to Sophie in 2060. Great-Aunt Sophie had worked for the State Department of the Free States, and Cassidy had always assumed she had purchased the deeds during one of her diplomatic missions, and that lunar deeds were issued by the Office of the President. But the weird thing was that Metolius had transferred the deeds to Sophie before the Global Alliance had even existed, and that particular transfer bore an ink stamp of the *Global Lunar Development Board.* To confuse things further, it was the transfer from Sophie to Cassidy in 2080 that bore the president's seal. She remembered it being there before she had signed the document, which was odd in and of itself. The gold foil seal pictured a big salmon fish leaping out of the water. Embossed clearly above the fish was *President Jared Michael Metolius.* Below the fish was embossed *Office of the President, Global Alliance.* Shivers ran up Cassidy's spine.

Grandma Leann had explained that Sophie and Metolius had been friends during school, saying, "Lines are made to be crossed and Sophie excels at crossing them, or at least blurring them. Life does not always fit into nice little boxes. All I know is they were close at one time, and she ran into him a couple times on Delos."

It was kind of creepy to have deeds issued by President Metolius, but Cassidy suddenly realized that not only did these deeds grant them land with rights to develop it, plus lunar citizenship, but Metolius's seal meant they were valid Global Alliance documents. She clutched the deeds to her chest, her head spinning.

6

LİEUTENANT JAMES

The Scripps Ranch company formed ranks on the concrete airfield that had been partially covered by the Shaman's Shield. Torr's squad had hiked the five miles west from their bunker in the hills to the main base. Before them loomed two white hangars, and a dozen Gaia United fighter aircraft sat idle on the cracked tarmac. Beyond the hangars were central command operations, administrative buildings, the infirmary, officers' housing, and a small golf course. There were also the buildings Torr frequented whenever he got the chance to rejoin civilization on a rare day of leave: bunkhouses with real beds in rooms with actual windows, a bathhouse with a sauna and steam room, a fully equipped gym, a mess hall, the commissary, communications center, weapons depot, game rooms, a swimming pool, movie theater, and three bars. The base had always seemed like a welcome retreat after living in the hills. Now it was buzzing like a disturbed beehive.

Their company was lined up by squad, waiting for Lieutenant James to speak. They'd been standing in ranks for an hour, waiting for all the Scripps Ranch squads to assemble. Each person's possessions from the bunkers sat on the tarmac next to them, as though they were waiting to board a plane. As squad leader, Torr stood at the front of his line.

The sun Torr hadn't seen in three years blazed hot in the afternoon sky, beating down on his head and neck. The only reminders that the Shaman's Shield had ever existed were a few wisps of white clouds painted across the blue sky.

He stared in front of him, anxiously awaiting their orders. Lieutenant James shifted heavily on his feet and cleared his throat. "As you all can see," his bass voice boomed across the yard, "the Shaman's Shield is gone. Actually, it shrank. It has retreated north and now encloses the territory from just south of Lassen and Shasta all the way up to Silverthrone in British Columbia. It still protects a large territory, but Los Angeles and San Francisco are now exposed. That means LAX and Moffett Field Spaceports are no longer under its protection."

Torr's stomach flip-flopped. If the San Francisco Bay Area and Moffett were no longer protected by the Shaman's Shield, that meant his home and family weren't, either. On the other hand, the Shaman's Shield was not completely gone, and Mt. Shasta City and Grandma Leann's house were still inside the shield. Fear and hope surged in his veins.

"You all know how strategic the spaceports are," Lieutenant James said. "I have been informed that Gaia United will relinquish control of Moffett Field and LAX to the Global Alliance."

A gasp escaped the ranks of soldiers, followed by mutters that faded to dead silence.

"That means," Lieutenant James continued, "that Los Angeles and San Francisco will also be handed over to the Global Alliance. And all the territories between here and the new southern border of the Shaman's Shield."

Torr's heart skipped a beat. Moans of despair rippled through the crowd. Torr held his tongue and stood at attention, his head reeling. Gaia United had surrendered most of California. Without a fight.

The two days of standing idly by while the Tegs stood unharassed across the hills now made sense. There was no plan to resist. There never had been. Hot rage took hold of Torr, melting the icy tendrils of fear. Why had they fielded an army if not to fight? They could at least show the Tegs that what they were doing was wrong. Show the Cephs that free people would rather die than be made slaves. Who had made that choice for all of them? He didn't even know who led Gaia United anymore. A group of generals whose names seemed to change by the month. Smith. Li. Waterford. Shankar. Richenbacher. Rodriguez. Faceless names. Cowards. He wanted to cry out in fury and frustration, but maintained his posture and stared straight ahead.

The troops shifted uneasily. Torr's feet were planted on the earth, his fists at his sides. The lieutenant continued, his voice bellowing across the airfield. "We are not moving north. The generals have surrendered our forces."

His voice echoed across the pavement and was answered by stunned silence. Fear sliced through Torr's body. He could not breathe.

"Male soldiers have the choice of joining the Teg forces ..." Cries and curses erupted. Lieutenant James held up a hand for silence. "... or surrendering themselves to be sent to work camps." Groans came from all around. "Females ..." His voice grew louder. "... are not allowed in the Teg forces. All females will report to work camps."

Torr's self-control broke. He looked over his shoulder at Reina. She stared straight ahead and would not meet his eyes.

"The handover of power takes place today at eighteen hundred hours." Torr looked at his wristwatch, along with every other person in the Scripps Ranch company. It was sixteen hundred hours. "At that time, you will surrender your weapons and get in line for the Teg army or the work camps. You have two hours to make your decision and gather your things."

Lieutenant James was staring into the distance. Torr wondered which option the lieutenant was going to choose. Torr knew which path he himself was going to take. The work camps. Let the Tegs work him to death. He was not going to kill one of his fellow soldiers for sport. Even if his dream was not true, he was not going to willingly defend a military state that enslaved its citizens. He raised his chin and held back tears of frustration. Thoughts of his sister and parents flooded through cracks of despair.

Torr could feel the ranks wanting to break. People wanting to scatter. To talk. To run and hide. The lieutenant nodded at someone in Torr's line.

Reina's voice rang through the air. "Are we still under Gaia United jurisdiction at this time, sir? Are we still bound by our oaths?"

The yard went silent. Shuffling and fidgeting stopped as Lieutenant James looked at Reina, his face like stone. Finally, he spoke. "Gaia United is a rebel force. Your oath was this: *I pledge to give my life for the defense of freedom and liberty, and to defend the Gaia United rebellion for as long as it shall stand.*" The lieutenant sniffed and a sneer curled his lip. "As far as I can tell, the rebellion no longer stands. Therefore, I think you have fulfilled your oaths, and are civilians for ..." He glanced at his wristwatch. "... one hour and fifty-seven minutes."

Lieutenant James had just said what amounted to treason. Signed his own death warrant. Torr looked at the man's bloodshot eyes. The lieutenant knew exactly what he had done. He had given all the females in his company, and anyone else who wanted it, the chance to escape to a tenuous freedom. Tears rose to Torr's eyes as he looked at the brave face of his lieutenant. The bravest man he had ever known.

Torr turned and met Reina's eyes as the company broke ranks.

"I'll go with you," he said breathlessly, grabbing her arm. She grabbed his, and they turned to their eight squadmates. The crew huddled, confused and scared. They were closer than siblings, having lived together in that stupid bunker for a solid year. Torr was their squad leader. They looked to him now. He stood straight, squaring his shoulders. "We'll go with Reina. We'll head north."

The men looked at one another, then started talking all at once.

"We'll get caught," Smiley said, clutching his rifle.

"We'll die," Jessimar said, his eyes bright and wild.

"Goddamn pussy motherfucker generals. We came here to fight, not lick balls," Johnson said, staring Torr straight in the eyes like it was his fault.

"So then you're coming with us," Torr said.

"No. That's suicide," Johnson said.

"So, what're you gonna do? Go to a work camp?" Torr asked.

Johnson glared stubbornly at Torr and hesitated, then said, "There's only one real option. We should join the Tegs."

"You should fuck your mother and die," Bobby said, pushing Johnson hard on the chest.

The two men shoved at one another. Torr pulled them apart. "Why should we join the army that wants to destroy us?" Torr demanded. "You know, they make you kill each other during Teg training. To see who's the meanest." He met Johnson's eyes. "You want to kill one of us?" The squad went silent and stared at Torr.

"They do not," Johnson said. "How do you know?"

Torr felt himself blush. It had only been a dream. He shrugged, embarrassed. "That's what I heard."

"No, they're just soldiers. Just normal guys, like us," Smiley said. "Choosing to be free instead of slaves."

"You call being a Teg free?" Bobby asked. "You got shit for brains?"

"Shut the fuck up," Smiley said, swatting Bobby's shoulder with the back of his hand. The two started scuffling, and the others pushed them apart.

"Would you really become one of *them?*" Mike asked, facing Johnson, Smiley, and Jessimar. Rashon and Bates stood to the side, shifting nervously as other squads rushed past. "Could you really drag people from their houses?" Mike pressed. "Grandmothers and kids? Women? Your neighbors? Your *mother?* Could you really send your mother to a work camp, Jessimar Jones?" Mike turned to Jessimar, who stared down at his feet.

Jessimar's weak voice laced through the hubbub. "She told me to do whatever I need to do to stay alive."

Torr couldn't believe Jessimar would send his own mother to a work camp. "Come with us," Torr pleaded. "Or go to a work camp. You'll stay alive at a work camp. Go there."

"I ain't gonna be no slave," Jessimar said, his voice sharp. He lifted his wide brown eyes and met Torr's evenly.

Torr felt his squadmates slipping away from him. He stood, frozen. He did not know what was best. His cheek felt as though a needle was jabbing into it as a wave of dizziness washed over him. Maybe he should go with them, fight the Tegs from the inside. Maybe they were not as bad as everyone said. Reina was looking at him, her intense gaze clearing his head. He fought against the intrusive thoughts and the strange sensation of a cold, dark weather front creeping across the field from the south.

"We have to stay together," Torr insisted, "We're a squad. We'll form a guerilla force. We swore to give our lives to defeat the Tegs."

He followed Bates's gaze to the endless ranks of Tegs lining the hills in the distance. He imagined them surging forward, streaming into the neighborhoods north of here, spreading into the sprawl of Los Angeles.

"A guerilla force? Against *that?*" Bates asked.

Torr swallowed. "We'll get others to join us. A guerilla force can put up resistance for months. Like in Chicago, and Houston."

"And Denver," Jessimar drawled sarcastically.

Bates and Rashon looked at Torr dejectedly. They had already given up.

"Johnson," Torr said, grabbing his friend's collar with both hands. "Tell them. Come with us."

"Lay off," Johnson said, pushing him hard against the chest and breaking his grip. Torr stumbled back a pace. Johnson had never lashed out at him like that before. "You ain't our squad leader no more." A fevered light burned in Johnson's eyes.

Torr stepped back another pace. At his side he could feel Donald's resolve wavering. Torr put out his arm to hold him and Mike back.

"Torr," said Reina. "We have to hurry. Let them go."

He took in a ragged breath. "I only ask this," he said, turning to Johnson and those who had lined up beside him: Jessimar, Smiley, Bates, and Rashon. Next to Torr and Reina stood Bobby, Donald, and Mike. The ground between the two groups felt deep and vast. "Remember, we're family," Torr said, his voice hoarse. "Everybody is family." He gestured to the scattering Scripps Ranch company. "No matter which side we're on. We're all in this together."

They did not respond, their expressions stony. It was as though the men facing him were suddenly strangers. He was filled with a chilling fear that they would have to face each other across enemy lines. He did not think he could shoot any of them, nor bear the heartbreak if they were to raise a gun against him.

Reina broke the uneasy silence and stepped across to hug Rashon. He clasped her tightly, lifting her off her feet. He set her gently onto the ground, and she moved on to hug Bates. Everyone relaxed their stiff stances and embraced. Tears made dark splotches on shoulders as they slapped each other roughly on the back and uttered short, inadequate words of goodbye. Finally they nodded awkwardly at one another, then trotted off in two separate groups towards the bunkhouses to prepare to leave.

———————)———————

Torr emptied his locker where he stored his civilian clothing and the few personal items he hadn't had room for in the bunker, staked out a small corner in a chaotic bunk room of the common male barracks, and sorted through his things. It seemed everyone had the same idea, crowding the aisles between the long rows of outdoor lockers, and squeezing into the rooms that were only made to accommodate the few soldiers who were on leave at any one time.

Torr took only what fit in his rucksack and small duffel bag. He rolled his blankets into their canvas cover and strapped them below the pack, then left his large duffel bag filled with his service uniform and extra clothing in his locker, and locked it just for the hell of it. He ducked into the showers to fill his canteen, not wanting to wait in line at the outdoor spigots.

He found Bobby, Mike, and Donald outside the female bunkhouse, waiting impatiently.

"It's about time," Bobby grumbled at Torr. "What'd you do, swab the floors and scrub the toilets? Call inside for Reina."

Bobby tossed pebbles at the small windows high on the cinder-block wall of the barracks.

"She'll be out," Torr said, watching soldiers pass by, wearing expressions of numbed shock, hard determination, or flat-out terror.

Reina emerged with Jenna, a blond woman from another squad whom Torr had only ever spoken to a couple of times. "Jenna's coming with us," Reina stated. The men nodded to Jenna. She looked as though she had been crying.

The group kept together as they made their way through the crowds of thousands who were converging near the processing tables. Troops from other companies that had been posted further out in the hills were pouring into the base and running in every direction. People were yelling, crying, or staring morosely as they shuffled towards one crowd or the other, while officers were trying to organize them into ranks. Lieutenant James was nowhere to be seen.

They walked up to the communications center and regarded the mass of people milling around a long line that snaked back on itself. Inside the building were a dozen wired phones in small, private rooms that everyone was allowed to use if they wanted privacy or didn't have access to a wired computer.

"Mike, try your phone," Torr said. They gathered around Mike, and Torr peered at the small screen. *No service.* Torr looked up at the clear sky. Far above, several dots slowly crossed the sky heading northeast. More Teg aircraft. He shivered.

Did they have time to stand in line to call home? What would he tell his family? Would the lines be tapped? He wouldn't be able to tell them he was deserting, so what was the point, except to tell them he loved them and that they should wait? Wait for what? Would they understand? Or maybe he should tell them not to wait. Urge them to flee before it was too late.

Torr had come here several days ago and called home, before the Shaman's Shield had fallen. The conversation had been short and pleasant. Torr had told them how bored he was. Cassidy had told him she had progressed to writing down magical properties of the plants. His parents were the same as always. Now he tried to remember exactly how their voices had sounded. What if that was the last time he would ever speak to them?

He pressed down a rising panic as the full realization struck him that if the Shaman's Shield stood south of Shasta, it meant they were all trapped outside of it. His family would be unable to get to Grandma Leann's house. What if they had left home already but hadn't reached Shasta before the Shaman's Shield moved? He'd never be able to find them. He tried to count back the days to when he had spoken to them. It had been five days ago. Would his mother have somehow known the Shaman's Shield was about to pull back and fled to Shasta in time? That would mean he'd be trapped outside without them. Every scenario was bad. He forced himself to stay rational. He would head home and see what the situation was, then figure out what to do next. That was all he could do.

People pushed past him. "Can't get through," someone said. "The phones say, 'All circuits are busy, try your call later.'" People in line moaned and looked nervously at their watches.

Torr's cheek was twitching in an annoyingly steady rhythm. He counted his racing heartbeat, slowing it down with the breathing exercises he practiced daily at his gun.

"Come on," Bobby said, tugging at Torr's sleeve. "We'll find a phone later. We've got to get out of here."

He was right. Torr trotted after his squadmates. They slowed to a walk as they came upon the racks where yelling men were collecting weapons. Torr exchanged glances with his buddies. He did not want to surrender any of his weapons. He had his

Dashiel, TAFT, Orbiter pistol, as many rounds of ammo as he could carry, and a combat knife. People pushed from all sides, anxious to drop off their weapons and leave. No one paid him and his crew any mind as they wandered past; everyone was too busy worrying about themselves.

The commissary was open, and people were streaming out with food and supplies piled in their arms. Torr realized the last time they had eaten had been that morning, an unusually paltry breakfast of cereal and milk, with overripe bananas and instant coffee. Everyone seemed to have forgotten about lunch, and it was already nearly dinnertime. The Tegs did not seem to be in any rush to arrange for their evening meal, and Torr wondered if it was intentional.

Torr and his buddies squeezed their way inside the food store. It was a free-for-all, and many of the shelves were already empty. Torr made his way to a refrigerated wall rack where people were grabbing packages of lunch meat. Hands were fighting with hands to get the last of them. Torr pushed his way in and snatched three packages of ham and got an elbow in the side. His heart was pounding and he pushed his way to the dairy case. The egg rack was empty. He grabbed a big block of yellow cheese and a couple gallons of milk. He moved on and stuffed his pockets with protein bars. His friends grabbed what they could: bread, chips, jerky, nuts, peanut butter, jelly, cookies, juice. They wanted canned goods, but that section was all the way on the other side of the store. It was too crowded, and their arms were full. And it was already sixteen-forty-five.

The cashiers were overrun, and people were rushing out without paying. Torr exchanged a look with Bobby and Mike, and they walked around the checkout lanes where cashiers were furiously scanning items. One cashier tore off his apron and walked out the door with the throng. People on his line rushed out the door behind him. Torr and his friends followed.

They passed the main mess hall and Torr peered through the wall of windows. It was dim inside. The tables were bare, and the serving lines were shut down.

They decided to try to find a vehicle and jogged towards the storage lot on the other side of the base. The crowds thinned out as they left the central area. Small groups and lone soldiers rushed past them with frantic glances. The residential units were abandoned, and the supply depot was gated shut.

The vehicle lot was unsecured and they stepped aside as a jeep sped out, two men glaring at them. Two other groups of men were in the lot, looking inside vehicles.

"We need one with keys," Mike said.

They fanned out and checked for unlocked doors and keys left inside vehicles. Torr attempted to get into the office trailer and the garage to look for keys, but all the doors were locked, and there were no windows. He was tempted to shoot out a lock, but that would be too loud. He walked between the rows of vehicles and found a new jeep with keys in the center console. The driver's door was unlocked. He threw his rucksack and food onto the passenger seat and got in.

"This one's ours," a voice said at the passenger side window. The man tugged at the locked door and rapped on the glass.

Another man appeared at the driver's side and flashed a military police badge. "Ours," he said to Torr. "Out."

Torr wanted to argue, but held his tongue and opened the door. He grabbed his things and stepped out, giving the MP a mock bow. The man ignored him and threw several packs into the back.

"Torr!" Bobby's voice rang out across the lot.

He trotted over to his friends. They were standing around a beat-up jeep. Its keys were on the dashboard, and the doors were unlocked.

"This'll do," Torr said as the MPs sped towards the gate, gravel flying from spinning tires.

They stuffed their bags and food supplies in the back. Bobby climbed into the driver's seat, and Mike sat in front. The back seat was too small for four people, and Reina ended up on Torr's lap, her arm wrapped around his neck. Donald was wedged in the middle, and Jenna sat against the other door. Bobby drove out of the parking lot and headed for the North Gate. They came upon several other groups of people fleeing like they were. Everyone had the same look of frenzied determination in their eyes. Most carried weapons. Some were in vehicles. Others were on foot.

They approached the gate and found a long line. Three guards stood in front of the gate, blocking soldiers who wanted to leave. Bobby drove through the people who were on foot, forcing them to part before the jeep. They reached the end of the line of vehicles. The MPs' jeep was not in the line, and Torr wondered if there was a better way out. Torr nudged Reina off his lap and hopped out of the jeep. Mike and Donald joined him and they walked towards the guards.

"Report to the processing center," one of the guards told a pleading female soldier, his arms crossed, standing in front of the gate. "I'm not authorized to let you pass."

The two other guards stood nearby, cradling assault rifles and glancing nervously towards the operations center. Torr, Mike, and Donald had been together so long, they didn't need to speak to communicate. They split up and walked casually towards the guards, as though wanting to politely ask permission to leave. Then with a flick of their eyes, they raised their guns in unison, and each guard found himself looking down a rifle barrel.

More guns clicked around them as others in line lifted weapons and trained them on the guards.

"Take their weapons," Torr commanded.

In seconds the guards were disarmed and lying face down, their hands secured behind their backs in their own handcuffs. Torr went into the guard shack and pressed the button to open the gate, and the crowd streamed out. Torr climbed into the jeep as it rolled up, and greeted Bobby, Reina, and Jenna with a smile. "See, that wasn't so hard."

The friends laughed nervously as they rolled out of Miramar and headed towards the freeway. It was seventeen-twenty.

7

FAMILY BONDS

Cassidy spread out the moon deeds on the kitchen table. Her parents stood around the table with her, perusing them skeptically.

"I don't know, Cassidy," Caden said. "I don't know how you would get there. And if you did, then what? Peary Dome is a rough frontier camp. And Peary Spaceport is a galactic trading hub with all sorts of who knows what passing through. I don't know if you'd be safe there."

"What about Jasper and Kai Manann? They're there."

Jasper's cocky grin filled her vision, his hazel eyes dancing with mischief. He was four and a half years older than she and Torr. When Kai had left for the Peary Dome moon colony, Jasper had been only fourteen and lived with the Dagdas while he finished high school.

"We haven't heard from Kai or Jasper since the Shaman's Shield went up," Brianna said. "We can't be certain they're still there. Besides, they're men, they can handle a rough environment. I don't want you going there, even if Jasper and Kai are there."

Cassidy's hackles rose. "Are you saying I can't take care of myself?"

Her mother sighed. "Cassidy. Be reasonable."

"I am being reasonable. I want to get away from the Tegs. As far away as possible. At least I'd be in a free, independent republic. Come with me, we can all go."

"No, Cassidy," her mother said. "I have to go to Shasta."

Cassidy propped her hands on her hips and glared at her mother. "Then I'm going by myself."

"How do you plan on getting there?" her father asked.

Cassidy shrugged. "Get a flight out of Moffett?" She had felt the distinctive pop of a takeoff just that morning.

"With what money?" Caden asked.

Cassidy looked down at the deeds. "I don't know." Her hopeful enthusiasm drained out of her. She looked up, meeting her father's kind eyes. He reached across the table and patted her hand.

"I'm sorry, honey," he said. "I wish we were rich. I'd buy you passage."

"How did Jasper and his dad get there, if it's so expensive?" she asked.

"Kai's airforce buddy arranged his passage. The guy who got him the pilot's job up there," Caden said. "Then it took Kai five years to save enough for Jasper's flight."

Jasper had often schemed of going to Moffett and smuggling himself onto a cargo ship to join his father. Maybe Cassidy could find some way to get there, too. Sneak onto the back of a freighter. Bribe or trade her way. Something.

"I own land there, that must be worth something," she said, looking hopefully at her frowning parents. "I could sell my deed for passage. But, then," she worried, "without the deed, I wouldn't have citizenship on the moon. Would that matter?"

The thought crossed her mind that she could sell Torr's deed and retain her own for citizenship, but that sounded too horribly selfish to say out loud.

Her father rubbed his chin. "I don't think you need citizenship to stay at Peary Dome. It's a trading colony. Or a refugee camp. Or some combination. I doubt very many people there have land claims." His eyes grew thoughtful. "Your land itself wouldn't be of much use to you. It's just a bunch of craters. You won't have the resources to develop it. In fact, I wouldn't be surprised if squatters are mining it already. There are illegal mines all over the place. So, yes, perhaps you could sell your deed."

"Who would buy it?" Cassidy wondered.

"I really don't know, honey," Caden said. "Even if I did think it was a good idea. We're fortunate to have a house in Shasta to go to. If we can get through the Shaman's Shield, that is." He glanced at Brianna. "Come on. Gather your things, we need to get going." He stood and held out a hand to his wife. "Cassie, get your pack, and help me carry the last of the water jugs to the truck."

Cassidy stood, tears in her eyes. "What about Torr?"

Caden frowned, and Brianna's mouth was a tight line.

"He'll be fine. He's a soldier," Brianna said stiffly. Her eyes betrayed worry, despite her confident words. "He's a grown man now." Brianna straightened her shoulders.

Cassidy understood the true meaning behind her words. That he was old enough to die on his own. With his buddies. He belonged to Gaia United now. His parents and sister no longer had rights to him unless he came home in a coffin.

"If we win the war, he'll find us in Shasta," Caden said softly. *If?* And if not? Cassidy couldn't speak the truth that hung in the air. "Bring his pack," Caden told her gently. "So the Tegs don't get it."

Cassidy nodded and swiped the back of her hand across her nose. The thought of Teg soldiers ransacking their house made her squirm. She grudgingly fetched her pack and Torr's, went out front, and placed them in the back of her father's refrigerated delivery truck, then lugged the last of the five-gallon water jugs to the curb.

"Do you have your passport and DNA papers?" her father asked.

She nodded, tapping the canvas bag that hung across her shoulder, wondering why it even mattered. She knew the Tegs required people to carry identification at all times, but she'd also heard that the Tegs gave their prisoners numbers.

Her mother emerged from the house with two daypacks. "Here," she said, handing Cassidy a green pack. "I split up the herbs, in case you and I need to separate at the border."

Cassidy eyed her unhappily. Brianna was afraid only she would get through the Shaman's Shield, with whatever shaman power she still possessed, and that Cassidy and her father would be left outside. Cassidy opened the pack and peeked inside. Mounds of small brown bottles sat in a nest of small paper sacks filled with loose, dried herbs. Wedged into the side was a notebook.

"You're giving me your red notebook?" Cassidy asked with surprise. It was the most magical of her mother's plant spirit medicine notebooks, written with the Black Guya ink. "Thank you." She smiled at her mother, who returned her smile and hugged her. With the red notebook, plus her own black, green, and yellow herb notebooks, Cassidy had a complete set of plant wisdom.

She watched her father lock up the house and walk slowly towards them, his eyes dark and hollow. Cassidy pulled away from her mother and stood on the curb. Her mind told her to get into the truck cab, but her legs would not move. Her feet stuck to Earth as though its iron core was anchoring her. She closed her eyes and searched for Torr at the front lines, bracing herself for an image of the Tegs advancing. Instead, she saw miles of freeway clogged with traffic. It did not make sense. But at least she had not been confronted with horrific battle scenes, or Torr standing in a line of prisoners of war. She had hoped that the Sweet Alyssum had torn a hole in the shielding blanket that dulled her extrasensory perception, but her power of second sight was as inaccessible as ever. She opened her eyes to see her parents waiting for her.

She slung the pack of herbs over her shoulders, resigned to her fate. But she could not continue forward. She was drawn to Torr as though a taut thread connected them, and if she took one more step away from him it would snap. If Torr came home, unlikely as that was, she'd be gone already and they'd never find one another. She and their parents would be stuck inside the Shaman's Shield, and Torr would be stuck outside. Or they'd all be trapped outside, hiding in the vast forests, never to cross paths. It was terrible enough if they never saw each other again because he was killed or taken prisoner at the front lines. That she could not control. But if he came here looking for them and they'd abandoned him, she'd never forgive herself.

She considered her options, knowing that if she waited for him and they were rounded up by the Tegs, Torr would blame himself. He would want her to leave. The best chance for her freedom and survival was to go with her parents and take her chances at the Shaman's Shield or in the wilderness up north, not stay here on the outskirts of Moffett Field Spaceport, which the Tegs would take first thing.

Then again, if the Shaman's Shield still stood, wouldn't General Tegea go after that? Wouldn't he focus on toppling the one defense that had stymied him? It must seem ridiculous to the Global Alliance that a magical shield erected by a bunch of fanatical Star Seekers had stemmed the tide of the most effective army in the history of the world, the army that was poised to control the entire planet for the first time ever. Tegea must be enraged by the Shaman's Shield, and would attack it with all the might he had. He had somehow forced it back already. He must have discovered the key to its power. Now it would be only a matter of time before he defeated it completely. Then he would go after the Shasta Shamans.

Cassidy balanced on the edge of the curb, surveying the neighborhood of wooden, ranch-style houses. A couple of people were in their driveways packing vehicles. Other houses were already abandoned. The whole street was muffled in an unearthly quiet. Even the birds were silent.

Her father stood by the open truck door, looking at her. Her mother was already sitting in the front. Cassidy knew she should go with them. They were older and wiser. She didn't need to decide anything, she just needed to follow them. They had already considered the alternatives and knew what was best. Her mind commanded her legs to move, but nothing happened.

She suddenly recognized the feelings she was having. Her mind was struggling to overpower her intuition. Her mind was trying to talk sense, wanting to follow the path someone else had laid out for her. This heavy feeling she had inside was her intuition bidding her to stay, regardless of what reason was telling her. Regardless of what her parents wanted, or even what Torr wanted.

She had ignored her intuition in the past, always with bad results. It was never obvious at the time why her instincts guided her in one direction when all signs pointed in another. But afterwards, her gut feeling had always proven correct. It was as though her intuition was connected with some larger pattern that was impossible to see from the perspective of current time and space. She'd sworn in the past she would always follow it in the future, no matter what. The trick was to recognize it in time. And she had recognized it now. It rang like a great bell, resounding and echoing through her soul. *Stay,* it said. *Wait. Trust in the stars.*

"Torr might come home," she said to her father. "I'm staying here to wait for him." She smiled as she said this, though she could barely breathe.

Her father's face fell.

Her mother stepped out of the cab and rushed around the truck. "Don't be silly, Cassidy."

Cassidy stood up straight, feeling her body and mind align with the rightness of her decision. Her throat tightened as she struggled to keep her voice even. "I am not silly. And I am not a child. I'm nearly twenty-one and I'm staying here, but you should go. *Go,"* she said. "Don't stay for me. Please. The stars will be with you." She could feel her eyes blazing.

Her mother returned her look with the same fiery determination. "Come," her mother said, stepping closer and taking Cassidy's arm. "Torr will be fine."

Cassidy stubbornly shook off her mother's grip. "Torr will *not* be fine. He's coming to meet us. *Here."* Yes, it was true. Her body knew, even as her mind struggled to believe it. She did not know how, but she could always feel Torr. Maybe it was because they were twins and had shared the womb. They were still connected by bonds that spanned the distance between them. Surely her mother felt it too, through the maternal bond, just as Cassidy felt her mother's strong emotions even when they were separated by miles. "You can feel he is coming to find us," she challenged her mother. "If I can feel it, you can too."

Her mother's brittle exterior cracked, and Cassidy knew she was right. Her mother could feel the truth of it—Torr was on his way. Cassidy took her and Torr's packs from the back of the truck and marched up to the house. She pressed her finger to the lock sensor, then pushed the door open. From the corner of her eye, she saw her parents slowly walking to join her as she entered the dim and silent house.

8

DANA POİNT

Torr rode quietly with his squadmates, squeezed in the back seat of the jeep. Miramar Base stood behind cement walls to their left, and they all breathed a sigh of relief when they passed the last gate and turned onto the 805. Reina was heavy and warm on his lap, and her hair tickled his cheek. He gently brushed it away, letting his fingers touch her skin. She pressed closer against him, resting her head against his. She smelled good.

Bobby drove fast, weaving around cars stuffed with families and belongings. Everyone was heading north, away from the Tegs.

"I have to find my family and help them escape," Torr said to no one in particular. "We live near Moffett." No one responded. They all knew where he lived, except Jenna, and she was staring east towards the hills. "Think cell phones will work now?" he asked, looking up through the open roof at blue sky.

Mike pulled out his phone. Torr could see the screen light up. "No service," Mike read despondently.

Bobby flicked on the jeep's radio and cycled through bands of static. It wasn't the static of the Shaman's Shield Torr had become accustomed to, which sounded like a constant wash of light rain pattering against a roof. Instead it was the rhythmic surge of intentional jamming, a roar of waves crashing over a faint backdrop of unintelligible voices. Bobby turned the radio off in disgust.

Their attention turned to the jeep's navigator panel, which was lit and read, "Welcome." Mike spoke to it. "Set current location," he said.

The screen responded in a sultry female voice. *"I'm sorry, I'm having trouble finding a connection. Is there something else I can do for you?"*

"You can blow me," Mike growled, and turned off the display.

Torr fidgeted, worrying. The Tegs had already jammed the airwaves and satellite communications. He wondered how many days his family had before the Tegs came to clear out their neighborhood. How long before his parents and sister would leave home to find a safe place? Maybe they had left already.

"We should build a guerilla force," Torr said, wondering if all the deserters should have banded together outside the gate instead of splitting up.

No one responded. They passed a car whose trunk was open and packed with furniture, its rear end sagging from the weight. Donald plugged his phone in and started playing the game he always played, an annoying beep sounding every time he killed one of the alien insects that crawled across the screen. *Beep. Beep. Beep beep.*

Finally, Reina answered Torr. "What happens when we run out of ammo?"

Torr tightened his jaws.

"I need to find my mother," Bobby said.

"We can't beat them," Mike said. "I just want to go home and get my parents out of here."

"Where will you go?" Torr asked.

Mike shrugged. "East into the hills. The desert, maybe. I don't know."

The wind from the open roof and windows whipped against Torr's face. He should go home too. Escape with his family to Shasta.

Beep. Beep beep. Beep.

"Shut that up for a minute, Donald," Torr snapped. "We need to figure out what we're doing."

It was a quick discussion. There was only one logical route. They would drive through Los Angeles, where Mike, Donald, and the girls were from, then Torr and Bobby would head up to the Bay Area. Bobby would drop off Torr, then continue north to his mother's apartment in San Francisco.

Beep. Beep beep beep beep beep. Beep beep.

"Will you turn the sound off, for crap's sake?" Torr asked.

Donald scowled, but turned off the sound, not taking his eyes off the screen.

Before long they reached the 5, merging into heavy traffic on the main north-south highway. By the time they got to Torrey Pines they realized they were in trouble. The road was red with brake lights. Northbound traffic ground to a halt.

A steady stream of Gaia United transports rolled by in the southbound lanes. Torr guessed they were coming from Camp Pendleton, heading for the Teg camp to surrender. Torr shrank at the sight of them, as if by sinking into his seat he could avoid detection. Fortunately, the jeep was surrounded by other civilian vehicles, while a median filled with tall, flowering bushes obscured much of the oncoming traffic. Reina's arm tightened around Torr's neck, and he pulled her closer, wrapping both his arms around her in a hug.

Traffic remained at a standstill. Bobby put the jeep in park. "What the fuck are we going to do now?" he asked, turning in his seat to look at them.

"Let me think," Torr said, loosening his hold on Reina. "The off ramp is backed up, and nothing is moving on the overpass. The coastal highway will be no better than the 5." The local road that ran through the towns along the shore might be even worse for them. They could be detected easily and hauled in for deserting. Here, at least, they were protected by the traffic jam.

"We'll never get to LA by eighteen hundred hours," Bobby grumbled. They all looked at their watches. It was seventeen-forty-five.

"We're not going to turn into pumpkins at eighteen hundred," Reina said. "It'll take time for them to process the troops. Could be days before they start dealing with civilians."

"Or deserters," Bobby said glumly.

Torr tried to relax. Reina pressed her cheek against the side of his head, and he rocked her gently. They had never been lovers, though he had often thought about it. There was no privacy in the bunker, and it didn't seem right to screw a squadmate, especially with him being squad leader, though now he wished they had found a way. They might never see each other again after this. He played with her hand and stroked the inside of her wrist, tracing the small tattoo of the Gaia United eagle that matched the larger one on his inside right forearm.

Traffic started slowly moving again. They sat back as the jeep inched forward. Eighteen hundred hours came and went, with no daggers of doom falling on them. Traffic continued to crawl, not moving at all for long periods of time.

By the time they reached Camp Pendleton, night had fallen. Torr was glad for the shelter of darkness. Gaia United convoys streamed onto the southbound lanes from the camp. There were vehicles of all sorts, many of them troop carriers. Torr clamped his teeth together and tried to keep his hands from shaking. He did not want to frighten Reina.

His cheek had started twitching as soon as they'd approached Pendleton. They passed the exit, and as they left it behind, the twitching subsided. They inched along for another couple miles, then traffic stopped completely. To their left stretched the flat, indigo ocean. To their right, bare, jutting hills towered like black sentinels below a full, yellow moon. He thought of Jasper up there at the lunar north pole, and his and Cassidy's land, sitting in the northwest quadrant, unused. They should be up there right now.

He pushed his regrets aside, vowing to enjoy the moon's beauty without punishing himself over past decisions. They got out of the jeep and stood on the side of the road, gazing up at the sky. He had gone three years without seeing the moon and stars and had forgotten how glorious they were. He hugged Reina and kissed her soft, eager lips. Moonlight bathed her skin and reflected off her bright eyes as he pulled his lips away and gazed at her.

She put her warm hand to his cheek, which was still spasming ever so slightly. "Are you scared?" she asked.

"Yeah," he said, taking her small hand in his big one and gently squeezing her fingers. "But that's not why my cheek is twitching. There's something not right at Pendleton. I don't know what it is."

"Probably Tegs are there already," she said.

Torr nodded. She had a way of knowing things.

They kissed until traffic started moving, then jumped back into the jeep. Traffic inched along, bumper to bumper.

By morning they hadn't even made it to Dana Point. It would take another day or more to get to Los Angeles at this rate, though they were less than sixty miles away. Traffic was only going to get worse the closer they got to the city. He sat cramped in the back of the jeep, Reina shifting her weight in his lap, his legs numb. The sun beat down on Torr's arm as it rose in the sky, and the jeep crept forward.

Jenna passed around a bag of pretzels and a jug of apple juice, and Donald opened a bag of beef jerky and distributed the salty strips. The little bits of food only made Torr hungrier. He split a protein bar with Reina, and passed out a couple for the others to share. He didn't know how long their food would need to last them.

Traffic ground to a halt again and the boys jumped out to piss at the side of the road into the bushes, and hopped back in as traffic started to roll. The girls had stayed in the jeep and complained about having to pee. They all grew silent and stared out the windows. He had never seen traffic this bad, and wondered if the Tegs had erected roadblocks up ahead somewhere.

He voiced his concern out loud.

"There's nowhere to escape to," Bobby said. "Except into the desert. Maybe we should make a run for it."

No one replied, and Torr gazed east. He knew the area a little bit. There were miles of suburbs, then a wilderness of scrubland, then eventually the Joshua Tree wilderness, and then Arizona, which was controlled by the Tegs.

"Even if there aren't any roadblocks," Torr said, "I don't know if we'll be able to make it through LA by car. You guys could head into the city on foot, and Bobby and I can take the jeep and try to go around and head north."

Reina looked at him, her eyes glistening. They were going to split up, sooner rather than later. His heart ached.

Bobby found a paper map of Los Angeles stuffed in a door pocket, and Mike unfolded it for everyone to look at. The four Los Angeles natives lived several miles apart, along a zigzagging line. Mike was the farthest north, in Glendale. If they had to go by foot, they could still drop off Jenna first, then Donald. Mike could take Reina home, then continue on by himself.

Traffic crawled, and they decided to take the Dana Point exit to find a bathroom, charge the jeep's battery, which was old and crappy, and stretch their legs. An hour later they had traveled the two hundred yards to the off ramp. Clearly, they could walk faster. It might even be safer for them to ditch their military vehicle. They were officially deserters now.

Once they got off the exit ramp, cars were lined up beyond the curve to get onto the northbound lanes, but the road leading away from the highway was nearly empty. They passed one car with an old man hunched over the steering wheel, his car packed solid with boxes and bags obscuring the back windows. A fast-charging station was backed up with a long queue of cars waiting their turn. They headed towards the marina, passing a strip mall. It was eerily abandoned, with shuttered shops and restaurants, and its large parking lot empty except for several cars waiting for the few parking spots with electric charging pods.

Bobby spotted a public phone booth, and pulled into the lot. Torr, Reina, and Mike crowded into the phone's glass enclosure. Torr took the receiver off the hook, while Reina slid a silver bit coin into the slot. There was no sound. Nothing. Torr hit the phone and Reina tried a different coin. They found another phone booth at the other side of the sprawling strip mall. Same thing. All the phones were dead.

"Damn Tegs," he said. He and Reina glared at each other in shared frustration.

They piled back into the jeep. Not much farther down the road, they turned into the marina parking lot and crossed the marina bridge to the harbor island. At the end of the small island, they found a parking spot with an available charging pod and plugged in the jeep. Mike tried another public phone, which was dead, while the girls rushed into the bathroom. Torr went into the men's side with the guys, and they changed out of their military fatigues into civilian clothing.

Torr put on a t-shirt and jeans that barely fit anymore, which made him realize how bulked up he had become with their daily workout regimen. He pulled on lightweight running shoes instead of the dusty boots he'd lived in for the past year, then gazed at himself in the mirror. He wasn't in the mood to shave but took the trouble to brush his teeth, for Reina's benefit.

He joined the girls on the rock jetty facing the sea wall and harbor mouth, where several craft were heading out to sea from the outer channel. They sat on the large rocks and shared a meal of peanut butter and jelly sandwiches, finished the rest of the warm milk, and watched brown pelicans fly overhead in a line. The water glittered blue and gold in the sun. Salt was tangy on the air, and Torr felt almost normal, as if life was as it should be.

After they finished eating they wandered over to the marina and gazed out over the hundreds of boats. Lines slapped against metal masts in a chorus of windchimes, and the cries of seagulls pierced the air. It was a large marina, with dozens of piers that reached out in a grid of long docks and slips. Large boats were moored at the end of each dock. The harbor island bridge spanned the central channel, with rows of docks on either side.

Torr leaned against a railing, standing between Bobby and Reina as they had been positioned for months in their bunker. He draped his arm loosely over Reina's shoulder as he regarded the boats. They were mostly leisure craft, with some fishing vessels moored at the last pier to the right, distinguishing themselves by their fishy stink, worn hulls, and stacks of crates and nets piled on the docks next to them.

"Bobby," he said, catching his friend's eyes. "What do you say we take a boat to San Francisco?"

Map of Dana Point Marina

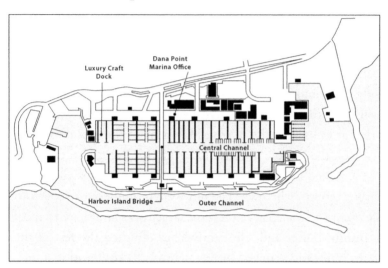

Reina leaned against him, and he met her pained gaze. She reached up and kissed his cheek, and he closed his eyes as her soft lips brushed his stubble, then found his mouth.

Bobby answered, "You mean steal one?"

Torr released his lips from Reina's and replied, "Borrow."

"I don't know anything about boats," Bobby said.

"Me neither. Except for canoes and kayaks. But it can't be that hard."

Torr examined the boats more closely. There was activity on some of them, people preparing to leave. The docks were fenced off with locked gates, and people were hauling supplies in on little orange carts. He and his buddies wandered along the railing. Torr told his idea to Mike and Donald, and Reina whispered to Jenna.

"What do you think?" Torr asked Mike.

His friend shrugged. "Might get you home faster. You could maybe hitch a ride."

Torr nodded, feeling like he was abandoning them. Things weren't going to get any easier by delaying the inevitable. He set his jaw and approached an older couple who were unlocking a pier gate. The woman held a small dog in her arms, and the man pulled a cart loaded with groceries.

"Hi," Torr said, introducing himself. They eyed him nervously. "We're looking to hitch a boat ride north. Two of us." He gestured to Bobby, who approached with a courteous nod.

The man glanced at Bobby and shook his head. "We're heading out to sea." He gave Torr an awkward wave and held the door open for his wife. The metal door slammed shut behind them, and Torr and Bobby exchanged a long glance.

They wandered down the sidewalk and waited until two young men rushed to a gate, lugging suitcases. Torr tried again, introducing himself and Bobby. The men nodded a silent greeting but did not shake his outstretched hand.

"Do you think we could hop up the coast with you guys?" Torr asked, as one of the men set down his bags and unlocked the gate.

"Can't. Sorry," the man said. "Our families are coming. We have too many people already. Good luck."

Torr held the door for them and lowered his eyebrows at Bobby, who followed the men with his eyes as they hurried down the dock without looking back. Torr let the gate click closed and joined their squadmates, who had been looking on from a bench.

"I like my 'borrowing' idea better," Torr said to Mike.

"Haha. Yeah," Mike said. "I doubt anyone who's not here already will miss their boat."

Torr didn't buy that, but pushed his misgivings aside. They walked across the harbor island bridge and turned left, pacing slowly past the piers. The back piers were lined with large luxury craft. They were sleek, white beauties, with dark windows glinting at them like sunglasses.

"We'll need a power boat," Torr said to Bobby. "Sailing takes skill. We need a boat with an engine and a steering wheel."

Bobby grunted his agreement.

They turned back the way they'd come, and passed the bridge and the harbor office.

"Come on," Reina said, and bounded up the stairs to the office.

Torr exchanged glances with Bobby and followed.

They opened the door into a waiting area filled with green vinyl chairs and racks of pamphlets. A man came out of a small office with a sign on the door that read HARBORMASTER. Thinning blond hair swept away from the harbormaster's high forehead as a salty breeze gusted in from the open balcony that faced the harbor. His face was lined and leathery.

"Morning," Reina said cheerfully. Jenna sidled up beside her and flashed a friendly smile.

The man nodded and a grin brightened his face. "Morning." His eyes darted over Jenna's long blond hair and halter top, then shifted to Reina, whose dark hair hung in waves over her tight t-shirt. The girls' long legs were bare below short shorts. Their civilian clothing had transformed the young women from worn, dusty soldiers to summer beach babes with not a care in the world.

"It's nice to see the sun, isn't it?" Reina asked, as though a simple storm had cleared.

"You can say that again," the man agreed, his eyes appraising Torr and Bobby and returning to the women. "Though I hear Teg ships are massing out at sea."

The bright mood in the room darkened. Reina wandered out to the balcony. The harbormaster and Jenna followed her, a gust of wind taking their words away. Bobby flipped through a pamphlet, and Torr glanced inside the harbormaster's office. Taking up the whole back wall was a pegboard marked with slip numbers and keys hanging below each one, on key chains with little red and white buoys. Of course. People who didn't live nearby would need the harbormaster to care for their boats, for maintenance, or in the event of a storm.

Torr walked to the balcony and heard Reina ask the harbormaster if anyone was offering sightseeing tours. What a stupid question, Torr thought tensely. Who in their right mind would sightsee on a day like today? But the harbormaster pointed left down the long line of docks and said, "Dave's Excursions said the waters are teeming with dolphins and whales. I guess the Shaman's Shield held them back and now they've all come rushing in. He counted close to four hundred dolphins yesterday."

Reina's eyes widened. "Wow, I'd love to see them."

"Dave should be back from his dawn tour by now. I was going to walk over there to ask him what he spotted."

"Ooh, can we come?" Reina gave him her best smile, and the harbormaster grinned pleasantly. "Want to come?" Reina asked Torr, looking over her shoulder at him. An intensity in her gaze told him she had no interest in Dave's Excursions.

Torr swallowed. "Nah, we're going to rinse off at the outdoor showers."

Reina shrugged as though she didn't care, and the harbormaster didn't seem disappointed to have the females all to himself. The man led the girls to the stairs and looked behind him, waiting for Torr and Bobby.

"Hang on," Bobby said distractedly, his attention focused on a pamphlet about riptides.

"We'll be down in a second," Torr assured the harbormaster as he studied a marina map mounted on the wall.

The man led the girls down the stairs and out into the sunshine. Torr slipped into the small office and hurriedly shoved
several keys into his jeans pockets. A key at the lower left corner
of the pegboard was marked MASTER, and Torr took it.

His heart hammered as he left the small office and tugged
on Bobby's shirtsleeve. "Come on," he said, grabbing a marina
map from the rack, and loped down the stairs and out into the
bright daylight.

The harbormaster locked the door behind them while he
chatted with Jenna, then walked with her away from the bridge.

Reina lingered behind, and Torr hugged her. "We're going
to try to slip out," he murmured in her ear. "This might be
goodbye." She hugged him tightly, and he kissed her. Their lips
lingered for a long moment, and he wished he could stay with
her. He kissed her cheek. It was wet with tears.

"I'll pray for you," she whispered.

"Me too," he said. He stepped back, his stomach in a knot.

Reina wiped at her cheeks and tore her eyes away. She hurried
to join Jenna and the harbormaster, stealing a parting glance at
Torr. He tried to smile, but her look wrenched his heart.

He forced himself to turn away and joined Mike and Donald
at the railing overlooking a long pier. They turned to him expectantly. They knew him well enough to know he had a plan.

"I've got some keys," he told them quietly. "Me and Bobby will
go to the other end and look for a boat. You guys stay here, and
sound a whistle if the harbormaster discovers his keys are missing."

Mike and Donald stared at him. They understood. Torr
watched as the girls and the harbormaster walked through a
gate several piers down, stepped onto a dock, and were soon
hidden by boats.

"Take care of the girls," he said to Mike and Donald, his
voice suddenly hoarse. They nodded, their eyes big and shiny.

He gave Mike a rough hug. "Don't cry," Torr said. "You'll make me cry."

"Knock 'em dead," Donald said as they embraced and pounded each other's backs.

Torr turned away without looking back. He and Bobby headed in the opposite direction from where the harbormaster had taken Reina and Jenna. They walked across the bridge, then ran to the jeep to grab their belongings. Weighed down with their packs, bags, and weapons, they went back to the nearest docks, hoping the harbormaster could not see them through the forest of ship masts.

Torr pulled the keys from his pockets. Names of boats and berth numbers were written on plastic tags. Bobby unfolded the marina map and searched for matching slip numbers. Torr had pulled most of the keys from consecutive hooks, and several boats were clustered together. They found a pier on their side of the bridge with a bunch of matching tags, and Torr unlocked the gate with the master key. They quickly walked up and down the dock, identified the boats, and weighed their options.

Wind Goddess was a sailboat. *Mojo* was an old fishing boat that stank. *Wanderlust* had a crew on board. *Johnny Jane* had clothes drying on the front hatch and a cat staring at them from a small round window. *Serenity* was a two-seater with a tarped roof covering the little wheelhouse—Torr wasn't sure the boat was even made for the open sea. *Wet Dream* was another sailboat with a tall mast in the center, and a shorter mast at the stern. The berths for *Golden Dragonfly* and *Chantyman* were empty.

Another batch of keys was for a dock across the channel right near where the harbormaster had taken the girls. One last key was for a boat named *Moon Star,* across the bridge and all the way to the back of the marina, which they decided to skip.

They reviewed their closest options again, stopping in front of *Mojo*. The stink of rotting fish made Torr want to hold his nose. The paint had worn off the wooden hull leaving broad, bare patches, and the winches and chains were covered in rust. Torr recognized a water pump sitting on the deck. The boat creaked as the rising and falling water moved it gently against the moorings.

"No," Bobby said, shaking his head. "That thing looks like a floating coffin."

"My thoughts exactly," Torr agreed. Creeping anxiety met with cowardly relief. They should just forget the whole thing. Ditch the keys and take their chances on the road. He recalled the blocked traffic, and tried to calculate the chances of making it through Los Angeles by car. They would probably end up abandoning the jeep and continuing on foot. Then what?

"Might as well check out *Moon Star,*" Bobby said, sensing his mood.

Torr nodded. They crossed the bridge, then strode down the line to the second-to-last pier. Torr let them through the gate, and Bobby grinned at him. Torr felt slightly nauseous. The boat at the very end of the pier was a sleek, white motor yacht, bigger than any of the other large luxury craft. Moon Star was painted on its side in fancy gold script.

Torr and Bobby looked at one another, then back at the yacht, then at each other again. Torr ignored his racing pulse, took a breath, and then hopped onto the back of the boat and clambered across the afterdeck. He pointed the key at the cabin door, and the lock flashed green and clicked open. His heart pounded as he dumped his belongings onto a bench molded into the afterdeck and signaled to Bobby to untie the boat from the cleats. Torr caught the ropes as Bobby tossed them on board, and gave Bobby a hand up as the boat started rocking away from the dock. Torr tossed the other keys overboard where they landed with a soft splash. Gurgles announced each buoy as one by one they popped to the surface, and soon a dozen little red and white buoys were bobbing in the water.

"Leave them," Bobby said, and held the door open for Torr.

Torr whistled with admiration as they entered the spacious cabin. It was elegant, with polished mahogany cabinets and white leather furniture. Torr hurried to the front and sat in the black leather captain's chair, trying to figure out the controls. He pressed the ignition, and the engine rumbled to life. The control panel lit up and started beeping at him, and red lights flashed as the stern of the boat thumped against the dock. Bobby came over, and Torr hit a glowing red button, which quieted the beeping. Bobby looked like he wanted to take the helm. Torr moved over to the co-captain's chair, and Bobby gripped the wheel, clamping his tongue between his lips like an eight-year-old taking his dad's car out for a spin.

The yacht fishtailed and the stern thudded against the dock. "Hey!!"

The yell came from outside, and a rapping on the metal railing brought Torr to his feet. Outside the small side window, a man was waving a fishing rod at them. Bobby gripped the wheel more tightly, and Torr ran out to the afterdeck.

The white-haired man eyed Torr suspiciously. "Who are you?" the man demanded.

Torr stared dumbly and fumbled with a response. "We're, uh ... I'm ... his cousin. Nephew. Second cousin."

The man's eyes narrowed.

Torr dove into his lie. "He asked me to get the boat and come get him. He's stuck up at Santa Barbara, and the roads in LA are blocked. I'm the only one nearby. I was attending Miramar College. The crazy Shaman's Shield is gone."

The man frowned. "How did he ask you?"

Torr swallowed. "My wired phone. Back at the dorm."

"How are you related, again? He never talked about you. What's your name?"

"John. Look, we don't have time," Torr said. "My mom's his first cousin. They grew up together. We need to go. Tegs are coming. You should go, too."

The man's frown deepened. "Yes. Yes, you're right. I have family in Costa Rica."

Torr said, "I'd go north if I were you. But that's just me. Good luck."

The man gave him a small wave. "Tell Earl I wish him well. Tell him Marty said so."

"Sure thing, Marty," Torr said. "I'll tell Uncle Earl."

Torr went inside, his legs trembling.

"Bloody stars, that was close," he muttered to Bobby, and sat heavily in the co-captain's chair.

Bobby held his breath and pushed on the throttle.

Marty was still outside, guiding them forward. "Use the side thrusters," Marty called through the glass. "The joystick."

Bobby found the side thrusters and moved the long craft away from the dock. Marty turned away and hopped onto the afterdeck of a neighboring yacht. Torr exhaled and wiped his sweaty palms on his pants.

It was like driving a huge tour bus, and Bobby frantically corrected his course as the boat angled towards another large yacht moored at the end of the next dock. They zigzagged out into the channel until they were in the center and facing away from Reina and the harbormaster. Bobby pushed on the throttle and motored towards the rear cove to sneak out the back way. They putted slowly across the quiet cove and rounded the bend into the outer channel.

"Five miles per hour," Torr said, reading the sign. Bobby pulled back on the throttle and chewed on his lip as the boat crept along, cutting through the glassy blue water.

The parking lots were on their left, and the sea wall was on their right. The mouth of the harbor opened straight ahead. They were safely hidden behind the tinted glass of the wheelhouse, and the docks were out of view behind the parking lots that were built up on the stone jetty. Even so, Torr's heart pounded in his chest and his brow was beaded with sweat. He looked for the jeep and saw it just as Mike and Donald jogged into view. They ran onto the grass and waved.

Tears sprang to Torr's eyes. "I'm going out back," he said, and went to the afterdeck, hopped up onto a bench, and waved to Mike and Donald. They were shouting at him. Torr thought for a second they were trying to warn him that the harbormaster was coming, but they did not look afraid.

"What? I can't hear you!" Torr yelled back. The sea was calling with a low roar, waves churning at the outlet, and sea gulls cried to one another on the wind.

His buddies hopped across the large jetty rocks until they stood at the point as the yacht motored slowly past. Tears were streaming down Donald's face.

Mike cupped his hands around his mouth and yelled into the breeze. "Learn ... to ... be ... a ... shaman!"

Torr's heart was in his throat. "I will!" he promised. "Stars be with you!" He struck his fist on his chest and pumped it up into the air.

His friends returned the salute.

Moon Star lurched as it hit the cross currents of the outlet. Bobby opened the throttle, and Torr hopped down to the floor and gazed back at his two friends who waved and grew smaller. The yacht angled off to the right towards the open ocean. Mike and Donald disappeared behind the sea wall, passing out of view forever.

9

TREASURES

Cassidy stood in her bedroom, wondering if her idea of fleeing to the moon was crazy. Of course it was, but she found herself continually drawn to the notion. What would Torr say? He would look at her with those practical eyes and tell her it was too expensive. Then he would insist they see their parents safely to Shasta, then maybe they could discuss it more after that. Her idea would die a quiet death, and she would always wonder what could have been.

If Jasper were here, he'd understand. He would get that excited glint in his eye and examine the deeds with her. He would talk about how they could get rich from mining minerals and trading with far-off planets. He would tell her that she was almost twenty-one, a full-grown woman who needed to make her own decisions. If he were here he would encourage her to gamble everything for her freedom. Jasper, who was up there already, far from the threat of the Tegs, while she was down here with a noose slowly tightening around her neck.

She racked her brain for a way to get enough money to buy passage to the moon. They could sell their house, but who would buy it? All homes would be turned over to the Global Alliance soon, or else razed. No one would be stupid enough to move here now. She tried to get online to see if she could find any information about passage to the moon, but the WestWeb was still down. She took out her cell phone. No signal. She threw the phone on her bed. "Useless piece of garbage," she muttered.

She went to her dresser, and her eyes wandered over the knick-knacks she had collected over the years, coated in a thin film of dust. Most of them were gifts from Great-Aunt Sophie. Cassidy took a small crystal ball and polished it with her sleeve. Her elderly aunt claimed the crystals she sent her and Torr had special powers, though Cassidy had never discovered any. She held the sphere in her palm. It was not much bigger than a ping-pong ball, small enough that her hand nearly hid it when she closed her fingers around it. It was clear quartz, with glistening rainbows within. If it truly had magical powers, maybe Cassidy could sell it for a good price.

Regardless, who would believe the crystal ball was magical and pay her lots of money for it if she couldn't demonstrate any-thing? She gazed into it but only saw a reflection of herself and a fisheye view of her bedroom. She set aside the sphere and picked up a crystal shaft. It was a clear quartz crystal, reaching from her fingertips to wrist in length, with a width of two fingers. Its sides were long and narrow and terminated in a sharp faceted point at one end. She dusted it off and stashed the shaft and crystal ball in a front pocket of her pack.

Back at the dresser her eye caught a shimmer of gold among a tangle of necklaces that hung from a little stand. She untwined the gold chain from the others and held the pendant in her palm. This would be worth something, she thought with a tingle of excitement. It was a good-sized coin pendant, and heavy. Twenty-four carat gold and as big as a one-ounce gold

Eagle, which was worth one thousand global credits. It depicted a nude woman on the front, and on the back were a triangle and strange runes. Great-Aunt Sophie had given her the necklace when Cassidy's family had visited her in her little cottage in the Great Isles. Cassidy had been only nine. She had never thought of the necklace as money before, though clearly it was. It was not from Earth; Sophie had brought it back from one of her trips to the planet Delos. That should make it even more valuable. Cassidy held back her excitement and went in search of her parents.

She found them sitting on the couch watching the wall screen. The same newsfeed was being broadcast on all the channels. They had been watching it all morning. Cassidy sat on the couch next to her mother.

Two male newscasters with smiling faces spoke of a treaty between the Global Alliance and Gaia United, whom they referred to as "the rebels." They did not say if the treaty was a peace deal or a surrender. They did not say if California would retain its free status, but Cassidy did not think so.

Earlier, she and her parents had gone out to talk with their neighbors who had not fled yet. Mr. Thompson met them at his door with an assault rifle in his hands, a cigarette hanging from his lips, and a frenzied look in his eyes. "The world as we know it has ended," he said ominously. His house reeked of smoke, and his coffee table was stacked with boxes of ammunition. He'd invited them in for a beer, but they had declined. Their other neighbors, Mr. Wimble and his wife, Kathy, refused to watch the newscast. "Propaganda," Kathy had stated decisively. "They are starting to brainwash us already. Preparing us for the camps. We're leaving tomorrow before dawn. Heading north."

Cassidy closed her eyes and tried to sense Torr. All she saw was empty ocean. This was as confusing as the traffic she had seen before. She thought maybe she would be able to see through his eyes as the Sweet Alyssum had implied, but if so he wasn't where she'd expected him to be. Maybe his unit had been sent out on a naval mission. But they were foot soldiers. It didn't make sense.

She returned her attention to the newscasters, neither of whom Cassidy had ever seen before. When they started repeating themselves again, Caden turned it off in disgust and glanced at Cassidy. He had black circles under his eyes. He rose from the couch and cracked open the front door, peering up and down the street, then locked the door and paced back and forth across the living room floor.

"Look," Cassidy said, dangling the necklace from her fingers. "You think this will buy passage to the moon?"

"Are you still thinking about that?" Caden asked. He walked over and took the necklace. "Well, it is pure gold, and close in size to an Eagle. But I don't know what passage to the moon costs anymore. I say it'd cost at least a Solidi, if not more, in times like these."

"A Solidi!" Cassidy's hopes plummeted. A Solidi was a million global credits. More than her parents made in ten years. "But it's from another planet. Doesn't that make it worth more?"

Her mother inspected the medallion. "Yes," Brianna said softly. "Aunt Sophie claimed this was from Iliad, if that's possible."

"Iliad!" The planet's civilization had been destroyed by a thousand-year war that was still smoldering. "I thought trade with Iliad was closed," Cassidy said.

Brianna shrugged. "Maybe it's ancient and made its way to Delos before the Cephs invaded Iliad a millennium ago, during the time when Iliad colonized Delos."

Cassidy's great-aunt rarely spoke of her trips to Delos, as much as they had tried to get details. She was happy to describe the landscape and its peoples, and to bring them back gifts, but everything else was "State Department business." She'd traveled there a couple times even after she'd retired. She wouldn't say how she had afforded the interstellar travel, nor with whom she had gone other than a vague "Friends from the Department," and "It's a lovely place to vacation. It has a gorgeous coast."

Listening to her aunt speak of her trips, Cassidy had realized off-world travel was possible, even for normal people like them. Cassidy suspected Great-Aunt Sophie's "friend" was President Metolius, and the connection made Cassidy question everything. Who was Great-Aunt Sophie, really? How could a member of their family associate with a cruel dictator? Nothing made sense anymore, except that Cassidy wanted to get as far away from the whole mess as possible. But where was there to go? It seemed the whole galaxy was threatened by the darkness of the Cephs. But anywhere was better than here, in the direct path of the Teg army.

In addition to her great-aunt, others from their close circle of Shasta friends had also journeyed away from Earth. Their family friend, Doctor Ramesh, had departed for the moon, then onto the planet Muria. The next year, Jasper's mother, Melanie, had left him and his father, heading off on a quest to discover the golden pathways to the Star People. Melanie had been able to go off-world somehow; she had found a way to afford it. She hadn't been heard from since. Two years later, Kai had gone to the moon, and eventually sent for Jasper. Cassidy had always dreamed of traveling to distant planets, with a mixture of anticipation and fear.

"If the necklace is from Iliad, then it should be priceless, don't you think?" Cassidy asked.

Her mother raised her eyebrows. "Yes, you would think. But I don't know who would buy such a thing during wartime, or how to find a buyer. I suppose a museum or something, but the timing is not good, Cassidy."

Cassidy took the pendant and inspected it. The nude woman was on her knees pouring water from an urn, and was surrounded by stars. The back had a simple triangle with three eyes in it and small runes etched along the edges. A shiver ran up the nape of Cassidy's neck. She hung the coin around her neck, wondering if there were any rich, eccentric collectors in San Francisco who would buy it, and how she would ever find them. She ran to her room and returned with the quartz shaft and crystal ball. "What about these?" she asked. "What do you think these are worth?"

"Not much," her father said. "They're just quartz. A tenth-gold bit if you're lucky."

A mere ten global credits. She couldn't buy anything with that. "But Aunt Sophie says they're magic," Cassidy insisted.

"Aunt Sophie says everything's magic," her father retorted.

Cassidy scowled and looked at her mother. "Maybe they are magic. Right, Mom?"

"Maybe," Brianna said doubtfully. "We can ask Balor if we make it to Shasta. He might know."

Cassidy's mood deflated. *If* they made it to Shasta? Her mother didn't sound very confident. Cassidy went to Torr's room to search for gifts Great-Aunt Sophie had sent him. The top drawer of his dresser was a junk drawer. She rifled through it and found four crystals in the back. One was similar to her shaft, but thinner and longer, like a dagger. The second crystal was more of a big blocky chunk than a shaft, and heavy. Each of its clear, rectangular facets was the size of her whole hand, and transitioned into triangular facets that terminated in a point like a giant, fat pencil. The third was a pale green fluorite crystal with an eight-sided, double pyramid shape. The octahedron was bigger than the crystal ball, but still fit nicely in her hand. The fourth was a multi-faceted dark red garnet, smaller than the crystal ball by half. She tucked them all into the side pockets of Torr's pack that was sitting inside his bedroom doorway waiting for him.

She closed up the pack and went to the kitchen window to look for him. She did not know why she thought he would come in through the back, except that their yard bordered a dry streambed that cut through the suburban neighborhoods in a cement channel. If the roads were blocked, that's how she would come. She closed her eyes, trying to feel for him, and felt nauseous. She exhaled and opened her eyes, and watched the tree limbs dance in the wind.

10

MOON STAR

"Go straight," Torr told Bobby, who chewed on his lip and nodded.

Torr sat in the co-captain's chair and looked through the yacht's operations manual. The control panels were supposed to show their location on a live map via satellite, as well as track ocean depth, currents, distance to shore and other craft, even locate sea mammals and schools of fish. They should have been able to set their destination to San Francisco, and the craft would navigate on autopilot. None of those systems were working. The navigation screen just jumped around in random patterns.

Torr unfolded a paper marine chart he had found stuffed in the seat pocket and looked at his compass. They were headed northwest, following the coast that curved westward until it turned northward past Santa Barbara.

Through the window on their right, land rose in low, hazy brown hills. From what Torr could decipher from the marine charts, if they kept to the channel between the mainland and the islands until they got past Santa Barbara, they should be okay.

He was a bit concerned about currents that were marked in orange with all sorts of swirls. He climbed out onto the bow and inspected the waters for signs of dangerous currents, but really did not know what he was looking for. He scanned the ocean for Coast Guard craft, afraid the harbormaster had discovered the missing yacht by now and reported it stolen. Torr didn't know what the punishment was for stealing a yacht, but he was sure he and Bobby would end up in jail. Or a Teg torture chamber. He hadn't considered that at the time. He hoped law enforcement officials had more important things to worry about at the moment than a stolen yacht.

There were no boats chasing them. He walked around the deck, coiling ropes and pulling up three bumpers that hung from the starboard side railing to protect the hull from the dock.

As they passed Long Beach they were joined by several more craft headed in the same direction: fishing boats, sailboats, and yachts like their own. None of them were Coast Guard. Bobby and Torr decided to follow the other boats, assuming their pilots knew how to navigate the channel. The fishing boats and sailboats soon dropped behind while the yachts sped ahead. *Moon Star* kept pace with the luxury craft.

After a time they realized they were motoring out to sea and had lost sight of the coast. Torr and Bobby looked anxiously at one another. They could follow the yachts, not knowing where they were headed. Or they could turn around and hug the coast, looking for other boats to follow in order to navigate the channels and currents.

Torr went to the bow and looked through his binoculars at the nearest yacht. It was called *Seas the Day.* A woman was standing at the stern looking through binoculars out to sea. After a minute she turned his way, and he gestured for her to approach. She understood and disappeared into the cabin, then returned on deck. *Seas the Day* slowed, and Bobby navigated to her side at a safe distance and matched speed.

Torr called across the waves, "Where are you headed?"

"Monterey."

Torr called back, "San Francisco. Can we follow you? We don't know these waters." Monterey was only a few miles south of San Francisco. She nodded and waved. A yacht that had been following them pulled up at his left. "Where are you headed?" Torr called to the man standing on the deck of *Tide Runner.*

"Anchorage."

"San Francisco," Torr called back.

The man waved. *Seas the Day* took the lead, *Moon Star* followed them, and *Tide Runner* took up the rear. The three boats resumed cruising speed, motoring into the wind. Torr breathed deeply, and thanked the stars for their companions.

Inside, Torr discovered more charts stashed in the coffee table that doubled as a chest. Among the charts were two star maps. One was a map of the sky as seen from the northern hemisphere, and one from the southern. In the old days people knew how to navigate the seas using the stars. He searched the maps for the constellation Cepheus. He found the star system where the ruling race of Cephs was from. They called their star Blessed Fire. There were two ruling planets that orbited Blessed Fire. One was Thunder Walker, which was said to have massive lightning and thunder storms. The second was Tree Nut, which at one time had been heavily forested but had since been stripped of its trees, and was now a desert planet relegated primarily to mining and metallurgy. The Cephs supposedly worshipped trees as a result of their mismanagement of Tree Nut, and that was one reason they had chosen to colonize Earth. A neighboring star was orbited by the first two planetary colonies conquered by the ruling planets, and were now full members of the Cephean

Federation. More planets in the Federation were in the Draco constellation, but Torr knew of them only vaguely.

He rolled the two star maps together, folded the roll in half, and stuffed it into his rucksack. Next, Torr looked through paperwork he found in a drawer. There was a copy of the yacht's title of ownership and a registration certificate. The owner was named Earl T. Morrow. Guilt stabbed at Torr. What if Morrow came to escape on his boat, only to find it gone? Torr's face heated, and his stomach felt upset. He was a horrible person.

"Bobby. What if the owner needed his boat to escape?"

Bobby cast him a sharp glance, then sighed and shrugged. "Bad luck, I guess."

Torr didn't know if he meant bad luck for Earl T. Morrow, or bad luck for Torr and Bobby. Torr didn't ask. They weren't going to turn around.

Torr explored the boat. The upper cabin held the sitting room, a round dining table with built-in, curved, cushioned benches, the wheelhouse, and a galley stocked with boxes of noodles, crackers, canned food, and beer. He grabbed a couple warm beers, plugged in the refrigerator, and opened a box of crackers and a can of tuna fish for each of them. They made short work of it, and Torr continued exploring.

Below decks were four staterooms, each with its own bathroom. One of the rooms had a large bed nestled up into the point of the bow, surrounded by a row of little windows at eye level, built into the mahogany paneling. On the bed was a fluffy white down comforter, as though the bed had been freshly made before the owners departed. Another was the master bedroom, with a king bed, a couch, large closets, and a good-sized bathroom. The two other cabins were tiny. Two twin beds were stuffed into each, with barely enough room to walk between the beds. Each had a bathroom so small Torr could wash his hands in the basin while sitting on the toilet, with a showerhead over the whole thing and a drain in the floor.

A whole family could live aboard this boat. Reina, Mike, Donald, and Jenna could have come with them, and they could have lived out at sea. Too late. His friends were sure to have sped from the parking lot the moment the girls were finished with the harbormaster. Besides, they would need food, and the ship's water tanks would run dry at some point. And although he had read in the manual that the boat's electric motor and several battery banks were powered by prop generation as well as solar panels on the roof, the engine would need recharging every several hundred miles, and the backup diesel tank would need to be refilled.

He climbed back upstairs and out to the afterdeck. It was lined with molded, fiberglass benches with slots for fishing poles and had a folding ladder off the back. He went around to the foredeck and climbed onto a large hatch cover, which was rubberized and kept his feet from slipping as he faced into the wind. The sea was beautiful with the waves and the sun. If he wasn't so nervous, he'd be in heaven.

He lay on his back on top of the hatch and watched the blue sky as they passed beneath it, wishing the Shaman's Shield was still up there. The rocking motion started to make him feel nauseous, and he retreated inside the cabin. The waves got larger as their little fleet went further out to sea, heading into the sun. Torr hoped they would adjust course soon and head north. He took a turn at the steering wheel while Bobby went out to the afterdeck, where Torr could hear him throwing up, bringing the taste of bile to his own mouth.

They settled into a rhythm, taking turns steering the boat and hurling over the side. Night fell and they finally headed north, following the coastline from several miles out. Torr went out onto the foredeck. Stars spanned the sky, brightening in layers as the night deepened. He watched, mesmerized, as the moon rose in the east, huge and yellow, reflecting off the water in a path of golden light that seemed to point at him, beckoning him to follow.

He gazed up at the moon. It was large and bright enough to show some detail. Jasper was up there right now. Torr fetched his binoculars and zoomed in until he could discern large craters and vast seas of black. He tried to detect Peary Dome at the moon's north pole on the rim of Peary Crater, but couldn't find anything that looked man-made. He tried to imagine for the millionth time what life would be like in the Peary colony. He'd seen photos of the magnificent Peary Dome structure, an enormous glass geodesic dome, but images of the inside of the dome looked like a depressing refugee camp, a tent city in a barren desert wasteland. But at least the moon was still free.

He sat on the hatch cover and hung on as they rode the waves. The sea moved with relentless power, in a whispering silence with the soft shushing of the bow slicing through the water. *Seas the Day* was still in the lead, and they followed her red lights, which disappeared and reappeared as the boats dipped into wide troughs then rose over smooth crests. The moon slowly climbed overhead and illuminated the endless sea.

Torr's thoughts turned to Reina and how they had kissed under the moonlight. He would never see her again. It was painful to leave her and his buddies, yet his family was more important to him. The bond he had with his sister was something he couldn't explain. It flowed beneath his consciousness like a powerful underground river. Yet it was because of Reina that he had decided to flee in the first place. Now he would never know her fate. Chances were she and the others would end up in a work camp. Torr and Bobby probably would as well.

Worse yet were the ones who had chosen to join the Tegs: Johnson and Smiley, Rashon, Jessimar, and Bates. Flipped to the other side so easily, thinking it would save their lives. They were his brothers, yet they had been so quick to abandon the tribe for the enemy. The betrayal stabbed like a knife.

He lay back on the hatch, trying to calm his heart, his mind, his stomach. Every part of him was upset. His cheek twitched lightly, as though a feather were stroking it. He stood up, lurched to the railing, and emptied his stomach over the side, trying to expel his churning emotions into the black sea.

11

JACOBSEN'S

The next morning Cassidy found herself alone. Her father had left in the middle of the night to make a farm run, insisting he might as well continue to supply the troops as long as he was still here. Regardless of the political situation, Torr and the other soldiers needed food. Traffic was getting worse and worse, and Caden said that if he didn't leave and return before sunrise he'd be caught in it all day. It was nearly ten o'clock, so he must have left too late.

Brianna had also left in the middle of the night, to go to a neighbor's house to help deliver a baby. Life continued, regardless of who won the war. Maybe the child would be raised in a work camp and grow up thinking that way of life was normal. Cassidy wondered if they'd all end up in work camps, and if the rumors were true that young women were sent to breeding centers. Her insides clenched, and she pushed the repulsive thought away.

She pulled on her leather jacket, went to the garage, and unplugged the motorcycle's engine battery from the wall charger. Cassidy recalled the night before Jasper had left for the moon, when he'd convinced her father to buy the bike. Caden never even rode it, but Torr did, and it had become his by default. After Torr left for the war, she'd practiced riding it up and down her street until she felt comfortable enough to drive herself to school and back.

She put on her helmet and daypack and motored out of the garage heading south, then took back roads towards the area surrounding her university. There were several jewelers and pawnshops in downtown San Jose. There was no reason to go all the way to San Francisco to sell her necklace and crystals.

She parked her bike on a street with several expensive-looking jewelry shops, and went to the nearest one. A *Closed* sign hung in the window, and the velvet display cases were bare. Although it was a weekday, the street had an abandoned feeling. Several shops were boarded up, and trash swirled in a sudden gust of wind. The few people she saw walked in a hurry as though they had somewhere important to be.

She tried three other shops before she found one that was open. A woman sitting behind a glass case raised her eyes as Cassidy entered the immaculate shop.

"I'm wondering if you buy gold jewelry?" Cassidy asked hesitantly.

The woman peered over reading glasses. "We *sell* gold jewelry," she said curtly. A man appeared from the back.

"It's an off-world antique," Cassidy said.

The man eyed Cassidy curiously. "Let's take a look," he said, his pinched face trying to smile. The woman threw him a side-long glance but did not object.

Cassidy slid the pack from her back and took out the gold medallion and set it on the counter. The man lifted it from the glass and examined it closely, putting on an eyepiece as he turned it over in his hand.

"It's Ilian," Cassidy said.

The man took out a small scale and weighed the pendant.

"Nearly an ounce," he said. "I'll give you one gold Eagle for it."

Cassidy gave a derisive chuckle. "An Eagle? It's *Ilian.*"

"I don't know if it's Ilian or not," the man said, arching his gray eyebrows at her. "Regardless, off-world coins are not official currency here. As far as I'm concerned, it's just gold, and weighs less than an ounce. I'm offering you an Eagle because it's an unusual piece."

"It's worth a Solidi," Cassidy said.

The man laughed haughtily, and the woman rolled her eyes. "Two Eagles," the man said. "No more."

Cassidy held out her hand, feeling the blood rise to her face. He dropped the pendant into her open palm. She closed her fingers around it and stalked out of the store.

Clutching the necklace in her fist, she felt herself shaking with anger. Why was she so upset? She'd known it would be hard to find a buyer. She calmed herself, then walked down the street. On the next block she spotted an antique store and entered the dim shop. The air was musty and the walls were crammed with dusty paintings and shelves of mismatched china. She stepped between an assortment of heavy wooden dressers and tables covered with knick-knacks. An elderly man sat behind a cluttered counter, taking apart an old clock.

He peered up at her with a delighted smile, as though no one ever came into the shop. "Hello, young lady," he greeted her cheerfully. "Nice day we're having. The sunshine is glorious."

"It is, indeed," she said, returning his smile and approaching the counter. "I have an Ilian antique to sell. I'm wondering if you might want to buy it."

The man's eyes brightened with interest. "Well. I don't have much gold to spare, but let me take a look. What have you got?"

She showed him the medallion, and he whistled. "Wow. Ilian? Really? I could never afford this," he said sadly.

"How much do you think it's worth? The jeweler down the street offered me two gold Eagles."

The man made a disapproving face. "Two gold Eagles? This is worth much more than that."

"How much? Do you think I could get a Solidi for it?"

The man examined the coin and rubbed the gray stubble on his chin as he considered. "Possibly, if you could find the right buyer."

Her pulse quickened with hope. "Like a museum?"

He wrinkled his brow. "No. Those committees take forever to decide on anything. You're better off with a private collector." He looked up at her. "Have you tried Jacobsen's?"

"Where's that?"

"San Francisco. Jacobsen is an old friend of mine. He might want it. Tell him Smitty sent you." He handed her the pendant. "This is really something you've got. A real treasure." His eyes glittered, and she felt her spirits lift, though she wasn't happy about needing to go to San Francisco.

"What about these?" she asked, taking out her two crystals and laying them on the scratched glass counter. She steadied the crystal ball as it rolled around.

"Hmmm," he said, holding the small globe. "Are they magic?"

Cassidy shrugged and said honestly, "I don't know. I think so, but I don't know how to make them work."

"Shame," he said. "I've been wanting to get my hands on something magical. Mostly to see if magic is real. You know?" He met her eyes. "They say the Shaman's Shield was magic, but I think maybe it was just technology."

Cassidy lifted one shoulder in a small shrug. "I don't know. What's the difference, really? Maybe magic is just technology we can't explain."

The man nodded. "Could be. Could be."

"Do you think these crystals are worth anything?" she asked.

He gave her the crystal ball, then examined the shaft. "Is this a magic wand, you think?" he asked hopefully.

She chuckled. "If it were, how much would it be worth?"

He laughed with her. "Well, if it were really a magic wand, it'd certainly be worth a Solidi. But a simple quartz crystal, even one as lovely as this, would be worth a gold bit at best."

She couldn't get to the moon with a measly one hundred global credits. He told her where to find Jacobsen's, then she gathered her crystals, thanked the kind man, and left him to his clock.

A couple blocks further on she found a pawnshop and stepped inside. It was a narrow space with a long counter running lengthwise along one wall. Dust covered everything. Hanging on the wall behind the counter were several guitars, a trumpet, a saxophone, some swords, an old musket loader, and a dusty suit of armor. A sallow-faced man who looked and smelled like he smoked too much glanced up from behind the counter.

"I've got an Ilian antique I'm selling for a Solidi," she said, taking the pendant from her pocket and dangling it in front of the man's rheumy eyes.

"And I'm selling my daughter for a Solidi." He coughed out a bitter laugh, spittle flying through the air.

She wrinkled her nose in disgust and left the shop.

Cassidy wandered the streets, feeling guilty. Here she was, trying to get a Solidi to buy passage for herself to the moon. She should be trying to get two Solidi. One for her and one for Torr. She was a hypocrite. She hadn't wanted to abandon him to go to Shasta, but she was more than willing to abandon him on Earth while she got herself safely off the planet. She kicked at a pebble and watched it bounce into the gutter. She should sell her deed and give the Solidi to Torr, so at least he could get away.

At the corner a sign stared her in the face. *Dream Realty.* She hesitated, then entered the office. She sat in the waiting area until an agent came out to greet her.

"I don't suppose you're in the market for a ten thousand square foot villa in the hills, are you?" the agent asked, smiling at Cassidy amiably.

Cassidy laughed. "No. I'd like to sell some land."

The woman sighed and shook her head. "Everyone wants to sell, but no one wants to buy."

"It's an unusual property," Cassidy said. "At least let me explain."

"Okay, why not. Come on back. Coffee?" she asked.

"No, thanks," Cassidy said, and followed the woman into a tiny office with photos of mansions on the walls. She removed her pack and motorcycle jacket and sat across the desk from her.

"A moon parcel," the agent said thoughtfully as she examined Cassidy's deed. "I heard these existed, but never saw one myself."

"How much do you think it's worth?" Cassidy asked.

The woman shook her head. "I have no idea. I suppose it depends on how big it is and what minerals are on it." She examined the map. "Moon land seems to be good only for mining, from what I hear. I can't tell what the scale is. Do you know how big the parcel is?"

Cassidy shook her head.

"Looks big," the realtor said. "How much did you pay for it? There are no prices listed."

"I inherited it."

"Hmmm. Well, I don't know how to get comps. It's not an open market. In fact, I don't even know what market trades in moon property anymore." She paused, her eyes scanning the document. "Office of the President. Wow." The woman looked up at her, one eyebrow cocked.

Cassidy ignored the unspoken question. "Do you think it's worth a Solidi?" she asked.

"Oh, I would imagine so. Buildable lots around here go for a Solidi or more. But I really wouldn't know how to find a buyer. Maybe you should ask someone at the spaceport if they know."

Cassidy nodded. She did not want to go near the spaceport. Not until she had enough gold for passage. The Tegs could show up there anytime, if they weren't there already. "Okay. Thanks for looking," she said, and rose to leave.

"Probably that's the only land that will be worth anything," the woman said as she walked Cassidy to the door. "All the land around here will be confiscated, and we'll all end up in camps. It's just a matter of time." Cassidy met the realtor's eyes, a look of despair passing between them. She shook the woman's hand and left.

On her way home she took a detour by the houses of her two closest girlfriends. Beth's house looked vacant. Neither of her parents' cars was parked out front, and when Cassidy knocked at the door only silence greeted her. The shades were drawn on all the windows. She went to Jessica's house next. It was the same story. Her friends hadn't even said goodbye. Loneliness followed her as she rode home. Maybe she and her parents were making a big mistake by waiting for Torr.

———————)———————

Cassidy slept fitfully and woke up early the next morning to the buzz of her father's truck fading into the distance. The sun was already up, but her mother was still asleep. Cassidy found a note on the kitchen counter saying the baby was a healthy boy. She got dressed and left a note that she was headed to San Francisco and would be back before dark. She wheeled the motorcycle out to the street, then rode through the neighborhood and onto the freeway.

Traffic was heavier than she'd expected at this hour. A hovercraft was causing everyone to slow down up ahead. Cars honked angrily as the sleek, bullet-shaped craft bobbed above the traffic jam then tried to cut into normal traffic, unable to maintain its speed and elevation without the charged hovercraft lanes. The cars around it swerved out of the way as it fell to manual hover height then finally clunked to a stop on the shoulder.

Further up the peninsula, the routes to the bridges were backed up to a standstill. Everyone was leaving town. Cars were laden with people and belongings. Cassidy gritted her teeth and got off at a South San Francisco exit and navigated the surface roads to downtown.

She found the antiquities neighborhood and parked on a side street. Homes and shops were boarded up. The plate glass window of a hair salon was shattered on the cement sidewalk. Cassidy picked her way around the shards of glass and turned onto the main thoroughfare. It was early yet, and only coffee shops and convenience stores were open. Several storefronts with plywood over their windows were painted with fresh graffiti. One wall was spray painted with a large, red Teg insignia, and "Teg Scum" was scrawled in big black letters.

The street was busy with people crossing this way and that, lugging their precious belongings, like ants in a disturbed nest. Bus stops and trolley medians were packed with families and stacks of suitcases. Parents clutched toddlers' hands, and elderly people leaned on walkers. But it was oddly quiet. People silently scanned the streets with haunted eyes. The clanging and screech of a trolley car announced its arrival, and people pushed to climb aboard.

Cassidy spotted an empty booth in a coffee shop through its grimy window. She went inside and slid onto the cracked, red vinyl seat. The waiter was a hunched-over old man, and brought her a cup of coffee without her asking. He took her bagel order with a pencil on a little scratchpad without uttering one word or looking at her.

The coffee was hot and bitter. She sipped at it and nibbled at the plain bagel that tasted like it was from yesterday's batch. She piled on strawberry jam and stared out the window, watching people hurry down the sidewalk, dragging suitcases behind them. She checked her wristwatch. It was only seven-thirty.

A couple in the booth behind her were talking about joining family in Nevada. They were going to take back roads and risk the mountain passes. Cassidy gripped her coffee cup until the dark liquid shook. Maybe what she'd interpreted as intuition had only been fear. Maybe her family should have left town like her parents had wanted. Maybe it was too late now. Or ... what would happen if she got her wish and gathered enough gold to get off the planet; what if Torr returned and they escaped together? Her parents would still be stuck on Earth.

She slowly finished the bagel and drank more coffee as the morning crawled by. Finally she got up, left five silver bits on the table, and used the café's tiny bathroom. Out on the sidewalk a homeless man cut in front of her, pushing a shopping cart piled high with stuffed garbage bags. She dodged pedestrians and walked the city streets aimlessly until shops began to open, then made her way back to where the antiquity stores were clustered, looking for Jacobsen's. A sign in a shop window caught her attention. *Pegasus. Off-world artifacts bought and sold. We deal in only the finest.* Her pulse quickened. She pushed the glass door open and closed it behind her, wincing as cowbells hanging from the door rang loudly, disturbing the hushed space.

Three men looked up from where they were gathered around a glass counter examining a piece of jewelry. A shopkeeper stood behind the counter. Large red Persian rugs covered the floor, and a crystal chandelier hung from a high gilded ceiling. Glass cases tastefully displayed a collection of gold jewelry, ornate boxes, and daggers. A clothing rack held an assortment of garments of leather, velvet, white frills, and fur.

The men watched her cross the carpeted floor. On the counter sat a gold cuff bracelet with a large, bright green gem set in the center. The three customers were tall and tanned, with dark hair and light eyes. They were young and healthy, and Cassidy's eyes wandered over their muscular physiques. The man behind the counter was small and mouselike, with thinning hair and wire-framed glasses. He glanced up at the men nervously and wrung his hands together.

"May I help you?" he asked in a high-pitched voice.

The three young men returned her physical appraisal, and she brushed her hair away from her face. She cleared her throat. "I, uh, can come back later."

"No, no," one of the three men said, backing away from the counter. "We'll likely be here all day." He waved her forward, and the three men crossed the large room to another row of display cases.

The shopkeeper set the bracelet aside and greeted her with a quivering smile. "What can I do for you?"

"I, uh, have some things to sell. Or to get appraised."

The man nodded and smoothed the black velvet cloth that lay on the glass countertop. Cassidy took the gold medallion from her pack and set it on the velvet. The man leaned forward, his eyes blinking quickly. He lifted it and turned it over, then inspected it with an eyepiece.

He lifted his small eyes to hers. "Where did you get this?" His voice was nearly a whisper.

Cassidy shrugged. "My aunt got it on Delos, I think."

"It's Ilian, I believe," he said softly.

"Yes," Cassidy said, drawing in a short breath. "That's what I understand. How much do you think it's worth?"

The man's brow rose and fell, and he kept his gaze fastened on the pendant. After several long moments he replied, "Well, it depends on if I can find the right buyer for such a rare artifact." He cast a glance towards the three men.

The merchant bent behind the counter and pulled out an old leather-bound book, turning the fragile pages delicately. He landed on a page. "Ah," he said, studying illustrations of three coins and comparing them to her pendant. The writing was in hieroglyphics she did not understand. He turned the book so she could see. The top drawing was a perfect likeness to her coin, both the obverse side with the woman pouring water from an urn, and the reverse side with the triangle and three eyes. Excitement rushed through her.

The illustration of the second coin was of a man kneeling on one knee and drawing a bow, with a quiver of arrows at his hip. The reverse side had the same triangle containing three eyes. The third coin on the page depicted a man holding a glowing orb in his upturned palm, and a short rod in the other hand. The reverse was the same triangle.

The merchant's skin was flushed, and his fingers shook as he turned the coin over and over.

"How much do you think it's worth?" she asked again, her heart racing.

"I don't know. Priceless," he muttered, and met her eyes. "But what it would bring in this day and age ...?" He glanced at the three men again, then dropped his eyes. "Perhaps I would add it to my personal collection," he said wistfully, and closed the book. He laid the medallion gently on the velvet.

She pulled the crystals from her backpack and laid them on the cloth, desperate for him to offer her a Solidi. Two Solidi. He had confirmed the pendant was a priceless artifact. Now it was a matter of finding a buyer. Maybe the men behind her were rich. Perhaps between the pendant and the crystals she could get the gold she needed. The men had grown silent and she felt them wanting to come closer. She glanced at the merchant's face, but he had turned his attention to the crystals. He was clearly a successful dealer; he would know the proper timing to call the buyers over. Let them sweat a bit.

He handled the crystals one at a time, but did not ask if they were magic. He kept his lips sealed and examined them with his eyepiece. Cassidy looked into the glass case and noticed several crystal shafts of various sizes. A couple were similar to hers. One was bigger, but most were smaller, the size of fingers, and polished so that they gleamed. He cupped the crystal ball in his palm, staring into it, and then set it gently on the velvet.

"Do you have anything else?" he asked, his expression unreadable. She should have brought Torr's crystals. They were different from anything in his case.

She pulled out her moon deed and map and unrolled them in front of him. "I don't know if you deal in property." She had a burning curiosity to understand the worth of her land, though she wouldn't need to sell it if she could get enough money from the pendant and crystals for passage for both her and Torr.

The merchant leaned over to inspect the documents. "A moon parcel," he said softly, "with the Salmon Seal of Metolius." She could feel the men watching them, setting the hairs on her arms on end.

"How much do you think it's worth?" she asked. Footsteps crossed the floor, treading softly on the carpets.

The merchant rolled up the parchments and placed them firmly in her hand with a pointed look as a hand fell beside her on the glass. She flinched as one of the men leaned over her shoulder and peered at the gold medallion and crystals. He smelled of cologne. The eyes of the man behind him followed her hands as she tucked the moon deed into her pack. There had been something odd about the men from the start, and it suddenly came to her. Their skin did not have the grayish pallor everyone's had from living three years under the gloom of the Shaman's Shield. Theirs was ruddy and healthy. *They had been outside the Shaman's Shield.*

"Looks like a fake," the merchant said of the deed, for the men to hear. "And this is probably a replica as well," he said as he handed her the medallion. She reluctantly slipped it into her pants pocket and took the crystals as he pushed them towards her, heeding his veiled warning. "As for these," he continued, "I have more than enough crystals, as you can see, and of higher quality."

The tall man at her side scowled as she put the crystals into her bag. She wanted to stay and barter with the merchant and get her two Solidi, but something about the three men made her skin crawl.

"Good day, young lady," the merchant said curtly, turning away. He retrieved the gold bracelet with the green gem and said to the men, "Now, this here is genuine Delosian ceremonial gold. A bracelet the Priestesses wore to summon the Star People."

Cassidy crept from the shop, vowing to return after the three men left. Maybe the merchant really did want to buy the medallion but did not want to let the men in on the deal. She stepped onto the sidewalk, glancing back over her shoulder into the shop. Two of the men were striding across the carpets after her. She wondered for a moment if they wanted to buy her goods, but the hair on the nape of her neck rose in warning. She sprang into a run, stealing a glance over her shoulder as the men stepped out onto the sidewalk and started in her direction. She flew around the corner and ducked into a side street. JACOBSEN's was in front of her. She hopped inside and closed the door quickly behind her.

She scurried to the back of the shop and hid behind an ornate, carved wooden panel flanked by two potted trees. Tall urns and a shoulder-high marble statue of a griffin stood at her side. A man was behind the counter packing things into a cardboard box. He looked up at her with surprise.

"Two men are following me," she told him breathlessly. Her pulse pounded in her ears.

The man inspected her for a moment, then strode to the front of the shop. She heard him bolt the door, and a scraping of plastic told her he had turned the sign over to indicate that the shop was closed. The overhead lights extinguished, plunging the shop into muted shadows. The man's footsteps approached, and he stepped behind the screen to join her.

"Smitty said I should see you," she whispered awkwardly. She breathed to calm her heartbeat, wondering if she had overreacted. Probably the men had just wanted some fresh air.

"Smitty?"

"An antique dealer in San Jose," she said.

"Oh, that old geezer. Yes." Cassidy's eyes were adjusting to the low light, and she could see the man examining her curiously. "Jacobsen," he said, introducing himself with a firm handshake. "Who's chasing you?"

"A couple customers from a shop around the corner. Pegasus. I showed the shopkeeper some off-world artifacts I'm selling, but I don't think he trusted the men so he sent me away, and two of the men followed me. There were three of them."

"What did they look like?"

"Tall. Dark-haired. *Tan.*"

Jacobsen nodded. "They were in here yesterday. They've been combing all the shops for off-world trinkets and magical tools, and asking all sorts of questions. I don't trust them either."

"Why not?" she asked, her skin tingling.

"They're not your normal antiquity buyers. They look more like ... soldiers."

Alarm gripped Cassidy's throat. *"Tegs."*

Jacobsen held her eyes levelly, and sweat broke out on her brow.

"General Tegea probably wants to glean all the knowledge he can from us before he throws us into camps and steals all our stuff," he said, giving her a wan smile.

A wave of dizziness passed over her. A chair sat by the back counter and she sank into it. She noticed several stacks of sealed cardboard boxes. It looked as though he was packing up his wares.

"Are you leaving?" she asked.

"No." He shrugged. "Yes. Maybe. I don't know what I'm doing, actually. Where am I going to go? This shop is my life. I've been boxing up my favorite pieces, but where can we hide from the Tegs?"

She nodded glumly. When the Tegs came, it would be the end of everything.

"What have you got?" he asked.

"An Ilian medallion the shopkeeper found in a book." She took it from her pocket and handed it to him.

He whistled. "Wow. An Ilian amulet. I didn't know there were any of these on Earth. Where'd you get it?" He inspected it curiously.

"I inherited it. I also have some crystals, and a deed to land on the moon. That's what got the soldiers really interested."

The owner raised his eyebrows and handed her the medallion. She pulled the gold chain over her head, resting the warm gold coin against her skin. She took the crystals and parchments from her bag and showed them to him. He quickly looked over the crystals then gave them back to her, but held onto the deed, reading it carefully.

"Seems genuine," he said. "It's got Metolius's Salmon Seal. I've only seen that in pictures. It's his personal seal." He rubbed his chin. "And his fingerprints. That's something."

She met his gaze, feeling a bit queasy. His expression deepened, and she could almost hear the question burning in his mind. *Who are you?*

He carefully rolled the parchments and gave them back to her. "I don't know much about land."

"Do you think I could get two Solidi for the medallion?"

"I do. Under the right circumstances. In another place and time. It's a piece any collector would die for. I would buy it myself, and the dealer at Pegasus probably would too, but we're all short on gold these days. Everyone's hoarding their currency."

"But you have gold all over the place, and so did he," she said, gesturing to a display case filled with gold jewelry.

"Yeah, but this stuff is not official currency. It's not liquid. Tetras and Solidi are in short supply. All my money is tied up in antiquities. It's worthless without a buyer. Yeah, I could give some priceless amulet away for a loaf of bread, but why would I do that? Even Tegea's spies weren't offering gold currency. They're just casing the neighborhood to come in later and steal it all." His voice was gruff, and Cassidy sensed hopelessness and fear behind his words. "Besides," he said, looking at her sadly, "some things are not worth selling. Keep the medallion for yourself."

"But I want to sell it to buy passage to the moon for me and my brother. And I need two Solidi for that. Otherwise, when the Tegs take me, they'll have the medallion anyway."

"I'm sorry. I would buy it if I could. Maybe the other dealer can buy it, but I would ask him another day, if I were you."

She would. She would come back and get two Solidi, and then she and Torr would escape to the moon. Suddenly, the dream felt like it could become reality. She had the urge to run back to Pegasus, but the unsettling presence of the three soldiers held her back.

She waited in Jacobsen's shop for an hour, looking through his jewelry and listening to stories of how he had traveled the world to collect it all. He had been planning a trip to Delos when the Shaman's Shield appeared and the spaceports closed.

Jacobsen stepped outside, then returned and told her the Tegs were not in sight. Cassidy thanked him and crept out onto the sidewalk. She hurried away, glancing nervously over her shoulder the whole time, and found the street where she'd parked her motorcycle. It was halfway down the block. She stepped into a recessed doorway and examined the shadows of the street. Dark trunks of trees stood in a line. Nothing moved except leaves fluttering in a soft breeze, and a piece of paper that lifted off the sidewalk and slowly settled again. The shadows were still. A couple walked quickly down the sidewalk towards her, their heads bowed together as they talked intently. They passed by without noticing her.

Cassidy held her breath and darted to her bike, pulled on her helmet, and started the engine. With shaking hands she maneuvered the bike out of its parking spot and drove as fast as she could towards home.

12

WAVES

Morning came in a glorious burst of pink and orange. The seas had calmed and Torr's nausea had eased. He felt almost normal as he stood on the hatch cover, stretching and scanning the glistening waters. The coast was a hazy ribbon on the eastern horizon. *Seas the Day* and *Tide Runner* were still within sight, as were two other boats, clearly visible with the naked eye. He trained his binoculars on the newcomers. They were more luxury yachts, white and sleek. On one boat's foredeck a woman stood against the rail gazing out over the water, wearing a red bikini top, a blue wrap skirt that flapped in the wind, and a straw sun hat. She was looking through binoculars, but not at him. She was facing west. He panned the horizon with his binoculars and froze, losing his footing as his legs straightened by reflex. A fleet of gray ships hovered like mirages where sea met sky.

He counted seven large ships, and could not count all the smaller ones, there were so many. From this distance, they seemed to be standing still, their prows pointed north. They were definitely Teg boats. Gray with the red shield insignia painted on the hulls. Big guns. One aircraft carrier. If he could see them, they could see him, and would have more powerful scopes.

His cheek was twitching. Once every three seconds an electrical current shot from his cheek up to his eye, making his left eye squint slightly each time. It was fucking annoying. He was a misfit, and had been teased and bullied as a child because of it. His fellow soldiers had been kind enough to ignore it, after he'd beaten everyone in target practice. He went inside to the wheelhouse and pointed out the armada to Bobby.

"Algol's hell," Bobby muttered. "Teg Navy."

Torr leaned over Bobby and pushed on the throttle, but it was already at maximum speed. His cheek was still twitching, and he focused on calming his nerves, not liking how his face betrayed his feelings so easily. He knew Bobby didn't need to see his face to know Torr was scared. After months of lying side-by-side on the shooting platform they could sense each other's feelings with their eyes closed.

"What should we do?" Bobby asked, his brow gleaming with sweat. "We should turn around. Head back to shore."

Torr nodded. "We could go back to Long Beach, steal a car, and try to get through LA. Or Santa Barbara might be better." They had to decide quickly. Suddenly, standing still in a traffic jam felt infinitely safer than cruising in the gunsights of Teg warships.

Bobby flinched, covering his head. "Duck!"

Splashes in the water drove Torr to his knees. He crouched and peeked over the dashboard as the sea erupted with artillery shells. But nothing was exploding. Torr stood up slowly. Three miles was too far for such accuracy, even by the Tegs. He raised his binoculars to his eyes. "Those aren't artillery shells," he said, and ran on deck.

Dolphins. Hundreds of dolphins surrounded *Moon Star* and their small fleet of yachts, racing across the sea. Their slick, gray bodies flowed like waves, leaping through the water, guiding the boats forward. *Stay the course,* they seemed to be saying. *Follow the North Star.*

Torr whooped and broke out in laughter. "Dolphins!" he called to Bobby.

Bobby whooped in response, and Torr threw back his head and opened his arms wide to the wind.

———————)———————

"How are we supposed to know when we get to San Francisco?" Bobby asked later that morning, his voice bordering on a whine.

"We'll be closer to land by then if we follow *Seas the Day.* They're going to Monterey. We'll see the bridge and the bay."

"What if we passed it during the night? Shouldn't we be there already?"

"Seas the Day is still in front of us," Torr said, but hopped out of his chair and ran out on deck. The dolphins had long gone, but the naval ships were pacing them and appeared to have moved closer.

Seas the Day slowed at his hand signals, and the two yachts closed to within shouting distance. "Where are we?" Torr called to the woman who stood on her afterdeck.

"Morro Bay."

Torr smiled and waved.

Morro Bay? Bloody stars, they had barely made any progress in an entire day and night. It would have been faster to drive. Well, maybe. At least they hadn't overshot San Francisco. Torr surveyed the empty sky for aircraft, then went inside to tell Bobby their location.

"Morro Bay?" Bobby cried. "You must be fucking kidding me. We could walk faster."

Torr nodded his head in exasperation, went to the refrigerator, and chugged a bottle of beer. He handed a beer to Bobby and dropped to the couch, looked through books from the coffee table chest, and found one on navigating the west coast. "If we'd been coming south, we'd have made it faster," he said. "Heading north, we're going against the current."

Bobby cursed under his breath and slouched in his seat.

Torr inspected a map of the coast, locating all the small ports between Morro Bay and San Francisco, if it came to that. He did not want to cruise right into the open jaws of the Teg Navy.

Torr went back on deck and peered through his binoculars at the enemy ships. They were definitely closer. He told himself that a few yachts escaping probably weren't very important to the Tegs when they had a whole rebel army and all of California to deal with. But it was a race to see who would get to San Francisco first, assuming that was the Tegs' destination. The Tegs would probably win. Even if he and Bobby did get there first, it would take another whole day to get there at the rate they were going, and then it would take another day for Torr to hike home. His family would never wait that long. He'd arrive home to an empty house. Possibly run into Teg infantry on the way.

Maybe he and Bobby should go to Alaska with *Tide Runner*. Hang back until the Teg armada moved north, and then escape westward. He took in a deep, worried breath. He didn't want to go to Alaska. He would take his chances and head home.

Thoughts of his sister nudged at him, like ripples against his skin. He felt worry, anxiousness. Fear. Was he projecting his own feelings, or were they hers? The twins had always felt each other when they tried. And often when they did not try. They had tested this connection many times, and their perceptions were usually correct. Many of the feelings they thought they shared were probably just natural; of course they were both worried right now. But sometimes unexpected events would trigger feelings the other could never have predicted. Like when he'd fallen rock-climbing and broken his leg and she'd sent their father out to look for him, and when she'd paraglided and he'd experienced the elation of flying.

He wondered if she'd felt it when he'd killed those men. What would she have felt? A painful numbness? A part of himself dying when each soul was extinguished? He closed his eyes. It felt as though he and Cassidy were submerged in the depths of the dark ocean and she was pushing water towards him, hoping the waves would get his attention.

"I'm coming," he whispered, pushing back. "I'm coming."

13

LİNEAGE

Each day that Torr did not arrive found Cassidy and her parents more and more on edge, jumping at every noise or shadow. When she went looking for him in her mind's eye, all she saw was water. Still, she stood fast and refused to listen to her rational mind's arguments for leaving. Every day another neighbor came to say goodbye, encouraging them to flee to the desert or the mountains. Caden explained that they were waiting for Torr, and the neighbors gazed at them with silent pity. Everyone knew he was at the front lines and was not coming home.

Cassidy stepped out front and looked up and down the street. Most people were already gone. The front yard of the house directly across the street was strewn with garbage, and its windows were boarded up. Just at that moment, the abandoned home's lawn sprinkler turned on with a sudden, violent burst of water, making Cassidy jump. Misty streams arced across the patchy lawn, splattering on clumps of clothing, aluminum cans, and broken furniture.

The neighbors down the street were loading up a van, trying to shove a wooden crib into the back. Their two toddlers were playing out in the empty street. Two cat carriers stood on the sidewalk next to the van, and a stray dog nosed through garbage from a toppled trash can a few doors further down.

Cassidy felt lightheaded and went back inside.

Caden was home that morning, having spent sixteen hours on the road each of the past two days, on routes that should have taken six. The night before, he had tried to buy meat for their dinner, but two grocery stores had been closed, and their windows boarded over. A third store was sold out of all meat, fresh and frozen, and most of the canned goods were gone.

The farms Caden bought from grew produce, but one also had a flock of chickens. Another had goats they milked to make cheese, and another had a few head of cattle. "I'll try to get some meat next time out," he said, not sounding very confident.

They had made an evening meal of the last of their eggs, and vegetables from the garden. This morning, they'd had a breakfast of toast, cheese, and tomatoes. Her mother was soaking dried beans for their dinner tonight, and Cassidy had promised to make zucchini soup.

Her parents had prepared backpacks for themselves in case they would need to abandon the truck somewhere along the road to Shasta. Their two packs sat outside their bedroom door, filled with clothing, food for the road, water, and whatever odds and ends they could jam into them, plus bedrolls strapped to the frames.

They took turns keeping watch, her dad toting Torr's green rifle across his back. One person was stationed at the front window, scanning the street. Another stood at the back fence watching the dry streambed. The third person paced nervously through the house, looking for anything else that couldn't be left behind. Cassidy knew it had come down to a race between Torr getting home and the Tegs arriving.

It felt like the time in Mt. Shasta when a forest fire had raged to the west, the sky smothered in smoke. They had huddled in Grandma Leann's house, afraid a wall of flames would appear over the ridge at any moment. They had finally packed up the essentials and left. Now here they were again, with something worse than fire threatening just beyond the horizon. It was a terrible gamble to wait, but leaving too soon was just as bad.

It was Cassidy's turn to take a break. She crossed the living room to the side table, and picked up a small framed photo of her parents when they were Cassidy and Torr's age. Cassidy had always loved this photo. It reminded her that her parents were real people, just like Cassidy and Torr, only older. Torr bore a likeness to their father: wide cheekbones, straight nose, sharp eyebrows. Both wore their hair short. In the photo, their father's was a sandy brown like Torr's. Only their eyes were different. Torr's eyes were gray and piercing. Stormy like the Shaman's Shield. It was Cassidy who had her father's eyes. Large and slanting up at the outer corners, and a penetrating blue that her mother said was like the sapphire waters of Lake Tahoe. Other than the eyes, Cassidy looked more like her mother, with high cheekbones, strong nose, a full mouth, and long dark hair. Her mother's eyes were a gem-like green. Cassidy liked to call them faerie-green. Her parents' faces in the photo were ruddy and cheerful. They stood in front of a row of sentinel pines with the snowy slopes of Mount Shasta in the background.

Cassidy went to her bedroom and slid the picture into her pack, then looked around the room. Pinned to her corkboard was a strip of two small photos of her and Jasper. They had taken them in an old-fashioned photo booth at the boardwalk on Santa Cruz beach, the spring before their world changed. She had been fifteen, he was nineteen. Their cheeks were red and hair mussed from spending the day on his motorcycle, riding over the winding mountain roads and along the coastal highway. They'd explored the series of beaches north of town, climbing over the bluffs and down to the secluded, rocky inlets where waves crashed against the rocks and sprayed huge water plumes into the air. They had ended up at the boardwalk and squeezed into the booth together, goofing around.

Cassidy bit her lip and took down the stiff paper, holding it tenderly in her fingers, and remembered the day she had said goodbye to him, the week after Pensacola had been bombed.

Jasper had moved out to room with some university class-mates, but moved back to their house after the Pensacola attack. Then he got word that his father had enough money for his passage to the moon. Cassidy's family sat around the table with Jasper as he tried to decide whether to join the resistance as he had planned or take Kai up on his offer. In the end, he decided to go to the moon.

He was to depart the following morning, and spent the night getting ready. Cassidy had tossed and turned in bed, listening to rustling and soft voices in the next room as he stayed up late, packing and talking with Torr.

Cassidy caught him alone in the boys' bedroom in the early morning. Clutched in her hand was a trinket Great-Aunt Sophie had given her that Jasper had always liked. It was an off-world pin in the shape of a shooting star, made of strange minerals. The star itself was a burnished orange stone, and the trailing tail was a stone of midnight blue. The whole thing was as long as her pinky, and was set into twenty-four carat gold, with a strange inscription etched into the back.

"Here," Cassidy said, holding out the pin in her open hand. "You can have this."

Jasper looked up from where he was trying to stuff books

into an already full duffel bag. "Really?" he asked, straightening up and taking the pin from her. "Thanks, Cassafrass." A smile lit his face. His auburn hair was short on the sides and back, but the top was long, with messy waves tumbling over his forehead. He put the pin into his pants pocket and pushed the hair away from his eyes to look at her.

"So you don't forget me," she said, her voice suddenly breaking. She had sworn she would not cry.

"Awww, I could never forget you. I'll think of you every time I look at Earth."

"You will? And I'll think of you every time I look at the moon."

His eyes locked onto hers and she held his gaze.

"Here," he said, turning to his dresser top that was nearly cleared off. "Look what I found." He held out a strip of four small photos from the boardwalk photo booth. In one photo they were making funny faces. In another they were laughing. In the third she was kissing his cheek while he rolled his eyes. In the fourth their heads were pressed together, and they were both laughing with their eyes closed.

Cassidy's tightly reined emotions broke, and tears pooled in her eyes. She looked up at Jasper, whose face fell at the sight of her trembling mouth.

"Don't cry, Cass," he said anxiously. "Here, we'll each take two." He grabbed scissors from Torr's dresser and snipped the strip in half. "Which ones do you want?"

She took the half with her kissing him. "I'm never going to see you again," she said, choking on her words. At that, tears spilled over and ran down her cheeks, and he pulled her into his arms, squeezing her tight.

"Of course you will. Don't say that. You'll take your deeds, and you and Torr will come to the moon. We'll be together there. I promise."

Cassidy pulled away, sniffling. "Those deeds are garbage."

"No, they're not," he said, holding her shoulders and looking at her seriously. "You'll see." He leaned down and kissed her on the mouth. She kissed him back, breathing in his scent and holding onto him one last time.

She came back to the present, looking at the faces in the photos. Two teenagers in love. She had to get to the moon and find him. But how? She felt as if she were standing on a high ridge overlooking an abyss. She could either keep her balance against a howling wind and creep along the ridgeline, or fall headlong into the darkness.

She carefully tucked the photo strip into her backpack with the picture of her parents, steeling her resolve to find a way to get to the moon. She would go back to Pegasus. Beg the dealer to buy the medallion. The memory of the three Tegs leering at her like cats hunting a bird made her want to flutter away and hide. Better yet, she would wait, and she and Torr would go to Pegasus together.

Cassidy stepped into Torr's room, looking around for anything else he might want. Her eyes settled on his bow and quiver of arrows hanging from the back of his door. He would want those. If they had to live in the woods, he could use them to hunt. She took them down from the hook and clipped them to the back of his pack where it waited at the front door. Her father glanced at her and nodded with approval.

Tired of wandering the house, she went out to the backyard and took over her mother's watch at the fence. After a time, her father joined her. He held out a handful of pine nuts and clicked his tongue. A squirrel hopped down from a branch and approached tentatively along the top of the fence. Caden had always had a strange way with animals. Brianna called him an animal talker. He spoke to the squirrel softly, and soon it ventured up and swiped a nut from his palm, then scurried along the fence a few feet before turning and watching them as it stood on its hind legs and munched at its treat. Soon a pair of Steller's jays were squawking down at them from a tree limb. One landed on the fence and hopped over, tilting its head side to side before grabbing a nut from Caden's hand and flying away. The other followed suit. Word spread, and before long several other jays had arrived and all the nuts were gone. The squirrel and birds chattered and screeched at Caden for more.

"What's going to happen to them when the Cyclops come?" Cassidy asked.

Caden looked off towards the green hills. "They'll go up into the forest," he said. "They'll hear them coming."

"Warn them," Cassidy said, urgency tugging at her.

Caden turned to the squirrel and birds and said, "When the big, one-eyed, metal monsters come, you'll have to go live up in the mountains. Okay?"

The squirrel and birds stared down at him, making soft chitters and chirps. Caden turned to her. "They said they know. The monsters only eat the valleys. They won't touch the trees in the mountains."

"How do they know that?"

Caden shrugged. "Their cousins probably told them." He smiled a kind, sad smile, and rested his hand on her back. "They'll be fine."

"What about all the cats and dogs left behind?"

"They might survive—the ones who can get outdoors. The others will probably die."

Cassidy felt empty inside and stared off towards the hills.

———————)———————

The day dragged on with no sign of the enemy, nor of Torr. Fear and unease wore at Cassidy, making her exhausted even though she'd done nothing but take turns standing watch all day. She was at the back fence again, and her mother was sitting at the picnic table in the sun, poring over a book and a stack of papers.

"Oh, my," her mother muttered. "*Oh. My stars.*"

Cassidy glanced at her mother, whose face had gone a deathly white.

"What?" Cassidy left her post to look over her mother's shoulder.

Brianna's face twisted with concentration as she looked from the book to the papers and back again. She shuffled through more papers and traced over the top sheet with her finger. "Golden light from above," she murmured. "Stars in heaven. Merciful goodness." Her hair rose with static electricity.

"What?" Cassidy insisted. "What are you 'stars in heavening' about?"

Brianna's face was a thicket of emotions. Cassidy couldn't tell if she was perplexed, excited, or scared. "I finally finished the key stanza." Brianna said, her voice shaking. "You remember this book Aunt Sophie sent?" She showed Cassidy the front cover. It was a small hardbound book with a faded blue fabric cover, gilt-edged pages, and gold embossed lettering that looked like hieroglyphics.

"Yeah," Cassidy said. It was a book written in ancient Ilian that Great-Aunt Sophie had brought back from one of her trips to Delos. Her great-aunt had bemoaned the fact that she had not been able to bring back a Delosian-Globalish dictionary, never mind an Ilian-Globalish dictionary. She said she had never even come across a dictionary translating Ilian to Globalish, only Ilian to Delosian, one of which she had seen in the Delosian Royal Library on display, and another at the State Department that she wished she had stolen.

So Brianna had set about translating the blue and gold book years ago by cross-referencing translated passages from scraps of text Great-Aunt Sophie had collected, to create her own dictionary. It was a slow process.

"Yes. Well, I think I've found something quite … intriguing. Astounding in its coincidence." Brianna's green eyes were churning.

The nape of Cassidy's neck tingled. "Wait a second. Let me see the cover again." She pulled the gold medallion out from under her shirt and turned the coin over. The triangle containing three eyes stared at her, and she stared at her mother, who stared at the cover of the book, which also bore the triangle with three eyes above a line of other symbols. A shiver went up Cassidy's spine.

"Oh my stars, oh my stars," her mother gushed. "It's another sign." She pressed the back of her hand to her forehead. "I knew it, I knew it. Look."

Cassidy perused the open book. The right-hand page bore a set of off-world symbols. The left-hand page was filled with her mother's flowing, Globalish script.

Moon and stars
Spheres of light
Paths of flight

The sister who sees, leads the way
The brother who dreams, slays the beasts
The friend who travels, opens doors

The Star Children of the twenty-ninth age
Twins with unbroken lineage
Shall be found on the moon of crystal sand
Of the blue planet and white star

From there they shall travel to gather seeds of the ancestors
Follow the song
Take us home

A sheen of sweat broke out over Cassidy's skin. She had never told her mother about the star music. "Let me see that." She took the book and read the passage again. "Okay, so we're twins. That's not such a coincidence. There are plenty of twins. What else has you so freaked out?" She met her mother's burning gaze.

Her mother and grandmother had always whispered that maybe she and Torr were the Star Children. It had seemed like a fairy tale to Cassidy, one that lost its glamour as she'd grown older. Talk of it had completely stopped after Grandma Leann had passed away. By that time, Cassidy and Torr had reached their teenage years and had more important things to think about than some ancient legend the Star Seekers obsessed over.

Torr's childhood dream of the golden people flashed across her mind. Torr had always had strange dreams. They never meant anything real. The important thing right now was for Torr to get home already, so they could escape from the Tegs before it was too late.

"Look," her mother said, pressing on the stack of papers. On top was Cassidy's DNA birth certificate. The document was four pages filled front and back with data and diagrams. Cassidy had examined it a few times, but most of it was too complicated to understand. Her mother pointed to a diagram that looked like an upside-down tree with branches fanning out below a thin trunk. "This charts the matrilineal mitochondrial DNA. Look."

"What am I looking at?" Cassidy asked. The tree had hundreds of upside-down branches in black, and a central, red line that went directly from the single root at the top to an end node at the bottom.

"This is you," her mother said breathlessly, pointing at the red end node. "These black branches chart mutations in the population. There are hundreds of them. You have none." Her mother shuffled through the papers and pulled out two more.

"This is Torr's. Same thing. And mine." Torr's and her mother's diagrams showed the same, unbroken line. Cassidy still did not understand.

"This tree shows two hundred thousand years of genetic mutation across Earth's human population from the oldest known common female ancestor. But you and Torr don't have any mutations. You have a direct, unbroken line. *Twins with unbroken lineage.*"

Cassidy felt prickles of excitement, or was it foreboding? They had discussed their genetic heritage before, one that Grandma Leann and Great-Aunt Sophie shared. It was fun to think they were unusual, but it had made no practical difference in their lives. But now her mother was tying that fact to an ancient manuscript, thinking it proved they were truly the Star Children. Brianna loved anything mysterious. The more outlandish the better. If it wasn't for her father's practical, grounding influence, Cassidy thought her mother would be off exploring the galaxy with Jasper's mother. "So, you think this passage is about us? Me and Torr?"

"Yes! Don't you see? And you'll be found on the moon of crystal sand. That's *our* moon. The *blue planet,* the *white star.* That's us!" Her mother's voice was trembling with conviction. Brianna stood up, the papers shaking in her hand.

Cassidy raised one eyebrow. "Yes," she said slowly, true excitement surging through her veins. This was perfect. This passage made her mother believe she and Torr should be on the moon. A sly smile spread across Cassidy's face. "Well. This sounds very important," she said, nodding at her mother. "Torr and I had better find a way to get to the moon, then, don't you think?"

"Yes," her mother said, shoving the birth certificate into Cassidy's hand. "I need to go tell your father."

14

SOLİDİ

Torr stood over the corpse, reaching slowly for the black sidearm clutched in the dead man's hands, and then jerked up as a squawk startled him. A turkey vulture with a wingspan as wide as the sprawled body landed next to the man's head. Torr stepped back. The vulture jumped forward and darted its ugly orange head out and back, clutching an eyeball in its beak like an oversized marble. Torr gagged and stomped his foot at the bird. It hopped away and was mobbed by a dozen other vultures, fighting over the bloody morsel.

Torr took a deep breath and held it in, then leaned over the rotting corpse and tugged at the Lectro. Edgemont's hands were clamped around it, fingers rigid. Torr took the butt of his rifle and hammered at the fingers until they broke, and jerked the gun from the bony grip. It was lighter than he'd imagined. He set it to the side and leaned forward again to pull at the man's clothing, looking for the snake jaw ammunition. A large pouch hung from the Teg's belt. Torr quickly opened it and found clips of the deadly ammo. Each clip held six wedge-shaped snake jaws. He unfastened the pouch, took the Lectro from the ground, and ran a few paces away where he let his breath out and breathed in gulps of air away from the fetid stench of the decomposing body.

"Here, wanna see how that works?"

Torr jumped.

Edgemont stood next to him, a gaping red hole where his eye should have been. "Damned buzzard," he said, wiping at a trickle of blood that ran down his cheek. "Now I match my buddy." He smirked at Torr, who shrank at the memory of aiming at the second soldier's eye and squeezing the trigger.

Edgemont took the Lectro from Torr's hand. "Here," he said. "You load a clip in here like this." He removed the clip and snapped it back in. He popped it back out, and Torr practiced loading and unloading the gun. "It's pretty basic," Edgemont said. He pulled a snake jaw from a clip and tossed it up and down in his hand. "It can't hurt you until it's discharged from a Lectro. The gun activates it, and then as soon as it hits anything, it's done. A one-shot wonder."

"So they're sort of like bullets," Torr said, handling a snake jaw.

"More or less. Only they don't pierce or explode. They release a charge."

"So it clamps onto you, like snake jaws?"

"No, that's a myth. They just kind of look like jaws, and they kill instantly, like a certain Cephean snake. They stick to whatever they hit with their little teeth. Watch." Edgemont aimed the Lectro at the ground and fired it, then pulled the snake jaw from the dirt. Little soft metal hairs like cilia covered it and held onto clumps of soil.

"The charge doesn't transmit through the ground?"

"No. It travels through the electromagnetic fields of living animals. If you were touching someone who got hit, you'd die too because your fields would be linked."

"I heard it has to clamp onto a nerve."

"No. It simply stops the flow of life force through the body. But the snake jaw has to discharge within the person's electromagnetic field to do that. The best way to ensure that happens is for it to attach to the body, be it skin or clothing or whatever. Most people's fields extend a couple inches beyond their bodies. Some people's, more."

"What about armor?" Torr asked.

"There's supposedly a way to shield against Lectros, but they won't tell us how. But I happen to know from experience that crystal deflects the Lectro's force. Glass, that is, and glass-based ceramic. Somebody told me the old-style body armor with ceramic plates will protect you if the snake jaw hits it."

"What's the gun's range?" Torr asked, snapping the clip into the chamber.

"A mile."

"No shit," Torr said, looking at the oddly shaped jaws, which did not look particularly aerodynamic. "How precise are they?"

"As good as your rifle there." The man glanced at Torr's Dashiel.

"Do you have to be a sharpshooter to work one of these?"

"No, the sights take care of most of the hard stuff." He showed Torr how it locked onto the target, signaled for release, and confirmed the kill.

"Then, you almost got me," Torr said, remembering Edgemont lifting the gun and his eyes seeking the gunsight.

"Almost. You already had me in your sights, though. If you'd hesitated another second, you would have been a goner." The man smiled, showing straight white teeth.

Torr jerked awake and sat up. He was in the bed at the bow of *Moon Star*, the boat humming as it sped through the water. The pink light of dawn illuminated the small, oblong windows flanking the bed. He sat for a moment, trying to quiet his pounding heart. He waited for the dream to fade, then slipped out from between soft white sheets and looked out a window. The rose-colored sky reflected off glassy water. The sun was just peeking over the horizon. Teg ships loomed like ghosts, silhouetted against the pale sky. Torr's heart pounded in his throat.

He pulled on his pants, and his eyes wandered around the stateroom. A small wooden triptych was displayed on a recessed shelf in the mahogany wall. The triptych had two side panels that folded out like window shutters to frame the center panel. It was colorfully painted with highlights of gold that glistening in the morning light. He stepped over and inspected it more closely.

The intricately detailed art was Christian in nature, complete with golden halos and winged angels. Torr had not been raised Christian, nor any religion for that matter, unless one considered shamanism a religion, or the Star Seekers. But he recognized Christ sitting on a gold throne with rays of golden light radiating from his head and body. Christ held a globe in his lap, and surrounding him was a field of gold stars on an indigo background, with the sun and moon at his feet. One of the side panels was of Mary holding baby Jesus in her lap, mother and child surrounded by a halo of gold. At Mary's shoulders and feet were tiny, meticulously painted angels blowing horns, working a loom, playing a harp, holding a key, and drinking from a goblet. The second side panel was of a man descending on a shaft of light, surrounded by little angels; some angels balanced urns on their heads, some poured water from the urns, others held children on their shoulders, and still other angels were sleeping and dreaming at the base of the shaft. The image reminded Torr of Star Seeker legends of a golden race descending on shafts of light to bring glory to humankind. Torr had always suspected the Star Seeker faith was simply a blending of Earth's religions and myths, combined with off-world legends—the same old stories repackaged for a new age.

Even so, he found the images strangely beautiful, and if this journey did not end well he would be praying for a ladder of light to descend from heaven and angels to spirit him away. He gently removed the triptych from little blobs of putty that secured it to the shelf and looked at the back, which bore another, simpler painting of a long, thin, golden angel that stretched horizontally across all three panels. Its arms were thrust forward, the thin form flying through a sea of gold stars in a midnight-blue sky. Its serene face looked forward. Wings streamed from its back, and its bare toes were pointed. He folded the panels closed so that the outstretched hands and feet met in the center, like two sets of golden hands touching their fingertips together. Folded, it was not much bigger than his palm.

Torr guiltily slipped the triptych into his cargo pants leg pocket. If he was stealing a whole yacht, what harm was there in taking a little knick-knack? He released the top latch of a dresser and pulled the drawer open. It was empty except for a black glasses case. The aviator sunglasses inside looked expensive. He tried them on, and the room took on an amber glow. He looked at himself in the mirror and ran his fingers over his short hair and rough stubble. He should take another shower while he still could, remembering the hot shower he'd luxuriated in the day before in the yacht's master bathroom, but dismissed the thought and opened the second drawer. It held stacks of neatly folded t-shirts. He rifled through them and pulled out a navy blue one. Printed in yellow on the left chest pocket was a small image of a crescent moon and a shining star. Moon Star was printed below the crescent in simple block letters. He slipped the shirt on. It fit well, tight enough to show off his muscles but still comfortable. He stretched his shoulders, and found a navy

Moon Star polo shirt and tucked it under his arm. He unzipped his rifle bag, took the sniper scope from its case, and bounded up the stairs two at a time.

"Teg Navy's closing in," Bobby told him.

"I know," Torr said, tossing him the polo shirt, and went outside.

The ships had inched ahead of them while he'd slept. But *Moon Star* was closer to shore. He tried to calculate distance, speed, and angles to see if they would beat the armada. It was a close call. He zoomed in on one of the battleships, the powerful scope providing detail. A hulking 5-inch gun sat alone on the foredeck. Another boat carried missile launchers. Men were walking the empty decks of the aircraft carrier. Another ship's decks were lined with sailors looking towards shore. Torr slunk back inside and put his scope away. They were sitting ducks. He returned to the wheelhouse and put on his brave face.

"Go on downstairs. Get some rest," Torr said.

"No. We're almost there. *Seas the Day* said it's an hour to Monterey."

"An hour? Were you going to wake me up? San Francisco is only a short ways past Monterey."

"No, I was going to leave you on the boat." Bobby smirked at Torr, then pulled off his t-shirt and put on the polo shirt. "Where're my fancy shades?"

"Sorry, I only found these. Finders keepers."

They playfully punched at one another.

"Teg Navy's going to beat us there," Bobby said quietly.

"I know, we may need to find a smaller port. Turning back would be no better."

Torr sat in the co-captain's chair, and they stared straight ahead.

Torr leaned back, trying to pretend they were on a pleasure cruise enjoying the last leg of their excursion. What would it be like to own a boat like this during peacetime? He'd never find out. Torr wondered what would happen to luxury craft when most of the population was sent to camps. He supposed Teg officers and Metolius's cronies got the spoils. And the Cephs. Would they start migrating to Earth in larger numbers once it was under total submission? Or maybe they would destroy the yacht, thinking it a useless, unproductive plaything.

Bobby followed *Seas the Day* as it angled towards the coastline. *Tide Runner* had headed further out to sea sometime during the night. They must have looped south, hoping to bypass the fleet of destroyers before heading up to Alaska. Torr hoped, for their sakes, that the Tegs were not interested in the northern reaches, but for all anyone knew they were already up there. *Seas the Day* turned east into Monterey Bay. The woman waved at them from her afterdeck.

"Maybe we should follow them," Bobby said.

"No," Torr said, considering their options. "We can pull in at Half Moon Bay if we have to. Pillar Point's too small for naval ships, they won't follow us there. It's not too far to San Francisco for you."

"What about for you?" Bobby asked.

"It's about halfway between your mom's place and my house."

Torr went out on deck and waved at the departing yacht as Bobby veered north. He lifted his binoculars and scanned the waters, frowning with concern as he spotted a large powerboat speeding towards them, its bow raised out of the water, spitting out a wide wake. Torr focused in on it.

"Coast Guard!" he called out. A second, smaller boat, a cutter, appeared from behind the larger craft, with a gunner stationed at its bow.

Torr's heart hammered as he froze in a moment of indecision, then ran inside.

Bobby clutched the wheel and looked frantically out the window at the approaching boats. "Get our guns," Bobby said, leaving the captain's chair and running down below.

Torr yelled after him, grabbing the wheel. "No. Why? If we kill them, they'll kill us. There's more of them."

"We're better shots," Bobby yelled back. He returned from belowdecks with his TAFT and Torr's Dashiel. "You're a better shot. Shoot them in the head." He shoved Torr's rifle in his arms.

"Then what?" Torr asked.

Bobby loaded his gun and sprinted for the afterdeck. Torr stared at his own rifle. If they killed the Coast Guard crew, then they'd really be criminals. They'd get caught and be thrown in jail. The Tegs would come. It would be all over.

Torr pulled back on the throttle and abandoned the helm, set his rifle on the couch, and ran out to the afterdeck. The Coast Guard boats were approaching fast. Their gunner had his weapon pointed at them and was watching them through his scope. Torr pushed Bobby's muzzle down and waved at the gunner.

"We're not fighting them," Torr said sternly, holding out his hands for the gun.

Bobby reluctantly snapped on the safety and grudgingly handed over his rifle. Torr placed the TAFT on the bench while Bobby glared at him.

An amplified voice boomed over the water. *"Turn your boat back. Proceed into the bay."*

Torr's legs and hands trembled from adrenaline. "You heard the man," he said to Bobby, who was fidgeting with anger and fear. Torr used his squad leader's voice. "Go inside and take the wheel. Turn the boat around."

Torr could tell Bobby wanted to reach for his gun, but Torr stood in his way. With a huff of defeat Bobby turned and went into the cabin.

The large Coast Guard boat was angling away, but the cutter sidled up next to *Moon Star*. Torr stood bravely and met the man's eyes. He would go peacefully. He wasn't going to kill anyone else, not when the odds were stacked so heavily against them. The gunner pivoted his gun aside and tapped his forehead in greeting.

Another crewmember stood on the cutter's afterdeck, hanging onto the small cabin's roof with one hand. He spoke into a handset. *"Tegs in San Francisco Bay."* His amplified voice was sharp and tinny over the whirr of the motorboat.

Torr grasped the handrail. Tension drained from his limbs, his knees nearly buckling with relief. He held onto the rail and found himself nodding and smiling idiotically at the men. His smile was quickly replaced with a grimace as newfound terror worked its way into his blood as the man's words sank in. The Coast Guard crewmen waved, and the cutter sped off to alert another craft.

Torr stumbled into the cabin. "They're not after us. They're warning us. Tegs in San Francisco Bay." Torr watched the same emotions play across Bobby's face. Relief. Joy. Comprehension. Grave despair.

If Tegs were in San Francisco Bay already, then Bobby's mother was in imminent danger. There was a good chance Moffett had been taken as well, Torr's neighborhood cleared out, and the path to Shasta blocked. Tendrils of fear constricted Torr's throat. He tried not to think of his family's fate, afraid he'd break down; he couldn't afford to do that now. He sucked in a deep breath.

"Should we go back to Monterey?" Bobby asked, his face stricken.

"Let's dock at Santa Cruz. It's at the upper curve of Monterey Bay. I know that harbor. We can hike home from there. Maybe there's still time." They had to stick to their plan. They couldn't let panic deter them.

Bobby agreed, and they changed course. Santa Cruz would actually be better for Torr, but worse for Bobby. Torr's nerves were raw. He wanted to take over the steering wheel, but Bobby's fingers were clamped around it like talons.

Torr went out onto the foredeck and surveyed the shore to locate the small boat harbor he was targeting. He found the lighthouse and jetty he'd explored many times, and directed Bobby to it. Currents battered them from every direction as Bobby guided the boat through the narrow channel that led into the marina. They passed through the mouth and slowed the craft to a quiet putt-putt, navigating past a parade of other, smaller boats heading out to sea, their pilots gazing warily towards the Teg navy. Bobby steered the yacht to a long dock, gliding up alongside it. A man who appeared to be the harbormaster ran over. Torr hung the bumpers over the side and tossed ropes to his waiting hands. The harbormaster secured the boat and Torr hopped off, standing unsteadily as his sea legs adjusted to the motionless dock. He looked nervously at the man, wondering if he had been notified about the theft of *Moon Star*.

"How is it out there?" the harbormaster asked, looking concerned but not suspicious.

"Tegs in San Francisco Bay," Torr said evenly, trying to steady his pulse.

"Already, huh?" The weathered man gazed out towards the horizon. The man did not seem ready to challenge them about the stolen yacht. Everyone had Tegs on their mind.

Torr's worries shifted to his family. Was he too late? Had they already gone? He tried to keep his face neutral and his eyes level. He had landed somewhere safe, somewhere familiar, yet everything was about to fall apart around him.

Bobby killed the boat's engine and joined him on the dock.

The harbormaster turned to them. "You looking for a berth, or you heading back out?"

Torr shifted on his feet, wanting to disappear into the mountains and away from the eyes of the navy. "A berth?" he asked blankly. He had no idea how much a berth cost. Between him and Bobby they might have enough; there hadn't been much opportunity to spend their modest soldiers' salaries living in a bunker. Or they could just walk away and leave the man to deal with the boat, but Torr did not want to cause a scene and draw any more attention to themselves.

His thoughts were interrupted by a man who came hurrying down the ramp onto the dock.

"We need a charter. You taking on passengers?" The man's eyes were round with panic. A woman ran down the dock after him, clutching a toddler in her arms. Two other adults followed, and another small group huddled behind a railing above, looking down at them: an elderly couple, two more adults, and four teenagers. Piles of luggage were stacked next to them.

Torr and Bobby exchanged glances.

"How many people?" Torr asked.

"Thirteen," the man said, grabbing Torr's arm. "Please. Please help us. We'll pay." His hand went into his pocket and emerged with a fistful of Solidi.

Torr tried to keep his eyes from bulging as he stared at the solid gold pyramids. His pulse pounded in his neck. He swallowed, took a breath, and met the man's eyes. "Possibly," he said, adopting the casual tone his father had instilled in him during years of helping with the trading business. He gave Bobby a warning look to keep quiet. Bobby pressed his lips together, his eyes darting to the glinting Solidi. Torr counted them in one glance. There were six. "I don't know," Torr said, rubbing his chin and letting his eyes pass over the hovering clan.

He felt cruel, but it was habit. In his mind he was calculating the worth of the boat. Hell, it was invaluable right now if people thought they could escape the Tegs with it. He wondered again if he and Bobby should reconsider and keep the boat. Stock up on food and water and take to the sea. Better yet, dock here for a couple days, fetch their families, and head out to some remote island. No. He didn't know the ocean, and certainly didn't want to die out there. He'd rather die on land, trying to get to Shasta. "Two Solidi per person," Torr told him.

The man's eyes shifted nervously to his wife, and her face went pale. Her eyes flew to the man and woman behind her, then to those watching from above.

The man's face turned red. "That's highway robbery."

Torr shrugged and smiled coolly. He held his gaze until sweat trickled down the man's cheek.

"Wait here," the man said gruffly, and pulled his companions aside. They climbed the stairs and whispered with the others. Torr watched as they opened bags and counted gold.

Bobby's eyes were big, but Torr scowled at him. The harbormaster looked on with interest, one eyebrow raised.

The man returned, his chin in the air. "One Solidi per person," he said. "Not counting the baby," he added, nodding at the three-year-old in his wife's arms. Not exactly a baby, but Torr didn't argue. "Twelve total," the man said crossly, as though Torr was ripping him off. He took the Solidi from his pocket. It took two hands to hold them all. Torr wanted to lick his lips. What he couldn't do with so much gold, he thought hungrily. He'd never held even a single Solidi, never mind a dozen. "But you'll take us wherever we want," the man demanded. "We are going to South America."

Torr looked at Bobby, who glared at him with a look that said, *Take it, you fucking idiot.*

Torr felt horrible letting the man think he could make it safely to South America with a net of Teg ships out there. But maybe he knew what he was doing. The ocean was vast, maybe he could slip past them and go far out to sea, then circle back and find a safe port.

"Tell you what," Torr said, hooking his thumbs through his belt loops to keep his hands from shaking. "Twenty Solidi total and you can have the boat outright. Take it for yourselves. Go wherever you want."

Sweat dripped down the man's face and he wiped it away. His eyes shone with desperation. "Really?"

"Yeah, I'll get the paperwork." Torr left the man on the dock and returned with the title of ownership in his hand. "I'll sign it over to you right now. Deal?"

The man had been consulting with his companions, and they dug into their bags again. The family came up with a total of sixteen Solidi, handfuls of the smaller, pyramid-shaped, gold Tetras, ten of which equaled one Solidi, and a paper sack filled with Eagles, gold bits, and tenth-gold bits. He could tell Bobby wanted to kick him as Torr scowled at the man, making his wife pull off her diamond ring and add it to the pile. The other adults threw in various items of jewelry, and Torr relented. Bobby scooped up the Solidi and the rest of the gold and jewels, and Torr rested the title of ownership on the harbormaster's clipboard. He scrawled something official sounding and signed *Earl Torrance Morrow.* The man signed his name, and the harbormaster signed as witness.

The harbormaster held the family back while Torr and Bobby climbed on board to gather their things. Torr grabbed his Dashiel and went below. He had put on his green forest

camo pants that morning by habit. They were much more comfortable than his jeans, so he kept them on. He would be hiking
through the forested hills to get home, anyway. He pulled on
his vest and stuffed his desert camo pants and field jacket into
his rucksack. He decided to leave behind his jeans, along with
most of his other clothing. He kicked off his running shoes and
pulled on his dusty army boots, which formed to his feet.

From the bottom of the duffel bag glinted his Gaia United
Expert Marksman badge, two rifles crossed over the globe of
Earth. It reminded him of his kills. One rifle for each dead man,
he thought with a stab of pain. The badge had been the inspi-
ration for the Light Fighter tattoo he wore on his left bicep as a
symbol of his longing to free Earth from the Global Alliance. He
supposed he had done his small part. He'd tried to make a difference. A flash of pride ran through him as he fingered the cold
metal badge. It signified his skill and accomplishments. Then
why did he feel so ashamed? He shoved it into his pants pocket.

He put everything he didn't want into his duffel bag and
stuffed it away in a closet. He filled his rucksack with ammo,
a couple t-shirts, underwear and socks, toiletries, and the star
maps. He strapped his bedroll underneath, pulled the rucksack
over his shoulders, and clipped on his weapons belt. Lastly, he
took the long bag for his two rifles, placed the Dashiel inside
with his TAFT, and hung the strap across his chest. He made
one last pass through the cabins and wheelhouse, kissed *Moon
Star's* dashboard, and stepped onto the dock.

The family streamed aboard to inspect the yacht, their faces
relieved and happy. Who wouldn't be happy with such a beauty?
Torr felt a sudden sentimental attachment to the vessel, and
wondered if they were making a mistake letting it go. He reluctantly handed the new owner the key. The grinning man shook

Torr's hand vigorously before turning to load suitcases, trunks, and cases of food and water.

Torr thanked the harbormaster, who eyed their weapons. "You guys Gaia United?" he asked.

"We were," Bobby said.

"Is it true there was a peace accord?"

"No," Torr said. "We flat out surrendered."

The man's pained expression reflected Torr's own despair.

"Aren't you going to leave soon?" Torr asked him.

"Nah. I'll take my chances here."

"Don't you have a boat?"

"Sure I do. Right over there. I live on it." He gestured down the dock. "I don't want to die at sea."

"Me neither," Torr agreed.

The harbormaster advised them that the safest path through town was to follow the stream that flowed down from the mountains and fed the marina. Tegs were starting to patrol the roads and had blocked the major mountain passes. They would need to hike the trails through the redwood forest, which was what Torr had been planning to do anyway. He knew the trails well. Bobby could split off at Skyline ridge and head north. Torr would continue down into the valley on his own and follow the water channels, which were dry beds this time of year, to get to his house. It was already nine o'clock, and he had thirty miles of walking ahead of him. It was doubtful he could get home before darkness fell, but the moon would be up, and he had a flashlight.

Bobby and Torr split their spoils, giggling uncontrollably. Torr shook his head with astonishment as he examined the Solidi and Tetras: large, square-based pyramids etched with a pattern of spirals, and smaller, triangle-based pyramids etched with a repeating wave pattern. He had never held either, and now he had a king's ransom. He took his eight Solidi and stuffed them into his vest pockets, weighing the front pockets down as though loaded with coal. The rest of his share went into a side pocket of his pack, save for two gold Eagles, which he gave to the surprised harbormaster.

They stopped at the harbor bathrooms and filled their canteens from the outdoor spigots. Torr placed his hand on Bobby's shoulder as they walked towards the back of the marina. They crossed over the footbridge, turned onto the grassy path that followed alongside the small creek, and left the harbor and *Moon Star* behind.

15

CROW'S NEST

Cassidy watched with a sick feeling in her belly as the wall screen showed the same newscast over and over. Two smiling young women in a lush orchard held a bushel of shiny red apples. Miners weighed small chunks of gold on a scale. A tractor rolled off an assembly line as President Metolius clapped. President Metolius cut the ribbon to a new spaceport in Germany. A sign over the entry to the spaceport read, *Global Alliance. Health and Prosperity.*

The newscasters were no longer pretending that Gaia United was still in control. They no longer spoke of negotiations or a peaceful accord. In fact, they never mentioned Gaia United at all, as if the rebel force and the Shaman's Shield had never existed. As though life under the Global Alliance would be business as usual. Better than before. The media transition had taken but a few days. How long would it take to bring in Teg forces and transition the population to work camps? The newscasters never talked about that.

Cassidy flicked off the screen as Caden stomped in the front door. He had left two hours before in search of more ammunition but returned empty-handed. He gathered Cassidy and her mother, and said with a shaking voice, "The freeway to San Francisco is blockaded by Tegs, at the reservoir. I managed to get off and take back roads home. I was afraid that was the end of me."

Brianna clutched his hands, and they all jumped at a knock at the door. Caden peeked through the peephole, then opened the door. It was Bernie from down the street, looking even more distraught than her father. Caden let him in and offered him a seat, but he was too nervous to sit down.

He twisted his ball cap in his hands. "Moffett has been taken. All non-essential personnel were sent home, and the Tegs moved in. My manager said they've been controlling spaceflights for days now. Security simply put down their guns and let them in. The Tegs lined us all up. I thought they were going to execute us. They told us to go home and pack our things and prepare to move to the camps. I'm going to try to cross the pass and get to Reno."

Cassidy's mind grew numb. It was happening. It was really happening. The Tegs were ten miles away. They had locked down the spaceport. Soon they would empty the neighborhood. She couldn't breathe.

Bernie left, leaving Cassidy and her parents staring at each other.

"It's been nearly a week, Cassidy," Caden said softly. "We may need to accept that Torr is not coming home. We should get out while we still can."

She turned away and retreated outside to the far corner of the backyard under the redwoods and the eucalyptus, whose pungent perfume hung heavily in the air. It was a hot summer day but the air under the trees was cool. Draping branches and thick trunks created a peaceful cocoon that was rudely pierced from above by a screeching jay and a chattering squirrel. She stared up at them, and they stared back. When the squirrel started screaming at her, she thought maybe they were trying to tell her something.

"I know," she said to the squirrel. "We're trapped."

The jay launched from its branch, its bright blue wings flapping noisily as it rose over the trees and disappeared from view. The squirrel twitched its tail then jumped to another branch, the thick green bough shaking as it scurried out of sight.

Cassidy sat on the carpet of redwood needles, her head hanging down. She wished she could fade into the shadows and disappear too. Maybe the Tegs would pass her by if she held her breath long enough. She closed her eyes, feeling for Torr. First it was dark and quiet. Then the familiar sense of him nudged at her, as though they were in their dark childhood bedroom and she could feel his presence. She calmed her mind, emptying it, waiting for images to appear. She saw trunks of trees. Redwood branches.

She opened her eyes in frustration, fighting back tears. Her own surroundings were reflecting back at her in her mind. She had taken Sweet Alyssum again this morning, but it was no use. She could not call upon her second sight at will as she had hoped. First she had seen roads, then the ocean, now woods. A bunch of random images spawned by her imagination. She was deluding herself by believing in magic. She glared at the bed of Sweet Alyssum bobbing in the wind as if everything was as it should be.

She tried to resist the part of herself she felt numbing out, slowly acquiescing to a new reality that would take her and absorb her into its new form. If things were changing, she must wield whatever power she had to shift the trajectory towards the light, away from the darkness that hovered at the edges of her vision.

She could hear her father out in the garage. He was probably starting to pack up the truck. He still believed the three of them could escape and somehow make it to Shasta by sneaking across the Diablo Range and the Central Valley to the Sierra Foothills. It was brave that he still held out hope despite all signs that it was too late. She had brought them to this fate with her desperate fantasies of reuniting with Torr.

She got to her feet, filled with a deep, aching sadness.

"Dad," she said, finding him in the garage digging through crates. "You're right. We have to leave." She could not deny him a last, courageous act. If she had to watch him march out of their house and surrender to the Tegs because of her stupidity, she thought she would die.

He met her eyes with his tired blue ones, then pulled her into the circle of his arms and inhaled a shaking breath. Together they went to find Brianna.

They found her at the kitchen sink, her hair floating. Her big eyes looked up at them, darker and greener than usual.

"What's wrong?" Cassidy asked, the nape of her neck tingling.

Brianna turned the faucet handle. The faucet coughed and gurgled, but no water came out.

"They turned the water off," Cassidy said, a chill running up her spine.

"It's time to go," Caden said, pulling his wife into his arms and smoothing her wild hair.

They decided to leave Torr's pack on his bed with a note that said they were going to find Nana, and that they loved him. Cassidy hoped Torr wouldn't interpret it to mean they were seeking their graves. After some debate, they left his lunar deed and DNA birth certificate in his pack, with a note advising him to escape to the moon if he could.

Cassidy changed out of her favorite pink t-shirt with the big sparkly butterfly and into a plain gray t-shirt that would blend into the surroundings as they tried to escape. She hoisted the pack onto her back and left her bedroom with a last, wistful look.

Caden thought it too risky to take the truck on the roads, so they decided to set out on foot via the aqueduct, head south to bypass the bay and urban areas, then follow the hiking trails through the coastal hills before striking east and then north. He left the front door unlocked so the Tegs wouldn't break it down.

"I don't know why it even matters," she said to him. "The Tegs are going to knock the whole neighborhood down with their Cyclops monstrosities anyway."

He stared at her, his lips tight. It was the truth and he knew it. She followed him back into the garage where he took the two rifles and pistol from the workbench, then into the living room where Brianna stood, hands on her hips.

"We're not taking those," Brianna said. "We talked about this."

"We might need to defend ourselves," he said, meeting his wife's stubborn glare. "Or hunt for food." His tone said he was going to take the guns whether she liked it or not.

"If the Tegs see us with those," Brianna said, "they will kill us."

"Yeah? So?" he countered, suddenly sounding like a pugnacious teenager.

Cassidy watched as her parents stood in a standoff, vying wordlessly for dominance. She wondered if it would be better to be killed than to be taken to a camp. It was a toss-up. "What about Torr?" she asked.

"What about him?" her father said, not taking his eyes from his wife's.

"If he gets captured and you're dead, you won't be able to meet him in the camps."

She saw her father's resolve waver.

"If they are the Star Children," Brianna said, taking advantage of the chink in his armor, "they need to stay alive. No matter what."

"If they are the Star Children, then they shouldn't be captured by Tegs."

"Why not? How do we know their path? Who knows how the Star Children are supposed to find the Star People? But don't worry, when the Star People come, no Teg army will be able to stand up to them."

Caden rolled his eyes. "Yeah? What if General Tegea doesn't want the Star People to come? Have you ever thought about that? What better way than to kill the Star Children?"

"My point exactly," Brianna said with a sly grin. "Bury them."

He stared at her for a moment. "The guns?"

The look on Brianna's face sent Caden out to the backyard where he took a shovel, dug a shallow grave, wrapped the guns and ammo in a canvas tarp, and threw dirt over top. Then he hid the fresh dirt under a pile of mulch.

"Satisfied?" Caden asked, as he wiped his hands on a kitchen towel.

Cassidy filled her canteen from a five-gallon jug, clipped it to her pack, then pulled on the heavy pack and tightened the straps. Her parents did likewise, and the three of them stood for a moment in the kitchen, staring at each other.

They left through the back door. Cassidy stepped through the garden, picturing the zucchini and tomatoes growing ripe and dropping one by one onto the ground to rot. Plants they had nurtured all season would shrivel up from lack of water. Deer would find their way down from the hills and scavenge in the abandoned yards. Then one day the Cyclops would come and kill everything.

They took one last, long look at their house and garden. One by one they climbed over the wooden fence, then slid down the steep cement embankment to the dry streambed twenty feet below. Caden led the way southwest. They picked their way over gravel washes and sandy islands dotted with tufts of grass.

I should be crying, Cassidy thought, knowing she was leaving their home forever. But she felt dead inside. Torr wasn't with them. That meant chances were she would never see him again. Anguish was etched in her parents' faces, but they shed no tears either.

The gully was quiet. They peered nervously up at the fences and trees that bordered the channel on either side. The streambed curved, and Cassidy looked behind her as they passed beyond visible range of their fence. Their clumps of towering redwoods and eucalyptus waved in farewell. Cassidy faced forward and marched on.

Their boots crunched over the ground as the warm afternoon made Cassidy sweat. Her heart was empty and her mind was blank, but every sense was on high alert. She flinched as she saw movement in a tree nearby. She stopped next to her parents, frozen mid-stride as they held their breaths. A squirrel jumped from a branch and scurried across another. Cassidy exhaled, her heart pounding in her chest. They went on, walking as silently as they could.

They had reached the next neighborhood when they heard a rhythmic whooshing sound. Two large ravens flew past them, one behind the other, their wide wings beating in time as they followed the curve of the streambed.

Her mother grabbed her arm. "Caden," she whispered loudly. "Stop." He halted and his eyes followed the huge black ravens as they disappeared around the bend behind them. "Stay here," her mother said, and crept forward to peek around the curve of the sloping cement wall, then scurried back like a startled spider. "I knew it," she hissed. "Tegs."

Cassidy and her father crept up as Brianna tried to push them back. Cassidy elbowed past her mother and craned her neck, jerking back as she caught a quick glimpse of three gray-uniformed soldiers standing in the channel a couple hundred yards down. They were looking up towards a fence with assault rifles in their hands. She felt her parents grab her arms, one on each side, and the three of them ran back the way they had come, hopping over rocks and debris, packs bouncing on their backs.

They ran past their fence, sprinted around the next bend, and skidded to a stop. Far up ahead on an overpass, lines of large gray military vehicles rumbled over a bridge. Cassidy and her parents reversed direction and ran. She didn't dare look back to see if they had been spotted. They stopped below their fence, looking frantically at one another, then scrambled up the steep slope, clutching at the rough cement. Cassidy and her mother climbed over the fence, and her father dropped down after them.

Caden led the way inside the house and peered out the living room window. Cassidy huddled next to him. At the end of the street, armored vehicles blocked the main intersection. Soldiers were climbing out of them. She pulled back, and her father dropped the shade.

"The treehouse," Cassidy blurted out. "We'll hide in the Crow's Nest."

She ran into Torr's room and pulled his heavy pack from his bed, clutching it to her chest as she stumbled down the hallway and out the back door. Her parents followed close behind as they rushed across the yard to the grove that held the treehouse hidden in its upper limbs. She gave Torr's pack to her father and climbed onto the tall redwood stump in the center of the clump of trees and reached for the lowest branch of the nearest redwood. Scrambling up the ridged, fuzzy bark, she pulled herself onto the branch and reached for the next.

Branches caught at her pack, snagging the smaller pack of herbs that was clipped to the outside. She tugged it free and climbed, branch over branch. Her mother climbed after her. Halfway up the towering tree she hoisted herself onto the wide wooden plank that connected the redwood to the eucalyptus. The squirrel screamed at her from high above.

Looking down, she saw her father laboring up the tree and trying to navigate the branches. Torr's pack was strapped to his own, giving him a heavy and awkward load, and she cringed as the bow and arrows caught on a branch. He jiggled them loose and kept climbing. Cassidy held the straight pole of a branch above her as she walked across the plank and onto the square wooden platform that was built into the reaching arms of the eucalyptus. Its thick, bushy branches intertwined with redwood boughs, concealing the structure.

The floor was covered with redwood needles and curled strips of pungent eucalyptus bark, and enclosed with waist-high plywood walls. Her mother stepped through the gap in the wall onto the platform and waited for Caden, who trod heavily over the plank. Cassidy helped him with the packs as he slid them to the floor. His brow furrowed as he caught his breath and surveyed their hidden fortress. "Good idea, Cassidy." His voice was low, and she nodded, afraid to make a sound.

It was a well-built treehouse with sturdy benches built into one corner around a little table. The other furnishings included a large white bucket, an empty cooler, and two large wooden lockers set against the back wall. A coil of rope was tied to a plastic crate for ferrying cargo from the ground. Cassidy found a small gap in the screen of leaves and peered through with her father's binoculars. From a certain angle she could see a portion of the southwest channel they had ventured down. No Teg soldiers were in sight.

She and her parents sat on the floor and leaned back against the lockers, pressed next to each other with Cassidy in the middle. The squirrel screamed from above, and she could hear him running across the branches.

They sat like that—still as stone—for hours. The spicy scent of the eucalyptus took her back to the time she and Jasper had come up here not long before he'd left for the moon. During the weeks before, they had made out on the couch and on the beach, kissing and holding and exploring each other's bodies. Then one afternoon they had stood on this deck and looked at each other. They had been home alone, and if they had lain down together in the bed of redwood needles and bark, she was sure they would have had sex for the first time. They'd looked into each other's eyes for a long, breathless moment, a pace apart and not touching, then wordlessly turned around, climbed down the tree, and went indoors to play cards.

She jerked out of her reverie to the rumbling of vehicles and slamming of metal doors drifting over the rooftops. Shouts. Barking dogs. A wailing child. She closed her eyes and leaned against the solid wood of the locker. Her mother took her hand and squeezed it. Her father's arm stretched behind her head and rested on her shoulders, his hand reaching across for his wife. They sat there, legs pressed against one another, shaking. Her mother's hand was clawlike, and Cassidy tried to loosen the painful grip. Cassidy's other hand was clasping her father's knee, and he laid his hand over it. His hand was cold and heavy. Her breathing sounded loud in her head, and she tried to quiet it, afraid the soldiers would hear her through the trees.

Painful, agonizing minutes dragged on. Cassidy tracked the sounds of the soldiers as they made their way methodically down the street, going house to house. Most of the houses had been abandoned. That meant some of the houses still had people in them—her neighbors for the past thirteen years. She recognized their frantic voices as they came out to the street. Yelling. Pleading. Bribing. Crying. Each ended the same, their voices drifting off towards the intersection where the transports waited to haul them away. The soldiers were calm and efficient. They did not mock, or yell, or laugh. They were professionals. They had a job to do, and they did it well.

The soldiers were next door. She heard voices talking over two-way radios. The house was empty.

Suddenly, the soldiers were at their house. Cassidy sat like wood as she heard their boots crunching up the driveway. Then it became eerily quiet. She knew they were indoors, but they were not making a sound. A couple of minutes passed. Cassidy's heart grew weary from its frantic pace. The spring on the back door squeaked. Footsteps fell in the yard. Her parents were rigid and cold as corpses beside her. Noise came from inside the shed, crates being moved. Rustling in the yard, soft beating against the bushes. Her blood chilled as she heard the snuffling of a dog, and she squeezed her eyes shut. Her father's hand pressed on hers. The handler talked softly to his dog as the snuffling approached the grove of trees.

"You find something, boy?" The soldier's voice was kind. Gentle.

Cassidy tensed as her father started humming with a strange soft moaning sound. Her eyes popped open, and she looked at him. His eyes were closed, his face serene. It was the game he used to play with their old German Shepherd, Silver. The snuffling below stopped.

"What is it, boy?"

Soft whimpers came from below. Just like Silver used to make. Her father had said he imitated the sound of the mother dog calling the pups to nurse. Cassidy wondered if the soldier's dog was down on its haunches, wagging its tail expectantly like Silver used to do.

Her mother sat up straight, eyes closed, hands rising into the air with palms turned up. Her hair was floating.

Eucalyptus leaves fluttered in a whispering melody as a breeze sifted through the trees. The wind picked up, and the long limbs that held the Crow's Nest swayed, rocking them like a creaking cradle. The wind came in violent gusts, leaves clattering, branches writhing. A shower of leaves and bark fell around them. The wind whistled as it descended from the hills and rushed down the channel, tossing the towering trees from side to side.

Cassidy pressed her hands against the swaying floor of the treehouse, startled by the sudden windstorm. The squirrel chattered from the redwood tree. A loud crack pierced the air, and Cassidy heard a redwood branch crash through other branches and thud loudly onto the ground. The dog yelped and the soldier exclaimed, "What in Algol's hell?"

Another crack resounded, and a second limb crashed through the branches. The screaming of the squirrel followed its downward trajectory, followed by a thunk and a mad scrambling as the squirrel dashed back up the tree.

"Is that squirrel what's got you whining? You know better." The wind picked up again, rocking the treehouse. A third crack rang out, followed by urgent yells. This time it was a gunshot. The rapid fire of automatic weapons followed.

"Nobody out here," the handler said through the sweeping wind.

Another voice rang out from the yard below. "Beta point, empty nest at two-two-seven-one." Their address. Cassidy let out a breath.

A tinny voice came from a radio. *"Check, beta point."*

Another voice came from down in the streambed and simultaneously through the radio. "Beta flank, clear."

A third voice came through the radio. *"Beta front, clear."* The tinny voice intertwined with the receding wind, *"Beta team, assist at two-two-three-five."*

"Check. Beta team to assist. Move out, beta point."

"Clear!" a different voice called from near the back door as the screen door slammed shut.

Rustling in the garden below revealed more soldiers. Cassidy could not tell how many. Two? Three? Her pulse raced. Footsteps ran along the streambed as the treehouse swayed gently in the dying wind. Cassidy jerked as gunfire started up again. The rat-a-tat of automatic rifles. The crash of a window shattering.

Boots clomped through their house and pounded down the street in the direction of the gunfire. Cassidy felt a sharp pain in her chest and her breath left her. Mr. Thompson lived in that house. The shots stopped suddenly. Taut yells and commands followed.

The wind gusted faintly, then quieted.

Cassidy shook her head and inhaled a rasping breath. Her mother lowered her hands and her eyes opened. Cassidy's father was gazing at his wife with a look of proud wonder.

"I guess I haven't forgotten everything," her mother whispered, returning his look with an impish grin. "And neither have you."

--------------------)--------------------

Cassidy and her parents stayed in the Crow's Nest until darkness fell, moving only to relieve themselves in the bucket, which they layered with redwood needles to dull any noise. The soldiers had been so quiet when they'd scouted the yard, Cassidy was nervous some might still be lurking below. The other noises had faded hours ago. Yells. Crying. Radio chatter. Vehicles rumbling by. Then there was only silence.

The moon rose, sending glimpses of yellow light through the leaves. She thought of Jasper up there, somewhere. Was he looking down at Earth? Did he ever think of her? A familiar ache throbbed inside her. She remembered his kisses, and wished things had been different. *Good night sweet Jasper, may the stars shine down upon you.*

Crickets chirped loudly, growing more insistent in their rhythmic chant as the moon rose in the night sky. Cassidy curled up on the floor between her parents and tried to sleep.

The faint light of dawn woke her. The crickets had quieted, and birds twittered merrily. Dozens of them. They were easy to hear in the silence of the desolate neighborhood. She wondered how many abandoned cats would need to rely on those songbirds for dinner.

Cassidy and her parents decided to wait in the treehouse for a few hours, listen for soldiers, and try to determine where the Tegs were and what direction they were heading. It was possible that they had finished with this neighborhood and moved on, or it was just as possible that they would evacuate the neighborhood across the canal and scout along the streambed all day. Or maybe they were a few miles away, and would intercept Cassidy and her parents if they tried to flee via the water channels or the roads. How long before the Tegs would do another sweep of the neighborhood? When would they raze the buildings and replace them with factories or farmland? Or a work camp ...

She and her parents would have to make a run for it sooner or later. Cassidy felt a sickening emptiness in her belly.

The morning dragged on. She glanced at her watch. It was only eight o'clock. The days were long this time of year, and she and her parents had been up since five-thirty. How would they know when it was the right time to leave?

She listened for soldiers, but all she heard were the sounds of animals, emboldened by the absence of humans. Flocks of birds stopped to feed in the garden. The squirrel sat on a branch and looked down at Cassidy, then leapt to another limb and ran off.

Cassidy trained her father's binoculars on a small patch of dry streambed that was visible through the gap in the leaves. Sure enough, she spotted a soldier. She froze and held her hands steady, trying to focus on the figure as it appeared then disappeared behind the thick screen of branches. She found him again. He was creeping. Scouting. But no, he was not wearing the gray uniform of a Teg. He was in green pants and vest, carrying a pack. Perhaps he was a neighbor trying to escape as they hoped to do. She got a glimpse of his face. The man wore sunglasses, and had short brown hair and the shadow of a beard.

"*Torr,*" she said softly. "*Torr!*" so her parents could hear. The breath left her lungs in a painful gasp of joy and relief.

Her mother wrested the binoculars from her trembling hands. The fear and worry Cassidy had held so tightly snapped like a violin string, leaving her sagging and weak as she choked back tears.

She waited, clutching her mother and father, until she heard the scrape of boots climbing the steep cement bank and a brushing sound as Torr pulled himself over the fence, then a soft thud as his feet hit the ground. Her father held her back as she went to step onto the plank. Caden reached past her and tossed a eucalyptus pod over the edge. It bounced onto the ground. Torr's footsteps stilled. Caden tossed another.

After several moments of silence Cassidy caught glimpses of movement around the perimeter of the yard. She heard a soft creak as Torr opened the shed, then the squeak of the back door. Her heart pounded relentlessly as the minutes ticked by. Only when he finally emerged from the house did she relax.

Branches crackled and swayed as he made his way up the redwood tree. His hands came into view, then his head, shoulders, and hips as he pulled himself onto the plank and strode across it. A broad smile lit his face as he stepped onto the platform and pulled the three of them into his arms.

16

MOFFETT FIELD

Torr scolded his family for waiting for him, while silently thanking the stars that they had. He didn't know what madness had made them stay, any more than he knew what had made him run the gauntlet of Teg patrols to make his way home. He'd nearly headed south more than once, but an inexorable pull had brought him here.

He sat with his family on the littered floor of the Crow's Nest, surveying with satisfaction the solid construction of the fort and grateful for how thoroughly it was camouflaged. They quietly told him how the Tegs had come through the day before, and how they'd barely escaped being discovered. The Tegs were gone, for the time being. Still, his family could not linger long.

He related a short version of Gaia United's surrender and told them his commander had allowed them to leave, without going into any more detail. How could he tell them that half his brothers had turned Teg? He didn't think he could force the words from his throat, even if he'd wanted to. He briefly described the clogged roadways, his boat trip up the coastline, and his journey over the mountain trails. Cassidy's eyes widened as he spoke, and he reached for her arm and squeezed it. He hadn't realized how much he'd missed her. She'd grown up since the last time he'd seen her, a year ago, when he'd come home for a few days of leave. Her dark hair was longer and hung in smooth waves. Her face was more mature and her blue eyes held a depth and gravity he'd never noticed before. She smiled at him. She was beautiful.

He told them how he had hidden under a bridge the previous night while Teg transports had rumbled over the road above him and foot patrols walked the gully below. He'd buried himself in a trench behind a bridge piling, covering himself with dirt and leaves.

"Are we heading to Shasta?" he asked his father, relieved that Caden was here to take charge. He was exhausted. He'd barely slept since the Shaman's Shield had started coming apart, and what little sleep he'd stolen had been riddled with nightmares. At least the biggest drag on him was lifted: the worry and uncertainty over the fate of his family. He had made the right choice.

He listened as his parents and sister talked of their plans. As he'd feared, Moffett was already under Teg control. They discussed the best route to Shasta and the problem of getting through the Shaman's Shield once they got there. They tried to calculate whether waiting longer would ensure a clearer path for them to flee, or make it worse. There was no way to know, but Torr preferred movement to waiting and voted for leaving within the hour. The streambed had been clear this morning; they should take advantage of that fact. Still, it was risky. With Moffett already taken and the Tegs aggressively clearing the neighborhoods, they were bound to run into Teg forces sooner or later, and a group might not be able to evade them as easily as he had solo.

Cassidy tugged at his sleeve. She spoke breathlessly, a child-like hope glinting in her eyes. "I had this idea, Sundance," she said, using his nickname. "I found our deeds to the moon. Remember them?"

He nodded. "Yes, I remember."

"Did you know the deeds grant us citizenship there?"

"Yeah, I suppose."

She went to her pack and pulled out a roll of parchments. "Look," she said, pointing to a section about citizenship. "And look. The personal Salmon Seal of President Metolius." Her voice lowered to a whisper. "And his fingerprints. The Tegs would have to honor them. They'd have to let us leave Moffett for the moon, don't you think?"

His eyes met hers. Great-Aunt Sophie had told him once that Metolius had been a good man in his youth but power destroyed him, and that Torr should take a lesson from that— no matter how good a person is, he can always be turned to bad if he finds himself on the wrong side of life. Torr hadn't understood it then. But he had just watched five men he thought of as brothers join the Tegs. And within twenty breaths, Torr had shot two men dead. He had thought he'd be okay with doing his duty and killing the enemy, but guilt kept poking its finger into his chest. He didn't know which way was up anymore.

He read the deed. It did provide for citizenship. An "independent republic," they called it. He furrowed his brow. That was an enticing concept. But could it be real? If the Office of the President had authorized the deed transfer, then the Global Alliance must have some claim to the moon, therefore how independent could it really be?

"Is Peary Spaceport under Global Alliance control?" he asked his father. They had been out of communication behind the Shaman's Shield so long, how could they even be sure the moonport was still free?

"Last I knew it was still a neutral zone," Caden said. "The

Tegs don't even have all the spaceports on Earth under their control. They wouldn't waste resources on the moon. Think of the logistics."

Torr frowned. With LAX and Moffett lost, that did not leave many spaceports free: only Seattle Chief and Whidbey in Washington state, which hopefully were still behind the Shaman's Shield; and Glamorgan in the Great Isles, which was under the protection of a mist even more mysterious than the Shaman's Shield. Still, the moon was so far away, his father was probably right. There had been almost no talk of Peary Spaceport at Miramar, and then only in the context of off-world trading and the black market.

He nodded and perused the deed again, and examined the map. Their parcel contained a cluster of three big craters, labeled Anaximenes. What would they do with undeveloped moon land? There was no atmosphere, and importing building materials would be impossible.

Cassidy continued speaking, the excitement in her voice waning. "But we could never afford to get there. Passage would be a fortune right now. A Solidi for each of us, at least." Her expression was sullen as she took the parchments and rolled them up.

He shrugged his shoulders, mischievous delight brightening his mood. "That's not so much," he said smugly.

Cassidy frowned. "Right," she muttered. "I had a buyer lined up for this," she said, pulling a gold necklace out from under her shirt. "But he was in San Francisco, and we can't get there anymore. The Tegs blockaded the roads and bridges north of here."

"When did they block the roads?" Torr asked, worrying about Bobby.

"Yesterday," Caden said.

Maybe Bobby would be forced to retrace his steps, hoping to find Torr. Torr should go back to the ridgeline to meet him.

He tightened his jaw. No, Bobby was on his own now. They all were. Torr had to take care of his family. Bobby could sneak past the Tegs just as Torr had, or bribe his way to safety with his share of gold and jewels. Torr ground his teeth and returned his attention to his sister.

"Maybe we could be stowaways," she said, her eyebrows lifting tentatively. "You know, like Jasper always talked about."

Torr reached into his chest pocket, took Cassidy's hand, and placed two Solidi into her open palm. The shocked look on her face made the whole yacht excursion worth it. He chuckled and dug out more Solidi, handing one to each of his parents, who stared at him, dumbfounded.

"Where on Earth did you ever ...?" his mother exclaimed.

"Don't ask," he said with a chuckle. "Keep those." He gently pushed away their hands.

His parents stared at one another, then back at Torr, who smirked proudly. His sister was still staring at the chunks of gold in her hand, turning them over and inspecting the inscriptions on the bases of the four-sided pyramids.

"Cassidy," he asked, "are you serious about going to the moon?" The idea brought to mind all kinds of crazy possibilities.

"Well," Cassidy said slowly. "The moon and the planets are the new frontier. People always flee to new frontiers in times of oppression. Right? It's always been like that, throughout history."

Torr sighed, scratching the stubble on his cheek. She'd been listening to her college professors for too long. He'd expected a simple answer like, *It's either that or the camps.*

She continued, her voice growing more urgent. "Maybe we'll find a solution out there. One we could never find here. We'd be free. We can explore the galaxy. Find allies. Free Earth." Her eyes were gleaming, sparkling with that overly enthusiastic nature she shared with their mother. She saw his scowl and tightened her lips. "Why are you frowning at me, Torr? You always look at the dark side of things."

Easy for her to say. She hadn't had to live in a bunker and kill people. "And you are innocent in your optimism," he said.

Her eyes narrowed. "You are not the only one who has been suffering, Torrance Brenon."

"Sorry," he said to appease her, though he still thought she was spoiled. And she didn't exactly have a thought-out plan. He wanted to go to the moon, too, but it was insane to think they could leave from the Teg-controlled spaceport.

"How would we sneak past security at Moffett?" he challenged her. "Tegs control it now."

"We won't sneak. We'll walk right up to them and present our documents. They have Metolius's seal on them. The guards will have to honor them."

Torr was stunned for a moment at the outrageous bravery of such a plan. He searched his sister's determined face. Was she serious? His face twisted into a grimace. "Walk straight up to Tegs?"

The idea frightened him, but he tempered his emotions to consider the idea. If Tegs were simply normal men doing a job—if they were former Gaia United soldiers like Bates and Smiley—then they would be reasonable men, not bloodthirsty killers, his dream of fratricide aside. Regardless, from what he'd heard, Tegs were extremely disciplined. That meant it would all come down to the rules. But Torr did not know the rules. Would Metolius's seal grant them safe passage? Torr had never seen a document with that seal before. It must be something special. But how special? What if the deeds were simple documents and the seal was a common administrative stamp? It could mean nothing. Or it could mean everything. It was a huge gamble. He breathed deeply, trying to stay calm.

Even if they did get through and made it to the moon, then what? Cassidy's dream was too grand. "What makes you think we can help Earth? We won't be able to settle our land, even with our Solidi. We've considered that before." He and Jasper had formed a plan to flee to the moon years ago, when Kai was living at the Peary colony without Jasper. They had drawn plans for a dome and everything. The cost and logistics had quickly become overwhelming, and they had built the Crow's Nest instead.

Torr met Cassidy's eyes. She was examining him, as though searching for something she had lost. "Don't you believe there's any hope for us? For Earth?" she asked. "Do you really believe the Global Alliance will end up controlling everything and we'll live as slaves forever?"

He swallowed. *What did he believe?* "No," he said, hesitating. "No, I ... I."

"What do you think will happen to us if we stay on Earth?" she insisted.

"I think," he said slowly, "that we will make it to Shasta and hide out. If we're stuck outside the Shaman's Shield, we'll find others and form a guerilla force." *Or eventually be caught and sent to a camp, or hunted down and killed.* "Or if we can get inside the Shaman's Shield, we'll be safe. How do you think we can get through it?" he asked his mother. "Nobody could get through before."

"I never tried before," she said. "I'll have to use some tricks I learned when I was younger." Her face was drawn. "If that doesn't work, we'll hide out. What else can we do? We can't stay here. In the forests up north, there are lots of places to hide. Food to scavenge. Fresh water."

And if they got inside the Shaman's Shield, and it kept shrinking, then they'd live inside a little bubble under siege until it disappeared completely. None of the possible futures were good. He looked despondently at his parents who were watching with lips closed. Even if he and Cassidy could escape somehow, they would abandon their parents to one of those fates.

"Look," Cassidy said, digging into her pack and pulling out their mother's faded blue book with the gilded edges. Cassidy opened it at a bookmark and pointed to a passage. It was written in their mother's flowing hand. On the opposite page were strange runes.

He took the book and scanned the lines of script. Star Seeker bullshit that spoke of the Star Children. The mythical twins who were supposed to save Earth. The Star Children whom his mother and grandmother had thought were Torr and Cassidy until they turned out to be just normal children. Grandma Leann used to weave the tale for him at bedtime: how Torr would unite the forces of the galaxy and lead an army of golden angels, and Cassidy would welcome the Star People to Earth wearing a halo of gold around her head.

"You can't really believe this refers to us," he said, glowering at his mother, but he could tell that she did. His father was keeping his feelings masked. Torr handed the book back to Cassidy.

"Wait," she said, going into the pack she had prepared for him and handing him his DNA birth certificate. She explained how they were part of an unbroken lineage.

He looked over the tree diagram on the birth certificate. "Interesting coincidence," he said. "But this is a practical decision, not one to be based on speculation and Star Seeker fanaticism."

"You think it's nonsense," Cassidy said.

"I didn't say that," he said. "It's just kind of, well, farfetched. And risky."

"What about your dream?" she asked.

How did she know about his dreams? Edgemont's face leered at him. "What dream?" he asked warily.

"The golden people singing to you."

"Oh, that," he said with relief. He could vaguely recall the glowing faces from his childhood dream and tried for the millionth time to recall their song, but it was like a distant murmur lost in the wind. "What about it?"

"Maybe it's true."

"Maybe what's true?"

She stared at him impatiently. "Maybe they are the Star People, and we're the Star Children."

He thought for a moment that maybe she was right, then dismissed the idea. She was talking nonsense again, cracking from the stress of the invasion. Even if they were the Star Children, it wasn't like anyone was handing them a map and an instruction manual. They were on their own, as far as he could tell. Those golden people had never visited him in his dreams again, they'd just left him with a dim memory of a song he couldn't sing. And if it were true, which it surely was not, then their first duty would be to stay alive.

He sighed, his exhaustion returning. "What do you think, Dad? Should we risk our lives and abandon you two to follow some rash scheme cooked up by our, excuse me, star-addled females?"

Cassidy threw him a sour look, and his mother's face was pinched. Too bad, it was true. They were always head-in-the-stars. Fascinated by every mystical tale they heard. Entranced by some wild fantasy that they clung to as if it could change the cruel fate of the world.

"Can we really believe some ancient prophecy from another planet?" he asked his father. "Risk handing ourselves over to the Tegs with only the questionable authority of the deeds standing between us and the slave camps?" It sounded like bad odds to him. Shasta seemed like a sure bet next to gambling everything on getting through Teg security and finding a flight to the moon. He sought his father's eyes, seeking reason.

"I can't answer that for you, son. It feels like we're stuck in a cell with no doors. Any crack in the wall is worth investigating."

He looked at his father, the man who'd seen him off to war, knowing what that meant. His son had come back to him, alive. And he was prepared to let him go again. Torr felt tears rising, and pushed them back. He did not want to leave his parents so soon. Leave them to an unknown fate. Take his sister on a dangerous journey that would surely end in tragedy.

But he didn't want to hide out from the Tegs forever, either. Or stay huddled inside a shrinking Shaman's Shield, trapped in a defensive position again, wondering when the barrier would fall.

His father said, "If Shasta and the Great Isles fall to the Tegs, the moon colony might be the only hope for our kind. For our way of life to survive."

"For our lineage to survive," his mother added.

Cassidy's eyes had grown huge, and Torr was finding it hard to breathe. Their parents were willing to send them into the unknown, in a desperate effort to save them.

"Do you think there's any chance the Tegs will let us through at Moffett Field?" he asked his father.

His father's expression was sad. "As much chance as making it to Shasta, or getting through the Shaman's Shield." His eyes were dark and deep like the ocean. "I don't think it's impossible."

Torr inhaled, then exhaled. *Not impossible.* That was beginning to sound pretty good.

———————)———————

His father had buried their guns. Torr dug them up while his mother and father argued about it. But no one stopped him.

"I don't think you kids should carry guns," his mother grumbled, saying something under her breath about Star Children.

Torr ignored her. He kept his Dashiel and the Orbiter pistol. Cassidy would carry the .22. He gave his father the TAFT and handed his mother the Browning 6 Creed he'd used for competitions, noting a smug look his father tried to conceal as Brianna reluctantly accepted the weapon. Torr quickly showed his father how to operate and clean the TAFT. His father had his own handgun, and took Torr's bow and arrows. Torr and Cassidy would have to ditch their weapons before they reached the spaceport. His Dashiel would be the hardest to part with, even if it was a killing machine. He had hoped for the chance to talk to his father about what he had done, but there was no time.

He gave his parents half of his gold Tetras and coins to add to their Solidi, gave Cassidy a handful of Tetras and coins, and pocketed the rest for himself.

He went into his bedroom, which was stale and dusty and reminded him of Jasper. All the pants in his drawers were too small. He quickly changed into his desert camo, convincing himself that many civilians wore fatigues, even though they weren't supposed to. Besides, his pants were patched and worn enough to look surplus. The cargo pants and field vest were comfortable and had lots of pockets. He would have to abandon the vest, which had the Gaia United eagle emblazoned on the chest pocket, before they reached the spaceport. He drank the rest of his water and traded his Gaia United canteen for the water skin that hung from the back of his pack. He filled it from a five-gallon jug his family had prepared, filled two more metal water bottles, then went back into the bedroom and clipped them to his rucksack.

He was stuffing his vest and pants pockets full of ammo when he stopped with his hand midair. The Gaia United eagle stared at him from his inside forearm. The tattoo he had been so proud of now marked him as a deserter.

Shit. Now what? He couldn't let Cassidy go to the spaceport alone. Maybe they should forget the whole crazy idea.

He heard the door creak open behind him. His mother peeked in.

"You okay, honey?" she asked.

"No." He held his arm up, and her eyes landed on the tattoo.

"Oh," she said, echoing his distress.

"I can't go to the spaceport with this."

"Yes, you can, wait one second." She left and returned with a little jar of makeup, smearing the flesh-colored cream over the tattoo.

He examined it skeptically. "You can still see there's something there," he said worriedly, the shadow of black ink visible through the makeup.

She rubbed in more, then returned with a powder and patted it on. "There, now, no one will ever know," she said, forcing a smile.

She rummaged in his closet and emerged with a black and white flannel shirt. "Here, wear this."

It still fit, and he buttoned the cuffs at his wrists. "It's hot out," he said. "I look ridiculous."

"You look handsome," she said, and kissed his cheek. "I'm so proud of you."

He pulled his vest on over the shirt, and pulled his dog tags from around his neck. He dropped them into his mother's hand. "Keep these," he said.

She cupped them in her palm.

"And give this to Dad," he said, taking his metal marksmanship badge from his bag and placing it in her trembling hand.

"I'll be out in a minute," he said.

She clutched the dog tags and badge and disappeared down the hall, leaving him to the silence of his bedroom.

Torr transferred some of the contents from the backpack Cassidy had prepared into his rucksack, keeping his army blankets and leaving behind the winter-weight sleeping bag. He had heard it was warm in Peary Dome. He sorted through the clothing Cassidy had packed. Most was too small for him. He hesitated over the red Shasta Mountaineering t-shirt, finally deciding to take it.

Cassidy had packed four crystals that Great-Aunt Sophie had given him. He weighed the largest crystal in his hand. It was as heavy as a big river rock. Why would she think he would want to carry a rock to the moon? More magical superstition, no doubt. He could maybe take the two small ones, a fluorite octahedron and a garnet dodecahedron. They would be a nice memory of Earth. But he left the long thin shaft and the squarish one on his dresser for the Tegs to find.

When he was done, he gazed around the room. It was a child's room, holding memories of who he used to be. He would never step foot in here again. He turned and left, closing the door behind him.

His parents and sister stood by the back fence. Torr joined them, and they looked at one another with tightly contained terror in their eyes.

"Where's your pack?" Cassidy asked, fear turning to indignation.

"This is all I need," he said, shrugging the medium-sized rucksack on his shoulders.

"Did you bring the crystals?"

He met her gaze. "Yeah."

"Liar."

He rolled his eyes. "I took the small ones."

She stomped inside the house and returned with the two larger ones, stuffing them into his rucksack like he was a pack mule.

"They want to come," she stated matter-of-factly.

"Yeah, whatever," he mumbled, catching his father's eyes. They traded grins that quickly turned to trembling frowns as they faced one another, dreading what was to come next.

Brianna stepped between them and pulled Torr and Cassidy into an embrace, one in each arm. "Oh, my beautiful twins," she said, pulling their heads in close. "Remember everything I taught you. Be hard and soft at the same time. Listen to the plants and animals. Feel the air and water. Look to the stars."

The moon had none of those things, Torr thought vaguely, except for the stars. Brianna released Cassidy and hugged Torr. She kissed his cheeks, his forehead, his eyelids. He clung to her, suddenly a small child afraid to leave his mother. She slipped from his grasp and turned to Cassidy, hugging and kissing her.

"Dad," Torr said, grabbing his father's hands. "Loop around the bay and go north, and if the Shaman's Shield falls, hurry up and get a flight out of Seattle Chief and come to the moon and find us. We'll go to our land and build a place for all of us."

His father shook his head sadly. "I wouldn't count on that, Torr."

"I can't just leave you here," Torr complained. His hands shook in his father's warm, steady grip.

His father released his hands and took him by the shoulders. "Son. Look at me. Look at me," he repeated, forcing Torr to meet his eyes. "You have to survive and go on without us. If you and Cassidy make it, then your mother and I will continue through you. Do you understand?" Caden shook him gently.

Torr nodded and pulled his father into a hug, not wanting to let go. All the words he wanted to say stuck in his throat. How much he loved him. How he had been such a good father. Brave and smart, compassionate and forgiving. How Torr wanted nothing more in the world than to be the man Caden imagined him to be.

"Be strong, son," his father said. "And kind. Always be kind."

Torr nodded and tried to smile. "Thank you, Dad," was all he could manage to say. "For everything."

His father seemed to understand, and kissed his lips firmly, tasting of salt. Torr watched as his father hugged Cassidy. All the strength his father had just shown Torr fell away as Caden hid his face in her hair. They all knew they would never see each other again.

Torr took a deep breath, then examined the streambed through his binoculars. When he was satisfied it was clear, he cast one parting glance at the house and yard, then led the way over the fence. They skidded down the steep embankment, then stood, children facing parents. None of them sobbed, but their eyes shed silent tears. Without a word, they turned in opposite directions. Cassidy held onto Torr's sleeve as the two of them left their parents and headed north towards Moffett Field.

———————)———————

Despite the nearly intolerable tension, Torr and Cassidy navigated the ten miles to Moffett Field without encountering any Teg troops. The dry streambed met the bay, where they hid their guns and knives in a gully. Torr transferred the Solidi from his vest to his flannel shirt's chest pockets, and stashed the flashlight and binoculars in his rucksack. He laid his vest and ammo over the weapons, then added his belt and belt buckle etched with its telltale eagle emblem into the hole and covered it all with leaves.

Cassidy removed their deeds and parcel maps from her pack and handed him his. They were either their tickets out or their death sentences. Torr and Cassidy hugged for a long, frantic moment, then walked out onto the bay trail where the scrubby marshland offered no cover. Torr forced himself to breathe and pretend it was just another day. The midday sun was hot, and a salty breeze blew in off the bay. They walked wordlessly, their boots crunching on the gravel path.

They rounded a curve of the bay, and the spaceport loomed in the distance, alone in the middle of a flat, drained marshland. The massive, modern structure was shaped like a seagull in flight, with two curved, outstretched wings and a long, white, cylindrical body. Torr had been inside many times, helping his father with his trading business, and it had always felt friendly. Now the building looked cold and forbidding. Nestled in the crook of the nearest wing was the launchpad: a sunken, cylindrical pit built with Cephean technology that allowed Cephean-designed, single-stage spacecraft to hurtle through the atmosphere with a single thrust.

Torr turned his attention to a contingent of gray-uniformed Tegs manning cement barricades along the perimeter road. The soldiers had seen them, and several rifles were pointed their way. The air was silent except for the buzz of a small drone passing overhead. Torr took a deep breath and nodded confidently to Cassidy. She managed a sick smile. It was almost a relief to finally be here and face their fates head on. They exchanged a look that brought up a memory of when they were kids about to jump off the cliff into the American River. Torr broke their gaze and they stepped forward together.

Torr's heartbeat pounded throughout his body. He had to be strong, for Cassidy's sake. They had decided to do this, and it was too late to turn back now. They crossed the wide field, hands in plain sight. Torr raised his chin and tried to identify an officer. He was not hard to spot, standing with his thumbs through his belt loops, while everyone else was toting a gun. Torr marched forward, with Cassidy at his side.

There was no fear in the officer's eyes. He was a Teg, after all, heavily armed and backed by dozens of soldiers with armored vehicles parked every hundred yards. When they got within speaking distance, he and Cassidy stopped walking.

"Hello," Torr called out, keeping his voice steady. "We're looking for the entry gate."

The man's eyebrows rose a millimeter. "There are no civilian flights launching out of here." Torr had a sinking feeling in the pit of his stomach. "All civilians are to report to a camp processing center," the officer said, not unkindly. "I'll provide you an escort."

"We have authorization to leave the planet," Torr said quickly, raising his scroll, resisting the rabid fear that was trying to claw its way up his throat. Torr read the name GROLSCH on the officer's right chest pocket.

Grolsch's eyes narrowed, and he folded his arms across his chest. "What kind of authorization?"

Torr had rehearsed the words a hundred times in his head, but his tongue tripped over itself as he forced them out of his mouth. "We have *citi* ... citizenship papers for the moon, issued by President Metolius." Torr's legs were shaking, and his damned cheek was twitching. There was no reason to believe deeds to the moon gave them the right to leave the planet. He held the man's eyes. If these were to be his last moments of freedom, he would spend them bravely.

Grolsch hesitated, examining him and Cassidy. The troops exchanged glances. "Let me see," he said, holding out his hand.

Torr took Cassidy's parchments, stepped forward, and handed the officer their deeds, then stepped back to stand with his sister.

Grolsch unrolled the documents and perused the first deed slowly, his brow furrowed. Torr could tell when he found Metolius's seal; Grolsch's eyes stopped and widened. He glanced up at Torr and Cassidy for a moment before returning his attention to the deed. His brow furrowed further, over what Torr judged were Metolius's signature and fingerprints. Grolsch examined the deed for several long seconds before inspecting the other documents.

He finally lowered the parchments. "IDs, please."

They fumbled in their bags and Torr stepped forward again, handing him their Free States passports and DNA birth certificates.

The man examined their papers for several agonizing minutes. "Wait here," he said curtly, and walked down the line where he stopped at a vehicle and disappeared inside.

Torr and Cassidy stood silently in the sun. Sweat trickled down Torr's temples and neck. The Tegs were eyeing them curiously. Torr's gaze slid to the left and he felt oddly detached, as though time had slowed and he was watching from above. The bay rippled with tiny, scalloped waves, and seven geese flew in a V formation. His cheek twitched in a steady rhythm, with a faint electrical pulse that no one else could see, but which reminded Torr relentlessly that something was very wrong.

Torr faced forward as Grolsch rolled up in the vehicle. Torr's stomach grew heavy, and his thighs started trembling again. He heard Cassidy's breathing quicken. *Stars in heaven,* he prayed silently, *shine down upon us. Let your golden light wash over us.* He reached out and found Cassidy's hand, which was sweaty and shaking. He thought of his parents making their way to Shasta. Torr and Cassidy had made a bet and they had lost. His heart pounded hollowly, a sense of doom settling coldly into his bones.

Grolsch hopped out of the passenger side and motioned to the back of the transport. "We'll take you to the gate."

Torr nodded and squeezed Cassidy's hand. They stood with their arms out to the sides while two soldiers scanned them for weapons, patted them down, and inspected their bags. The soldiers raised their eyebrows at the Solidi in their pockets and the stash of gold coins and jewelry that filled a side pocket of Torr's rucksack. Easy spoils for the men. Torr half-expected them to slyly pocket the gold, or maybe hand it over to Grolsch. They did neither, returning the gold to where they had found it.

They were disciplined soldiers, Torr deduced, and did not have the authority to confiscate their goods. They handled the crystals curiously, but it was Torr's binoculars and flashlight that caught the men's attention. A wave of nausea overtook Torr as the men huddled over the Gaia United equipment. They were not marked with the Gaia United emblem, but the flashlight was Gaia United green and the binoculars were military grade. The soldiers looked up, noting Torr's camo pants and rucksack. Torr closed his eyes as the men called Grolsch over. Torr silently cursed himself for his idiocy, sweat beading on his upper lip. Why hadn't he left the flashlight and binoculars in the ditch along with everything else? Why hadn't he worn his tight jeans and taken the hiking backpack? Next they would discover his tattoo and he would get a rifle butt to the side of the head. He opened his eyes and did not dare look at Cassidy.

Grolsch cast a look their way, then spoke softly to the men, who returned the binoculars and flashlight to Torr's rucksack. Torr felt sick. One of them handed Torr his rucksack while the other returned Cassidy's pack to her. Grolsch directed them towards the vehicle.

Torr helped Cassidy into the back, then climbed in after her. Grolsch climbed in as well. Torr swallowed painfully.

The vehicle had a long bench on one side where three soldiers were sitting with rifles across their knees. A table was built into the other side where three more soldiers sat in front of communications equipment. The soldiers got up from the bench and squatted on the floor, giving up their seats for them.

Torr sat thankfully, bathed in sweat, and took a sip of water from his water skin and passed it to Cassidy. The vehicle made a U-turn and headed towards the port. No one spoke during the five minute ride. Torr kept his eyes lowered, slyly examining the soldiers, their weapons, and the equipment in the vehicle. It looked like a typical communications station. The screens were blank, probably because he and Cassidy were there. Each soldier had an assault rifle, as well as a handgun and knives. No one carried Lectros.

They reached the gate, and Grolsch motioned for them to step down from the vehicle. The guards at the gate seemed to be expecting them. An officer took their documents from Grolsch and disappeared into the guard shack while Torr and Cassidy stood under the curious eyes of the guards. Torr breathed shallowly. Cassidy's face was unnaturally pale.

A red-haired officer emerged from the shack. He nodded curtly and held out the documents to Torr. "They will take you to the entrance," he said, tilting his head towards the armored vehicle. "Someone will meet you and escort you to a gate. Do you have passage?"

Torr stared at the man. Slowly it sank in. Did he have passage. To the moon.

Torr shook his head, relief flooding through him along with an uncomfortable urge to pee. He cleared his throat, trying to gather his composure and act as though he'd known all along that they were sending them to their freedom. Cassidy's mouth was hanging open. "No, we'll have to buy it," Torr said hoarsely, then blurted out the next thing that came into his head. "I assume flights have resumed to the moon colony?"

The officer nodded. "Yes. But passage is expensive." His eyes ran over Torr's faded, patched pants and dusty pack. Torr reached into his shirt pocket and pulled out a Solidi. The man stared at the gold pyramid for a moment, then nodded and stepped back to allow Torr and Cassidy to climb into the vehicle.

————————)————————

Torr and Cassidy walked behind Grolsch across the empty cement sidewalks that fronted Moffett Field Spaceport.

Grolsch led them to the main entrance and handed them off to a young officer named Brent. Brent led them past a throng of guards who stared straight ahead, and into the airy structure with its towering ceilings of glass. Brent's heels clicked against the tile floors, the sharp tap-taps echoing across the otherwise hushed building.

Teg soldiers were stationed at each doorway and juncture, standing two per position, eyes forward and hands clasped behind their backs. The ticketing counters were closed, and there were no passengers in sight except for an elderly couple walking briskly across the floor, flanked by two Tegs. The couple looked rich.

The soldiers were alert, but the mood was calm. Evidently, the spaceport had been handed over without a struggle.

Brent led them around a corner and into a small, windowless office. A Teg officer, Clark, was seated behind a desk working at a screen, and looked up as they entered. Clark stood and shook Torr's hand, then Cassidy's, and offered them seats in black guest chairs facing the desk. Torr and Cassidy sat stiffly, while Brent stood at the door, hands behind his back.

"May I see your deeds?" Clark asked. Torr handed him the rolled parchments. Clark studied them silently for several minutes, referencing something displayed on his screen that Torr could not see, then passed the deeds over a sensing device. "Passports and DNA certificates?"

Torr and Cassidy handed over the documents, which Clark also passed over the sensor.

"Touch here, please," Clark said, pointing to a black pad on the table.

Torr and Cassidy each laid their hands on the DNA sensor, and Clark's screen beeped.

He seemed satisfied and handed the deeds and identification papers back to them. "There are no flights scheduled for Peary Dome at this time. I assume that's where you're headed?"

Torr nodded, clutching the documents to keep his hands from shaking.

"There is a cargo ship bound for Ridge Gandoop later today. I can see if they'll take you. You'll have to arrange passage from there to Peary once you're moonside."

Torr exchanged glances with Cassidy. Torr assumed Ridge Gandoop was another lunar spaceport, but he had no idea how they would arrange passage from there. He turned to the officer. "How long until the next flight to Peary?"

The officer shrugged. "I don't know. Seems all moon traffic is being routed through Gandoop. I'd take the freighter, if I were you. If they have room, that is. Let me check." He turned to his screen and typed silently. After a long while, he looked up. "They said they'd need to remove some cargo to make room for you, so you'll have to pay enough to compensate for the lost freight."

"How much?" Torr asked.

The man frowned. "Best you negotiate with them directly. Come, I'll take you there."

Clark and Brent led them through the cavernous building into a cargo hangar. Torr had been in this hangar a dozen times, helping his father with loads bound for the moon or other international Earth ports, back before the Shaman's Shield cut off long distance air travel. Several ships were being loaded, and pallets and shipping containers were lined up on the floor. All of the ships, except one, were Earth orbit freighters, which delivered to ports across the globe. The only moon freighter had CALICO JACK painted in large red script on the hull. It was a beat-up, dusty thing with its loading hatch open, revealing a cargo hold packed solid with goods.

A thin, haggard man leaned against *Calico Jack's* hull and watched them approach. He wore a faded brown flight suit. His shoulder-length hair was as gray as his complexion, and he rubbed his hands together as they stopped in front of him. He looked Cassidy up and down, then spoke to Torr without offering his hand in greeting.

"Name's Captain Herbert. I hear you want to buy passage on the *Calico Jack*. I'll have to remove some freight to carry you," he said, as though it was a great inconvenience. He glanced at the officers, then back to Torr as if the only reason he was even discussing it was because the Tegs were there. A husky man with a bald head and a jutting chin came up behind Herbert, towering over the skinny captain.

Torr kept his face blank, wondering if they should trust these men. He and Cassidy didn't have a lot of options.

He met Herbert's gaze. Torr had been brought up working at his father's side in his trading business and had negotiated with worse-looking characters than these, but not for his own passage and that of his sister. Torr knew the man intended to take them on, otherwise he wouldn't even bother speaking with them. It was now only a matter of what the man could get in exchange. Torr hoped all he had in mind was gold.

"One Solidi for the both of us," Torr said.

Herbert threw back his head and laughed, then sneered. "Don't insult me."

Torr's eyes slid to the open back of the cargo ship. It was tightly packed floor to ceiling with fifty-gallon drums and fifty-pound sacks. Everything was strapped down and secured to the metal floor, walls, and ceiling. RICE was printed on the edges of the top sacks. Others lower down read WHEAT FLOUR. Others, RED BEANS. The men would need to remove a few dozen sacks to make room for him and Cassidy. Torr was certain Herbert could not get anything close to a whole Solidi in exchange for the goods he'd need to remove to accommodate them. However, the shipping fee itself would be steep, far beyond the value of the cargo itself. He did not know how the captain's shipping deal was structured.

The man spoke, his voice dry and raspy. "I'll be short on my shipment. It's not good for my reputation. I'm taking a risk carrying you two. Humans are a pain in the ass to transport. They piss and shit, and use my oxygen. Two Solidi apiece, take it or leave it." The man glared at Torr.

Torr could feel Cassidy's anxiety. She wanted him to take it, but Torr forced himself to be calm. They had six Solidi between them. They could accept his offer and be done with it, and still have gold in their pockets. But then the man would be dissatisfied, thinking he could have gotten more, and might demand additional compensation of some sort at the other end. Besides, Torr would not part so easily with the gold.

Torr's lip curled into a snarl. "I could buy your entire load twenty times over for four Solidi." Torr leveled his eyes at the man, whose lids narrowed.

"Yeah, but you can't get it to the moon, now can you?"

Torr shrugged. "No, that's why I'm offering you one Solidi. More than a fair price."

After going back and forth, with the captain adding insults at each round, they finally settled on one Solidi apiece. Torr showed him the two gold pyramids, then handed him one. "The other when we get there safely," Torr said.

The man frowned but accepted it. The Teg officers watched as the wiry captain directed a loading crew to remove several rice sacks from the top left quadrant of the wall of grain, leaving a small hole.

"Not big enough," Brent said, frowning at the captain.

"It's plenty," Herbert said crossly. "Trip's only twelve hours."

"They're paying you two Solidi, at least give them some room to move around. Eight by eight should do it."

Herbert cursed and directed the crew to remove another section of the wall of rice. At Brent's insistence they removed another layer deeper into the wall, leaving an eight-foot cube of open space. Herbert climbed onto a ladder, complaining all the while as he spread a tarp over the newly exposed grain sacks and strapped it all down.

The captain threw them an annoyed look as he descended the ladder. "Piss or shit on my cargo and that'll be another Solidi."

It wasn't what Torr had pictured when he'd imagined traveling to the moon, but, given their situation, he supposed they could tolerate a day in a rice cell.

Herbert and the large man he called Junior disappeared into the front cab and returned with their arms full. They tossed two ancient-looking pressure suits, helmets, and harnesses to the ground. The suits had probably been white once, but now were a dingy gray. The men made another trip and returned with oxygen tanks, cables, hoses, and a small crate. In the crate were four two-liter bags filled with water. Two were labeled GENUINE WATER, the others SALT WATER.

Junior pointed at a bag of salt water. "Drink one of these when we drop into moon orbit."

"How will we know when that is?" Cassidy asked.

"You'll know," Junior said.

"When's the last time you ate?" Herbert demanded.

They hadn't eaten since they'd forced down a few bites of bread and cheese while walking the streambed on their way to Moffett.

"Lunchtime," Cassidy said.

"Well, don't eat anything else unless you want to clean yourself up like a baby." Herbert handed them each a pair of large white underpants. "These are space diapers."

Torr stared at him, then quickly tried to mask his disgust.

"Wear these at all times. I don't want a drop of your bodily fluids touching my cargo, and there ain't no toilet in the cargo hold." Herbert glowered at them, his eyebrows joining together in a scowl. "But if you're stupid and stubborn and sneak some food, and you don't mind shitting yourself, then absolutely no bread. Nothing crumbly to clog up my air system. Got it?"

"We won't eat," Cassidy said, glancing at Torr.

He nodded in agreement. He had no desire to shit himself.

"There's a toilet over there," Herbert said. "Take a crap and put these on. Hurry up."

Brent led Torr and Cassidy to bathrooms at the end of the cargo floor. Torr changed into the adult diaper and tried not to think about pissing his pants. He had never really thought through the details of space flight before.

They met back out on the floor, and Herbert removed a stack of folded white bags from the crate. "If you have to puke, use one of these, then wipe your face and tie it up. Don't puke into your helmets or you'll be sorry, and don't take your helmets off until we stop accelerating. So that means don't puke during launch."

Torr swallowed.

"Here," the captain said gruffly. "This will help with zero gravity sickness." He pulled two squares of plastic from his breast pocket and peeled one open. It was a small round patch. Herbert took Torr's right forearm, his dirty fingers closing over where Torr's Gaia United tattoo hid under his shirtsleeve. Torr twisted his wrist free and offered his left arm instead. Herbert frowned impatiently as Torr unbuttoned and rolled up his sleeve so that Herbert could adhere the patch onto his inner wrist. Torr helped Cassidy unwrap her patch, his shaking fingers fumbling with the plastic.

"I've got it," she said, and took the patch from him, applying it to her wrist.

Herbert stashed the motion sickness bags and water sacks in the crate, which he sealed and secured to a bracket on the cargo ramp next to where Junior was clamping down two chairs. The chairs were more like padded boards with a cushioned bracket at the head and a raised block at the feet. The freighter loading ramp doubled as the cargo bay door, which he and Cassidy were apparently to be strapped onto. It looked like they would be lying on their backs, heads down on the sloping ramp. He didn't want his sister to sense his nervousness and gave her an encouraging smile. Cassidy tried to smile back, but she looked as uneasy as he was.

Junior handed them each a pressure suit, which they proceeded to step into and pull over their shoes and clothes. The suits were heavy, and Brent and Clark helped pull them up over their shoulders where they hung loosely. Big boots and gloves were built in. Herbert tightened the chest straps and handed them each a helmet, then stepped away to help Junior finish bolting down the chairs.

"You'll be fine," Clark assured them. Torr nodded and shook the officer's hand with his gloved one.

"Thank you," Torr said to him and Brent.

"Sure thing. Good luck out there," Clark said, and clapped

him on the shoulder. Brent shook their hands, and the Teg offi-cers stepped back as Torr and Cassidy walked onto the ramp to inspect their seats.

Herbert strapped their packs and the oxygen tanks to metal brackets on the floor next to the seats. "If you take off your suits, you'll need your blankets. It gets cold back here. There'll be oxygen and normal Earth air pressure, but no lights. You got flashlights?"

Torr nodded.

Herbert and Junior helped them step into their harnesses and pulled the straps over their shoulders. The captain spoke as he tightened the straps around Cassidy's shoulders and hips. "Tighten your stomachs to help withstand the force of takeoff. Take big breaths. It'll feel pretty heavy at first, but it'll be over in a few minutes. Your suits will protect you. You might start feeling sick from zero gravity a couple hours after that." He smiled at them, showing yellowed teeth.

Torr tried to return the smile. His first spaceflight. He should be excited, but instead he was sweating and his stomach felt like he'd been punched.

Herbert helped Torr put on his helmet and sealed the airlock at the neck, attached a hose that led from the oxygen tank into the side of the neck, then showed Torr how to turn the oxygen on and off with a valve at the neck. "Turn it off when you remove the helmet," Herbert said loudly through the glass of the helmet. Finally, he plugged in cables at Torr's wrist and ankles. Suddenly the legs of the spacesuit tightened around his calves and thighs. Herbert felt Torr's legs and seemed satisfied. Junior hooked Cassidy up the same way.

"Ready?" Herbert asked, almost cheerfully, and pointed to the chairs mounted to the lowered cargo bay door.

They lay on their backs in the reclined chairs, heads down-hill and feet resting on the raised leg rests. Herbert and Junior clipped their harnesses to brackets on the chairs and tightened the straps. Their arms were left free but Herbert instructed them to hang onto the arm rests during takeoff.

Torr couldn't move his torso or legs, and sound was muffled by the helmet. He turned his head to check on Cassidy. She smiled tensely at him through her face shield. They were helpless. If Herbert and Junior wanted to do anything to them now, they were at their mercy. His cheek was twitching again, but no one would notice with his helmet on. He tried to hold onto his courage, and looked up at the girders of the spaceport ceiling that loomed far overhead. His last moments on Earth. He wondered if he would ever return. A warm tear left the outside corner of his eye and trickled down his temple. There was no way to wipe it away, and he fought shedding any more.

Herbert and Junior disappeared from view. The ramp underneath them shuddered then slowly started rising, lifting them with it. Soon they were sitting high up on the metal ramp that would seal them inside the cargo bay. They approached the cube-shaped gap in the wall of grain sacks. The light shrank to a sliver, then the ramp clanged shut and plunged them into total darkness. A sucking thud sealed the chamber.

Torr felt the ship slide onto the tracks that led out to the launch platform. The craft crawled along for several minutes, lurched to a stop, then slowly tilted up until Torr was lying flat on his back again. A shudder signaled their descent into the launch cylinder, then all was still. Time dragged on in blind silence. Torr gripped the arms of his chair and waited, trapped inside his airtight suit and breathing oxygen through the face mask.

It began as a faint vibration that grew until Torr's bones shook from the noiseless tremors. He worked to steady his breathing and wished he could see. He remembered Herbert had told them to tighten their abdomens, and he tensed his muscles. Without warning, he was slammed back against his seat. He held on and squeezed his eyes shut as the weight of acceleration flattened him. His chest felt as though it was being crushed by a pile of rocks, and he tightened his muscles against the relentless force. A shiver of panic passed through him as he struggled to take deep breaths. He began counting in his head, wishing he had asked exactly how many minutes this would last. *Ten. Twenty. Sixty. One hundred and twenty. One hundred and eighty.* He stopped counting and surrendered to the rhythm of his pulse as his heart labored in his chest.

As abruptly as it had started, the pressure dropped away, and Torr's body was suddenly light and free. He drew in deep breaths, every part of him trembling. He reached out, searching for Cassidy's arm.

She grabbed his gloved hand. She was okay. He let go and felt for the release latch on his helmet. He held his breath, shut off the oxygen, broke the air seal, and lifted the helmet off. The air pressure seemed normal, and he took a tentative breath. He fumbled with his bulky gloves to release himself from his harness, then worked himself free of the chair and floated over to Cassidy to help her. He found her helmeted head in the dark and hung onto it, his weightless body and feet floating up behind him as laughter shook him.

"I'm floating," he said as he pulled off her helmet.

"Oh, my God," she said, her voice shaking. "I thought I was going to die there for a minute."

"Me too."

"We need light," she said.

He could hear her fumbling with her harness. He found a strap and loosened it for her, then left her to free herself. He detached the pressure cables from his suit and the tightness around his legs relaxed. Climbing out of the bulky suit, he let it float away and immediately bumped up against a wall of rice. He kicked off gently, glided back, and did a slow flip.

"I'm flying," he said.

"Me too," Cassidy said, giggling. She bumped against him in the darkness and pushed against his shoulders to propel herself, sending him back against the stacks of rice.

It was like floating in the ocean. Torr pulled himself hand over hand across the rice sacks and found the metal wall and his rucksack. Its top contents drifted away as he found his flashlight.

The light beam illuminated their little rice cave, reflecting off a swarm of floating dust particles. The white ghost of a pressure suit swam across the pool of darkness, and he pushed it aside. Cables and straps snaked slowly through the air, and articles of clothing floated in all directions. He gathered them one by one, stuffed them into his pack, and fastened the flap before they could escape again.

The space was small, and after bouncing around a few times, the novelty of zero gravity wore off, and Torr was overcome with exhaustion.

He tried resting with his arms folded across his chest. It was hard to hold that position, and he found himself naturally curling up into the fetal position and bumping against surfaces like an untethered balloon. He experimented with tying himself to the wall. He ended up tying one ankle to a cargo strap that secured a wall of rice, and a shoulder to the opposite wall, stretching himself across the space. Cassidy rigged her sleeping bag like a hammock, crawled inside, and floated silently next to him. Torr mused about the phenomenon of gravity and how important it was to hold everything in place. He admired Herbert's and Junior's stowing skills—hundreds of grain sacks and barrels stayed securely moored to their spots regardless of which way was down.

Not much later, Torr felt the need to pee. He held it in and tried to ignore a feeling of nausea that welled up in his chest. He hadn't eaten in hours, which added to his lightheadedness, but he was afraid eating might make things even worse. He breathed deeply and closed his eyes.

———————)———————

It grew cold in the cargo hold, as Herbert had warned, but Torr didn't think they'd let it get below freezing, not with all the foodstuffs on board. Torr untethered himself and rolled up in his blankets, clipped the bungee cords around his body so the blankets wouldn't float away, then attached to his anchors again. Cassidy was cocooned in her sleeping bag. He kept his flashlight on to dispel the inky blackness. Aside from the takeoff, Torr couldn't tell they were on a ship hurtling through space. It was totally silent and felt as though they were suspended and not moving at all, though he knew they were traveling at several kilometers per second.

He checked his watch. It was still working. They had left Earth four hours ago. Eight hours to go. He closed his eyes and tried not to worry about what awaited them on the moon. They were landing at some unknown spaceport and would need to find their way to Peary Dome. He calmed his mind. He would deal with that when they got there. They had plenty of gold. They would get to Peary Dome, then look for Jasper.

Cassidy tried to start a conversation, but Torr didn't feel much like talking. She went on in a steady monologue. He could tell she was too excited and nervous to sleep and needed the comfort of his presence. He listened and said, "Uh-huh," once in a while to let her know he was listening. She spoke of her past year at the university and her herbal apprenticeship with their mother. She showed him her gold coin pendant from Great-Aunt Sophie, which was supposedly from Iliad and had been pictured in some antique dealer's book in San Francisco.

"I was so worried about you," she said. "I kept trying to check to see if you were okay. You know, the way I used to do when we were little."

The tone of her voice made the hairs on the nape of his neck stand on end. "I thought you couldn't do that anymore."

"I know. I didn't think I could either. I kept getting random images. First, I saw Teg soldiers spread across the hills. Thousands of them. That scared me. Then I saw traffic jams. Then the open ocean. And the forest. It made no sense at all, until you told us about your escape."

Shivers ran up his arms. "How did you make that work?"

"I'm not sure. I tried water scrying, but that was useless. I think it might have been an herb I found."

"Ah," he said. While he had spent his younger years helping his dad with the trading business, Cassidy had been learning about herbs from their mother. He avoided his mother's herbs as much as possible. They felt like spirits watching him. His nightmares were bad enough; he didn't need plant spirits following him through his waking life.

"I hope that wasn't too intrusive," she said. "I didn't realize the visions were real until you described your journey."

He thought he'd felt her presence tugging at him since the Shaman's Shield had fallen, and now he knew it had been real. They were connected, like they had been their whole lives. It didn't matter that he'd moved hundreds of miles away; when she reached out to him emotionally, he felt it. "It's fine," he said. "We're twins."

He didn't dare ask if she'd felt it when he'd killed the Tegs. He pulled at his tethers and rolled to his side, away from her.

"I'm worried about Mom and Dad," she said to his back.

"Me too," he muttered.

"And my friends. I went by Beth's and Jessica's houses. They were empty. They left without even saying goodbye."

Her voice was strained. She paused, waiting for him to say something. He wished he could just fall into a dreamless sleep and not think about any of it. He could feel her sadness seeping across the narrow space between them.

"I'm sorry," he finally said.

"What about your friends?" she asked.

He sighed to himself. She was not going to stop talking, and he didn't have the heart to ask her to be quiet.

"Did you make close friends in the army?"

"Yes."

He had forgotten about his squadmates for a brief time. Now their faces crowded his consciousness.

"Are they okay?"

He bit his lip. "I don't know."

He thought of each of them. Bobby. Reina. Mike. Donald. His squadmates turned Teg. Johnson's cynical sneer. Rashon's silly dance. Jessimar's baby face. Smiley's missing front tooth. Bates's eagerness to please. Then, despite his efforts to avoid it, he thought of the soldiers he had killed. He wondered if they were still lying on the hillside, their bodies slowly rotting into the soil. Probably the Tegs had retrieved them by now. Pain twisted in his belly.

He took in a deep breath and thought of his parents creeping across dry streambeds, sneaking down fire roads, ducking into the bushes every time a craft flew overhead.

Cassidy finally was silent.

He extinguished the flashlight and surrendered himself to the darkness, trying to empty his mind.

Cassidy's voice broke the stillness. "What's bothering you?"

That was a stupid question, he thought. Everything was bothering him.

But she could tell there was something more going on than concern for their parents and his friends, something besides leaving Earth and traveling into the unknown, or the dystopian tragedy of the Teg invasion. He knew she felt the hard knot of pain in his gut, but he didn't want to speak of it. How could he tell her he'd killed two men and that he felt partly dead himself? It felt like whining. He was a soldier. That's what soldiers did. They killed the enemy. He was a Designated Marksman, and they had been clean kills. A normal guy would feel proud. He should be spending his energy praying for his parents and friends, and mourning the death of their nation and their whole way of life. Besides, those men were Tegs. They deserved it.

Cassidy was waiting for him to respond, but he couldn't voice any of it. He knew his silence was hurtful to her. He could feel her across the darkness. Better hurtful silence than what she would feel if he confessed to her what he'd done. She never wanted to kill anything. Not even spiders, or rats in the attic. She always wanted to rescue and release the pests into the yard, even though they would just come right back inside. She would be horrified and repulsed if she knew he'd shot two men, even though that was his job. She'd try not to judge him, but she would anyway. Then she'd feel sorry for him. Then she'd try to comfort him, asking him all sorts of questions like he was a patient at one of her herbal consultations.

He hadn't needed to talk about it when he was with his buddies. They had seen him do it. They knew he had a job to do, and he had done it well. They were proud, slapping him on the back. They interpreted his silence as humility. Only Reina and Bobby knew it bothered him a little. Reina had watched them die through her spotting scope. It had shaken her a bit, too, but they hadn't spoken of it. What good would it do? The men were dead.

He hadn't really thought of Tegs as people before. Not until he'd seen their eyes—living one moment and dead the next. Not until they'd visited him in his dreams. Not until his friends turned Teg.

Now he had to face the confusion by himself. Being with Cassidy was almost worse than suffering alone. She was like a tender part of his heart. Her sorrow would be even more painful than his own.

"Don't you want to talk about it?" she ventured.

"No," he snapped, his voice harsh. He could feel her shrink away from him. Too bad. If he told her, he would fly apart. He forced his emotions into a tight ball in his belly, then wrapped his arms around himself and stared into the blackness.

17

GOLDEN TENDRILS

Zero gravity had been fun for a while, but now Cassidy's head was stuffed up, her bladder was pressing at her painfully, and she was afraid that if her nausea got any worse she would be reaching for the motion sickness bags. She tried to calm herself. Torr must be as uncomfortable as she was, but he wasn't complaining.

He was in no mood to talk. Something had happened that hurt too much to speak about. He had always needed to process things by himself. She pulled the sleeping bag over her head for warmth. The ship was silent and still. Despite her discomfort and Torr's obvious distress, it was gloriously peaceful out here. She hadn't noticed that her mind had been constantly buzzing on Earth. Out here, the intense silence made her aware of who she was when she wasn't constantly bombarded by the energy of everyone around her.

The star music welled up the way the chirping of crickets emerges when the noises of the city subside late at night. She held her breath and listened, trying to discern a melody, but it remained elusive, as if a string orchestra was playing at a festival on a distant hilltop, the sound drifting to her in snatches but the whole of it lifted away by the wind before she could recognize the tune. Still, the resonance of it was comforting, and she let it join the rushing of her blood that whispered softly in her eardrums.

She nestled her hands up under her chin, and the gold coin pendant floated out from under her shirt collar. She captured it in a cupped palm. The metal was warm from having rested against her skin, and she rubbed it between her thumb and forefingers, wondering how Great-Aunt Sophie had ever found such a treasure. If President Metolius had something to do with it, she didn't want to know, although she was sure his Salmon Seal and fingerprints on the deeds had allowed them to leave Earth. She had literally almost peed her pants sitting in the transport with the Tegs, thinking she was headed to a camp. Or a breeding center. For the first time she had fully understood the danger she was in. All the Tegs in the transport were men. They could have easily gang-raped her and there was nothing she or Torr could have done about it. But she was okay now. They would find Jasper and Kai on the moon, and everything would be all right.

She listened for the star music again, wanting it to drown out the fearful voices that kept trying to get her attention. A memory surfaced of a conversation when she was small—a scene she had forgotten until now. It was a cold winter morning, and just the females—Cassidy, her mother, grandmother, Great-Aunt Sophie, and Jasper's mother, Melanie—were seated around Grandma Leann's kitchen table. Cassidy was munching a fresh-baked chocolate chip cookie.

"You shouldn't have shielded Cassidy like that," Brianna said to Grandma Leann. "You need to undo it."

Cassidy looked from her mother to her grandmother, who were staring daggers at one another and speaking as though Cassidy were not sitting right there.

"First of all, I can't undo it. Secondly, even if I could, I wouldn't. She'll need to do it herself."

"What do you mean, you can't undo it? What did you do?" Brianna's dark hair floated around her head.

"Calm down, Brianna. She's already rebuilding her connections with those in her life, like a normal person. Her attachment to Torr is stronger than ever, and she's firmly connected to you, me, and Caden. And Jasper. She's a normal, healthy girl now."

"Now? What do you think she was before?"

"Abnormal. Don't look at me like that, you know it's true. She was connected to everything, Brianna. She had golden threads feeding into each of her chakras like nothing I've ever seen. Masses so thick they were like solid pillars of gold, streaming the connected consciousness through her so strongly, it was burning her out. No child has the capacity to handle that much energy in a constant flood. No one does. Not without help."

"We were helping her," Brianna said, tears of frustration glinting in her eyes.

"Everything is intensified near the mountain," Melanie said, gesturing to the window where the snowy peak loomed over the small town. "Shasta heightens everyone's awareness."

"That's why we have to move away from here," Brianna said. "It's too much, it's making everybody crazy." She turned her attention back to Grandma Leann. "Torr's connected to everything, too, but you didn't feel the need to shield him."

"Torr is connected through the back, through the subconscious. He experiences everything in his dreams, like your father did. Sleep serves as a natural buffer. Cassidy was connected through the front, through her conscious being. She sensed everything. She was aware of everything, all at once. It was drowning her, Brianna, you saw it yourself. She was always distracted. Upset. She couldn't sleep, she was always screaming and crying, wide awake in the middle of the night. And not from dreams. No. From the world battling for her attention. She was seeing the *war*, Brianna. No child should suffer like that."

Grandma Leann waved her hand, hushing Brianna before she could interrupt. "And it wasn't just the war," she went on. "It was everything. She perceived too much. Remember how she was always running up to strangers on the street as if she knew them, sharing their grief over something there was no way she could have known? Do you remember when she ran up to that pregnant woman and said she was sorry her baby was dead? Then the woman went into labor that night and had a stillbirth? It was too much, and not just for her. People were growing afraid of her."

Tears were trickling down Brianna's face. Her voice was almost a whimper. "But I didn't want to cut her off from everything. Not like that. What exactly did you do?"

"I just got really upset seeing her suffer so. So I cut it all. I severed it."

"Severed what?"

"Everything. All her connections, the golden threads. I just sliced through them. I hadn't intended to, I just … got impulsive."

"Impulsive! You got impulsive?!" Sobs of anger shook Brianna's shoulders. "What if she really is who we suspect she is? One of the Star Children? What have you done?" Brianna broke down and wept into her hands. "You've ruined everything. Crippled my baby. Doomed the whole galaxy."

"She's far from crippled. And they're not the Star Children," Grandma Leann said, leaning across the table to pat Brianna's arm. "The Star Children don't come from Earth."

"*Didn't* come," Great-Aunt Sophie corrected, the first words she had uttered.

Brianna lifted her head, staring down Grandma Leann. "If you damaged one of the Star Children, then we are all doomed."

The elderly woman shrugged in a sort of surrender. "Perhaps, perhaps. But if she really is a Star Child, then she'll figure out how to get everything back. Perhaps it's better she learn on her own how to connect to everything. She'll be stronger that way. Besides, if she had burnt out or gone crazy, she'd have failed anyway."

"You don't know that," Brianna said.

"Now, now," Great-Aunt Sophie broke in. "Cassidy's a smart girl. She can figure it out."

All eyes turned to Cassidy. She looked around at the women and turned up her little hands. "I don't know," she said, not understanding what they expected of her. "When are Torr and Jasper getting home? Jasper said we could build a snow fort."

The women's lips pursed in unison, and they turned back to their adult conversation. Great-Aunt Sophie took charge. "We'll just have to get her some tools. And some training."

"I'm not handing her over to the shamans for training," Brianna said. "They're worse than you," she said, shooting Grandma Leann a scathing look. "Thinking they know what's best for everyone. Unable to control their 'impulses.'"

Grandma Leann glared back at Brianna. "They are my friends, with the best of intentions. And brilliant, to boot. We have a new idea for harnessing the power of the mountain."

"You're changing the subject."

"I'll get her some tools," Great-Aunt Sophie said. "Magical tools for her and Torr. I have some connections. I'll be going to Delos in the spring." She smiled, as if that settled that, then turned to Cassidy and grasped her hand. "Don't you worry, little princess, everything will be fine."

Cassidy pulled her hand free and reached for the last cookie on the plate.

"That's perfect," Grandma Leann declared, smiling brightly at her sister. "Tools make things so much safer."

"How?" Melanie asked.

"Well," Great-Aunt Sophie said slowly, "it's like stirring a fire with an iron poker instead of your hand. You know? It puts distance between you and the fire. Tools are like that. They offer protection. Filters. Safety mechanisms. Crystal balls, for example. You can see all sorts of things when you look into a crystal ball, but when you've had enough, you just put the crystal ball away. Imagine seeing life through a crystal ball all the time. That's what it used to be like for Cassidy, I'll bet."

"More like a thousand crystal balls," Grandma Leann said.

Great-Aunt Sophie nodded. "How exhausting would that be, having to manage such a constant onslaught of information while trying to live her own life at the same time? If I get her a couple of crystals, then she can access the energy field at her leisure and wield her power when she wants, but not be bothered when she doesn't want to. She just puts the crystals away, and she's back to normal. Living a regular, serene life."

"Exactly," Grandma Leann said smugly. "Couldn't have said it better myself."

Cassidy shook herself free of the vivid memory and opened her eyes to the thick darkness of the ship. She could tell by his breathing that Torr was awake.

"Turn the flashlight on, Torr."

He grunted in response and lit their small space. The smell of the cargo hold reminded her of Grandma Leann's pantry: forgotten bags of flour and old spice tins hidden in the back shelves. She unzipped her sleeping bag and pulled herself over to the metal wall where their belongings were secured. It was cold in the cargo hold. Floating in a cross-legged position, she kept the pack's contents from floating away with one hand. With the other hand, she felt around inside the main compartment and front pockets until she found her sweatshirt and the small crystal ball Great-Aunt Sophie had given her. She fastened the pack shut, pulled the sweatshirt over her head, and stared into the glassy globe.

All she saw was the reflection of the flashlight and a distorted view of Torr's floating body. Great-Aunt Sophie and her mother had tried to teach her how to use it, but even they could not get it to respond. Maybe it was a dud. Just a polished quartz sphere. Less powerful than a pool of water.

"I'm turning the light out," Torr said gruffly. "We shouldn't waste batteries."

Her reflex was to snap back at him, but she stopped herself. She could feel he was hurting inside. "Okay," she said. She stuffed the crystal ball into the front pocket of her sweatshirt, and pushed off the wall with her feet to propel herself slowly across the shadowy space. When she had zipped herself back into the sleeping bag, Torr flicked off the light.

"Try to get some sleep," he told her.

18

CARGO⊙HOLD

It was bitter cold. Torr lay still to let a thin sheath of body heat collect inside the blankets. Cassidy had gotten up again and found her own flashlight, and was huddled in her sleeping bag staring into the crystal ball Great-Aunt Sophie had given her. Torr checked his watch. Only two hours had passed since he'd last looked. They had six hours to go.

When Cassidy finally turned the flashlight off and her breathing settled into an even rhythm, Torr stared into the blackness. It felt like a tomb. If it wasn't for Cassidy's presence, he thought he might very well lose his mind. His rational mind knew they were on a trajectory to the moon, but in the meantime they were surrounded by nothingness, with demons taunting him from the edges of his consciousness.

He tried to keep his eyes open, though there was nothing but infinite darkness before him. He didn't want sleep to come, but it took hold and pulled him under.

The hills of Scripps Ranch were dry. All was quiet except for the chirping of insects. Torr stepped over Edgemont's corpse and crept around the upside-down vehicle to where the second body was sprawled.

Torr bent and shook the young Teg's shoulder. A bullet wound showed itself as a bloody stain between the shoulder blades. The back of the head had a clean exit wound, but the hair was bloody and matted like Edgemont's. Torr pulled the body over. The corpse opened his one eye and moaned, then raised himself on an elbow and climbed painfully to his feet. "You didn't have to take out my eye," he said crossly, looking at Torr with the remaining one. "I was dead already."

"I wasn't sure," Torr said apologetically, and strode next to him towards the Teg encampment. "Sorry."

"Come on," the man said grudgingly, turning east. "We can still get out of here."

"How?" Torr asked.

They crossed to the next hill where a different Teg scout vehicle was disabled. Limbs hung out of opened doors, two dead soldiers strapped into the front seats.

"Come on," Torr's companion said, unbuckling one of the bodies and dragging it onto the ground. Torr went around to the passenger door and hauled out the second corpse, then took a seat in the cab.

The vehicle was suddenly brand new, the black dashboard housing unfamiliar controls and a display that showed a top-down view of their vehicle and the surrounding terrain. They rode over the bumpy ground and soon were driving down a paved street in a neatly manicured suburb.

"Here we are," the dead man said, and led Torr to the door of a slate-blue house with white trim. They walked up the sidewalk, their footsteps echoing off the cement. He opened the door and led Torr into a front hallway with a stairway leading to the second floor. "Mama!" he called out. His bullet wounds were gone, and he had red acne blotches and the sparse facial hair of an eighteen-year-old.

"There you are, Matthew," a woman's voice answered from the top of the stairs. She ran down and pulled Torr's companion into a small kitchen where another young man stood. They were obviously brothers, and Matthew was older. Their mother pulled them both in front of her and looked them up and down.

"The Tegs will accept you for sure," she said. "They take sixteen-year-olds now. That's what I heard. Just be polite and do as you're told. Listen to the officers."

"Yes, ma'am," they said.

"Now, Matthew, you take care of your brother," she said.

"Yes, Mama," he said somberly. "I will."

"And you do what Matthew tells you," she said to the younger one.

The brother rolled his eyes.

She kissed both of her sons and handed them each a duffel bag. "Go now," she said, fighting back tears, and pushed them down the hallway and out the door. "Do like I said. Just go right up to their blockade on Main Street and volunteer yourselves, you understand?"

"Yes, Mama," the boys said, fear rising in their voices.

"Go on, now," she urged. They exchanged awkward hugs with their mother, then she took their shoulders and turned them away from her, and watched as they trudged slowly down the street. "I love you," she called.

The brothers looked back, but were too choked up to say anything in response.

Torr stood by her side. When her sons disappeared from view, she locked herself inside and crumpled slowly to the floor, sobbing against the closed front door.

———————)———————

Matthew and his brother were in the pit, and Torr stood on the rim. A rabid crowd pressed around Torr, chanting and yelling. He hopped down inside and tugged at Matthew's bare arm.

"You don't have to," Torr said sharply, over the catcalls and chants of the onlookers.

"Go away," Matthew said. He gave Torr a shove.

Torr regained his footing and stood behind Matthew's shoulder.

"You're going to have to kill me," the brother said to Matthew.

"No," Matthew replied, his voice pitched high. "You kill me. I'll let you. Just strangle me." The brothers' eyes bulged as they lightly held each other's necks and circled slowly.

"Kill him!" someone yelled, and a rock struck Matthew's brother in the ribs. The youth stumbled, and Matthew held him up by the neck.

"You're okay," Matthew said hoarsely. "Squeeze my arteries. Feel them pumping?"

"I can't. Besides, you're stronger," the brother said, their feet slowly pacing around each other. "I'll just die in the next round, anyway. You stay alive. For Mama."

"No, I can't," Matthew objected in a panic.

"You can. You have to. Just squeeze. It will be fast."

The chanting grew louder and handfuls of mud rained on them from all sides.

Torr tried to jump between them, but he was as insubstantial as a shadow. "No, no!" Torr yelled, trying to pull them apart as Matthew grimaced and tightened his grip around his brother's neck. "Stop it!" Torr screamed, as the raucous yells of the crowd drowned him out.

The two brothers locked eyes. The younger brother did not put up much of a struggle, but merely stared at Matthew as life left him and his dead weight brought Matthew to his knees.

———————————)———————————

"No!" Torr yelled. "Stop it!" He lurched backwards, flailing against arms that held him at the side of the pit. Ropes were tightening around him, and he twisted around in a panic, trying to free himself. It was pitch black, and he struggled to breathe. He bounced against his restraints and hit his head against the side of the pit.

A light blinded him. "Torr!"

He squeezed his eyes shut, and air surged into his lungs.

"Torr, are you okay? What's wrong?" It was his sister's voice.

His heart pounded, and sweat soaked his face and neck. He realized in a flash where he was. He was floating inside a freighter on his way to the moon, wrapped in blankets and bungee cords, surrounded by walls of grain sacks and dark shadows. He exhaled with quivering relief.

"You were dreaming," Cassidy said. She lowered the flashlight beam and gazed at him with concern. She was floating in the air next to him, her loose hair billowing up around her head, reminding him of their mother. "You okay?" she asked, her eyes following droplets of sweat that had left his forehead and were drifting slowly away from him.

Torr became mesmerized by a droplet and pressed his sleeve against his face and neck to absorb his sweat. The despair of his dream fell away, replaced by the overwhelming reality of where they were and where they were headed. He was filled with a surge of excitement and pain, then cursed softly as he felt his bladder release and spread hot fluid into the cloth of his space diaper.

Cassidy didn't notice. "We're almost there," she said, as she tightened the blanket around his shoulders and tucked it under the bungee cord, then pushed off the rice sacks to propel herself back to her sleeping bag.

"Keep the light on," he said, afraid of returning to his nightmare.

"Okay." She zipped herself into her sleeping bag.

He watched as she gazed into her crystal ball. "What do you see?"

"Nothing," she said with an edge of frustration, and stashed the crystal sphere out of sight. "But do you hear the star music?"

He cocked his head and listened. A deep silence resonated in the cargo hold. Torr pictured the infinite vacuum that lay just on the other side of the thin metal walls and tried to stay calm. "No."

"Well, it's out there, and it goes something like this."

She hummed to him, and he closed his eyes.

That tune. That elusive tune. She almost had it right, but not quite. He tried to recall the images of the golden people from his childhood dream, but their faces merged into glowing orbs that danced across the insides of his eyelids. Her humming reminded him of being safe in Grandma Leann's attic bedroom.

He slowly drifted off to sleep and wandered aimlessly through his dreams. He found himself on a vast rocky plain surrounded by a ring of stone mountains, red lava streaming down the slopes and dark clouds of ash covering the sky. Funnels of smoke rose from numerous small blazes in the foothills. The air was hot and dry and stank of sulfur. He adjusted his rucksack on his back and headed off in search of the golden people.

PART TWO

THE MOON

Map of the Northwest Sector of the Near Side of the Moon

Map of the North Pole of the Moon

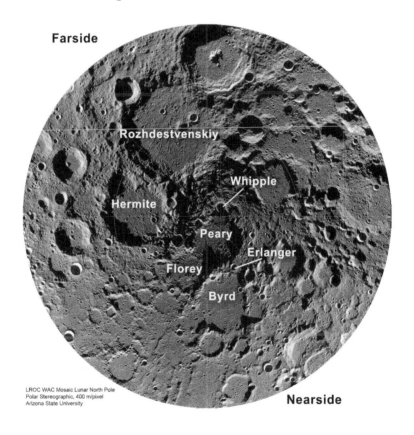

LROC WAC Mosaic Lunar North Pole
Polar Stereographic, 400 m/pixel
Arizona State University

Map of Peary Crater (Peaks of Eternal Light)

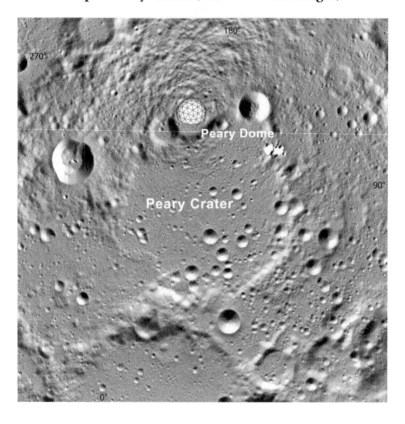

19

HALF-BREEDS

Location: Anaximenes craters, Earth's moon

THREE YEARS AGO: OCTOBER, 2087

"Ridge." Balty's sharp voice broke the dead silence. Ridge had set the ship's radio volume to low, but still the voice made him jump. Balty's tone was more intense than usual. Angry.

Ridge had settled his speedster into the dark shadow of one of the impact craters inside the massive Anaximenes G crater, lights out, speedster idling noiselessly. He gazed up through the curved windshield at the billions of stars. It was the best way he'd found to relax. But he couldn't get away from Balty. Not even here.

"What's up, Balty?"

"Get back here before I kill this motherfucker."

"Who?" Ridge sat upright and flicked the navigation controls to ON.

"Murphy, that's who, the little cockbreath motherfucker. My guards found a stash of gold watches under his bunk. He's been stealing from me. From us. I bought those watches special from Wenchang. I'm gonna kill this little prick."

Ridge could hear Murphy moaning in the background. He rose up out of Anaximenes G and accelerated towards the spaceport, the ground racing by below him. The bleak moon terrain stretched in every direction—miles of gray regolith and black shadows.

Earth floated in the southern sky, a brilliant blue and white jewel, half-lit, and the sun blazed to the west, a fireball in a sea of black. The main Anaximenes crater opened up before him. Fifty miles wide and one-and-a-half miles deep, the floor of the crater was dotted with small, round craters and crisscrossed with furrows from the moon dust harvesters. Dominating the center of the crater was Ridge's architectural masterpiece, Gandoop Spaceport. Its elegant, curved, white titanium roof stood in stark contrast to the four monstrous black cubes and rectangular towers that housed the biggest mineral processing facility on the moon. Ridge decelerated and swooped down to the hangar's compression bay that was opening for him.

"Hang on, Balty. I'm here. Don't do anything." Fuck.

The radio was silent, and Ridge gripped the throttle while the door closed behind him. He glared at the external pressure gauge as it slowly climbed. The door before him opened and closed behind him as he glided into the second airlock and waited for the rear door to seal. He cursed himself for designing the dual airlocks when one was nearly as good. He counted the seconds until the interior door opened for him to pass through.

He pulled the speedster into its parking spot, hopped out, and ran into the main hangar.

"Where are you?" Ridge said into his hand-radio as he ran across the floor towards the office. The hangar was oddly devoid of people. Ships stood in various stages of loading and unloading. He spotted two Earth freighter pilots peering out a cockpit window, and two of Balty's guards flanked the doorway of the passage to Cube One.

"In the metal shop." Balty's voice had that weird flatness to it.

The metal shop? A guard opened the door, and Ridge ran down the long passageway, his footfalls echoing against the titanium walls.

"Ali, get to the metal shop, now," Ridge barked into his radio.

His brother replied, his voice strained, "I'm here. Hurry up."

Ridge reached the metal shop and flung the door open. Spaceport and mine laborers huddled between drill presses, 3D printers, and laser cutters, the air thick with the acrid stench of sweat.

"Just in time," Balty called to Ridge across the room in a gleeful tone that belied the sinister flashing of his eyes. "I've gathered everyone to witness what happens to thieves and traitors." Ridge spotted his father, Ishmar, hovering behind Balty, trying to talk him down.

"Balty, no!" Ridge yelled, pushing through the crowd.

Ali tugged at Balty's shoulder as Murphy pleaded, "Please, Mr. Balty, I'm sorry, I'm sorry."

Ridge broke through as three of Balty's thugs restrained Murphy and the fourth held his arm against the plate under the chop saw. Balty grabbed Murphy's wrist and lowered the saw. Murphy's scream was drowned out by the buzz of the blade slicing through flesh and bone. Ridge lunged forward and grabbed Balty's forearm as he raised Murphy's severed hand into the air, and Murphy collapsed against the guards, blood spurting from the raw stub.

TWO YEARS AGO: JUNE, 2088

"I need your help with something," Balty said from Ridge's black leather office chair behind the large metal desk.

"Yeah, sure," Ridge replied. He hated when Balty "needed help with something." Ridge glanced through the glass wall. Gandoop's spaceport hangar floor was bustling as usual, but no one could see them through the one-way glass. Two workers walked by. One averted his eyes but the other forgot himself, glancing at the mirrored glass and adjusting his hat.

Ridge avoided looking at the man seated across from him. The confusing conflation of love and hatred Ridge felt for Balty reflected his fascination and contempt for the half of himself that he tried to deny, or had until Balty had stepped off the ship into Gandoop Spaceport three years before. The two half-breeds had shaken hands and their eyes locked, recognizing the Cephean blood in each other immediately. It wasn't hard. They both had the brilliant emerald-green eyes, the tall stature, though Balty's bulky frame dwarfed Ridge's lean one, and glossy black hair with the distinctive hairline and facial hair pattern. And they began attacking each other right away with their energy tentacles. Not attacking really, exploring, more like. It was strange to Ridge that Balty did not see the tentacles as Ridge did. Balty could wield them and sense them, but, as far as Ridge could tell, he did not see them. That was one advantage Ridge had over Balty.

"Shinuha," Balty had said, using the Cephean greeting reserved for one Ceph to another.

Ridge had managed to mumble "Shinuha" in return, and was filled with warmth at being respectfully acknowledged. This man, this stranger, Balty, with one simple word had made Ridge feel normal for the first time in his life.

For several months Ridge had floated through his days proud and lighthearted. Finally he had found someone who accepted him for who he was, even celebrated it. Someone who had struggled through discrimination like Ridge had, and had come out on top. Ridge had found a true brother. They exchanged stories about growing up as half-breeds, and discovered more about themselves through each other. They laughed together until their sides hurt, sharing observations only they could understand, comforted in each other's presence.

Ridge was not used to people honoring and enjoying his Cephean heritage. He had spent his life being bullied for it and trying to hide. Balty had taken the opposite survival tactic: he had become a bully himself, and worked his way up through the ranks of the Cephean half-breed gangs. He had ended up a two-star general in the half-breed Tegea's army, only to be stripped of his stars for bad behavior, and assigned to work security for Cephean diplomatic and trade delegations on Earth. As part of that duty he had landed one day at Gandoop Spaceport, and never left.

Balty was tapping his fingers on the desk impatiently, waiting for Ridge to give him his undivided attention. Ridge ignored him and panned the live video feed on his hand screen. Nothing exciting was going on out at the oxygen mining field, but he watched his fleet of moon soil harvesters kick up dust in a slowly moving line just to make Balty wait.

The finger-drumming became more insistent. Ridge snapped his hand screen closed and slipped it into its belt case. He leaned back in the green leather guest chair, folded his hands across his abdomen, and casually crossed his ankles. Somehow, at some point in time that Ridge could not precisely recall, Ridge had ended up in the guest chair and Balty had taken over Ridge's desk.

"Let's go," Balty said. Broad-shouldered and wearing desert camo, Balty looked like the general he once had been. Square chin with a black shadow of stubble, he held his jaw tight as though daring Ridge to punch him. Balty came out from behind the desk and Ridge followed him, walking briskly across the large hangar floor and into the smaller hangar where they parked their personal vehicles.

"In here," Balty said, directing Ridge to the passenger side of Balty's speedster, the wing door rising silently.

"What the fuck, Balty," Ridge said. Wedged into the narrow floor space behind the two seats was a body wrapped head to toe in a colorful tapestry. "What have you done now?" The body was petite, and there was a sickening scent of perfume and urine.

"I got a little rough," Balty said with a sheepish chuckle.

"A little rough?" Ridge demanded, blood rising to his face.

"Yeah. Can you ... You know. Get rid of it?"

"Get rid of it," Ridge muttered, wondering which of Balty's two sex slaves it was. Probably the blond. She was tiny.

"Yeah. You know. In that grinder thing you have."

Ridge swallowed. He stared at the body, looking for some sign of life. The small rise and fall of a lingering breath. A twitch. But she was motionless. It could just as well have been sacks of grain wrapped in the tapestry.

"Yeah. Yeah, sure, Balty." Ridge turned his gaze to the man he used to call his friend. Balty's voice feigned guilt and shame, but his eyes showed no emotion, sending a chill up Ridge's spine. "You can go," Ridge said. "I'll take care of it."

"Thanks, Ridge, buddy." Balty smiled and strode across the floor, back straight. The door clicked closed behind him and the soft hum of the air system filled the hangar.

Ridge thought back to when Balty had first arrived, a few months after the Gandoops had negotiated the deal with the Global Alliance to use their new spaceport as a waystation between the Cephean Federation and Earth. The port had gradually turned into a holding facility for Cephean goods and black market cargo. The Gandoops negotiated a ten percent cut of everything passing through the spaceport, which filled their warehouse and their coffers to overflowing.

One day Ridge had been inspecting a Cephean Federation freighter, and instead of dusty crates of minerals, food, or other hard goods, he found a cargo hold full of young women. They were somewhere between the ages of fifteen and twenty-five, and all drop-dead gorgeous. If they hadn't been so scared. And dirty. It was sad. He had tried to talk to Balty about it—about how he didn't want females trafficked through Gandoop. How it sickened him.

"Oh, Ridge," Balty had said. "Don't be such a prude. You get ten percent of everything. That means," he said, pointing at the cowering girls and counting out loud, "... thirteen, fourteen, fifteen. That means you get one. And a half." He laughed his velvety, syrupy laugh. "Your brother didn't want one either. You guys monks or something? No worries, I'll take yours." He had gone into the cargo hold and grabbed two girls by the wrists and dragged them out of the ship. They had ended up locked in Balty's private suite at Ridge's house until the next shipment came, when Balty traded them out for two fresh girls.

Ridge looked glumly at Balty's victim. She had escaped once and for all. Probably better this way. The human trafficking cartels sold primarily to the Nommos lords on Delos, and from what Ridge had heard those fish men did not treat the girls any better than Balty did.

Ridge bent inside the speedster and poked gently at the wrapped corpse. It was cold. He pulled at the legs until he was able to get his arms under her knees and stiff torso and lift her out, propping her head on his shoulder. He had never carried a woman in his arms like this, and it was not how he had imagined it would happen.

He hesitated at the doorway. He really did not want the entire shipping crew to see him carry a dead woman across the hangar. Nor did he want to feed her into the recycler. The grinding sound always sickened him when he had to dispose of a body, and he didn't think he could get himself to push a young woman through it, even if she was dead. He turned and awkwardly set her on the floor, closed Balty's speedster door, then fumbled for his own speedster controls and opened his wing doors. After some consideration he took his spacesuit out of the stowage compartment behind the seat, pulled it on over his sleek black flightsuit, buckled his utility belt outside the stretchy white fabric, and placed the helmet and oxygen tank on the floor behind the seats. He set the corpse in the passenger seat and tried to arrange her so she wouldn't fall over, not bothering with the harness that was made to come down across the chest and clip between the legs, wrapped as she was like a mummy.

Ridge climbed into the pilot's chair. The cockpit stank of death as he passed through the decompression chambers and flew out over the sterile moonscape. He crested the mountainous southern rim then veered east towards the uninhabited zone north of Herschel crater.

When he reached the center of the sector, he randomly chose a small crater and maneuvered the speedster inside, settling on a flat spot at the northern edge, in the light. The crater was about a half mile wide and half as deep, the center a roughly concave dish, pockmarked with smaller craters. Otherwise, the soil was untouched. No one ever came here except him. He had explored many of the large craters in the near side's northwest quadrant, but he rarely saw any signs of other humans. The sparse population who braved the harsh life on the moon staked out their territory, built their little dome enclaves, and stayed put. When they wanted to be part of civilization, they went to Peary Dome. He was the only weirdo who lurked in the small, unclaimed craters, seeking the solace of emptiness whenever he could.

The corpse was slumped against the door. She could have been asleep.

"At least he can't hurt you now," he said to her softly. "I'm sorry I couldn't protect you from him."

He had fantasized in great detail about various methods of killing Balty, from shutting off the air to the house, to shooting him with one of his own Lectro guns, poisoning him, tying him up and throwing him in the iron smelter, running him through the recycler alive, or simply throwing him outdoors and watching him swell up like a balloon. But Balty's guards and his connections to the Teg army and Cephean Federation smothered Ridge's courage whenever it flared up. Besides, Balty was not a renegade working on his own. He was backed by powerful forces and sent to the moon for a reason. Ridge was thankful the Gandoops had maintained control of their property as much as they had. Of course, the Gandoops did the hard work of running the mining operation and the spaceport. Balty needed them. At least for now. But he did not need the girls. They were toys to him.

Morbid curiosity got the better of Ridge, and he carefully unwrapped the tapestry from around the girl's face. It was the blond. Her whole face was swollen, the skin ashen, with one side purplish-yellow from an old bruise. The skin around one eye was puffy and red from a recent blow, and her pointy little nose was crusted with yellow snot above parted, swollen lips. Dried saliva made white track marks down the side of her chin. She looked about sixteen.

Her blue eyes were half open, staring blankly at him. He peered into them, wondering if any part of her was still alive. He waved his hand in front of her face, but her eyes were like glass.

Ridge swallowed and unwrapped her to her shoulders. Dark red and purple bruises ringed her neck. The bastard had strangled her.

Ridge felt queasy and wrapped her up again. She would probably swell up even more when he left her in the vacuum of the moon's surface.

He strapped the oxygen tank to his back, locked on the helmet and gloves, connected the air, and then set the pressure, which inflated the thin spacesuit against his muscles. Opening his door, he swung outside the craft, guided himself around the back using his hands to tether himself, and raised the passenger door. He lifted her out, much lighter now in the moon's low gravity, held her to his chest, and bounded slowly across the dust to a little crater that was not much wider than an empty grave.

He hopped down into it with her in his arms, landing gently. Half the crater was in shadow, and he debated whether she would rather mummify in the sun or freeze in the narrow cusp of permanent shadow. He chose the sun, and laid her gently on her back in the gray bed of dust. He straightened her out as best he could. Getting on his knees, he fumbled in his bulky gloves to unwrap her head. Her accusing eyes stared back at him through narrow slits, her face puffing up already. He watched in fascination as she continued to swell. He had always wondered what people would look like thrown out into space without a pressure suit. Living people probably swelled faster. He was pretty sure her skin would not burst.

He covered her face with the tapestry, leaving only her eyes exposed. "This way you can look at the stars," he said into his mask, and looked up to see what she would see. The brightest stars were scattered like diamonds against the black sky. His only regret was that she could not see Earth. There would be no way for her to see it unless he removed her from the shelter of the crater.

"The stars are good enough, right?" He gazed down at her. She was dead. She did not care.

He should have brought a shovel, he realized, and sacks of moon dust. He felt the ground with his glove, and, as he suspected, the layer of dust in the crater was only a couple inches deep over the crusty regolith. He scraped up handfuls and covered her wrapped body as best he could, a dust cloud enveloping them. By the time he had made a small mound, her eyes were completely swollen shut. He pulled the tapestry over her eyes and patted a layer of dust over it.

"Sorry," he murmured, and left her there.

ONE WEEK AGO: JULY 8, 2090

Ridge looked at the name painted on the side of his speedster where it was parked in the private hangar at the spaceport. RIDGE GANDOOP. It still bothered him slightly. His actual name was Rjidna, but no one could pronounce it right. His father had started informally calling the mine Rjidna Gandoop after him because he was the one who had figured out how to extract elements from the moon soil, and the name stuck. But all the men who worked at the mine had thought his name was Ridge, like the ridge on the rim of craters. He gave up trying to correct people, and decided to officially name the mine Ridge Gandoop, and adopted the name himself.

As their mining operation grew, lines of moon freighters waited to land in their one-ship hangar. They ended up doing a lot of loading outside, which created all sorts of challenges. Ishmar and Ridge drew up plans for a new hangar that got larger and larger with every draft. Ridge designed dual compression chambers to avoid any chance of a breach. They made one of their chamber pairs big enough to accommodate interstellar cargo ships. It had taken more than five years to build the facility, but finally they had the only interstellar spaceport on the moon, aside from Peary. This had bumped up their business five-fold, but it also brought complications: illicit Global Alliance traffic, and Balty.

Ridge strapped himself into the speedster's pilot's seat and sealed the airtight doors, then passed through the decompression chambers and glided out into the light. Anaximenes had turned to face the sun a day ago. There would be fourteen more days of relentless light blazing down from the naked sun, reflecting off the steely gray regolith and casting harsh shadows across the colorless landscape.

Ridge sped low across the crater floor. He knew every hillock and pockmark of his land. Well, technically it wasn't his land, but for all intents and purposes it was. He had read an old property law that said if land was settled and the owners put up no resistance to the settlement, then eventually the settlers had legal claim to the land. So, therefore he and his father and brother were on the land legally.

Ridge climbed vertical altitude and rose above the crater. Its vastness still impressed him. From this vantage point a mile and a half above the crater floor, the mining facility looked like a collection of children's building blocks. Most everything on the moon was round. Round craters. Round domes. The globe of Earth. Ridge's industrial buildings were black cubes. Sharp, angular edges in a world of smooth curves. That's how Ridge felt. Out of place, never quite fitting in. So he embraced it, finding power and beauty in the clean lines.

He navigated over the worn northeast rim and across the flatlands of the adjacent crater, Anaximenes G. Earth was in the sky like a loyal friend, showing a waning crescent of blue ocean today. Unlike the sun, which came and went, Earth was always there, changing shape and mood, but faithful nonetheless. He appreciated the sun—it pumped solar power into his extensive banks of batteries. But Ridge preferred the dark days. The darkness quieted his mind. Plus, he didn't really need the solar power since he'd installed the nuclear generators. The small generators had cost them every last ounce of gold and minerals they'd had, but they were worth it. The family had already refilled their coffers many times over in the years since.

He sped towards the geological survey station he had set up to take samples of the moon soil at the far edge of crater G. He hadn't tested this area before. Most likely it was the same composition as the rest of the regolith layer, but maybe they would get lucky. They had been pleasantly surprised on another occasion when they'd discovered high levels of dysprosium and terbium in a large crater within Anaximenes H. Rare-earths had made the Gandoops rich. Well, richer.

Back on Earth, Ishmar had amassed a good amount of gold managing large construction projects across Eurasia, but spent most of it buying their passage to the moon and building their original mining operation. The soil harvester Ridge had invented gave them a stake in the lunar economy, and the gold started flowing in. Ridge had been inventing gadgets since he was a kid, and held a special fascination for chemistry. He invented the harvester when he was sixteen, after two years on the moon. Back then, it had been the Gandoops and a few workers doing everything. He'd tired of wearing a pressure suit and loading soil into transports, then carrying it back to the small facility to extract oxygen, their first product, then carting the tons of soil back outside again. His harvester scooped up soil and fed it into trailers, where his mobile labs extracted oxygen, hydrogen, nitrogen, and helium-3 from the soil. Everyone knew those elements were there, but Ridge had been the one who'd perfected the process to isolate and store them. They transported the captured gases to the main facility to be compressed and stored in huge pressurized cryogenic chambers, then eventually transferred them to smaller canisters to sell. Aside from the fact that oxygen and hydrogen gases were extremely combustible, the process worked like a dream. He'd only had one explosion to date, which had killed the worker who'd been inside the mobile lab, and left a new crater on the floor of Anaximenes.

They sold the canisters to spaceships and were now the biggest suppliers on the moon, stocking interplanetary freighters who wanted to trade with Earth without actually going there. The freighters could drop off and pick up Earth shipments on the moon and avoid Earth's atmosphere and gravity, and, more importantly, political and military entanglements.

Ridge also invented an oxygenator for facilities: a contraption that fed moon soil into a processing unit and released oxygen directly into the air control system. It was a cheap way to produce oxygen. Many moon facilities, including Peary Dome, had bought units from him. *Him. Them.* Whatever. Ridge was the technologist who kept to himself. His father was the businessman who made the deals. And his brother was the nice guy everybody liked. They made a good team.

Ridge approached the mobile geological survey trailer, toured around the exterior, and checked in with the technicians by radio. All was well. They had just started collecting samples.

The radio crackled again, and Ridge stiffened. It was not the technician. It was Balty. "Ridge, buddy. Where'd you slip off to?"

Ridge rolled his eyes and replied, struggling to keep his voice friendly, "Checking on the new survey site."

"Ah. Well, I want to talk to you. Meet me back at the house."

"Okay." Ridge clicked off the radio. "For the love of Perseus," he muttered, and banked the craft. Half of him wanted to head out over the barren terrain towards Last Chance, the small outpost he was building on the outer rim, but he gritted his teeth and headed towards his house. He couldn't risk angering Balty by making him wait. *Balthazar.* What a noble name for a scumbag. He hated Balty for two reasons. One, the man was a despicable creature. Two, Balty was living in Ridge's house.

He thought sourly of the most beloved of his accomplishments: an Earth-like dwelling on the surface of the moon that he'd placed in a secluded location on a narrow plain at the juncture of the three large Anaximenes craters. The home was like a desert adobe, built into the contours of the dunes, coated with a composite of moon dust and graphene, perfectly camouflaged and radar absorbing, making the structure virtually invisible.

During the fourteen days of daylight the roof was closed to shield against the brutal sun. For those days, Ridge had designed skylights from a complex matrix of overlapping triangles of alternating stone and glass filters that helixed down to allow in reflected light but kept out the most damaging rays. The rainbow skylights, as he called them, lit up a room like a summer's early morning. If one looked up into the spiraling structures, a crisscross of colored light beams wove across the tubular space as the light bounced off the helix walls and refracted through itself. The rainbow skylights were dazzling gems. Kaleidoscopes whose jewels were the rays of light themselves. Recessed chandeliers of the highest order.

During the fourteen days of darkness the roof retracted, exposing thick, clear sheets of one-way glass that provided an unobstructed view of the stars. The glass was coated with a pure graphene layer—not quite as radar absorbent as the moon dust composite, but it was transparent. Some tradeoffs needed to be made for beauty, after all.

The house was perfectly climate controlled with proper air pressure and optimal relative humidity. He'd shipped in a few small gravity bars from Delos for the house, mining facility, and spaceport so they could walk around normally. He hadn't been able to reverse engineer the white stone gravity bars, which fascinated him. He liked puzzles. He had to give those dwarf-like Scrids some respect for having invented something so ingenious.

Needless to say, there were bathrooms with hot running water, and marble tubs big enough for two, with little seats in the corners. And furniture: couches, chairs, beds, wooden armoires, wooden tables, hand-woven wool carpets with birds and flowers. A fully functional chef's kitchen with stoves, ovens, sinks. Refrigerator, stocked with fresh food. Zero freezer, full. It was like being back on Earth.

Everyone who'd been in his house lusted after it. Balty was no exception, and had effectively taken it over and kicked the Gandoops out. Not that they weren't welcome to stay. They each still had their private quarters: bedroom, sitting room, bathroom, kitchenette. It's just that they had to live with Balty.

Ridge's brother, Ali, had been the first to move out. He'd found a nice office in the bowels of the mining facility that he'd filled with rugs and cushions from the house. He said it was easier to stay over there since he was responsible for managing the personnel, and they ran two twelve-hour shifts back to back. It was the only way to keep an eye on things. Balty had to agree.

Next was Ishmar. He had eye problems and the rainbow skylights hurt his eyes in the day, and the starlight pierced his eyes in the night. No one wanted to close the roof, so he spent most of his time at the facility, where the lights were soft reds and yellows. He slept on cushions in Ali's office, and brought over a small metal tea table and tea set they had imported from Baikonur.

Ridge was the last holdout. Why should he have to move out of his own house? He had designed the structure down to every square millimeter and knew it better than his own body. It was an engineering marvel. A thing of beauty. The only problem was, Balty lived there. He and his girls. Whichever girls had caught Balty's eye that shipment. Balty wasn't one to get attached. He got sick of the girls after a few days, and it was painful how he treated them until the next shipment came. Actually, the worst was the first day. Ridge made sure he wasn't around when a new shipment arrived.

If Ridge was honest with himself, he only stayed out of stubbornness. It didn't feel like home anymore. He was always walking around on eggshells, trying not to annoy Balty. The reasonable thing would be to move to Last Chance when it was completed, far from Balty on the lonely banks of the Black Mare, the basalt sea. The growing compound sat on a plot of land they'd received in exchange for letting a ship filled with stolen artifacts from Alexandria sit in their hangar for a couple years until a suitable buyer was found.

Ridge slowed as he approached his house and flashed his coded beam to open the gate to the outer compression chamber. The sensor was a simple invention he hadn't shared with anyone. Everyone else needed to manually key in a light code that Ridge changed all the time. Ridge couldn't be bothered with that for himself, not when a light matrix worked just as well. Of course he had a key code too, which he used whenever he had a passenger. He had to keep some ideas to himself with Balty around, ready to steal all his inventions.

He made his way slowly through the two chambers and glided into the residence's hangar. He stepped out of the craft and nodded to one of Balty's thugs, who was perched on a stool on guard duty.

Ridge strode towards the living room, where he heard the clinking of ice in a glass. Balty was standing at the wet bar with his back to Ridge. Balty was a tall man with broad shoulders and strong hips and legs. Short, black hair topped his long, thick neck. He turned and greeted Ridge with a smile that only touched his lips. Ridge's abdomen tightened. Balty had that look in his eye that warned Ridge to tread carefully.

Ridge sat uncomfortably on one of his brown leather couches, and Balty sat in Ishmar's rocking recliner, swirling ice and amber liquid in his glass. Shafts of multi-colored light streamed down from the rainbow skylights, filling the room with a pleasant glow. He had to get out of here. Take a vacation on Delos to get away from this prick.

"What can I do for you?" Ridge asked casually, leaning back and giving Balty a collegial smile.

He could smell the current girls, but thankfully they were out of sight. He glanced up as another of Balty's thugs walked silently through the end of the long, open living room, on his way from the kitchen to the hangar, the only places Balty allowed them to hang out aside from the guest suite that his four personal guards shared.

Ridge regarded Balty's infuriatingly handsome face. Shiny, sleek hair and an immaculately groomed beard and moustache. Olive skin. A long, straight nose that accentuated his eyes. While all of his features were artistically sculpted, it was his eyes that made him beautiful. Like a woman's eyes. Exotic. Wide with a delicate slant. Emerald-green with long, thick lashes.

Ridge's eyes were the same color, but small and plainly shaped, with short eyelashes. His nose was pudgy and his lips were thin. At least he had a strong jawline and chin.

Like Balty, Ridge had the triple widow's peak that, along with their eye color, gave their half-breed heritage away: a sharp peak at the top of his forehead, and two more points arcing down to the temples where they nearly met the ends of the eyebrows. The beard line was triple peaked as well: one arrowhead pointing up from the chin to the lower lip, and one on each cheek pointing towards the corners of the mouth. Cephs called this shape the Angel's Star.

Balty drained his glass. "Drink?" he asked Ridge, springing to his feet and sauntering to the wet bar.

"Sure, thanks," Ridge said, not liking the delay. If Balty wanted something simple he would have stated it straight away. He only stalled when it was something important. It always went the same way. Balty would serve Ridge a drink from his own bar like Ridge was a guest. Wait for him to drink it. Then present him with something delicate or unpleasant. A shipment that had gone missing. A dignitary from the Cephean Federation who needed secret passage to some planet using one of the Gandoops' ships. A dead girl.

Ridge took the drink Balty offered and braced himself. Balty watched as Ridge tilted the glass and drank it in a few gulps, letting the cold liquor burn down his throat. No sense prolonging the suspense.

Balty smiled at Ridge in that overly-friendly way he had. Ridge could feel Balty's energy tendrils creeping over his back like they always did when Balty wanted something. Ridge had come to expect them and had his guard up, causing the tentacles to shear off Ridge's body the way rain runs off glass.

Balty's smile wavered when he sensed his probes had no place to grab hold and he was forced to rely on other means of persuasion. By now, Balty should know Ridge was immune to his powers, but he always tried anyway. Ridge had determined the man was unaware of what he was doing.

If Ridge allowed himself to, he could see the energy streamers coming at him. Balty's looked like gray tentacles, making Ridge think of a giant squid trolling the inky depths of the ocean, reaching for prey. Normally Ridge suppressed his vision, otherwise he'd be constantly distracted with the garlands of light that crisscrossed everywhere.

He'd learned that not everyone could actually see, or even consciously feel, the lines of light. In fact, sometimes he suspected he was the only one who could. Some freak of nature, destined to be tormented with seeing and knowing more than anyone else—isolated in his perceptions. It was lonely, and he tried to turn off his awareness to fit in, while maintaining a minimal level of alertness to protect himself from pernicious attacks. Ridge had always thought his sight was due to his Cephean heritage, but when he'd realized Balty could not see as he did, it made him question his assumption. He longed to test his theory with a purebred Ceph, but they scared him and he avoided them as much as possible.

Even though normal people couldn't see them, everyone connected with everyone else through lines of energy. It was part of how people related. Most people connected with each other through the front of the body with fine, translucent filaments of shimmering gold or silver. Only the devious people, those with bad intentions, tried to attach through the back. Their tendrils were often thick and dark. At their worst, they were black and sticky, though he had only seen those kind on a couple of purebred Cephs who had passed through Gandoop Spaceport. One of them had tried to lash out at him with a long tendril that looked like a tar-covered whip. It had taken all the focus he had to deflect the attack. The Ceph had stared at him for a long moment before retracting his tentacle and stalking off. Ridge was sure the visitor was aware he had been unable to connect to Ridge, but Ridge could not tell if the Ceph could visualize what was going on or if he sensed it in some other way.

"I've agreed to host some guests," Balty said casually.

Ridge smiled. "Oh?" He mentally brushed away another tendril that was trying to dig into the small of his back. This time he sent a jolt through the tentacle as he flicked it away, making Balty's face flinch like he'd been bitten by a bug. Ridge watched him carefully. Balty really did not know what had just happened; he had felt something but did not know what, and reacted with startled annoyance.

Balty took a sharp breath and replied, "Yes. Needs to be hush-hush, if you know what I mean."

Ridge settled back into the couch, content that they were on equal footing, and continued in a conversational tone. "Someone important, then? No worries, I don't talk to anyone." Ridge tried to laugh good-naturedly, but it sounded pathetic. It was true. He didn't trust anyone enough to confide in them. He avoided discussing anything related to Balty with even his brother and father. It would only cause them grief. Better Ali and Ishmar focus on the mining and shipping operations and let Ridge deal with the sadistic maniac on his own. "We've got plenty of space. How many people? I'll prepare my father's and brother's quarters. They aren't using them at present."

"No need, they'll be staying at the main facility."

Ridge raised an eyebrow. "At the mine? It's not very comfortable there."

"Yes, yes. They're fine. That is, they arrived a few days ago. I've been meaning to tell you, but you spend so much time joy-riding in your speedster we keep missing each other. Another shipment is due in today. I was glad to be able to get hold of you. I didn't want you to be caught off guard."

Guests were staying in the cubes and he hadn't known? Ridge's blood seethed. His father and brother must not have been informed either or they would have told him. How had Balty snuck people into the facility without any of the Gandoops knowing about it? Balty was gaining too much control. Ridge breathed slowly. *Another shipment?* He hoped it wasn't a shipload of women. He was not going to make Gandoop a holding pen for human traffickers. Or, knowing Balty, next he'd want to open a whorehouse.

Ridge could feel heat rising to his face and suddenly he was on his feet, his hand clutched around the icy glass. Balty's face melted into a soothing grin as Ridge's muscles hardened with anger. It could not continue like this, with Ridge pretending everything was okay while Balty trampled over him like he did his girls. Ridge took a breath and spoke, trying to keep his voice calm but authoritative. "No holding slaves at the facility. And no prostitution." Ridge stood tall as Balty threw back his head and laughed a gay, pleasing laugh.

Ridge relaxed for a moment as Balty's laughter washed over him, then he snapped back to full attention. Charm was one of Balty's manipulative tricks. He made people feel good somehow. They would let down their guard, and Balty would hook them with one of his tendrils. Ridge had seen it happen a thousand times, even to his brother and father. Ridge wished he knew how to protect others, but he only knew how to defend himself. He met Balty's hypnotic gaze with his stone-cold one.

"No, no," Balty said. "I wouldn't dare insult you with something you obviously find repulsive. Good sport you are about my girlfriends, though, I must say. No, these are men. They've come to help dig out the tunnels. You know, expand the facility. You don't have enough workers here, and the ones you do have are working the mine and the spaceport. I thought we could use a little help."

We. Ridge hated it when Balty said "we," as if they were all in this together.

"I understand your priorities," Balty said, "but it seems a shame to let all that work you started underground just sit there unfinished, wouldn't you agree?"

Balty was sounding magnanimous, a sure sign that there was more to the story. Ridge sat down. It was true that they could use more manpower to continue excavating the underground facility. More space would allow them to house more workers and increase their productivity. Not that they needed any more gold. It was coming in faster than they could spend it. He leaned back, his blood pressure slowly equalizing. But he didn't trust Balty. "Tell me more."

Balty crunched an ice cube between straight, white teeth. "Let's go over and meet the fellows, shall we?" Balty asked congenially.

Ridge tensed again. This could be anything. A trap. A takeover. Balty could be intending to imprison him and his family. Maybe Ishmar and Ali were already in custody. Ridge got stiffly to his feet. There wasn't much he could do, with Balty's thugs lurking about. A Lectro hung from a strap across Balty's solid torso, and an Earth pistol and combat knife hung at his waist. Ridge carried a small pistol but he'd never actually shot anyone with it, and if he tried it on Balty he knew which one of them would die. Not that Ridge could do anything if Balty were not armed; the general was nearly seven feet tall with powerful limbs, and was trained to kill. Balty pulled a tan canvas field jacket over his weapons and asked if Ridge was ready to go.

Ridge followed Balty to the hangar and climbed into his own speedster, and noted that one of Balty's thugs climbed into the passenger side of Balty's. The two craft passed in tandem through the dual decompression chambers and glided out over the plain on their approach to the main Anaximenes crater.

Ridge's speedster crested the rim of the crater, and the block-shaped buildings and towers shone black against the silvery land below. Unease churned in Ridge's gut as he sped through the deafening silence. They entered the spaceport through a small set of compression chambers that opened into the private hangar, where Murphy met them. The man's good hand held a stylus, and his prosthesis held a small screen between two metal pincers.

Murphy looked apprehensively at Ridge, making Ridge's skin break out in goosebumps. What did Murphy know that Ridge did not? Did he know about Balty's "guests" and hadn't told Ridge, choosing to risk Ridge's displeasure over Balty's wrath? Ridge couldn't blame him.

Murphy followed them into the main hangar and motioned to an Earth freighter that was being unloaded. "She arrived from Alcantara with a shipment of food bound for Peary Dome," Murphy said, staring at Ridge's and Balty's feet as though unsure whom he should be addressing. "Forty casks of wine, two five-hundred-gallon tanks of spring water, six hundred pounds of dried meat, two hundred pounds of dried fish, fifty crates of eggs, four dozen wheels of cheese, eight dozen fifty-pound sacks of rice..." Balty cut him off with the wave of his hand.

"Pay them in gold and have them unload into the warehouse, as usual," Balty said. Murphy's eyes darted to Ridge, who kept his expression neutral.

Murphy scuttled away towards the South American vessel. Balty led Ridge through a side door and along a passageway. Balty's guard trailed closely behind Ridge. Balty opened the door to the stairway that led down to the half-finished tunnels under the spaceport, dank air hitting Ridge's nostrils. Someone had turned on the humidifiers. Ridge hadn't been down here since he'd abandoned the tunneling effort a couple years ago, when he'd turned his attention to constructing the Last Chance facility. The stairway looked freshly swept and strands of new solar filaments snaked along the roughly hewn ceiling, lighting the way as they descended. Ridge wondered how long the "guests" had actually been here.

They reached the tunnel with its raw stone floor, walls, and ceiling. Balty stopped at a door that led to the largest of the excavated rooms and knocked. The door opened, and Ridge followed Balty inside. Several men stood up from where they'd been sitting on cots or turned-up crates arranged around makeshift tables.

Ridge quickly counted twenty men filling the space. They were of medium height or taller, and well muscled. Although most everyone wore surplus Earth military clothing in the moon colonies, the way these men stood so erect, their faces like stone and eyes facing forward, it was obvious they were soldiers. Their hands hung straight at their sides, fingers pressed together, rigid and unmoving. It must have been all they could do not to salute Balty. Ridge imagined Balty gathering random articles of clothing to replace their uniforms and ordering them not to salute. Not on the moon. Not at Gandoop. They were undercover.

Mission accomplished, Ridge thought sarcastically. *I have no fucking idea I'm standing among a unit of Tegs.*

He wondered if they would take his head, or perhaps lock him in a storage room, or did Balty have some worse fate awaiting him?

Ridge masked his dread and nodded politely. "Hello, gentlemen. Welcome to Ridge Gandoop. I trust your trip here was pleasant?" He didn't even have to try to calm his voice. He was resigned to his fate. Balty had him trapped, plain and simple.

The soldiers relaxed their postures. The Teg who had opened the door stepped forward and held out his hand towards Ridge while Balty clapped the man on the back. "Fowler, meet Ridge Gandoop, the brains behind the operation." Fowler gripped Ridge's hand in a firm shake and met him with large brown eyes that displayed an even temperament.

"Fine facility you've constructed here," Fowler said. "Wonderful piece of engineering."

Ridge bowed his head graciously. "Thank you, we're proud of it."

Fowler seemed to be in charge, and it didn't appear Ridge was going to be introduced to the others, as they had already returned to their activities. Some were hunched over screens, some were playing cards, others were gathered at a small kitchen area opening cans of food and chopping onions and carrots. Balty and Fowler ushered Ridge out the door and proceeded further down the tunnel. Ridge could sense Balty's feelers trying to get into his back again, but he brushed them off without even thinking. He started to relax. If they were going to assault him, they would have done so already. He hoped. He glanced over his shoulder. The bodyguard was a pace behind him and avoided his eyes.

Balty was getting more and more brazen. He hadn't tried very hard to disguise the new men, unlike the few he'd infiltrated into the plant and mining crews in the past. It had not been difficult for Ridge to pick out those early additions. Straggly hair, unkempt beards, and dusty clothing do not a moon rat make. They would have needed a particular desperation in their eyes, which Balty's men could not fake. Ridge had asked his brother about them, but Ali hadn't noticed anything odd and said they were good workers. Then Ridge had seen Balty walk past one of them, and although Balty did not acknowledge the man, Ridge saw thick, silver threads connecting them. That evening after sharing dinner and a bottle of whiskey with Balty, Ridge had confronted him about it.

"I see you have some friends in the mining crew," Ridge had said, holding the man's bloodshot eyes with his own.

Balty's gaze did not waver, and Ridge could see him considering whether or not to lie.

Balty cracked a half-grin and said, "Sometimes men want to disappear."

Ridge was reminded of Balty's story of being relegated to the moon after bad behavior, and his own shadow-life as Jidna.

He had imagined Balty was handing out favors: helping miscreants escape the wrath of the Tegs. Either that, or the moon was a convenient dumping ground for Teg misfits who for some reason were spared imprisonment or exile to a Cephean planet. Now, in retrospect, Ridge admitted it had probably all been part of a larger, more sinister plan.

Ridge inhaled the stale, tunnel air and stood with Balty and Fowler at the boring machine, which stood right where Ridge had left it when they'd stopped tunneling. It was like a giant insect, its nose buried in the bedrock.

Balty pulled a small screen from his pocket and showed Ridge a series of plans and specifications: designs of underground dwellings and production facilities. Ridge bristled as he recognized several of his own drawings, wondering with rising indignation how Balty had accessed his data. He could have at least asked Ridge's permission. Balty seemed unconcerned that he had appropriated Ridge's plans and was happily waving his hands in various directions, describing his vision of a thriving underground facility as though he had thought of it himself.

Ridge bit his tongue and nodded as Balty talked excitedly. "And some of Fowler's men will be manning the spaceport from now on. Murphy has agreed to train them." Ridge stiffened, and Balty's face softened apologetically. "That way, some of your men will be freed up to resume the tunneling work down here. I thought it would be better if you could focus on expanding the facility and mining operations, seeing as that's your strong suit."

Ridge tried not to glare at the presumptuous green eyes that stared at him calmly while silently daring him to object. *Strong suit?* Ridge wanted to kick Balty in the testicles, but merely cracked a derisive grin. "Very thoughtful of you," he told Balty, who smiled with feigned relief towards Fowler.

"See? I told you he'd like the idea. Now, this facility will be able to hold…" Balty rattled on while Ridge's mind searched frantically for a way to free his domain from this infestation of vermin that had suddenly multiplied, and was about to multiply again.

Ridge politely excused himself, leaving Balty in the tunnels with Fowler and the bodyguard, and climbed up the stairs. He stood alone in the empty passageway and contemplated sealing the door to the stairwell, turning off the radio relay, and cutting off the oxygen supply. They would pound at the steel door but no one would hear them through the connecting door to the spaceport, with all the noise inside the hangar. But soon the other men Balty had strategically placed in the various build-ings would wonder where their boss was, and would slit Ridge's throat. And there were the guards at the house to consider. And the new "shipment" of Tegs that could arrive at any moment.

Maybe Ridge could trap Balty's moles somehow and not let in any more ships. The Gandoops had their own guards who had kept order at the port all this time. He should stage a revolt. In his own facility. His guards against Balty's men. Moon rats against Tegs.

The odds were not good. He was not built for this. He was an inventor, not a soldier. He exhaled loudly and walked away to find Ishmar and Ali, reflecting dully that he still had his life.

20

PEARY D⊙ME

E dgemont stared at Torr's left cheek as they stood on a dry hilltop south of Scripps Ranch.

"What're you looking at?" Torr asked angrily. He hated it when people stared at his twitch.

Edgemont reached out his hand, pointing towards his cheek. It took all Torr's self-control not to wrench Edgemont's wrist and take him to the ground. Edgemont wiggled his fingers in the air next to Torr's face, causing his cheek to tickle.

Torr knocked the Teg's hand away. "What're you doing?" Torr asked. "Stop that."

"What's this weird whisker growing out of the side of your face?" Edgemont asked, laughing, and continued to flick his fingers next to Torr's cheek. "It's like a cat whisker."

Torr pressed his hand to his cheek. "There's no cat whisker growing out of my face." He did have an extra-stiff whisker that grew straight out of a little mole on his cheek, which required extra care when shaving, but his facial hair was not long enough for anyone to notice. "You're an asshole," Torr said.

The Teg laughed out loud. "Look," Edgemont said, taking out his compass. Its brass cover was shiny, and he passed it to Torr.

Torr stared into the small reflective cover. A luminescent gold filament extended from his cheek like a strand of a spider web, stretching through the air beyond the view of his reflection. He waved his hand next to his face, trying to feel the filament, but his hand passed right through it.

"Here," Edgemont said, still chuckling. "You want me to get that for you?" The Teg reached out his hand and tugged at the golden thread.

Torr jerked awake, finding himself in the pitch-black cargo hold of the *Calico Jack*. He listened for Cassidy's breathing. She was asleep. He stared into the nothingness, trying to forget his weird dream and plan their next steps once they arrived on the moon. Much as he tried to imagine their arrival, he had no idea what to expect. He'd always thought he'd arrive on the moon at Peary Spaceport. He'd seen footage of the busy spaceport and the geodesic dome, even the tent city. He'd find Jasper and Kai, and things would fall into a sense of normalcy. Now it was anybody's guess. Ridge Gandoop Spaceport. What the heck kind of name was that?

The profound blackness of the cargo hold lulled him back to sleep, and he found himself on the hills of Scripps Ranch, lying prone on the hot dirt behind a screen of leafless bushes with Reina lying next to him, spotting.

"Movement in the brush at ten o'clock," she said.

Torr stared through the Dashiel's scope at the hilltop on the horizon to their left, his finger next to the trigger. Teg snipers had been infiltrating their zone all morning, taking out one Gaia United soldier after another.

"I don't see anything," he said. "Where?"

"I lost him," Reina said, frustrated.

The Tegs were good. Very good. Torr lifted his chin above the cheek rest and turned his head slowly to the right, eyes closed. He could feel his gold cheek filament stretching out through the air. He continued turning his head until he felt the filament snag on something, like a tripwire, sending a sharp impulse to his cheek. Torr shifted his gun by feel and fired, his right cheek already back on the cheek rest, the stock recoiling against his shoulder.

"Got him!" Reina said. She paused for a moment. "I didn't see him move. How did you spot him hidden in the brush like that?"

He opened his eyes and took in a breath. "It's a thing I have," he said. His cheek was still pulsing. There were more Tegs out there.

A lurch in Torr's stomach announced *Calico Jack's* drop into orbit. His body sank downward. His heart throbbed, but his cheek was still as stone. He turned on his flashlight and squinted against the sudden light. Everything drooped and settled with whispers and scrapes as the gentle gravity of the moon pulled at them.

He freed himself from his moorings and fell softly onto the tarped floor of grain sacks. Cassidy did the same, then found the salt water sacks and handed him one. He forced himself to drink it all, his face pinching from the gagging brine. They rolled up their bedding, gathered the pressure suits and cables, wadded them together, and waited.

A long while later, the craft jerked to a stop, then shook slowly. A loud clanging came from outside the cargo bay door, followed by the hiss of the airlock being released. Torr's ears popped painfully. Light cracked around the edges of the door then came streaming in, forcing him to cover his eyes. They crouched on the rice sacks as the cargo bay door slowly creaked open and clanked heavily to the floor. The air was sharp with the smell of spent gunpowder.

Herbert and Junior looked up at them. "Still alive, I see," Herbert said with a crooked grin. Junior set up a ladder for them. They passed him their suits and packs then climbed down.

Torr stood on the loading ramp and pulled the rucksack straps over his shoulders, the pack weighing him down. His muscles were shaky and he still felt slightly nauseous, but they had made it. They were on the moon.

Torr had been looking forward to experiencing the weak lunar gravity, but, if anything, the gravity here felt stronger than on Earth. They could have still been on the planet, except for the odd smell and the strange quiet that hung heavily in the background behind the clatter and hum of the spaceport.

The hangar was large, with clean cement floors. A curved ceiling supported by white girders soared overhead. There were no windows, but the hangar was lit brightly by electric light fixtures. Three large Earth freighters were parked in the middle of the floor near another large craft of odd proportions, whose head bulged out from its bulbous body like a vulture. He had never seen a Cephean ship in real life, and tried not to gawk as a group of dusty workers who were loading the strange ship glanced their way. Next to it stood an unfamiliar craft shaped like a square bronze mace head covered with large spikes. Several smaller craft were lined up against a side wall. Two small cargo loaders buzzed across the polished cement floor carrying stacks of plastic crates.

At the far wall, a large doorway led into a warehouse with rows upon rows of tightly packed crates and goods. Another group of thin, dusty men were loading one of the Earth ships on the other side of the floor. Two men carrying assault rifles broke away from the group and headed their way. They did not look beaten down like the loading crew, but stood straight, appearing robust and healthy.

"How was the trip?" Herbert asked in an almost friendly tone.

"Not as bad as I'd feared," Torr said, handing the man the second Solidi. "Thank you."

Herbert pocketed it and smiled. "And how's the pretty lady?" he asked, eyeing Cassidy, whose hair lay in a tangled mess across her shoulders, her eyes rimmed with dark circles.

She gave Herbert a wan smile. "Fine, thank you," she said, glancing at the approaching guards.

Herbert sighed. "Well, let's see who we can hand you off to."

Torr watched warily as the two guards stopped and hovered a few paces away. Three men in coveralls approached from the other direction, followed by a hunched, wiry man. His head was balding, and he held a screen in a prosthetic claw. His good right hand shook Herbert's and Junior's.

"Murphy," the hunched man said, introducing himself. "How was the trip?" Without waiting for an answer, Murphy tapped on his screen, then looked at the ship. *Calico Jack. Denver 523317,"* he muttered as he read the side of the ship and marked it on his screen. "We were expecting a food shipment. Not uh ... who are they?" Murphy's face twisted with concern as he peered at Torr and Cassidy.

"Just a couple passengers I had to add at the last minute," Herbert said, waving his hand through the air. "You know those Tegs. They said I had to take them, so who was I to argue?" Herbert gave a toothy smile, and Murphy's shoulders hunched closer to his ears.

Murphy's eyes darted nervously towards the guards then to Torr and Cassidy, resting on Cassidy's breasts before he glanced over his shoulder at another man who was approaching.

Tall, with a strong posture, the man strode with a sense of authority. His short blond hair and confident bearing reminded Torr of Johnson, his squadmate turned Teg. The two guards stood straight as the man passed them. What Torr wouldn't do for his TAFT and squad right now. He tightened his hands into fists, then relaxed them by force. He had to appear calm. He softened his expression, trying to subdue his cheek, which was pulsing with insistent jabs.

"What's this?" the man asked brusquely. His eyes fastened on Cassidy.

Cassidy stepped closer to Torr, and Torr met the man's eyes. Obviously, people were taking an interest in his sister. He straightened, giving the man his best, respectful gaze.

"We're on our way to Peary Dome," Torr said. "Came out of Moffett Field."

The man looked at Murphy, whose head sank lower into his shoulders, reminding Torr of a turtle. Murphy's voice squeaked, "We could send a ship to take them over there."

"What's the policy?" the blond man demanded.

Murphy's eyes shifted. "Um, we're not accustomed to receiving, um, passengers."

"I'll need to run this by Fowler," the man said curtly, and strode away.

The two guards scowled at them as Murphy looked apologetically at Torr. Torr's heart beat rapidly, and he glanced around him. He could feel the small tug of Cassidy's hand hanging onto his backpack. Torr suddenly felt trapped, and his skin was clammy. He wanted his guns. Herbert and Junior avoided his eyes. The three dusty men were examining the ship's cargo.

"Couldn't you just take us to Peary on your way out?" Torr asked Herbert, trying to keep the desperation out of his voice.

Herbert lifted his brows. "I'm going to have a full load," he said, eyeing Cassidy.

Torr couldn't tell if Herbert was negotiating or saying no, or perhaps had something worse in mind. Torr looked sideways at Cassidy, who was breathing with deep, even breaths, her eyes taking in every detail of the hangar. He matched her breathing and tried to stay calm, and surveyed the surroundings. There were several doors, but they all would lead deeper into the facility. Escaping outdoors was not an option on the moon. He inhaled and a prayer came unbidden to his lips. "*Golden stars, shine down upon us,*" he murmured softly. Cassidy looked at him. He hadn't meant to say it out loud.

Murphy's head popped up, his skinny neck straightening as he spotted something across the hangar. "Ali! Ali!" Murphy yelled, hailing a man who stopped and walked towards them while pointedly ignoring the guards. Ali was thin and of medium height, and had a soothing air about him. His skin was a pale olive tone, and his dark hair hung in waves around his ears. Large brown eyes examined Torr and Cassidy with grim curiosity.

"These two need to get to Peary. Hardman went to get Fowler," Murphy whispered to Ali, his voice rasping. The guards tilted their heads, trying to hear.

"I see," Ali said, frowning. "Where are you guys in from? You can't be from Denver," he said wryly, his eyes noting the markings on the ship.

"Moffett Field," Torr said.

Ali's eyes darted quickly around the hangar. He lifted a hand radio from his belt and spoke into it, looking across the floor to the group of men loading the ship at the other end of the hangar. "Hunter. I need you."

One of the men broke away and trotted towards them. Torr's pulsing cheek erupted into a full-blown twitch, and he turned his head, hoping they wouldn't notice. He detached his mind from the feeling of doom pressing in on him and focused on the miracle of having traversed space in a metal box. He was now standing on the moon. A ripple of excitement ran over his skin, and the twitch subsided.

"Take my speedster to Peary," Ali said to Hunter, who had joined them. "Find out the current price for oxygen canisters. We need to clear out some inventory. Murphy, you go with him. Give these kids a ride." Ali nodded curtly at Hunter and waved his fingers in a gesture to hurry up. The two armed guards stepped forward, but Ali put his arm out and the men stopped, eyes shifting.

"Yes, boss," Hunter said, and motioned for Torr and Cassidy to follow him. Torr took Cassidy's arm, and they hurried after Hunter. Torr stole a glance behind him. Herbert and Junior were watching with unreadable expressions. Ali had turned to face the guards and was speaking to them.

Murphy scurried to catch up, and Ali headed in the opposite direction towards the same door the blond officer had left through. The guards stood in the middle, looking back and forth between Ali and Hunter. Torr's heart pounded, and he and Cassidy quickened their pace to keep up with Hunter, whose long legs had already taken him through another doorway. They caught up with him, and Murphy shut the door behind them.

They were in a much smaller hangar with four silver-colored speedsters lined up precisely in the dim space. Against the back wall, four more speedsters were covered with tarps. Murphy went to a speedster in the center and popped a hatch open, then gestured for Torr and Cassidy to climb in behind the two pilot seats.

There were two small jumpseats in the back, and just enough room between the seats to fit their packs. Hunter and Murphy climbed into the front seats. The hatches lowered and clicked into place, and the airlock sealed. Torr and Cassidy imitated Murphy, pulling harnesses down over their shoulders and clipping them between their legs. The craft lifted into a hover and glided silently across the floor.

Torr's fingers gripped the chest harness, his pulse hammering. The agitation radiating from Murphy made it so Torr could barely enjoy his first ride in a moon speedster, something he'd dreamed about since he was a child.

Torr leaned his head back against the seat as they entered a decompression chamber and the door clanked down behind them, sealing them in. Everyone sat stiffly, the sound of their breathing loud in the small cabin. The wall in front of them blinked for what felt like an eternity, then opened slowly. The craft glided into a second chamber, and the wall behind them slid closed. A couple long, agonizing minutes later the outer gate opened, and the craft glided out into the glaring sunlight.

———————)———————

Torr gazed out the small tinted window by his shoulder. Prickles of excitement chased away his nervousness. They were inside a vast crater. The gray land below was flat, with tall peaks of the crater's rim looming in the distance. Above, the black sky marked the top of the deep pit they were in, speckled with bright stars despite the presence of the sun that blazed above the horizon like a fiery torch.

Torr stared, dumbfounded. He was really here, on the moon that he'd gazed upon his entire life. He had charted its phases, watched it rise and set, studied it through a telescope. Now it was Earth's last outpost, the new frontier, gateway to the stars.

He regarded the bleak terrain. It did not inspire hope. It was a lifeless desert, severe and forbidding. He looked behind him and examined the long spaceport building they'd just left. It had a curved, white roof that caught the sunshine—a bright beacon against the dull lunar soil. Beyond the spaceport stood enormous, black, cube-shaped buildings marked with blinking red lights. Rectangular towers thrust upwards alongside the buildings, and nearby was an array of dish-shaped solar collectors.

With a sudden, stomach-dropping bounce, the craft rose vertically, the floor of the crater spreading out below. Torr could see the true massiveness of the crater now. It stretched for miles in all directions. The crater's rim was a jagged mountain range. A cluster of antenna towers poked up from the highest peak like a stand of sentinel trees.

The speedster rose above the rim, revealing the vast surface of the moon. The exterior rim of the crater plunged down to meet a sea of irregular dunes that stretched as far as the eye could see. The pitch-black sky was thick with stars, and the Milky Way cut across the firmament in a river of light clouded by webs of darkness. Torr's breath caught at the striking beauty of it all.

As they gained altitude the barren wasteland spread out below them. Smooth sweeps of land were broken by round impact craters large and small. There were no buildings. No craft in the sky. He craned his neck and peered out the small window, scanning the sky behind them. No one had come chasing after them.

"Torr," Cassidy whispered with awe as she peered out her little window. He leaned over, and his mouth fell open.

Earth shone brightly in the dark heavens, a huge, fat blue crescent. The ocean was laced with strands of white clouds.

"Gaia," he said softly, suddenly understanding her name. Mother Earth. A living, breathing planet. He felt its pull as though its magnetic core still tugged at the iron in his blood.

"It's something, isn't it?" Hunter asked.

"Unbelievable," Torr murmured, gazing at it. It was a precious jewel. An invaluable treasure.

His parents were there, somewhere. And Reina, Bobby, Mike, Donald, and the others. Sadness flooded through him. Then guilt. Then anger. Why was he able to get off Earth and his parents and friends could not? Why him? Torr settled back into his seat. His stomach was in a knot. He was here now. It was done. He had to move on.

The craft tilted, and jabs of light made him close his eyes and raise his hand against the glare of the sun. He shielded his eyes and peeked out his window. The land below reflected sunlight back at him like brushed aluminum, but the sun's light did not brighten the sky. It did not make the air shine, neither gold nor blue. Torr realized that with no atmosphere there was nothing to catch the light. The sunrays simply hit the ground, illuminating the steely gray dust against a night sky. It was unexpected to have a black sky dotted with stars while the sun blazed in the heavens. *The sun.* Torr had never thought of it as a star. Now it was obvious. It was a raging ball of fire.

They rode in silence. Torr stared out his window, wondering how anything survived in such a hostile environment. No one seemed to live here at all. The only signs of life were one cluster of trailers arranged in a neat grid in one of the larger craters, and a tall antenna tower perched on the rim of another. There was nothing here. No air. No water. No plants. No animals. Nothing. Maybe it had been a mistake to come.

They followed the curve of the moon until towering mountain ranges came into view. Perched atop a high plateau was a large, white, glinting beacon like someone was pointing a mirror at them. A line of small bright specks flashed on either side of it, stretching out along the ridge.

"Peary Dome," Hunter said. "Sits a mile above the crater floor on the northwestern rim; the crater itself is fifty miles across."

Torr's pulse quickened with excitement. As they got closer, the glass geodesic dome caught the light of the sun on its facets, like a massive cut gem. The smaller lights were reflections from a row of large solar dish collectors and antenna dishes.

They flew over Peary Crater, its vast, flat floor slashed by long shadows and dotted with several large impact craters.

Hunter spoke at the control panel. *"Peary Control, this is Gandoop Meleager 556. Requesting permission to land."*

After a few moments, a voice from an unseen radio blared in the small cabin. *"Cleared for landing, Meleager. Bay Three."*

The craft sped along, the dome growing bigger as they approached Peary Rim. Torr could make out details of the dome now. A long white tunnel stuck out from the base and ran along the flat, gray land. Hunter decelerated, and they skimmed above the ground, which was covered with small craters rimmed with shadowy crescents. Torr held onto his harness as Hunter swooped into the wide mouth of the landing tunnel and came to a gentle stop outside the dimly lit hangar wall.

The wall before them formed a vertical slit and opened slowly, revealing a large metal bay, lit by solar filaments that snaked along the ceiling. The ship glided into it and waited as the door behind them closed. After the pressure equalized, the door in front of them opened and they moved forward, where they were sealed into a second bay.

The inner door finally parted, and Torr watched with fascination as a huge hangar appeared before them. Peary Spaceport was many times the scale of Gandoop Spaceport, with soaring ceilings and skylights that let in filtered light. Men were directing ships, unloading freight, or driving little transports.

They were guided to a parking spot between several small

craft, and *Meleager* settled onto the concrete hangar floor. The hatches opened, and Torr unfolded his stiff body and climbed out. He stood next to his sister and wanted to put his arm across her shoulders protectively, but she was sensing the surroundings and he didn't want to disturb her. His cheek had started subtly throbbing again, but not too much. There were some threats here, but not in their immediate vicinity.

Two guards in tan fatigues approached. One nodded to Hunter and Murphy with recognition, then looked at Torr and Cassidy.

"Refugees," Murphy said. "They came in from Moffett Field."

The guards looked Torr and Cassidy over. "Got any guns?" the man asked. He patted them down quickly, then took a quick look inside their packs. The other guard frisked Hunter and Murphy.

"Customs is at that door," one of the men said to Torr and Cassidy, pointing across the wide floor. "Then you should head over to the PCA, Peary Central Administration, in Center Ring. You'll need to get a tent and register for rations." The man nodded as if that was the end of it and turned to Hunter, who began speaking of oxygen canisters.

Torr turned to Murphy, who was fidgeting behind Hunter.

"Murphy," Torr said, reaching out to shake the man's good hand. "I think we owe you thanks for more than just a ride. Seems like you got us out of some trouble."

Murphy shifted nervously and shook his hand. "New administration at Gandoop. Not sure what they would have done with you two. Especially her," Murphy said, his eyes sliding sideways towards Cassidy, who was peering intently around the enormous hangar.

"I thank you kindly," Torr said. "What can I give you two, and Ali? What do we owe for the trip?" Torr dug into a pocket and pulled out some gold coins.

"Oh, no," Murphy said, raising his hand defensively. "No, you don't owe anything. Ali just wanted to help. Believe me, he has more gold than he knows what to do with."

"Here, then, you take it, and Hunter." Torr held out four gold Eagles, but Murphy stepped away, a look of fright flashing across his face. Torr pulled his hand back, surprised at the man's reaction.

"We couldn't. I can't." Murphy shook his head and lifted his metal claw of a hand as if in explanation.

Torr wrinkled his brow, confused, but shrugged and returned the coins to his pocket.

"Okay. Well, thanks anyway. I owe you one."

Murphy smiled awkwardly and gave him a jerky wave, then stepped away to join the other men.

Torr turned to Cassidy. "I think we narrowly avoided something ugly," he said quietly.

She met his eyes and nodded. "I don't think that blond guard, Hardman, wanted to let us leave. He looked like a Teg to me."

Torr's skin crawled. The same disturbing thought had crossed his mind. The man had behaved like he was on active duty, with the haughtiness of a soldier on the winning side. Torr frowned. He thought he'd seen the last of the Tegs when they'd left Moffett. Even the suggestion that Tegea's forces were on the moon made his limbs grow heavy with dread. "Do you think …?" he mumbled, loath to acknowledge the possibility.

Cassidy's lip rose in a sneer. "I don't know, but I didn't like the feel of him or the other two guards."

"Me neither." It felt better here at Peary. Free.

The hum of activity was all around. Brawny cargo handlers strode by, glancing at Cassidy as they passed. Several large spacecraft were lined up in rows. A slick, red speedster hovered above the floor and floated through a huge square doorway at the far end into another hangar, which appeared to be a shop. Torr could see a large engine hanging from a chain sling. A metal grinder buzzed, and an arc welder flashed from inside the shop.

A compression bay gasped behind him. An Earth freighter glided out over the hangar floor, and a waiting ship was guided towards the vacated airlock by a tug pod. The departing ship was black and oblong with short metal spikes protruding all around it, reminding Torr of a blowfish.

Another of the blocky craft he'd seen at Gandoop was parked midway down the row of large ships. It was a tarnished metal cube with a large cone projecting from each side, like some sort of giant spiked dice or square head of a mace. He looked for the owners of the strange ship, and identified them by what they wore. Their clothing reminded Torr of medieval garb or what he imagined pirates wore: grungy velvet doublets, leather arm guards, and leather pants. They were flamboyant, with soiled white ruffles at their necks and sleeves, and colorful scarves tied around their heads. They had narrow, lined faces with swarthy skin and short, pointed beards, and carried long, sheathed knives at their hips.

Earthlanders wore every manner of military surplus attire. Camouflage of various colors: forest green, desert sand, galaxy black. Pants were either worn long or cut off into knee-length shorts below the large cargo pockets. Dingy t-shirts were layered under field jackets or vests.

Torr looked down at his own clothing. Desert camo cargo pants. An old flannel shirt. He fit right in. Cassidy did not. Despite their harrowing trip and looking like she'd just spent a week hiking the backcountry, she was attracting far too many glances. Her tousled hair was long and her jeans were tight, and she wore an old gray sweatshirt that was sloppy for her, but hugged her curves. Torr reached to his empty belt, feeling for his Orbiter by habit. His jaws tightened.

He examined the men working the floor. A wide assortment of weapons hung from belts or shoulder straps. Guards who walked the floor and stood at the doorways carried handguns and assault rifles. The rest of the men wore various cutting and bludgeoning implements. Most had two-way radios on their belts, the bursts of chatter blending in with the din of the busy spaceport. Torr felt naked without the weapons he'd worn for two years. He needed to find some other weapons, and quickly.

The swagger of the guards made him feel better. Hopefully they had assembled a fighting force to defend against Tegea, should he try to invade this distant outpost. First Torr had to find Jasper and Kai. They would help him navigate the place. Then, once he got Cassidy settled in, he would find the local moon militia. He scanned the hangar, searching for Kai's tall, lanky build and narrow, serious face. Or Jasper. Tall like his father, but wider at the shoulders, even at nineteen when Torr had last seen him five years ago. Dark auburn hair. Cocky as all hell, with a sarcastic half-smile ever-present on his face. Torr inspected the assortment of men. No one looked familiar.

"Where's Jasper?" he thought out loud, catching Cassidy's eyes.

"I was wondering the same thing." She looked lost.

He adjusted the straps of his rucksack and asked one of the guards if he knew Jasper and Kai Mannan. The man shook his head.

"Names don't ring a bell."

Torr hid his disappointment and addressed the next urgent issue: bathrooms. The guard gestured to a far wall where three blue porta-potties were lined up. Apparently they were free to leave, so he and Cassidy crossed the floor, and Torr went inside one of the little huts. It stank, and a small puddle of urine was at his feet. He peeled off the damp diaper and shoved it into a small waste can. He felt like an idiot. He relieved himself in the hole that was half-filled with excrement, then met Cassidy outside the blue huts. They didn't talk about it. They had just flown to the moon; what was a little indignity in light of such an incredible journey?

They made their way to the customs station at the far doorway, which consisted of two long folding tables and two bored guards sitting on stools. The guards stood up as they approached, the sight of a young female apparently perking them up. One guard explained the layout of the camp while the other checked their passports, frisked them for weapons again, and did a cursory check of their packs' contents.

"Do you know Jasper and Kai Manann?" Torr asked.

The guards looked thoughtful for a moment, then one shook his head. "Don't think so."

"Kai's a Peary pilot," Torr said. "He works here." He glanced over his shoulder at the parked spacecraft and men in flight suits wandering the floor.

"Pilots come and go," the other guard said. "They stay here for a few months or a couple years, then get a gig on an interstellar craft and leave to explore the galaxy." The guard saw the disappointment on their faces, and his expression softened. "Hang on. Let me get one of the old-timers." He took a radio from his belt and spoke into it.

A couple minutes later, a mechanic crossed the floor and joined them. The man was pale and gaunt, his hands black with grease. He tightened his face for a moment, thinking. "Kyle?" he asked.

"No. Kai," Torr said. He spelled the name and described him.

The mechanic turned down his mouth and squinted his eyes in thought. "Nope. Don't know no Kyle."

Torr exhaled in exasperation then thanked the man politely. The man turned and left, and Torr thanked the guards for trying. Torr could feel Cassidy's disappointment more sharply than his own.

"Is there a rebel force here?" he asked the guards. "A militia?"

The first guard stared at him blankly. "You mean Gaia United? No. Peary is a neutral zone."

"No organized force at all?"

"No. The war's back on Earth. Not out here."

Torr felt a moment of empty confusion. "What about Tegs?" he asked. "Aren't you afraid they're going to take over the dome? Or maybe they're already here."

The men both shook their heads, and the second one answered, "No. They come through now and then to trade or fuel up. But that's about it."

Waves of relief and guilt washed over Torr. Had he really left all that behind? Left his parents and friends to suffer that madness while he and his sister slipped away?

"Come on," Cassidy said. "Let's go."

A guard held the door open for them, and they stepped out into the light. Torr squinted against the sudden glare.

They were standing on the edge of a wide road. Before them stood a vast tent city spread out under the high, clear glass dome. The land was perfectly flat, and peaks of dust-gray tents blended together into a monotonous landscape. The road under his feet felt hard like concrete, though it was the same color as the dust that was pushed like sand against the sides of buildings and tents. Girders and glass triangles formed an elaborate pattern of hexagons and stars above them, converging at the center far overhead with the black, star-filled heavens looking down at them through the glass. Not far above the tentline stood the sun, reflecting harshly off the dust and casting shadows from the ruts and ridges of the road.

Earth hung above the southern horizon to their left, drawing Torr's eyes and making his blood surge with longing. Overcome by a wave of homesickness, he found his binoculars and trained them on the planet, trying to determine which ocean was showing. He saw the edge of a continent in the southern hemisphere, but did not know which one. Perhaps Australia.

He passed the binoculars to Cassidy. She looked towards Earth, then lowered the binoculars.

"What's wrong?" Torr asked.

"Just worrying about Mom and Dad," she mumbled.

He patted her shoulder. "They'll be okay," he said reassuringly, though he wasn't sure at all.

She passed Torr the binoculars with calculation in her eyes. Probably she was counting the days and guessing how far their parents would have traveled by now. Better she try to feel them, that would give her a better clue. Torr closed his eyes for a moment and reached out to his father. He was flooded with nervousness and did not like the feeling, so he opened his eyes. Torr could do nothing to help his parents from here. He had to focus on his own survival and that of his sister right now.

He surveyed the interior of the dome as a transport rolled by, crunching over the road with its wide treads. Another small transport rolled by on rubber tires, little puffs of dust trailing it and settling slowly. Clusters of fist-sized rocks littered the sides of the roadway. The camp smelled like a pottery studio filled with raw clay and hot kilns, mixed with the flinty smell of gunpowder.

Torr squatted at the side of the road and scraped up a handful of dust layered on top of the hardened surface. It was a fine-grained sand, almost powdery. Gunmetal gray with minuscule flecks of silver, gold, white, green, and orange. He let it slip through his fingers and watched as it fell a little too fast in the fake gravitational field, the grains falling to the ground like filings to a magnet. Despite the pull of gravity, a faint dust cloud billowed around his hand and lingered in the air. A residue of the chalky dust clung to his skin and was already under his fingernails. He rose and wiped his hands on his pant legs.

The air was warm and dry like the desert east of Miramar, where he had been sent for a week during basic training. He had done a lot of crawling on hot rocky ground, avoiding spiky bushes and scorpions. Unlike the desert, there was no wind here, though vertical turbines jutted up from the tent city and rotated slowly, and little fan-looking pods floated in the upper reaches of the dome.

The curved structure created a subtly muffled environment with a hint of an echo. It was as though every sound bounced sharply off the glass and was amplified just a bit before being drowned out by the dust and canvas tents. Yells and laughter, the ping-ping of a hammer striking metal, and the distant croon of a harmonica floated over the city.

His eye was drawn to the center of the camp where a tall, white stone pillar protruded upward, terminating abruptly halfway to the peak of the dome. The stone looked similar to marble or alabaster, and slightly translucent, catching the sunlight and glowing subtly from within. The gleaming pillar and the gem-like, faceted dome cast a glimmering aura over the otherwise depressing tent city. He recognized the pillar from photos. It was the "gravity bar," made from an alien material that created Earth-type gravity within its range. The guard had said the dome was a mile and a half in diameter. That would mean the peak of the dome was three-quarters of a mile high, and therefore the pillar was over a quarter mile tall.

Torr craned his neck, looking overhead. The dome was a massive engineering feat. Each triangular panel of the interlocked grid was twice as tall as he was. He couldn't imagine the number of shiploads of materials that must have been brought from Earth to construct such a thing. A much smaller dome and spaceport had been installed on this site first, then this massive structure had been erected around it. The large dome had taken twenty years to build, as long as it had taken to build the Great Pyramid of Giza, or the Taj Majal, or the Star Labyrinth. A group of nations had worked together to build it, before the Global Alliance took hold of Earth and ruined everything. Torr's mood darkened at the thought, but lightened again. Somehow Peary Dome was still independent, and he and Cassidy had miraculously made their way here. His mood was buoyant suddenly. They had run a long and dangerous gauntlet, and had come out the other side.

A smile spread across his face, and he turned towards his sister. "Cass," he said, grabbing her shoulder. "We made it. We're here." Laughter welled up from his chest and tumbled out of his mouth. Cassidy's laughter joined his and they hugged, then pulled apart and hooted and hollered, and whistled sharply with thumbs and forefingers between their teeth like they used to do when they were kids, drawing curious glances from a pair of scruffy men walking by. Torr didn't care who was watching and danced the little jig he and his squadmates used to do. He and his sister were free. From here they could start a new life and explore the heavens. Everything was going to be all right.

Soon their joy dissipated as they observed their surroundings and the people passing by on the well-traveled road. They walked in groups of twos and threes and some in larger groups. Everyone's eyes were hollow and their faces gaunt. Some people wore bandanas or dingy white masks over their noses and mouths in an attempt to filter out the dust that coated everything.

The road arced away on either side, following the perimeter of the dome. To their right as they faced the center of camp, next to the spaceport and jutting in from the dome's edge, stood a line of metal shacks. Beyond the shacks were several rows of stacked shipping containers of various faded colors: red, yellow, green, and blue, stacked three high with ladders for accessing the upper levels of the makeshift dwellings. To their left, at the other end of the long spaceport, were more shipping containers. They were not stacked but formed a grid surrounded by tall, chain-link fencing topped with barbed wire. People were wandering around inside.

"Let's see what that is," he said, and walked with Cassidy towards the fenced-in area.

They passed several men walking the road with two women huddled amongst them. Scarves were wrapped around the women's heads, noses, and mouths. Their eyes followed Cassidy as they passed. The women were dressed as the men were, in dusty tan cargo pants and faded t-shirts. More transports, painted olive green, rolled slowly by. One was towing a wagon carrying two large plastic water tanks. Another was an enclosed box truck. Another carried a group of men hanging off the sides and the back, holding rakes and shovels.

The spaceport's front wall to their left housed a row of large loading bays. A couple of the tall garage doors were rolled up. Ground transports were parked inside, and one was being loaded by a forklift hoisting a plastic crate. Several five-hundred-gallon water tanks stood against one wall, and a small crane hung over them.

They got to the fence, and Torr examined the interior of the large pen. It was a market. Shipping containers stood in rows with their side doors open, revealing wares inside. Men huddled in small groups, examining merchandise. Some were arguing. Others laughed. Two men were attired in off-world clothing. One wore a dark blue velvet jacket that fell to his knees over dark brown leather leggings and boots. A long knife was strapped to his belt and a bright blue sash was tied around his head, holding back long black hair that was fastened in a neat ponytail. The other wore a black and gold striped tunic over black pants and boots, with white ruffles spilling over a high black collar, and a gold sash tied around his head.

Torr walked slowly with Cassidy alongside the fence to the second row, which was dedicated to fifty-gallon drums and sacks of grain. The third row was crowded with large wooden crates marked with off-world runes. Tall metal canisters stood in orderly lines up and down the fourth row. Torr spotted Murphy and Hunter at the end of the row, waving their hands at the canisters.

The men did not see them, and he and Cassidy moved on to the last row, which had the feel of a flea market, with various wares stacked on tables and inside containers. A woman sat on a stool in front of an open shipping container with three stools at her side. Two stools held small, green potted plants. The third held a cage with two small, twittering birds. The woman met his eyes and smiled. Cassidy's fingers wrapped around the chain-link fencing beside him, and Torr wondered if he should buy her a plant, or the birds. But they had nowhere to stay yet, and he had no idea how much water and food they would have to spare. The water they'd brought from Earth was nearly gone. He took a half-empty metal water bottle from his cargo pocket and swallowed a large gulp, then passed it to Cassidy. She took a mouthful and handed it back to him. Hunger gurgled in his belly.

They reached the end of the market. The chain-link fence turned at a right angle and terminated at the dome's edge. There were no gates in the tall fence; the only way into the market seemed to be through the spaceport building. To the right of the fencing, set end-to-end along the base of the dome, stood shoulder-high troughs of green plastic. A faint stink of pond scum reached his nose.

They moved away and crossed the wide, dusty road, heading towards the center of camp where the guard had said they would find the PCA. He'd said the camp was arranged like spokes of a wheel, with Center Ring at the hub and twelve roads radiating out, numbered like the hands of a clock. The southern spoke that pointed towards Earth was twelve o'clock. The road that ended at the spaceport was nine o'clock. The spoke at six o'clock pointed north towards a vista of descending ridges and rising peaks. There was open sky at three o'clock, where the dome perched at the edge of the high plateau. They walked towards the nearest intersection. At a corner stood a long pole topped with a hand-painted sign that read, "Spoke Road 9." They turned onto the spoke road and headed towards Center Ring.

21

REFUGEE CAMP

Cassidy glanced behind her at the massive hangar and resisted the urge to run inside and board the next ship back to Earth. Instead she placed one foot in front of the other and headed down the road. Spoke Road Nine was long and straight, carving a wide channel between clusters of identical tents. An occasional group of haggard men trudged past them. They looked numbingly bored. Their eyes followed her as she walked down the road.

The surface of the moon was not white or golden like she'd imagined, but soot gray like ash from a fireplace. She'd determined that the subtle smell of gunpowder was just how the dust smelled. A barren landscape stretched beyond the edges of the dome, a vast, colorless desert in sharp contrast to Earth, which glistened a brilliant blue and gold. The beautiful planet was a prison for her parents, who were suddenly and irrevocably separated from her and Torr.

She lifted her eyes to the stars that seemed to glow brighter the longer she gazed at them. Their music streamed like the rushing of her blood, pushing its way into her awareness. The star music seemed louder out here than on Earth. She tilted her head, trying to discern the direction of its source. Did it come from one star, or all the stars? Was it one sound, or many? It seemed to come from everywhere, like an orchestra in a great hall. She scanned the horizon, turning in a circle to take it all in. Yes, it was definitely louder at the horizon. When she tilted her head back to look up, the volume lessened a tiny bit. She lowered her eyes to the horizon again and the strange music subtly amplified and gained clarity, like tuning into a radio frequency.

Torr waited for her as she circled slowly. His joy had subsided, as had hers, worry creasing his brow. They were alone in this strange, hostile place, and were never going home. She put on a brave face for him and shuffled along at his side, checking out the tent city.

Lengths of canvas covered the ground in front of some tents, displaying a random collection of wares. They looked to be secondhand items from Earth. A few people were picking through them. A man pulled a small wagon loaded with mason jars of yellow liquid, and called out, "Sun tea. Sun tea for sale!"

"Piss tea," a man walking near them muttered.

"Ewww," Cassidy said, wrinkling her nose. She wondered how thirsty people had to get to drink their own urine, though she supposed all moisture here was recycled.

They came upon an intersection and a road sign marked Ring Road L. The ring road arced away on either side. The next crossroad was Ring Road K. More tarps were spread on the ground, filled with a motley collection of used clothing tinged with the pervasive dust. Most everyone wore faded army surplus gear, whereas she had obviously just arrived from Earth. From the looks of things, jeans were not in fashion here, and she didn't like the way men's eyes kept wandering over her breasts and hips.

She and Torr exchanged glances, approached a tarp, and started rummaging through the items. The sooner she blended in, the better. A pair of faded, black-galaxy camouflage pants seemed to be the right size, and not too stiff from the dust. She tucked the folded pants under her arm and rummaged through a box filled with belts, clasps, and dusty pouches. She found a black web belt of the proper length. Torr found a belt for himself, and handed her a tan canvas field vest that was in fairly good condition. She pulled it on over her sweatshirt. It was boxy and oversized, and hot, but would hide her breasts from wandering eyes. It had a collection of pouch-like pockets on the front, and deep side pockets.

"This'll work," she said. "And I need some more t-shirts. Most of mine are pink." And tight fitting. They were cute in San Jose. Here they would draw too much attention.

They looked through more mounds of clothing. She found a black, short-sleeved t-shirt with a faded red dragon on it, and Torr found her a plain olive-green t-shirt.

The dust was already irritating her nose and they considered buying a few of the white dust masks, but settled on black-and-white bandanas instead.

Torr went back and forth on the price with the seller, and ended up paying a few silver bits for everything. The man let her change her clothes in his tent, which doubled as a fitting room. The tent was filled with stacked crates and a bedroll, with a narrow space for her to stand. A dusty full-length mirror leaned against the crates. She looked a mess. She peeled off the sweatshirt and t-shirt she'd worn for the past few days, wincing at the sharp smell of her own sweat. She chose the dragon shirt, and pulled on the dusty pants and vest. They were surprisingly comfortable. She yanked Grandma Leann's brush through her knotted hair and quickly plaited it into one long braid, tied the bandana across her nose and mouth, and came out feeling much less conspicuous.

Torr was asking the man if he knew Jasper and Kai. He did not.

"We'll find them," she said. Torr frowned and nodded.

They wandered to other tarps. She needed a knife. She'd stashed her pocket knife in the ditch with the guns before they'd reached Moffett. She walked slowly, scanning the goods spread on the ground. She trailed behind Torr as he stopped to examine every knife on display. His back had broadened, and his legs were thick and strong. He'd removed his flannel shirt, and his navy blue t-shirt showed off wide shoulders, his tanned arms bulging like he'd been lifting weights. He strode with an easy confidence that turned heads as he walked by. She shook her head in wonder. He had changed into a man. But it wasn't just his body that had changed.

He had always liked knives, and bows and arrows. He was oddly talented at shooting guns, and had competed at the shooting range for years. Torr had always won, even against the older men. But now he looked like he wanted weapons to actually use them. She had avoided pressing him about what had happened at the Gaia United front lines, since something obviously had. She could tell it had been difficult to leave his friends, but something else was bothering him.

He stopped at a tarp and fished out a dusty vest from a pile of rumpled clothing. It was a simple vest with two chest panels connected by a wide waist belt and shoulder straps, with an open back. Rows of horizontal webbing lined the belt and chest panels.

"Is this Teg surplus?" he asked, and Cassidy tensed up. The vest was the steel gray of the Teg uniforms.

The man looked at a tag sewn into the seams. "Yep," he said, pointing at a red shield insignia.

Cassidy shivered, but Torr slipped it on. It fit him. He pawed through a pile of pouches and selected several of various camo patterns, shapes, and sizes. He wove their straps through the horizontal webbing, and ended up with a bunch of bulging, mismatched pockets hanging off the chest panels.

"Good," he said, and settled on a price, placing several silver bits into the seller's dirty hand, which closed around the shiny coins greedily. Torr thanked him and wandered slowly past the neighboring tarps.

Further down the line, Cassidy watched him as he crouched over a collection of knives. He had come home with two indigo tattoos. A hawk on his inside right forearm was the insignia for Gaia United, with an olive branch clutched in one claw and a rifle in the other. On his upper left arm was an image of Earth with two swords crossed above it, and the full moon sitting above the crossed blades. Above the image was the word *Light*. Below was *Fighters*.

Her eyes wandered to his profile. His nose was straight and his slate-gray eyes intense. He glanced up and caught her looking at him.

"What?" he asked.

"Nothing," she said, pulling the bandana off her face and letting it hang around her neck. "You've grown up is all."

He gave her a humorless grin and turned back to the knives. She watched as he skipped over the hunting knives that he normally would have wanted and focused instead on the black combat knives, and settled on two. He handed them to her while he paid for them. One was long with a black leather handle and came with a beat-up black leather sheath. The blade and hilt reached from her fingertips halfway to her elbow. The other was smaller with a smooth, sharp blade and a small serrated portion near the handle, which would be good for cutting rope. The hilt was a textured black synthetic material with finger indentations. It fit her hand nicely.

"Take this one," Torr said, slipping it into its black sheath.

"Thanks," she said happily, sliding the sheath onto her belt.

Torr asked the man if he knew Jasper and Kai. He shook his head no. This place was bigger than she'd imagined—a small city. Torr strapped his new knife to his belt and put on his sunglasses. She nodded that she was ready to go, and they continued on their way towards Center Ring.

At Ring Road G they came upon a ration trailer. People were lined up and moved slowly through the open shipping container, then left holding metal camp dishes, a small loaf of bread, and a gallon jug of water. Some people closed the metal cover over the camp dishes, others ate as they walked. The dishes contained a small amount of rice and beans, and what looked to be a quarter of a pale tomato. Her stomach complained. It had been a whole day since they'd last eaten. The customs guard had said they'd need to register before they could receive rations, so they continued on.

Next to the ration trailer stood a bank of blue plastic porta-potty shacks. Next to the porta-potties were three wooden huts that appeared to be bathhouses of some sort. People stood in line with towels over their shoulders, and two men leaving a hut were ruddy-faced and slick with sweat. She guessed they were saunas.

They stopped at the side of the road, dug into their food supplies, and made a small meal of stale bread and cheese. Several people stared at them as they ate, as though a sandwich of white bread and cheese was something special. She was still hungry, but they decided to save the rest of their food. Torr nudged her, and she followed his gaze. A man was selling plums out of a crate, the first foodstuffs she'd seen at any of the tents. People crowded around him, and Torr and Cassidy wedged their way in. Torr bought two, for a tenth-gold bit each. The price was easily ten times what they would have paid on Earth, but Torr handed over the coins without flinching. They stood to the side and ate them. They were hard and tart. Even so, she wished they'd bought more, but the man's crate was already empty.

They continued down the road and reached Center Ring. It was a vast circular yard of tramped down dust, hard and crusty like the roads, perhaps three hundred yards across. Dominating the center stood two large square tents Cassidy assumed housed the PCA. Behind the PCA tents huddled a collection of shipping containers. Thrusting up from amongst it all was the white gravity bar, sparkling in the sunlight. A ration trailer and accompanying shacks sat at one edge of the circular yard, and another ration trailer was visible at the opposite side. Small groups of people meandered across the yard. Cassidy noted few females and even fewer children. She and Torr crossed the yard and approached the nearest PCA tent, where a stern-faced man stood guard, dressed in khaki shorts and matching short-sleeved field shirt.

Torr approached him. "We came to get a tent and register for rations."

The man motioned to the side. "It's the tent around the corner." His attention returned to the yard. He was not unfriendly, but clearly had no interest in conversation.

Torr asked if he knew Jasper and Kai Mannan. The man examined Torr's face briefly, then shook his head and turned his gaze away. Cassidy steeled herself against disappointment. They had just gotten here. They would find them.

They located the entrance to the second tent. Inside, three long folding tables stood side by side with a man sitting behind each. Dusty shelves and a wide canvas curtain hung behind the tables, obscuring the rest of the tent. A line of four or five men per table waited their turn. Cassidy and Torr joined the shortest line.

The administrator at the middle table was talking to a tall, gaunt man who bent over the table, leaning on his palms and looking beseechingly at him. "Don't you have anything else?" the man pleaded.

"Ridge Gandoop's the only mine issuing work permits right now," said the administrator apologetically. Cassidy stiffened at the mention of Gandoop. "They're sending over a freighter to pick up workers tomorrow. Only two permits left. You want one or not?"

The man's bony face contorted into a scowl. "Don't you have any jobs here at Peary? I can shovel out the composting toilets. Oil the roads. Anything."

"We don't need more Peary staff. We've got more than enough. I can put you on the waiting list, but it's about two years out." The administrator looked sympathetic. "Listen, you can stay at Peary as long as you want, the refugee traffic has slowed. Not so many people coming from Earth these days. No one will bother you."

"But there's not enough food or water here," the man said hollowly. "I've been here six months and a man can't survive on a handful of rice and beans, a slice of cucumber, a small loaf of bread, and only four liters of water."

Cassidy could see the knobby bones of the man's wrists sticking out below the cuffs of his long sleeves, and his cheeks were sunken. She could feel his hunger as an ache deep in her belly. Her empathy for the man was crowded out by fear for herself and Torr.

"It's enough food to survive. Better than what we used to provide. It used to be just bread and water. You'll burn it off faster at the mines, believe me." The administrator sighed. "Come back next week, maybe one of the other mines will have sent over some permits."

The man's face sagged, and he shuffled off.

When they made it to the front of the line, the gray-bearded man looked at them through dusty glasses.

"We need to register," Torr said, stepping forward. "We need a tent and rations."

"Look here and don't blink," the man said, holding up a light gun.

They each leaned in, and he scanned their irises.

"One ration per day. You can go to any ration station. They'll give you a dish and jug your first time. You are allowed one sauna per week, and one extra ration of water every week for sauna day. Females get one extra water ration per month. I recommend you drink it to stay hydrated, don't use it to wash yourself. And no drinking the moat water. It's salt water and will make you sick. We use it for oxygen production, so don't dump anything into it or mess with it in any way. Anyone messing with the moats gets docked a week's rations. Second offense you get airlocked." The man pushed up his glasses. "Go outside and around to the back corner to pick up your tent. Closest open spots are near 6C. Be sure to return your tent when you leave." He stood and took a handie-talkie radio from the next table and spoke into it. "Tent pickup."

"Roger, tent pickup," a man's voice responded.

"Next!"

"Do you know if Jasper or Kai Manann are in Peary Dome?" Torr asked.

The administrator sat down and looked up at him. "No, sorry. Next!"

"Don't you have records of people here?" Cassidy asked, standing stubbornly in front of the table as he waved for the next person to approach.

"No," he said curtly, meeting her gaze.

"What's your iris scanner for, then?" she asked. "Can't you check to see if our friends are in the camp?"

"No. I have no way to look anybody up. We scan your irises to enter you into the ration system. The scanners know if you try to take more than your share."

"So you don't know who anybody is?"

"Why would we need to? This is a free zone. We just want to make sure you don't take more than your fair share of rations. Next!"

She and Torr exchanged frustrated glances.

"So everybody's anonymous here," Torr said under his breath as they walked towards the tent door. "And what the hell is 'airlocked'?"

"I don't know, but it doesn't sound good."

They left and found the storage shack where two young men threw a large, rolled-up tent into the back of an open jeep. Cassidy sat in the front next to the driver and the other man climbed into the back with Torr. They rode across the yard towards Spoke Road Six, and Cassidy asked if they knew Jasper and Kai.

The man thought for a moment and shook his head. "Nope. Lots of folks come through here." He swerved around a dusty patch on the road. "Damned dust," he said, and pulled a bandana up over his nose.

Cassidy did the same, not liking the smell of the dust and wondering how harmful it was to breathe in. She'd heard it was made of miniature glass crystals that would cut up your lungs.

She pressed her bandana against her nose and mouth and tried not to breathe.

They traveled down Spoke Road Six, turned right onto Ring Road C, and located a patch of empty dirt between two tents. The men helped Torr and Cassidy set up their tent, swinging sledgehammers to drive the stakes into the hard ground.

It looked to be a six or eight-man tent, rectangular with a straight roofline seven feet high. Guy wires pulled each corner taut, and the floor was the same khaki-colored canvas as the rest of the tent. Cassidy pushed aside the dusty door flap and went inside. She could stand straight if she stood in the middle. The back wall was solid canvas, and each side wall had a little window with a mesh screen and canvas flap.

The two men wished them well and took off. Cassidy and Torr arranged their things, each claiming a side of the tent. She took out the photo of their parents, and having no furniture, set it on the floor and propped it up against the back wall. Torr stared at it, then turned away and stepped outside, the canvas door flap falling closed behind him.

Cassidy regarded the tight space that was already filled with their few belongings. Her earlier euphoria at having escaped the Tegs and arriving at Peary was gone. Would they really be living in a tent? For how long? Forever? The tent was dim, the yellowed canvas creating a sickly glow. Not exactly her idea of a home. She sighed, knowing she should be grateful they had escaped Earth and were not in a Teg camp right now.

Her mind turned to her parents. She knelt in front of their photo, letting her eyes become unfocused, and tried to reach out to them with her feelings. She closed her eyes and breathed deeply. After a few breaths her heartbeat slowed. She could feel her mother's heartbeat as though her head was on her mother's chest. It was a trick she had done all her life, from when she was a small child and needed comfort. Even after Grandma Leann had shielded her, she could still find her mother's heartbeat if she tried. Her mother was sleeping. She was calm. Alive.

Cassidy tried to feel for her father. It was not something she normally did, but she reached out, traversing the connection her mother had with her father to locate him. His heartbeat was faster and more jagged. He was awake. Standing guard.

Cassidy breathed out, her concentration wavering. They were alive. They had not been captured. That was all she needed to know right now. She sucked in a deep breath, the effort of connecting with her parents making her head swim. She lay on her back on top of her sleeping bag and stared at the canvas ceiling, and cried.

The tent doorway faced Earth, and Cassidy gazed up at it while Torr talked with the neighbors in front of the next tent. She finally tore herself away from the planet that had cast her off like a seed in the wind, and went to join her brother.

The neighbors turned as she approached, four sets of shy eyes landing on her in wonder as though she were a mermaid emerging from the sea. She chose to meet the gaze of the youngest, a boy in his early teens, who returned her direct look with a blushing smile. They were a family of a father and three boys. The father, who introduced himself as Durham Boyer, had a quiet voice and a strong, dry handshake. He had only one leg and stood with crutches under his armpits. His older sons, Raleigh and Roanoke, were about Cassidy and Torr's age. Raleigh was tall and lean; Roanoke was shorter and compact. The youngest son, Hawk, had long, gangly limbs, indicating he would be tall like Raleigh. They all had shaggy brown hair that fell over brown eyes, and they spoke with a southern drawl.

They each had a small, two-way radio clipped to their belts, next to an assortment of knives and short wooden clubs. Cassidy nodded to the three boys.

"We were at Pensacola when the Tegs destroyed it," Durham said to Torr, continuing the conversation Cassidy had interrupted. "Me and the kids were home, outside the blast zone. My wife was at work, at the base." The man's jaws tightened, and the sons' faces showed lingering grief. "That was five years ago, of course. We fled to Houston, but left before the Tegs got there. Then we went to Denver and got passage to Peary from a pilot friend of mine from the Air Force. Good thing we didn't stay in Denver," he said with a sour look.

"Did you lose your leg in the Air Force?" Torr asked.

"Yeah, a long time ago, when my radar station got blasted in Alexandria during the Early Wars."

Cassidy noted the lines of sadness that scored his face. She smiled at Hawk, who had moved to her side and was looking at her with wide, timid eyes.

"Hi," she said, patting him on the back. He smiled at her, his eyes brightening. Durham glanced at them, and his expression softened.

Two more men walked between the tents, from the tent behind Cassidy and Torr's. They both were in their mid-twenties. The first one introduced himself as Sky. A couple days of blond whiskers covered pale cheeks, and his short yellow-blond hair stood up in greasy spikes on his head. His arms were covered with indigo tattoos. Curious blue eyes met hers. She smiled and shook his hand. The second man was named Thunder. He explained that his name was really Thor, but he preferred Thunder. He had dark brown skin and short fuzzy hair. He was tall and thin, and stooped to hide his height. He looked shy, but smiled when she shook his hand. His fingers barely squeezed hers. Sky told them they had been graduate students of Mineralogy at Denver and had come to the moon on a research project a few months before Denver was blown up.

Torr asked if they knew Kai and Jasper. They all shook their heads with blank looks.

"You guys have power," Torr noted, gesturing to a power strip coming off a battery the size of an ice chest, connected to a large square of solar cells mounted on a pedestal behind their tent. "Can I charge my laptop?"

"You have a laptop?" Raleigh asked. "Sure, plug it in."

"Yeah, I've got one. Why? Don't you?" Torr asked, pulling his laptop from his pack.

"Only my dad does," Raleigh said.

"For my radio business," Durham said, pointing to a bulky, black laptop sitting on a low, makeshift table in front of their tent. "Any electronics that are not ruggedized for the moon die after a few weeks. They can't take the dust. Can I buy yours when it goes?" he asked, with a half-smile. "I always need parts. What's it got inside?"

Torr and Durham went over to the table to discuss specs, and Thunder turned to Cassidy. "Do you have one too?"

"Yeah, and a phone," she said.

"Wow," Thunder said. "All of my music is on a stick, but I have nothing to listen to it on. I could load my music onto your laptop for you, if I can listen to it once in a while." His eyes were hopeful.

"Of course," she said. She got her laptop and plugged it in next to Torr's. "Is there Internet here?" she asked.

"Not really," Durham said.

"A lunar intranet?" Torr asked.

"Sort of. Spaceport has one, but it's not public. It's kind of the Wild West out here. People put up their own wireless networks. Most are locked. Some people share content, if you can get onto their network. I stopped trying because they come and go too fast. People's computers break and they give up. It's hard to get parts out here. Mostly people just rely on two-way radios to communicate."

Cassidy glanced up at Earth. All remnants of her life were slowly slipping away, one after another.

"Did you guys get your rations yet?" Durham asked.

"No, and I'm starving," Torr said.

"We can go with you. They close at eight." He glanced at his watch.

"What time is it here?" Cassidy asked as she and Torr looked at their watches.

It was noon, California time. Yesterday at this time she and Torr had been crossing the bay's marshland, facing the Tegs and Moffett Field. She understood courage now—it's something that allows you to walk into the belly of the beast with your eyes wide open.

"It's nineteen hundred hours," Durham said. "Seven at night. We use Zulu Time here. Greenwich Mean Time. The sun never sets here, but you get used to it."

Cassidy and Torr reset their watches.

"Let's get our food," Torr said.

One of the older brothers, Roanoke, volunteered to stay behind to guard the tents.

Cassidy and Torr ducked into theirs. Though Cassidy was grateful for the neighborliness, she stuffed anything of value into the small green daypack that held the herbs. Torr filled his vest and pants pockets with various items, including the crystals, she noted approvingly, and left his rucksack on his bedding. He slung the nearly empty water skin over his shoulder.

"Ready?" he asked.

She nodded, and they stepped outside.

"It'll be good to have more people to walk the camp with," Durham said as they waited for the others. "Things have been getting rough around here. Somebody went into our tent a few months ago while we were getting our rations and stole my radios. Good thing I carry my computer and my most important tools with me," he said, gesturing to the small pack on his back, "or I'd be screwed. Can't get new communications rigs these days. Shipments of electronics from Earth have been mighty rare this past year. Peary's not the port it used to be."

Cassidy examined his worried face. The depth of his eyes reminded her of Caden, in the way he exuded solid calmness even as he expressed concern. He did not look quite as old as her father but was more worn down.

"Gangs of a dozen or more have started walking the roads, causing mischief," he continued. "We're not enough."

"There's six of you, five if one stays behind," she observed.

Durham laughed. "Five if you count a cripple and a kid."

"I ain't a kid," Hawk said, emerging from their tent and standing tall. He was gawky, his long bony limbs seeming to have grown faster than his muscles could keep up with.

"Well, not much of one," Hawk's father said. "Not for much longer, anyway. But I'd be no good in a fight." He chuckled and swung a crutch playfully at Hawk's thigh, who deftly avoided it and struck a mock fighter's pose.

"But now we've got a girl to worry about," Sky said, coming up behind them and looking sideways at Cassidy. "We'll draw attention."

Thunder and the two older brothers gathered around.

"I've noticed people look at me a lot," Cassidy said. "I don't like it."

"Not too many young women live at the camp," Durham explained. "It's a small place. And you're new."

Cassidy shifted uncomfortably and looked at Torr, who met her eyes for a moment.

"Torr will more than make up for her," the older brother, Raleigh, said. "He looks like he could whoop your ass, Lady-Sky, and Thunder's too. Two-on-one." He threw a challenging look at Sky, who glared back.

"I didn't say nothin'," Thunder said.

"I didn't mean anything by it, I was just sayin'," Sky said.

"You talk too much," Raleigh drawled.

Roanoke grunted agreement as he took a seat on a crate in front of the table and opened Torr's laptop. Torr had offered to let them play games on his computer, and Cassidy wondered if that was why Roanoke had so readily volunteered for guard duty.

She suddenly felt like a burden as they left Roanoke behind and walked as a group towards Center Ring. Maybe she should have joined Gaia United like Torr and learned how to fight. They crossed the yard to the far canteen trailer and got in line with a collection of scruffy men. The nearest men eyed her up and down. She met some of their glances and checked them out in return. Others she ignored. There were no other females in the line, nor among the groups walking across the yard. She stepped closer to her brother and Raleigh.

"Why don't you find a bigger group to hang out with, if protection is such an issue?" she asked.

Raleigh shrugged. His nose was long and straight, and his eyes inspected hers curiously. "Haven't made that many friends here. Not everybody's nice. Or at least, I don't trust them."

"You trust us," she said.

"I can tell who's trustworthy and who's not."

Torr stepped forward, shielding Cassidy from the curious stares of a group of men passing by. Torr and Raleigh stood shoulder to shoulder and folded their arms. Thunder came up next to Cassidy and assumed the same cross-armed pose. If

Raleigh trusted Thunder and Sky, then she did too, even if Sky seemed a bit bristly. He stood a pace away, stone-faced. She felt no ill will coming from him, only nervousness.

"Why didn't we go to the nearest canteen?" she asked Thunder. They had passed right by the food trailer and cluster of shacks that stood near Spoke Road Six.

"Guards are friendlier here. Sometimes they'll slip you bigger portions."

The canteen stood halfway between the entrances to Spoke Roads Eleven and Twelve. It was an old corrugated metal shipping container that stuck out into the yard with its big side door open. The large door at the far end was also wide open and faced the PCA tents, with two water tanks sitting on a wagon just inside the shadow cast by the metal roof. A man in khaki shirt and shorts stood guard by the water tanks, observing the yard. People passed through the inside to collect their rations. Two khaki-clad men wearing dust masks stood at the side door where Cassidy and Torr entered. The first man was a guard and scanned their irises, waving them through as his scanner beeped. The other man handed each of them a hard brick of bread from an open crate.

"First-timers," the guard called to another worker inside, who handed them each a metal camp dish, metal camp utensils attached by a ring, and an empty, clear plastic, four-liter jug with a plastic carrying strap long enough to sling over a shoulder.

Cassidy stepped in front of a long table, took the cover off the plate and held it out while two men served her a ladleful of rice, beans, and a quarter of a tomato. The portions were child-sized, but she thanked the men. Behind the table stood a large electric stove and two industrial-sized pots with steam escaping from the edges of one of the lids. Several large rice cookers were lined up on the floor beside them. A stack of clear plastic containers held more tomatoes. She could see it might be tempting for people to raid the canteen, but the servers and guards seemed to be confidently in charge, and wore knives, wooden clubs, and radios on their belts.

She looked hungrily down at the steaming food and clamped the lid shut, grateful they were given warm food and fresh vegetables at all. Her father had sold produce bound for the moon colony before the Shaman's Shield had closed that trade route. He could get twice the money from the lunar cargo pilots at Moffett than he could from local grocers. The spaceport had been one of the reasons their parents had sold their little produce market in Mt. Shasta and chosen to move to San Jose. She wondered if the Tegs would resume shipping food to Peary out of Moffett, or if they would forget about the colonists.

They walked through the dim container to the water tanks at the far doorway and took turns filling their jugs. Torr tried to fill his waterskin but was reprimanded by the guard standing outside the door near the water tanks.

"One gallon per day," he said firmly.

"Sorry," Torr said, and hung the empty waterskin from his shoulder.

Cassidy stepped out into the sun. The guard nodded to her with a smile. She returned his smile, and lifted the heavy jug to her lips. The water was sour. She lowered the jug and made a face.

The guard laughed. "Tasty, huh?" Black hair fell in dusty waves over the faded red bandana tied across his forehead.

"What's wrong with it?" She wanted to spit, and told him about the piss tea.

He grinned, his eyes crinkling at the corners. "This isn't piss tea, they just load it with vitamins and minerals. The sour taste is vitamin C. Though if you imagine it's piss, it'll make you drink it slower, which is not a bad thing."

She took another tentative sip. "Where does the water come from? They can't possibly ship in enough water for so many people. How many people are here, anyway?"

"Around ten thousand, I think. Maybe more. The water comes from various sources. All moisture is recycled here." She glanced at the composting toilets that stood nearby. He saw her look and laughed. "Yes, from the toilets, too. But don't worry, the water system is pristine. They also collect moisture from the air." He gestured to the spinning posts that rose above the tentline. "It's like a terrarium in here. Not much place for the moisture to go but back into the system. They also mine ice out of Peary Lake." He pointed southeast. "Down there in Peary Crater. The sun never shines in some spots down there. Plus, people with money import water from Earth, which gets added to the supply eventually. It all works out, I guess."

"What are those things?" she asked, pointing to the little flying saucers the size of party balloons. They had long flanged wings and drifted in the upper reaches of the dome as though on a gentle wind. "And those things outside?" Several small triangular pods clung to the outside of the glass dome, moving slowly across the facets.

"The flying pods are fans to circulate the air, and the ones outside are polishers. My name's Pablo," he said. "What's yours?"

"Cassidy," she said, capping the jug and hanging it from her shoulder so she could shake his dusty hand.

"You new here?" he asked.

"Yeah, just came in from Moffett."

"Moffett? That's open again, huh?"

"Yeah, but the Tegs control it."

Pablo looked at her curiously. "How'd you get out?"

"Lucky, I guess."

"Yeah. I guess we're all lucky."

She said goodbye and joined her neighbors. They waited while Cassidy and Torr stood behind the ration trailer and ate their meal standing up. One minute and a few bites later, the hot food was gone. The tomato was pretty good, all things considered, but she wished there was more of it. She was nowhere near satisfied, and scraped up the few remaining rice grains and bean sauce with her spoon.

Hawk was watching her. "You can lick the dish. It's okay, everybody does it," he said.

She returned his grin and looked hesitantly at her plate.

"Or you can soak it up with your bread," Durham suggested.

"That sounds more polite," she said, and tore a corner off the loaf, cleaning the plate in two bites. Torr did the same. The bread was good and hearty, multi-grain with seeds and nuts added. She ate half of the small loaf before looking up again.

"You might want to save the rest," Durham said.

"There's really only one meal a day?" she asked.

Everyone nodded.

"We usually save some bread for a snack, and the rest for breakfast," Thunder said.

"We have some honey to put on it. We can share," Hawk said, looking at his father, who nodded.

"Can we use your hotplate?" Cassidy asked. "We can heat up some water in the morning. I brought some tea leaves."

"Yeah," they all responded, their excitement slightly depressing. Things were worse here than she had expected.

"Can people cook their own food?" she asked Durham.

"When they can get it," he said, frowning. "We've got the hot plate, and a little rice I've been hoarding for an emergency. But you need water to cook rice."

"Where'd you buy rice?" Torr asked, "At that market by the spaceport? I haven't seen any other food for sale, aside from a crate of plums we stumbled upon earlier."

"Plums?" Raleigh asked. "Where?"

"Spoke Road Nine." Cassidy said. "But they're gone already."

"Buying rice is not easy," Durham said, replying to Torr. "You have to be a Guild Trader to get inside the pen. It costs a Solidi to join the Guild, or you need to be sponsored and serve an apprenticeship. I'm not friends with any Guild members. They kind of keep to themselves. Once in a while we hear about a rice shipment over the radio. If we have enough coins saved and can get to the meeting point in time, sometimes we can score a small sack. Lately, it's always been gone by the time we get there. Shipments are running low, supposedly." His brow was wrinkled in a permanent horizontal crease.

They shuffled past the porta-potties and sauna huts. Sky walked next to her, matching her gait. He glanced at her downcast face. "Welcome to Peary," he said, and gave her a wry grin. He looked more relaxed now, and she could see that he was quite handsome. He wore a tight black t-shirt whose sleeves had been cut off, exposing the sculpted muscles of his tattooed arms. An Eye of Horus stared at her from his left shoulder. Below that, on his upper arm, flew a pyramid with wings, crowned with a glowing orb and flanked by two winged lions standing guard.

"Nice tattoos," she said.

"Thanks." He turned and showed her the tattoo on his right bicep, an ornate cross with a crown of thorns looped over the top, dripping blood. The artwork was meticulously detailed.

"Nice. Did you grow up in Denver?" she asked him.

"No, Vancouver."

"Do you still have family there? If so, you're lucky. I think Vancouver is still inside the Shaman's Shield."

"Only my mother, and she's trapped in there. Those crazy shamans, they'll be the death of us all."

"You think?" she asked, surprised at the distrust and fear in his voice.

"Yeah. Messing with forces they don't understand."

"But she's safe, at least."

"How do I know? I can't communicate with her."

"It's safe inside. I was inside for three years. It's like normal, only cloudy. Well, there's no radio or satellite communications. And you're right, you can't travel beyond the border of the shield."

His mouth curled into a sneer. "I'd rather live under the Tegs."

"She said it's safe." Thunder's low voice interrupted them. "I haven't heard from anybody in my family. They're not inside a protective Shaman's Shield. They're either dead or in a camp." Thunder glared at Sky. Cassidy felt she'd walked into an old argument.

"Where are you from?" she asked Thunder.

"Philly. At least you know where your mom is," he said to Sky. "You should be thankful."

"I trust in God to protect us. Not some evil wizards."

"Your so-called god abandoned us a long time ago," Thunder retorted bitterly.

Sky's face flushed, and Thunder stalked away to walk with Raleigh and Hawk. Sky strode with an upright posture and stared straight ahead, his lips drawn in a thin line.

"I think your mother's probably okay," she said gently, but he didn't respond. She supposed the Shaman's Shield would frighten some people. She wasn't about to tell him she was born in Shasta, or that she knew some of the shamans. Or that her mother and grandmother had been early members of the sect.

She tried to smile, and left his side to join Torr and Durham, pulling the bandana up around her nose and mouth. It seemed to help a little with the dust and made her feel a little more hidden, but it was hot and stuffy. Most people went without.

"Why doesn't the air system filter out the dust?" she asked Durham, needing to repeat herself because the bandana muffled her voice and he could not see her lips.

"It tries to," he said. "They say it used to be a lot worse before they started spraying the roads with soy oil."

She had noticed a couple people holding small tanks and long metal wands and spraying the little plots of ground surrounding their tents. Even so, the dust permeated everything and was already clogging her nose.

The group wandered slowly around the edge of Center Ring, looking over the various wares spread out on tarps and makeshift tables. A man played a flute as he spun and danced next to a hat that sat on the ground with a couple copper bits in it. A young woman wearing a red belly-dancing costume stood on a large ball with her bare feet. On her chin she balanced a long stick with a plate spinning on its tip. The men who stood around were focused on her bare belly, which was slightly pudgy with a deep dimple for a belly button, and her ample breasts spilling over her tight red beaded bra.

Cassidy continued walking, attracted to a pair of blond men, who looked like identical twins, playing a classical guitar duet. She was mesmerized by their flying fingers and the intricate, interweaving melody. Torr stood next to her, transfixed as well, while their companions moved on.

"Can you hear anything?" Torr asked her, his eyes squinting as he listened. The men were clearly accomplished musicians, and certain tones resonated with something similar to the music she heard from the heavens, but it evoked nothing more than echoes of a memory. Nothing she could grab onto and follow. She shook her head sadly, and Torr seemed disappointed.

"I thought you didn't believe in that anymore," she said.

He avoided her gaze sheepishly, and for a moment she recognized the brother she remembered. "What, is your rational construct of the world crumbling?" she teased, pulling her bandana off her chin and letting it hang from her neck.

"What's that supposed to mean?" he asked, his serious eyes meeting hers through the yellow tint of his aviators.

"You know, how you like to think everything fits together so logically, and magic has no place in our reality."

"I never said that."

"You act like it. You look at me like I'm crazy every time I mention anything to do with our crystals, or Great-Aunt Sophie, or the Star Children. I saw how you looked at me on the ship when I was gazing into the crystal ball."

He squared his shoulders. "Did you see anything?"

She shrugged. "No."

"Well, then," he said lightly, and threw her a bratty smile. She punched his arm playfully. "Ow," he laughed, pretending it hurt.

"Shut up," she said, trying not to laugh with him. "I'll see something in it one day, then you'll be scared."

"I'm already scared," he said, his laughter trailing off.

The blond twins finished their piece with a flourish. Cassidy and Torr clapped, and Cassidy tossed a copper bit into an open guitar case. The musicians bowed their thanks, then took up another tune and began singing. It was a space chanty that attracted more onlookers than the beautiful classical piece had. The song was about a ship's captain who found a star goddess who lured him to her lair, where he is trapped still.

Cassidy and Torr caught up with their neighbors, and the small group strolled on. Raleigh checked in with Roanoke on his radio; all was quiet back at the tents. They headed up Spoke Road Three, then made a long tour around Ring Road G. The camp was about the same all over. Grayish-yellow tents. Ration stations. People selling things in front of their tents, or offering services such as haircuts or leather repair. Mostly, people just looked bored.

She tried to fight off a creeping sense of despondency, reminding herself she was lucky to be here. She looked up at the stars, and her eyes were drawn to a prominent point of light she thought must be Jupiter. She wondered if there was a better world out there. They still had four Solidi. That should be enough to buy them passage. But to where? Which planet? No other planet in their solar system was habitable, though there was endless talk of colonizing Mars or one of Jupiter's moons. Delos was where most people seemed to go, because its civilization was closest to Earth's, and it was a peaceful planet. But it was so far away. What if they couldn't afford to come back?

She wanted to return to Earth. Wouldn't the Tegs be overthrown eventually? Earthlanders wouldn't tolerate the Cephean way of life forever. At some point they'd get fed up, and they'd rebel and win. Then she and Torr could go back home, find their parents, and life would return to normal. She and Torr would have to stick it out on the moon until then. They could use their gold to build a small dome on their land. They could import dirt and grow a garden and an orchard. They'd bring in animals and build a pond. They'd find Jasper and build huts to live in.

She sighed, searching the passersby for Jasper. Would she even recognize him? It had been five years. Most men here wore beards. Would she recognize Jasper in a beard? Everyone looked similar. Worn and scruffy. Like they hadn't taken a shower or laundered their clothes in forever.

She trudged along as they made their way back to their tent. Kicking off her shoes, she collapsed onto her sleeping bag and opened her laptop, put in her earphones, and randomly chose a music playlist. The first song immediately brought her back to Beth's house where they had sung and danced to it. She yanked out the earplugs, closed the laptop, and curled up on her side, overcome with sadness.

Faintly audible through the muffled background noise of the dome, strains of star music wormed their way into her awareness and lulled Cassidy to sleep.

———————)————————

Cassidy had experienced jet lag the couple times she'd flown on Earth, but she was not prepared for moon lag. Here she could barely walk. Her legs and eyelids were like cement, yet she could not sleep. She wandered around the camp with Torr and their neighbors in a fog, looking for Jasper and Kai.

The near side of the moon always faced Earth, which hung in the same spot in the inky black sky, waxing like a huge, multi-colored moon. The sun never set at Peary Rim, but circled around the horizon once every twenty-nine days. It was one long, endless day of oblique sunlight, broken only by gongs that rang at midnight and then again six hours later. Everyone set their watches by the gongs and organized their days around them. The gongs marked an arbitrary nighttime during which a curfew was imposed and when most people slept.

Cassidy dragged herself through the long days. It took all her effort to keep her eyes open. She napped whenever they returned to their tents, and then when night gong struck she would find herself staring at the tent ceiling, wide awake. She noticed Torr did the same, and was no more talkative than he'd been on the freighter. He acted almost normal with their new friends, but when she was alone with him in their tent, he would clam up again.

She started reading through her herb notebooks, choking up every time. She had taken living plants for granted, assuming they were inextricably tied to human life and would always be there. Her detailed drawings were so lovely she could hardly bear it. The occasional leaf or bloom she had pressed between the pages fell into her lap as cruel reminders of a world she would never see again. She finally buried the notebooks in the bottom of her pack.

One night alone in her tent, she unfurled her deed and map and studied the Anaximenes craters and the lay of their land. She tried to determine the scale and how far Peary was to their property. She really had no idea. The moonscape she had seen on their ride from Gandoop to Peary was vast and riddled with craters of all sizes. Hers could be any of them. If they could find Kai, she would ask him to take them out for a look. And if they did not find Kai, they would find another way to get out there.

She and Torr spent most of their waking hours with their neighbors, walking the twelve concentric ring roads of the camp and up and down the twelve spoke roads, searching for Jasper and Kai. They stopped at the spaceport every day, begging their way past the customs guards and inspecting the faces of the pilots who climbed in and out of various vessels, until eventually a security guard would usher them out. Cassidy soon became familiar with the camp's layout, but they did not find Jasper or his father.

Torr liked to spend his evenings talking with Durham, who was teaching him how to repair radios. Mornings, they scoured the secondhand tent markets for old equipment.

Hawk followed Cassidy like a puppy hungry for attention. Roanoke blushed anytime she talked to him. Raleigh liked to explain the workings of the camp to her but then would become flustered and find an excuse to leave at seemingly random moments.

Sky quickly got over his concern about having a woman as part of their group and turned out to have a sharp wit. She found herself talking and laughing with him and Thunder in their tent evenings, while Torr and the Boyers soldered radio parts outside their tent. Eventually, the boys would find their way to Sky and Thunder's tent and they would all play cards until well past night gong.

⸺⸺⸺⸺)⸺⸺⸺

Morning gong had rung already, but Cassidy stayed curled up in her sleeping bag.

"I'm not going out today," she told Torr. She listened as he got out of bed and got dressed.

"We have to keep searching for Jasper," he said. "He's not going to come find us; he doesn't know we're here."

"If he's even here," she mumbled.

"Come on, Cass," he said. "Don't give up."

"I hate it here."

"I know, me too." He paused. "We have to keep each other strong. This is hard, Cass, leaving Earth and being in this place. It's the hardest thing I've ever done. Well. Almost."

"What else is harder?" she asked, yawning loudly and dragging herself from her sleeping bag. "Leaving Mom and Dad?"

He pulled on his boots and did not respond.

"Fighting at the front lines?" she asked.

He straightened up and pushed open the door flaps.

"Did you have to fight?" she asked.

"Yeah," he grunted, and left the tent.

She watched his heels kick up dust as the tent flap fell behind him. She heard his boots crunch across the ground, and the low voices of him and Durham greeting each other.

She got dressed, grabbed her laptop, and joined Torr and the others in front of the Boyers' tent. Torr avoided her eyes, and she left him alone.

Sky drew guard duty. They left him sitting in front of the Boyers' tent at their table, putting in his earbuds and opening Cassidy's laptop. The rest of them headed out for their morning walk.

She lagged behind with Hawk, who chattered cheerfully about the flying pods and how he imagined they were little creatures. He had named them all and pointed out their unique markings that allowed him to tell them apart.

Cassidy listened with amusement as she examined the men they passed, looking for Jasper's auburn hair, though with all the dust it probably wouldn't appear red anymore. All the dome inhabitants looked the same. Gray and dusty. Worn and hungry. Men, women, they all blended together.

The only thing that got her excited were the greenhouses. They stopped there every day. Sometimes more than once. When they came upon them this time, she went straight to the second house back from the road, which was bursting with green. She found a spot in the steaming glass that was clear enough to see through, and pressed her nose to the warm glass. It was like a jungle, and she wished she could go inside. She even heard faint birdsong from within, which made her heart ache even more.

Masses of climbing vines filled every spare inch, with little purple flowers everywhere. Droplets of moisture dotted fuzzy stems and leaves. She walked to the next greenhouse. Stacked racks of identical seedlings filled the space from floor to ceiling. The dome's main crop was soy, with four large greenhouses dedicated to it. A fifth greenhouse grew a variety of vegetables. She went to that one and gazed inside, recognizing kale, Swiss chard, spinach, peppers, onions, carrots, beets, and tomatoes.

Her stomach growled. She wished she could go inside and pick handfuls of ripe cherry tomatoes that hung heavily on the vines. They were ready to be harvested. As large as the greenhouses were, there were not nearly enough vegetables to feed the entire camp. Plants did not grow that fast.

If she were in charge, she would fill every inch of open space in the dome with vertical gardens. If she could get glass somewhere she could build her own mini-greenhouse. But she would need a lot of water for that.

The men were waiting for her on the road, so she pulled herself away and trudged through the dust. The gray, ugly dust that covered this entire cursed rock they rode on. It filled her nose and eyes with gunk, even her ears, and made gross globs of phlegm in her lungs. Why had she ever wanted to come here? How had they let the Cephs steal their green, living planet? She curled her fists and glared at Torr, who looked in a worse mood than she was.

They took a spoke road and passed the ration station at the G ring intersection. People walked slowly out of the trailer, regarding the contents of their metal dishes: a cup of rice, a few small chunks of tofu, and some unidentifiable green and purple things.

They decided to wait and get their food at the southern Center Ring canteen as usual.

A commotion broke out ahead of them. Two men wrenched metal camp dishes from the hands of two startled men and ran off down the road, the victims yelling and chasing them. Torr took off at a run after them. Two ration guards and the Boyer brothers raced to catch up, turning a corner out of view. Cassidy stood with Durham and Thunder as other people gathered in concern.

A food server came outside and peered up and down the road. He shrugged helplessly. "What are we supposed to do?

People should travel in groups. It's been happening more and more lately." The server got on his radio and went back into the trailer. Cassidy could hear him reporting the theft.

A few minutes later her brother, the Boyer boys, and the two guards returned.

"They disappeared," Raleigh said, as the guards went inside to confer with their co-workers.

"They said there's not much law enforcement around here," Torr said.

"Nope," Thunder agreed.

"They guard the food, that's about it," Raleigh said.

"Yep," Durham said. "It's pretty much every man for himself unless something big happens, then the leader of the camp, Ramzy, gets involved. I've only heard about that happening twice, over murder."

Cassidy traded glances with Torr. "The server reported the theft," she said. "But nobody's come."

"That's crazy," Torr muttered.

Cassidy warily regarded a group of men passing by. She walked between Torr and Raleigh as they crossed Ring Road G and continued down the dusty spoke road.

———————)———————

They had been on the moon for a week, and Cassidy was finally getting over her moon lag. She had even started sleeping soundly during curfew, but it didn't cheer her up any. She had gone to bed early that night and was awoken by night gong. She listened from her sleeping bag to the sound of the card game in Sky and Thunder's tent. Cards were being shuffled, and she heard the muffled voices of Torr, Raleigh, and Roanoke as they argued over the rules of a game no one could remember exactly. She dozed off and was awoken again by Torr as he crept into the tent, stripped down to his shorts, and lay on his blankets, staring up at the ceiling. The camp was quiet, and Cassidy let her eyes close.

"Jasper's not here," Torr said, breaking the silence.

The declaration jerked her out of her half-sleep. She rose onto an elbow and looked at him. "I think he is," she said. "We just haven't found him yet."

"What if he's not?" Torr asked. "What if he and Kai left a long time ago, and we're wasting our time looking for them?"

Cassidy rolled onto her back and stared up at the faded yellow canvas.

"We have to move on with our lives," Torr said. "There's nothing for us here. We should leave."

She didn't want to admit that. Besides, where was there to move on to? Then again, why should they stay here? She remembered her father calling Peary Dome a refugee camp, and now she saw the truth of it. More like a large lifeboat floating in a vast, black sea, launched from a sinking ship.

She sighed and turned her head to look at him.

He glanced at her, his eyes haunted.

"We just got here," she said. "Though it feels like an eternity."

"I guess it's only been a week," he said. "Feels like forever."

Time had passed like a murky dream. A nightmare of walking endless circles in a labyrinth of dusty tents.

"We have to be strong," she said. "Remember? Yesterday you were telling me not to give up."

"Well, eventually we'll have to leave. Might as well start planning now."

"We'll find him," she said.

"If we don't, we should go to Muria and find Doctor Ramesh," he said.

"Muria? I heard that planet is wild. What makes you think Ramesh is still there? How do we know he actually went there?

Why not Delos? What about Mom and Dad?" she asked, sitting up.

"What about them?"

She had no response to that cold statement. She wanted to help her parents. To save them. But that was ridiculous. She and Torr had escaped, and her parents had not. No, she corrected herself, her parents *would* escape. To Shasta. They would be fine.

She felt tears rise to her eyes, and before she could stop them they spilled onto her cheeks.

Torr glanced at her then turned away, rolling onto his side to face the tent wall.

"What about our land?" she asked, wiping away her tears. "We're going to leave here before even seeing it?" He was silent. She spoke to his back. "We'll go to the spaceport tomorrow and hire someone to take us by our craters."

He answered, still facing the wall, "We need to save our gold for passage to Muria. Besides, we can't do anything with the land." He turned over onto his elbow and looked at her. "I talked with Durham. He agreed it would take millions of global credits to establish a settlement. Way more than we have. Most mines were developed by groups of wealthy investors from Earth."

They held each other's eyes. They were no closer to settling their land living here than they had been living on Earth.

"Maybe we can sell one parcel and get enough money to build a small dome on the other," she said.

"Maybe," he said doubtfully. "Sell it to who? Get the dome from where? Tegs control everything on Earth. It's not like you can just order a lunar dome from a catalog. I researched this before. It's a lot more complicated than you think. There's no atmosphere, for starters."

"I didn't say it was going to be easy. And what about Mom and Dad?" she asked. "Don't you want to save them?"

"Of course I do. But how can we? We can't develop our land. We can't do anything to help them from here. Look at this place, everyone is half starving."

"Regardless, I want to see our land," she said.

"Maybe if we find Ramesh, he can think of something."

"We haven't seen him since we were kids," she said. "Why do you think he would help us?"

"Grandma Leann said he would."

"She did? That was a long time ago," she said. "We don't know anything about Muria, except that it's really far away. How would we find him once we got there?"

He exhaled and flopped onto his back.

She looked at him. His taut muscles. His clenched jaws. She lay down and closed her eyes, shutting him out.

22

BROTHERS

Torr did want to see their land, but what good would it do? It would just taunt him with another impossible situation. Give him hope for a brief time until reality punched him in the gut again.

The tent was claustrophobic, and he kicked his blanket away. Beyond the tent was the glass dome, trapping them in its delicately balanced environment. They were all prisoners of desire, guilty of wanting to survive. Maybe if he gave up all hope it wouldn't hurt so much. But his sister was here, with that smoldering fire in her eyes that reminded him of his mother and grandmother. He couldn't give up. He had promised his father.

If they stayed on the moon they would have to live in this wretched camp, staring at an Earth they could never return to. His fantasies of returning with a fighting force were just that, childish fantasies of a helpless, beaten man. Tegea had won, and Torr had fled. He had left his parents behind; he had left his friends behind. All that was left was to save himself and his sister, and find some sort of life out in the galaxy.

He tossed and turned. Ramesh had gone to Muria. Why? What was there? His mother thought he and Cassidy were the Star Children. What did that mean? If the Star People were real, they could save Earth from the Tegs. Right?

He glanced across the tent at the still form of his sister huddled in her sleeping bag. When he was little, he had thought they were identical twins and that he looked just like her. He had always thought that when he looked at her it was like looking at himself. It had always made him happy. But now it hurt to look at her. It was as though he were looking into a mirror and seeing what he used to be. What he would never be again.

——————————)——————————

Torr lay on the shooting platform, looking through his scope at the overturned vehicle on the hillside in the wispy remnants of the Shaman's Shield. *Breathe in, breathe out.* A door opened and Edgemont swung out onto his feet and trained his Lectro at Torr's bunker.

Squeeze. The Dashiel recoiled on Torr's shoulder and spit out the shell casing as the bullet pierced Edgemont's forehead, dropping him to the ground.

A form emerged from the other side of the vehicle and Torr followed the man with his scope as the Teg glanced over his shoulder and ran for the hills. *Matthew.* Torr held his breath and watched him run. *Let him go,* he told himself. He brought his attention back to the vehicle, waiting to see if any other soldiers emerged.

A head poked out, then shoulders. The soldier crawled to his feet and peered at the bunker. *Johnson.* Torr's heart pounded.

"Come on!" Torr called to him, waving frantically at his squadmate to run to the safety of the bunker. "I've got you covered!" he yelled.

Johnson pulled a Lectro from his belt and slowly raised it, pointing it at the bunker.

"What are you doing?!" Torr yelled as Johnson pulled the trigger. With a thunk, Bobby collapsed beside Torr on the shooting platform.

"Do it!" Edgemont yelled, sitting up and urging Johnson on, blood trickling down the side of his nose.

Torr's heart hammered as he aimed at Johnson's head, locked onto the center of his forehead, and squeezed the trigger. Johnson fell to the ground as Smiley, Jessimar, Bates, and Rashon crawled from the vehicle and pointed Lectros at the bunker.

"Take aim!" Edgemont commanded.

"No!" Torr called, anguish ripping through him as he put his sights on Jessimar. Torr thought there was no way Jessimar would kill one of them, but the grim determination on his friend's face said differently. *She told me to do whatever I need to do to stay alive.*

Torr watched in horror as Jessimar grimaced and pulled the trigger. Mike fell against the rampart wall and slid to the floor. Torr gritted his teeth and took Jessimar out, then Rashon, pain lancing through his heart as each of his friends fell to his bullets.

He could hear Edgemont laughing. "Good shooting, Torr! You passed the test! You can be a Teg now."

Torr ignored Edgemont's taunts and held Smiley in his sights. Funny, tortured Smiley. Torr let it happen. Smiley pulled the Lectro's trigger, releasing a snake jaw, and Donald crumpled to the cement floor.

Torr became aware of Reina at his side firing her TAFT, the gun jerking in slow motion, silence ringing through Torr's ears. Bates was the last one. Gentle Bates. Bates aimed at them and shot just as Torr pulled his trigger. Reina and Bates fell together in one graceful motion, Bates folding on top of Jessimar, and

Reina relaxing with a little gasp onto the platform. She stared at Torr, her mouth open.

"Torr."

An insistent tugging at his arm made him look up. Cassidy was staring down at him.

"Torr," she repeated.

The bunker and hillside slowly faded away. He rose shakily to a seated position and looked around the dusty tent, disoriented. "It was a dream?" he asked, relief washing over him.

"You were yelling," Cassidy said.

He threw off his blanket and staggered to his feet, and then stumbled outside into the quiet of night curfew. The tent city was motionless under the glass dome. Earth shone in the black sky, hiding his squadmates on her shimmering surface, smoothing away the dream. The planet was waxing towards full and showed the brown and green landmasses of Asia and Australia surrounded by cobalt-blue oceans. The nightmare clung to him as he tried to sort out reality from the dream. Half of his squad had turned Teg. He had abandoned his friends. He would kill his brothers if he had to. He was no better than a Teg.

"Torr." It was Cassidy again, standing in the tent doorway.

He turned to her, annoyed at being disturbed. Hurt flashed in her eyes as she felt his rebuff. She stiffened and went back inside the tent. He couldn't help it. She didn't know what a horrible person her brother had become.

He turned back towards Earth, sure Edgemont was laughing at him.

23

———————)———————

PİNE FLOWER

Cassidy awoke to Torr's groans. He was dreaming again.
"No," he moaned, and continued to mutter incoherently. She lay still, trying to understand his words. He turned onto his side, still sleeping. His mouth hung open and he folded his hands under his cheek, his eyes jittering behind closed lids. She shut her eyes and fell back to sleep.

Morning gong rolled through the tent. Cassidy listened as Torr climbed to his feet and dressed.

"I'm going for a run," he said gruffly.

She opened her eyes. "Where?"

"A couple laps around the perimeter road," he said, and ducked out through the canvas flaps. She listened to his footsteps as he ran off.

Two laps would be ten miles. During one of his rare talkative moments, he'd told her he'd run five to ten miles almost every day at Miramar. It was a good sign that he wanted to run again. Probably his body missed it. She hoped it would lift his spirits.

Cassidy gazed idly at the dull canvas wall. She was trying to keep her own spirits up, but it was difficult. Maybe they should have stayed with their parents and tried to get to Shasta. At least they'd still be on Earth. Together. At least they'd still have fresh water. Plants and animals. Wind, rain, and the darkness of night.

It had all been her stupid idea. She thought back on the unrelated things she'd strung together into an irrational storyline that was quickly proving to be complete fantasy. The deeds. The prophecy of the old book. Their ancient and useless DNA. The dream of finding Jasper. Now she was stuck here, and so was Torr. No wonder he was hardly talking to her. He was probably furious at her, and at himself for going along with her idiotic plan. She sucked in her breath and got up.

Their new home was worse than a prison cell: an eight-by-twelve rectangle of canvas, coated in dust. She peeled off her pink butterfly t-shirt that she'd worn to bed and changed into the olive-green one, then slowly pulled on her camo pants of mottled black, white, and gray. Dull and faded like everything else in this star-forsaken place. She worked the brush through her matted hair and looked into Grandma Leann's mirror at her grimy face. She looked horrible. Her skin was dry and lined with dust, and her lips were cracked and peeling. She picked dust crust from the corners of her eyes and blew her nose into a washcloth to clear her sinuses, wondering if her body would ever get used to the dry, gritty environment.

Her parents' young faces smiled up at her from the photo propped up against the canvas wall. She could not bear looking at their happy faces any longer and guiltily slid the framed picture into her pack next to the herb notebooks, pulling out the red one.

She slowly leafed through the pages. Her mother's handwriting appeared to be indecipherable squiggles, like always when there was nothing for the mysterious book to tell her. She started at the beginning again and turned the pages slowly, scanning the scrawl for something she could read. When she found nothing, she took out her own black notebook that she had been using to record her plant spirit readings.

"Okay," she said out loud, "find me something to give me hope." She opened to the first page, but her own handwriting was illegible. She examined one page after another.

On the last written page, the writing resolved into her flowing script. *Sweet Alyssum.* Cassidy smiled. She had forgotten all about that old bone spinner woman. She read the prescription. *Take two drops and the eye of the moon will awaken within you. Seek its wisdom, for it illumines the path of spirit. See through the eyes of your blood-kin as the threads of life weave your destiny.*

Shivers ran up her spine. That reading had been a lifetime ago. She examined the words and remembered when she'd taken the herb back home. Her visions of Torr's whereabouts had been accurate. She had seen through his eyes.

Those visions had made Cassidy wait for him. That must mean they were supposed to be here. Her pulse quickened. She had accessed her power. Her second sight. Her ability to see things happening from far away.

Excitement thrilled her blood. Was it permanent? Had she torn a hole in the shield that her grandmother had placed over her? Or, would she have to rely on Sweet Alyssum to see? She closed her eyes and concentrated on finding Torr. Her mind wandered, but no visions came. She sensed that he was somewhere out there, but nothing more. Disappointed, the old anger at her grandmother flared up. Grandma Leann had insisted it would be safer for her to use tools rather than access her power directly. "Safe," she grumbled. "Forever crippled, more like."

She angrily searched for the bottle of Sweet Alyssum and placed two drops on her tongue, feeling the bitter herb absorb into her as she swallowed. A small shudder shook her body, and the scent of flowers touched her for a moment before fading away. She closed her eyes and forced herself to relax.

After a time she searched for Torr with her senses, reaching out, feeling for him. She could see the perimeter road pass by. Tents to the left, infrastructure buildings to the right. She could feel his heartbeat, pounding in a steady rhythm as his feet struck the ground. He held a deep anguish inside. A ball of tension about to explode in his belly. She sucked in her breath, taken aback by the intensity of it. She had only been aware of the surface of his agony. Underneath, the pressure was like a volcano ready to erupt. This was more than seeing through his eyes. She could feel him.

She had always been able to vaguely sense her brother, like a feather tickling her hair, which she had attributed to their being twins. But this was a direct connection, an unmistakable knowing, as though she had jumped into his body. It made her recoil from the intimacy of it. She pulled away from the uncanny perception, breaking the bond, and hoped he had not felt her.

She glanced at the bottle of Sweet Alyssum, wondering at its power. It was too much for her. She had crossed a boundary she was uncomfortable crossing, but it was too late to undo the sensing. Torr was in agony.

She reached for the red book and flipped anxiously through the pages. She did not know what was causing his suffering, but she knew it was intolerable. Her mother's script slithered like snakes across a page, then slowly formed words. *Pine Flower*

– Administer two drops to soothe the pain and sorrow of one who has taken the life of another.

Cassidy froze, staring at the page. That couldn't be right. He had said the Gaia United forces had surrendered. She read it again, her heart growing heavy. He had admitted he'd had to fight. He was a sharpshooter. His job as a soldier was to kill people. *Oh, Torr.*

She searched in the green daypack for a bottle of Pine Flower, praying that she had some. She found two bottles. She silently thanked her mother and tucked one into her vest pocket, then stood outside the tent, pacing nervously as she waited for his return.

An anxious hour passed before he finally came walking down the road, drenched in sweat and coated with dust, his face sagging like an old man's. "Torr," she said, but he brushed past her into the tent. She followed, but he acted like she was not there. She wondered if he had been conscious of her invasion of his privacy, but she was too ashamed to ask. He peeled off his soaked t-shirt and wiped down his face and chest with it, then guzzled the remainder of his water. Wiping his brow, he met her eyes. It was as though he were only half there. One eye looked out at her, while the other seemed to stare inward.

"Torr, I have an herb for you," she said, holding out the bottle of Pine Flower.

"Later," he said coldly, and turned away, dropping to the bare canvas patch of floor between their bedding, and faced the ground on his hands and knees. He straightened his legs and dropped into a pushup. She watched as his body rose and fell, his arms pumping. She closed her mouth and slid the bottle into her pocket, counting to herself as he did ten pushups. Twenty. Fifty. His arms bulged and his breath blew out with each pushup. At eighty he started grunting with each one, his pace slowing. Still he continued. At one hundred he stopped and knelt for a moment before straightening again. He moved his arms to a different position, with his elbows in close to his body, and began again. One, two, ten, twenty. Each pushup was now accompanied by an angry huff. At seventy the huffs became groans. Cassidy felt her own muscles burning, and finally turned and left the tent, unable to watch him tear himself to pieces.

She stood in the middle of the road. Earth was nearly full, a huge, glistening, blue sphere. Eurasia was a patchwork of browns and greens, dotted with puffs of white clouds. It was cruel the way Earth looked so fertile and alive, while they were stranded out here on this dead rock.

Torr's grunts were angry now, nearly yells. She met the eyes of Durham, who was sitting on a rolled up canvas tarp at the low table in front of his tent, one leg bent under him and the other an empty pant leg. A small radio lay in pieces on the table, a soldering iron in his hand. Durham returned her gaze calmly, as though listening to the agony of a man was normal. Through the gap of the tent flaps she could see Torr doing sit-ups. The painful groans of self-torture continued.

Finally, the moans ended with merciful silence. She gave him a few minutes, then timidly crept through the doorway. She'd expected him to be lying down, but he was standing, staring at nothing, his skin red from exertion.

"Here," she said, thrusting the bottle at him. "Take this. It will help ease the ... pain."

Both his eyes drilled into her. "I don't want to ease the pain."

Torr's anger was directed at her now, and it was harsh and bitter. Cassidy had half a mind to stalk away and leave him to his misery. But she stood her ground. Her mother had taught her that to be a healer she had to witness another's pain.

"Killing *yourself* isn't going to help anything," she said.

"It might." He glared at her, daring her to press him.

He and Cassidy had grown up with their mother pushing her plant medicine on them. As a child, Torr had started pushing back. Demanding to know what the herbs did before taking any, insisting on reading the book himself. Their mother said most people could not find meaning in the book, but those who did had their own plant spirit medicine. Those who found a prescription in its pages always took the herb. It had always proven so.

Cassidy got the red book and shoved it at his bare chest. "Look for yourself," she said, steeling herself to confront the fury that rippled off him.

He pressed his lips together, then grabbed the book and flipped quickly through it. He was nearly at its end when his fingers stopped and his eyes focused on a page. The blood slowly drained from his face, and she held her breath as his eyes became shiny with tears. She did not know what the plant medicine was telling him—it told everyone something different—but it had hit the mark.

"Pine Flower," he said stiffly.

"I know," she said, holding out the bottle. "Here."

He avoided her eyes as he handed her the book and plucked the bottle from her fingertips.

"Leave me alone," he said, and turned away.

She crept from the tent and heard him tie the door flaps closed. The sides of the tent shook as he shut the little window flaps. She would leave him alone, that was for certain. She had done what she could and wasn't going to suffer his anger any longer.

She stared at Earth, wishing her father were here. He was the only one who knew how to comfort Torr. Cassidy took a deep breath. The voices of the three Boyer brothers came from Sky and Thunder's tent. The snapping of cards being shuffled mingled with laughter. She went to join them, and as she passed alongside her tent, the faint sound of Torr's sobs followed her.

24

---)---

BERKELEY

As noon approached, Cassidy stood in front of her tent and gazed at the gravity bar soaring above the tent city. She was glad for it. She didn't know how they would manage if every step were a floating leap.

Torr was sitting on a square tarp outside the Boyers' tent with Durham and the brothers, sorting through scavenged radio parts. He looked up. "Durham's going to make us each a radio. After they finish three orders ahead of ours."

"Wow, that's great," Cassidy said.

"Could be a while," Durham warned. "Transistors are in short supply."

"That's okay," Torr said.

Hawk caught her eye and stood up, wiping his hands on his pant legs. He walked over and smiled up at her. "You can borrow my radio."

"No, Hawk," she said.

Disappointment shaded the youngster's eyes at her refusal.

"No," Torr echoed. "We can wait."

"Thank you, though, Kitty Hawk." she said. "That's very

kind of you." She tousled his hair, making him turn red. "Want to help me with a puzzle?" she asked.

"Yeah. I'm good at puzzles." His brown eyes brightened.

She led him into her tent and took out the blue book with the gold runes, and the thick folder of papers Great-Aunt Sophie had collected on her trips. The folder contained a variety of documents: dozens of loose pages, small slips of ragged parchment with tiny text and tight scribbles, and a thin notebook where her mother had started a dictionary of the symbols she had deciphered. The scraps of paper were the keys to the puzzle. Bits of Ilian had been translated into Delosian. Other papers had Delosian texts translated into Globalish. All they had to do was find three-way matches, which was not easy given that the handwritten Ilian and Delosian symbols were cryptic at best, distinguished by very subtle markings that were badly faded.

Cassidy turned to a random page of verse in the blue book. Five symbols of the long stanza had already been translated by her mother. They made no sense as disconnected words, but the theme was far from cheerful. The words were *dark, wrong, death, chains,* and *despair.* Cassidy shivered and started to look for a different page to work on, but Hawk took the book from her hand and squinted at the hieroglyphics.

"What is this?" he asked.

"Another language. Ancient Ilian. Here," she said, spreading out the loose pages. "We need to find symbols that match." She tried to show him how to tell Delosian from Ilian, though half the time they looked the same to her. No wonder it had taken her mother years to translate as much as she had.

Hawk nodded and studied the verse, then started examining the papers. She did the same. They worked silently for a time, then Hawk's face lit up. "I found one," he said excitedly.

"Let me see." Sure enough, he had found a match. The symbol translated to *emptiness.* She shuddered. "This is depressing," she said.

Hawk laughed. "It's fun." He dove into the papers again while Cassidy wrote the translation in the blue book and the dictionary notebook.

They worked quietly. It calmed her. The morning moved along, sounds of a guitar drifting through the open doorway. The clatter of a transport rolled by, and laughter floated over the tents from out in the dense tent city. The beating of a drum bounced across the dome, its repetitive rhythm blending into the background noise. Cassidy rubbed her nose. The air was dry and dusty and smelled of a desert baking in the sun.

Torr's head poked in through the doorway. "Ready to get our rations?" he asked.

She was. Her stomach ached from hunger, but she'd been trying to ignore it. She needed to get accustomed to eating less. She had no choice, anyway, since the food she and Torr had brought from Earth was almost gone. They had been sneaking small morsels when they were alone in their tent, feeling guilty that they weren't sharing with their neighbors.

She put away the books and papers, and they went to join the others.

The line at the canteen was long. She wondered how they would survive on such meager rations. Everyone else seemed to be surviving. People were thin in general, but not completely emaciated.

"I wish we could find more plums," she muttered. Her stomach rumbled.

"We got a can of sardines a few weeks ago from some guy, but we couldn't find him again," Thunder said.

"And those oranges a few months ago," Sky said. "But it took all the money we had."

"We could cook our rice for you," Hawk offered. "If you're extra hungry."

Durham met her eyes, and she smiled gently. "You raised a good boy."

"Yes," he agreed. "We're gonna save that rice, bud," he told his son.

"How does everyone make money to buy extra food?" Torr asked.

"People do what they can, but it's tough," Thunder said. "We used to sell minerals, but nobody's buying rocks these days. Traders Guild or black market's the only way to make real money on the moon. I heard you can get black market goods at some of the mines."

"Really?" Torr asked.

"Oh, yes," a man behind them said.

They all turned. Cassidy hadn't noticed the man standing there. He was a tall, slender man in his forties with big round brown eyes, finely chiseled features, dark brown skin, and long, dusty dreadlocks pulled into a fat ponytail. He had the strangest beard Cassidy had ever seen. It was long and fuzzy and forked down the middle, ending in two points that jutted down past his collarbone like some sort of crazy upside-down topiary bush.

She stared at the man. His big brown eyes stared back at her in anxious surprise, though she quickly realized that was just how his eyes were. Bulging, like a raccoon caught with its paws in the goldfish pond.

"All kinds of black market goods go through the mines," he said, his beard bobbing as he spoke. "Anything you could want from Earth, or even other planets."

"Don't any black market goods come through the camp?" Torr asked.

"They get smuggled in sometimes. But there's not much of a market here; most people can't afford that kind of stuff. Look around you." The man gestured to the men in line and loitering in the yard. "Almost no real money passes through this camp. It's all barter. Anyone with gold finds a Guild member and gets whatever they want to order. Most of the real trading is done at the spaceport, and the good stuff gets shipped off to the planets." His full brown lips puckered knowingly. "That's how it's done. Name's Berkeley," he said, flashing white teeth at Cassidy.

"I'm Cassidy, and this is my brother, Torr." Torr and Berkeley exchanged glances with a brief nod. "Do you know any Guild members?" Cassidy asked him.

Berkeley's round eyes narrowed. "I might. What's it worth to you?" He gave her a shrewd look.

She held her tongue and moved along as the line shifted forward. "Do you know Jasper or Kai Manann?" she asked. She described Jasper's skinny frame and short red hair and told him Kai was a pilot and was tall and stern.

Berkeley thought for a moment and shook his head. "Don't think so." Berkeley wore khaki cargo shorts and dusty boots, a faded red t-shirt, and a khaki cargo vest with colorful patches sewn onto the pockets and chest panels.

Cassidy examined the patches and stopped breathing for a moment. "Hey," she said indignantly. A patch on his pocket depicted the faceted gem of Peary Dome and was neatly embroidered with the lettering, Peary Dome Traders Guild. "You are a Guild member," she said, pointing her finger at him accusingly.

"Maybe I am, and maybe I'm not," he retorted, gesturing at his collection of patches, which depicted various Peary Dome organizations: Peary Pilots, Peary Dome Air Control, Peary

Dome Water Control, Peary Spaceport Security, Peary Space Control, Peary Greenhouse, Peary Maintenance. "Do you think I belong to all of these?" he asked. "Maybe I just collect patches." He smiled again, and Cassidy answered his smile with a frown.

"Well, can you get us some food?" she asked.

He shook his head. "No, I can't. Sorry." She didn't believe him. If there weren't so many people around, she would tempt him with her gold.

"How do you know about the mines?" Torr asked him.

"Worked at a bunch of 'em," Berkeley said, licking his fuzzy moustache. "Only the big ones. Won't risk working the outer rim mines. Might not get out alive. Hard enough getting out of Gandoop."

Cassidy's eyes flicked to her brother's. She and Torr had barely gotten out of there themselves.

The line moved forward and she entered the canteen, looked into the iris scanner, and picked up her small brick of bread. She moved to the serving table and held out her plate for the day's ration of one peeled hard-boiled egg, a pickled red beet, and three limp, raw green beans. There was no hot food or even rice today, but at least eggs were protein. After filling her jug she stepped out into the yard, nodded at the guard, Pablo, who responded with a wide smile, and waited for Torr and the others to leave the trailer.

A faint tinkling of bells drew her attention. Two squat, oddly proportioned men strode purposefully across the dirt on thick, powerful legs. They did not look like Earthlanders, and Cassidy found herself staring. They were as broad as a husky six-foot-tall man crunched down into a five-foot frame. Wide hips and wider shoulders were clothed in dusty desert gear and leather vests. Covering their thick forearms were leather armguards, dusty and well-worn. Their pants were tucked into knee-high brown leather boots, which had long leather fringes strung with tiny bells that jangled and flashed in the light as they walked. Leather vests and heavy leather belts were laden with various pouches and knives. Each man had a short stone club hanging at his hip: one was a dark gray stone with glints of white and a spiral pattern carved into it; the other was a reddish stone, smooth and polished.

She caught Berkeley's eyes as he left the canteen with Torr.

"Scrids," he said. "From the planet Scridland in the Orion system. They built the gravity bar." He gestured to the tall white column that jutted up from the PCA compound. "Some workers who erected it never left, and brought more of their kind here. They think they own the place."

Cassidy glanced at the pillar, then back at the strange men who were headed their way. She noticed they did have a bit of a swagger, resting broad hairy hands on the hilts of their long knives as though they were swords. Their hair was dark red streaked with gold. One wore a thick, messy ponytail, and the other's hair was loose and tangled with curls. They each had full beards and wide foreheads, and deep-set amber eyes that were nearly hidden behind hairy, drooping eyebrows. They were human, but not like any she'd ever seen.

Cassidy expected them to go to the back of the ration line, but the one with the ponytail walked straight at Torr, locking onto his eyes with wide amber ones. The Scrid did not stop walking but thrust his leather-clad chest at Torr, as if to chest-butt him.

Cassidy gasped, and Torr hopped backwards and drew his combat knife, dropping his water jug and crouching and sneering at the man who continued towards him. Water chugged from the jug into the dry dust, and Pablo sprang forward to rescue it. The scene unfolded in the span of a breath. Torr had the choice to either run, knife the man, or meet him chest to chest. He pushed his chest out as the solid, burly man hopped into the air and threw his weight against Torr. Torr staggered backwards, barely keeping his footing, as the man landed on his feet and the other man stepped forward. Torr's legs widened in a solid stance, his eyes flashing as his chest met that of the second Scrid.

"Whoa, wait a second," Berkeley said loudly, and pushed himself between Torr and the two hairy Scrids. Pablo shoved the water jug at Cassidy and helped Berkeley push the Scrids back as Raleigh, Thunder, and Sky rushed to Torr's side, glowering at the strange men.

"Jorimar, Helug, back off," Berkeley said in a commanding tone.

"Step away," Pablo ordered. Another ration guard appeared from the food trailer and stood threateningly at Pablo's side.

Cassidy and the others watched the Scrids warily as they spoke to Berkeley in a guttural glut of spits and stops, saliva flying from their mouths through bushy moustaches, their hands waving frantically at Torr. The Scrids' eyes turned to Cassidy and she cowered behind Durham as Torr and the others formed a defensive line between her and the strange men who pushed towards her. The Scrids looked strong as oxen, with heavy builds just like the lumbering beasts. Berkeley shoved his hands against the chest of one, but the Scrid did not budge, nor did he attack. The stench of dried sweat reached Cassidy's nose.

"What do they want?" Cassidy asked as a crowd gathered and someone handed her the cap to Torr's jug.

Berkeley yelled haltingly at the Scrids in their language. They backed away, red-faced, and did not follow as Cassidy, Torr, and their friends quickly strode across Center Ring.

Torr grabbed his water jug from her as they walked. "Algol's hell," he said at the jug, which had lost a third of its contents.

As they neared the edge of the yard, footsteps pounded up behind them. It was Berkeley, his nostrils flaring and eyes bulging. The Scrids had not followed him. He went with them as the group hurried onto Spoke Road Six, led by Durham, who swung swiftly on his crutches. They turned onto Ring Road C and stopped in front of their tents, eyes darting about to see if they'd been followed. Roanoke stood to meet them, and Raleigh and Hawk quickly told him what had happened. The Scrids did not appear, and Cassidy turned to Berkeley, who was inspecting her and Torr.

"What in Perseus's name was that all about?" Torr asked Berkeley, his face flushed.

"Crystals," Berkeley said. "They said you both are carrying crystals."

Cassidy's blood ran cold. "How do they know that?"

"They can feel them." He turned to Torr. "They said you're carrying a large one in your vest pocket. Can I see it?"

Cassidy tried to determine if she trusted this odd bird. He did not look devious. His eyes, though perpetually startled, seemed to take everything in with sharp appraisal. And he knew how to speak with the Scrids, who knew things no one could have guessed.

"Show him," Cassidy said.

Torr looked hesitantly between her and Berkeley. He unclasped the pouch, took out the fat crystal, and handed it to Berkeley. The man held it as though it was a jewel of great worth.

Torr asked, "How could they have felt it? What did they say?"

"They were saying something about a legend. I couldn't understand most of it." He peered at Torr. "Do you want to sell it?"

Torr's lips drew down in a scowl. "Sell it? I don't even know what it does. Besides, it's a family heirloom. No. It's not for sale."

Berkeley reluctantly placed the crystal in Torr's outstretched palm and tugged at one of his beard points, his mouth twisting to the side. "Okay. What are the others like? How many do you have?" He glanced sideways at Cassidy.

Torr stepped forward, distrust creeping across his face. "Thanks a lot for helping us back there, but I think you'd better go." Torr's face was hard, and Berkeley backed away, raising both hands, palms forward.

"No problem," Berkeley said in a calming tone. "I don't want to cause trouble, I just got a little excited, that's all. You don't see crystals like that every day."

He took another step backwards, then turned and headed down the road. At the intersection, he glanced over his shoulder with a wistful frown, then turned onto the spoke road and disappeared from view.

"What do you make of that?" Torr asked Cassidy as the two of them ducked inside their tent, leaving their friends standing outside, bewildered. Torr raised his eyebrows, his face betraying a hint of excitement.

She grinned, relieved to see some of Torr's old self shining through. "I think Peary Dome just got a lot more interesting," she said, chuckling.

"That's for sure," he said. "But we really have to watch our backs now. Those Scrids were very strong. We'll need to keep our friends close."

Torr pulled his other crystals from various pockets and pouches, and she retrieved hers from her bag and lined them up on his blanket. They handled the six crystals, gazing at them from different angles. She tried to think of what the shamans used to say about crystals. That they held ancient information, had special powers. But what kinds of powers?

Everyone knew crystal balls were for clairvoyance, but all she saw in the sphere was her own distorted reflection. Torr stood and waved the long, dagger-like crystal through the air as though he were fighting a ghost. "Yah," he yelled, slashing the crystal back and forth. She sat back, wrapping her arms around her knees, and watched as he did his quirky little dance.

She grinned happily. He was her brother again. The one who had left home lighthearted and full of life, and had returned from Gaia United heavy and broken. She slipped the crystal ball into her vest's deep side pocket and picked up her crystal shaft. Three of the six long, narrow facets were smooth and polished. The alternating three facets were striated crosswise with a series of small ridges. She ran her thumb over them, liking the texture. She pressed the cool shaft against her cheek and closed her eyes, trying to divine some meaning from the crystal. A sense of calm filled her, but nothing else.

Torr sat next to her, tossing the red garnet in his hand, then set it down and examined the big, fat crystal. "What do the Scrids want with this?" he wondered. "How could they have felt it?"

Cassidy shrugged, perplexed, and picked up the octahedron. She liked this one. It was cool and smooth, and a pale, icy green. She held it up to catch the light from the doorway, and ripples of rainbows glinted off the facets.

"Maybe the legend the Scrids were talking about was the same as the one in the book," she said, putting down the crystal and finding the blue and gold book. She turned to the page her mother had translated and read a couple passages aloud.

The sister who sees, leads the way
The brother who dreams, slays the beasts
The friend who travels, opens doors

The Star Children of the twenty-ninth age

Twins with unbroken lineage
Shall be found on the moon of crystal sand
Of the blue planet and white star

She looked up and her heart fell. The haunted look had returned to Torr's eyes, his face pale. Oh, no, ... *slays the beasts.* She had reminded him of his grief. His guilt. She reached out to touch his arm, but he pulled away, his eyes clouding over. He stuffed his crystals into his rucksack and stepped outside the tent, the flap falling behind him.

She sank her face into her hands, cursing herself. "Air-headed fool, you dull-witted dust cloud. Agh!" She shoved the shaft into her other side pocket, threw her pack onto her sleeping bag, and stormed from the tent. Torr was standing with Raleigh in front of Sky and Thunder's tent, his back to her, posture rigid.

Cassidy breathed deeply, furious with herself. Her eyes passed over the dreary tent city. Across the road, a neighbor she hadn't met waved. She waved back and turned her eyes away, not feeling sociable. Her eyes froze as she spotted Berkeley at the intersection, turning onto their road. She stiffened and called to Torr.

Another man was with Berkeley, a tall, strapping fellow who sauntered at his side, long legs striding with relaxed confidence. He was wearing tan cargo pants and a tan vest over a brown t-shirt. Dark auburn hair fell in waves to the man's shoulders, and he wore a close-cropped russet beard and dark green sunglasses. Something was familiar in the way he held himself. The easy, almost cocky swing of his arms.

"Jasper!" she called, tears rising as the breath left her lungs. She stepped forward hesitantly. Was it him? No one else had hair the color of autumn chestnuts. No one else had long knobby fingers like those that rose to take off his sunglasses and peer down the road at her, his eyes widening in disbelief.

"Cassidy? Cass! Bloody stars in hell!"

They ran towards each other, and she threw herself into his arms, laughing and crying as he lifted her off her feet and swung her around, their chests pressed together, their heads close. He put her down and broke away to grab Torr in a bear hug, the two men laughing and cursing and repeating each other's names.

"What in Algol's hell are you doing here?" Jasper cried. He released Torr and pulled Cassidy to him again, wrapping his arm around her shoulders and loudly kissing her cheek. "Holy stars, Cassandra Dagda, you are a sight for sore eyes. When did you get so beautiful?" His eyes sought hers, and heat rose to her face. Jasper's skin was flushed, his fair complexion ruddy and dark with freckles.

"I almost didn't recognize you with a beard," she said, reaching up to touch it.

"You like it?"

She smiled, joy and relief filling her like the swell of an ocean tide. His hand dropped to her waist and pulled her against his side as he grabbed Torr's shoulder with his other hand. "Torr, you're all grown up, man."

"You too. You look good." Torr was beaming, and Cassidy felt like a thousand pounds had been lifted from her shoulders. *Jasper was here. Everything would be all right.*

Berkeley watched from behind Jasper's shoulder.

"I thought you said you didn't know him," she said accusingly.

Berkeley shrugged. "What did you call him?"

"Jasper," she said.

"Is that your name?" Berkeley asked.

"Yeah." Jasper met Cassidy's curious glance. "Everyone here calls me Jaz."

"Jaz?" She raised her eyebrows. "That's what Mom used to call you when you were in trouble."

Jasper nodded proudly. "Exactly." He laughed, his hazel eyes sparkling with flecks of gold that caught the sunlight. Stars, she wanted to kiss him. She reluctantly let their bodies part, his hand lingering on her back and sending a shivering current to her toes.

"I suppose you know Kai, too, then?" she asked Berkeley. "Is your dad still here?" she asked, turning to Jasper.

"Yeah, he's here. He'll be so excited to see you."

"You mean Kujo?" Berkeley asked.

"Kujo," Cassidy repeated, twisting her mouth.

"Yeah," Jasper said. "That's what he goes by here. They called him that in the airforce. But how'd you get here? How long have you been here?"

Cassidy looked at her brother. He'd never said how he'd gotten all those Solidi. And they'd decided not to tell their neighbors about their deeds.

Torr glanced at her, then told Jasper, "We got passage out of Moffett Field a little over a week ago. Mom and Dad went to try to get to Shasta. The Shaman's Shield pulled back to south of the peaks. My mom's going to try to get them through." Jasper nodded, listening. "But we decided Cassidy and I should get out while we still could. The Tegs are taking over."

Jasper frowned and rubbed his chin. "Those fuckers. They're like a cancer. They won't stop till Earth's dead. Good thing you got out."

They went to sit on the Boyers' tarp, setting aside boxes of radio parts. Cassidy, Jasper, and Torr sat in a close circle while their friends gathered around to listen.

Torr told Jasper briefly of his time with Gaia United, and how he'd fled. *Deserted*, he called it, though Cassidy thought deserting an army that flipped to the other side so easily was the only honorable thing for a rebel to do. Cassidy told Jasper about her studies at the university and her history courses. Jasper had taken some of the same classes with the same professors, and got a wistful look in his eyes.

Jasper talked about his time on the moon, and proudly showed them the patch on his chest pocket. PEARY DOME TRADERS GUILD. Torr smiled slyly at him, and Cassidy's eyes darted to Berkeley, who shrugged guiltily.

"We need food," Torr said. "And water." He held up his partially empty ration jug.

Jasper rolled his eyes. "You and the rest of Peary Dome." Torr glared at him, and Jasper made a face. "Talk to me later," Jasper said, winking at Cassidy.

She blushed again. She felt like a teenager. Her eyes dropped to his other chest pocket. On the flap was the shooting star pin she had given him the day he'd left Earth. She reached out and touched the smooth orange and blue stones. He was wearing it, after all this time. Her heart grew tender, and she wanted to lift her hand to his face and stroke his cheek.

His eyes dropped to her hand resting on the pin, and he gently took her fingers, bringing the back of her hand to his lips. Her heart thrummed as his warm lips pressed against her skin, his forest-green eyes holding hers. His fingers intertwined with hers, and he lowered their hands to his leg. Cassidy's heart sang in her ears while the sounds of the camp faded to a distant drone.

"You guys have to move your tent to the Fen," Jasper said, squeezing her hand and gesturing behind him with his head. "We're at 7B. Come on, let's roll it up. We can carry everything between the four of us."

He gently released her hand and stood, shaking out his legs. His camp had been so close by, this whole time? Cassidy exhaled, tension draining away.

Hawk's and Roanoke's faces fell. Raleigh scowled, and Durham locked eyes with Torr. Even Sky and Thunder looked surprised and sad.

"What about our friends?" Cassidy asked. "They have to come with us. There's safety in numbers. We can't just leave them here."

"Really?" Jasper turned to her, his expression puzzled and a bit pained. "I don't know," he said hesitantly. "I have a bunch of guys at my camp."

"They make radios," she said, gesturing at the Boyers.

Jasper inspected their companions and the boxes of electronics, then turned his attention back to her. She pleaded with her eyes, and she could see him relenting.

"Okay, if you want," he said grudgingly. "There's room in our camp for ..." He looked around. "Three tents?"

Cassidy nodded happily. His face softened at her smile. Cassidy turned to Durham. "You want to come with us?"

Hawk stared at his father with begging eyes, and his two older sons nodded at him insistently. Durham leaned on his crutches and said, "Sure. That'd be fine. The more friends the better."

"What about you guys?" she asked.

Sky and Thunder traded glances.

"Okay," Sky said, shrugging.

"Why not?" Thunder agreed, a toothy smile lighting his face.

Hawk narrowed his eyes at her and said, "Y'all are the twins in that blue book. And he must be the friend."

Her skin prickled.

"What book?" Jasper asked.

Cassidy took in a breath and shook her head. "Something from Great-Aunt Sophie. I'll tell you later."

Jasper's eyebrows rose. "Ah. I understand now. The crystals ... they're the ones Aunt Sophie gave you?" His mouth turned up in a knowing smile. "It all makes sense now."

He pulled Cassidy into the crook of his arm, and she wrapped her arms around him in a hug, pressing her cheek to his warm neck and breathing in his woodsy scent that she realized she had been missing all these years. He returned her embrace, both his arms squeezing her tight and his lips brushing her hair in a soft kiss. She closed her eyes, suddenly ecstatic to be living on the moon.

25

THE FEN

Torr walked with Jasper on the way to his camp. Raleigh and Roanoke had insisted on carrying Torr and Cassidy's tent and walked single file in front of them, the rolled-up tent propped on opposite shoulders. Cassidy, Hawk, Sky, and Thunder were in the lead, and Durham had stayed behind to guard the other tents and pack up his radio gear. Hawk had insisted on carrying Cassidy's backpack, and bent forward from the weight. Berkeley had gone on ahead to warn their campmates.

Torr examined Jasper as they walked. Jasper returned the appraising look as though their more mature bodies could tell the story of the past five years. Jasper was wearing loose, dusty cargo pants like everyone else. His body was taut and hard, corded muscles lining his arms. His neck had thickened, and the planes of his face had smoothed and hardened. He wore a closely cropped beard, and his freckles were darker than ever. At his belt he wore a knife and a handie-talkie. Someone on the radio chirped something about a shipment of rice, and Jasper flicked the radio off.

"You bring the deeds?" Jasper asked, one eyebrow lifting hopefully.

Cassidy glanced back at them, and a smile curled one side of Jasper's mouth as he regarded Cassidy's curves. Torr shook his head. All Jasper needed was a patch, and he'd look exactly like a pirate, Torr thought to himself. Lecherous, greedy, sly, and cunning on one hand. Loving, generous, honest, and a bumbling fool on the other. Jasper was a bundle of conflicting passions. Torr had never laughed or cried so much as he had with Jasper, from when they were small boys exploring the fields and forests of Shasta, to when they had shared a room as awkward teenagers after Jasper's parents had left him.

He put his arm around Jasper's shoulders. "It's really good to see you," Torr said, his voice rough with emotion.

"You too. I can't even tell you how much. It's like hell here, sometimes."

Torr dropped his arm, and they fell into step together.

"What in Perseus's name happened to your sister? She's a blazing knockout." Jasper's eyes traveled over Cassidy's body as she walked in front of them with Hawk.

"Yeah, she's pretty good looking."

"Pretty good looking?! Are you blind?"

"Don't get any ideas," Torr growled, though who was he to say anything? Jasper and Cassidy had always loved each other, for as long as Torr could remember. Now, he supposed, they were adults and free to do something about it.

"Why not?" Jasper asked, his eyes still on Cassidy. "Does she have a boyfriend?"

Torr gave Jasper a sharp look.

"What," Jasper complained, looking genuinely concerned.

"That's an idiotic question. Look," Torr said, pointing at

Earth. "Even if she did, he's out there. Two hundred thousand miles away. Do you really think it matters?"

Jasper frowned and shrugged. "She could've met someone here." He glanced at Sky and Thunder.

"We've only been here a week, Jasper. She doesn't move that fast."

Jasper examined Hawk, who was gazing at her adoringly.

"He's fourteen," Torr said. Jasper forced a grin, and Torr shook his head again. Jasper was acting like a teenager himself. "She's practically your sister, Jasper."

Jasper threw him a sidelong glance. "I love her, but not like a sister." Jasper's lips curled up on both sides this time, and Torr punched him hard on the shoulder. Jasper winced and stepped away.

"Well, she's *my* sister, and I don't like you talking about her that way. Be careful with her, she's sensitive. You hurt her and I'll break your face."

Jasper scowled playfully. "I'll be careful." His eyes settled on Cassidy again. "You won't mind?"

Torr looked ahead, wishing Cassidy wouldn't toss her hair over her shoulder like that. She had no idea how distracting it was. And why wasn't it in her usual braid instead of tumbling down her back in waves? Torr didn't have any control over his sister, nor over Jasper. They had always done whatever they wanted, sneaking off together thinking no one noticed. Torr had seen his father talking seriously to Jasper in the backyard one morning after Jasper and Cassidy had spent all night in the living room together, as if no one in the house knew what was going on.

"It's up to her," Torr said. "Just don't break her heart."

"Ha!" Jasper laughed. "I'm more concerned about my heart, frankly."

Torr followed Jasper's gaze that took in Sky and Thunder before returning to Cassidy.

"She does seem to like Sky a bit," Torr teased. Jasper scowled for real this time, his playful expression turning dark as they took a few steps in silence.

"You didn't bring them?" Jasper asked.

"Bring what?"

"The deeds."

"Oh, those. Yeah, we brought them."

Jasper exhaled. "Oh, good. I thought you shook your head before."

"I was shaking my head because I can't believe you're such a lech. You're like a bear eyeing a honeypot." Jasper's gaze was still glued on Cassidy's swaying behind.

"Torr. There aren't many girls around here, in case you hadn't noticed. And now the flower of my heart shows up on a dusty Peary road and runs into my arms. How do you expect me to react?"

Torr rolled his eyes. He had noticed the lack of women, and it was quite depressing. It was an even worse ratio than at Miramar. "What can we do with the deeds?" he asked, kicking aside stray moon rocks as he walked. "We can't very well construct a dome on our own."

"Wait a sec. Turn in here," Jasper said, stopping and directing Raleigh and Roanoke through a gap in the tents. "Drop the tent in the open courtyard. You'll see it."

Cassidy went with the others, leaving Torr and Jasper alone on the roadside.

"I suppose we could sell the deeds," Torr said.

"Hell yeah," Jasper said, grinning. "Two parcels with big craters like yours will bring enough gold to buy passage anywhere in the galaxy."

"Yeah, I was thinking maybe we should go to Muria. It's just ... Cassidy was hoping ..." Torr said, looking up at Earth, "... that we could build a little place on our land, and you know, maybe our parents could join us and we could all be safe here."

"Yeah, maybe," Jasper said gently. "If you sold one parcel, maybe you'd get enough to build on the other."

"Yeah, we thought of that. But how would we get the materials and equipment to build a dome? And what if somebody's claimed the land already? I heard there are illegal mines all over the place."

"Yeah, there are a few. Especially in the big craters. A bunch of them have those white kit domes and small regolith mining operations. Then again, that might be the best scenario," Jasper said, his eyes getting that scheming look Torr knew so well. "If somebody's already set up a mining claim on your land, you could take it over."

"Hmm. You mean kick the miners out?"

Jasper shrugged. "Maybe you could work out some sort of deal. You'd own the land. They'd own the structures, I guess. Share the mineral deposits." Jasper's eyes narrowed. "Or yeah, kick them out."

Torr grew uncomfortable. "I don't think they'd take too kindly to that."

Jasper shrugged. "I'm just saying. It's your land. But you're right. The mining lords are mean. You'd have to go in strong."

Torr shook his head. "Forget it. I had to leave my guns behind."

"Guns? How many did you have?" Jasper's eyes glinted. "You got some good shit from Gaia United, I bet."

"I had a TAFT assault rifle and a Dashiel sniper rifle. And a SIG Sauer Orbiter pistol. My father took the TAFT, and I had to ditch my Dashiel and Orbiter before we left Earth. Do you have any guns? Where can I get one here?"

"No guns inside the dome."

"Yeah, right."

"No. Seriously. Only in the spaceport."

Torr didn't know if that was good news or bad. Jasper laid his hand on Torr's shoulder. "Come on, let's get your tent set up."

They headed through the gap in the tents, navigating guy wires and stakes marked with red plastic ribbons until they reached a clearing enclosed by a collection of tents. "Welcome to the Fen," Jasper said expansively, spreading his arms.

Torr looked around. The camp looked well lived-in, with two white plastic picnic tables with attached benches, several lawn chairs scattered about, and clotheslines strung between tents with men's underwear and socks hanging out to dry.

Raleigh and Roanoke had dropped Torr and Cassidy's tent in a gap between two others, and were headed back with Sky and Thunder to get their own tents. Two dark-haired and two blond men accompanied them and stopped while Jasper introduced them to Torr.

The first man was named Ming-Long. He was a tall Asian man with wide shoulders and thick arms, whose hairless, golden skin was marred by several straight scars. White, chipped teeth glinted from a broad smile that was pulled a bit to one side by a small scar near one corner of his mouth. The smile was not so much friendly as open to whatever life might bring. Another small scar split his right eyebrow in half.

A shorter, olive-skinned man with shiny black hair layered like crow's feathers was named Khaled. It was not only his hair that reminded Torr of a crow. His eyes were black and scanned the surroundings like he was looking for the next choice morsel to pounce on, and settled on Cassidy's rear end as she bent to retrieve something from her pack. Torr suppressed the urge to punch him.

The two other men were clearly identical twins. He recognized them as the blond guitar players from Center Ring. They seemed to recognize Torr as well, and greeted him with friendly handshakes. Of medium stature, they were tautly muscled with strong hands. Their skin was fair, their wavy hair the color of golden wheat, and their eyes a piercing blue. Jasper introduced them as Frick and Frack.

"Fritz and Frank," Fritz told him, smiling cheerfully. They wore scruffy goatees and moustaches, and each sported several tattoos on their arms. Fritz's were of a celestial theme: stars, moons, Earth. Frank's were morbid: skulls, dripping knives, gravestones.

Another man appeared from the tent nearest them, the flap closing behind him. He strode to join them, mirrored sunglasses shading his eyes and a short ponytail pulling his thick black hair away from his face. He was smooth-shaven and unsmiling, as though he had just been woken from a nap; either that, or he found nothing amusing about a bunch of strangers invading his camp. He shook Torr's hand with a strong grip. "Faisal," he said.

"Prince Faisal," Jasper said.

"Prince of what?" Torr asked, inspecting the man, who appeared to be close to thirty.

"House of Saud," Faisal said simply, and looked about impatiently.

Last Torr knew, the family of thousands of Saudi descendants still held sway in their territory on Earth, albeit under Metolius's rule. He supposed there would be many young cousins and princes in such a family, searching for their places in the tribal hierarchy. Torr guessed Faisal was not very high up, since he was here on the moon. Or perhaps it was the opposite.

All the men were fit. They wore the typical Peary Dome military surplus garb, dust-imbued and drab, aside from Faisal's t-shirt, which was a sparkling white. They wore tactical vests with a multitude of pouches, and belts with knives hanging from them. Jasper had surrounded himself with a bunch of former soldiers, from the looks of them. Torr felt comfortable with these men. He nodded respectfully as they turned away and trailed Raleigh, Roanoke, Sky, and Thunder through the gap that led to Ring Road B.

Cassidy, Berkeley, and Hawk were unrolling Torr and Cassidy's tent between Faisal's and what turned out to be Jasper's, who ducked into the tent and emerged with a small black leather daypack.

Jasper stood with Torr, watching Cassidy with a love-struck grin on his face. Cassidy pretended she didn't notice him standing there, but every word out of her mouth was a giggle and her hands flapped around when she talked, the way they always did when she got excited.

Torr sighed and looked around the compound Jasper had called the Fen. The dry, dusty ground was the opposite of a marshy fen, but he supposed the name wasn't any stranger than calling the basalt expanses of the moon "maria," the Latin word for "seas."

Torr wandered around the camp. Across the circular yard from Jasper's tent, on the eastern edge, the two picnic tables stood end-to-end. Two open supply tents formed a rear boundary, with a small gap that led to a back alley. In front of the supply tents, stacks of plastic crates were topped with the side of a large wooden packing crate that served as a kitchen counter. An array of solar panels was perched above the supply tents, powering three hot plates, several power strips with orange extension cords that snaked across the yard, and battery charging stations set up on crates. Buckets sat to the side of the supply tents for waste. Sitting on a wagon next to the kitchen was a half-full, five-hundred-gallon plastic water tank. The kitchen, dining area, and water wagon were shaded by blue plastic tarps.

Things were definitely looking up. It had become painfully apparent this morning that he wouldn't be able to sustain his regimen of long runs and strength training on four liters of water a day. Not in this warm, arid environment. He had gone into a near panic after spilling his water at the ration trailer, thanks to those smelly, hairy Scrids, who had some serious boundary issues and the densest bodies he had ever encountered—their chests felt like cinderblocks. At least now the water problem was solved. He noted cases of canned goods and sacks of grain stacked in the supply tents, as well as a cask of olive oil, and shelves filled with a variety of food storage containers and kitchen implements. *Jasper Manann, Peary Dome Traders Guild.* Jasper was enterprising, that was for certain. *Jaz.* Torr chuckled.

Lined up on the south side of the yard were three tents, which Torr assumed belonged to the men who'd just left. On the north side stood a gray, half-sized shipping container bordering a gap through which Torr could see a smaller yard and more tents.

Jasper walked over, noting the direction of his gaze, and said, "Come on, I'll introduce you to the rest of the crew."

Torr followed Jasper past the water wagon into a sheltered area formed by four tents and the closed container, which had a large padlock on it. Jasper introduced two small men who were straddling a wooden plank that rested on two crates and formed a bench. They were facing each other, and the younger man rested his forearm on a stack of towels. The older man was holding a needle gun and was laying down a colorful tattoo on the smooth fleshy part of the man's inside forearm. New red ink formed the shape of a dragon. They glanced up and bowed their heads in a friendly way, and continued with the dragon.

The older one with the tattoo gun was Tatsuya, and the younger one was his son, Hiroshi. Tatsuya was gray-haired and nearing seventy, and Hiroshi was in his mid-thirties with glossy black hair. Both had small black eyes, long ponytails, and stringy goatees and moustaches.

Torr eyed the vials of colorful ink that were laid out on Tatsuya's tray, which sat on a plastic crate next to him. He glanced down at the Light Fighter tattoo on his upper left arm that he'd intended to get colored in one day. On his inner right forearm was the indigo Gaia United eagle, clutching a rifle and olive branch. He stared at the tattoo, seeing Reina's inner wrist and her smaller Gaia United eagle, feeling her smooth skin under his fingertips. He pulled in a breath and looked up to find Hiroshi's gaze resting on his face.

Berkeley passed behind them and opened the container. He disappeared into the dark shadows and came out with a sledge-hammer and several lengths of rebar.

"Leave it open," Jasper said.

"You meet Tatty and Hiro?" Berkeley asked.

Torr nodded. "Is that your tent?" he asked, nodding to a tent across the small yard. The door was tied open, revealing an interior festooned with brightly colored tapestries and a small table covered with carved figurines. In the center of the doorway hung a rope strung with shells and pieces of driftwood, making him homesick for Earth and the ocean.

"How'd you know?" Berkeley asked, his eyes round as though every moment was a wonder.

Torr raised one eyebrow. "It wasn't hard."

Next to Berkeley's tent was another tent with its doors tied open, revealing a cluttered craft shop, with a table and shelving made of open crates.

"What's that contraption?" Torr asked, shifting his attention to a large sewing machine that sat on a table outside the craft tent, beneath the shade of a huge shiny black umbrella made with solar panels.

"Ah, that's my own little cottage industry. Need new pants?" Folded on a crate next to the sewing machine was a stack of brand-new cargo pants made from the same dun-colored canvas as all the tents.

"Not at the moment."

"Well, you just let me know. I'll make 'em custom for you." Berkeley smiled, and left with the sledgehammer and steel bars, walking in a smooth, catlike prowl.

Torr wondered what kind of role he could adopt in this rugged frontier economy. What did he have to offer? All he'd done at Miramar was dig trenches, build bunkers, work out, and shoot guns. Not much use for any of that here. He couldn't think of anything he knew how to do well enough to make himself useful. He could learn about radios from Durham, but there didn't seem to be enough scrap parts around to keep Durham's own sons busy. Torr had been raised a trader's son. Maybe he could join the Traders Guild with Jasper.

Jasper caught his eye and put his arm around his shoulder. "Don't worry, Sundance," Jasper said, giving his shoulder a shake. "Everything's going to be fine."

"Yeah, I guess," Torr said, silently thanking the stars they'd found him.

26

ANTLER KRALJ CRATE

"Help me carry something," Jasper said.

Torr followed him into the dim, dusty container. It was filled with stacks of plastic crates, rolls of tent fabric, shovels, pickaxes, and the skeleton of a four-wheeler. A large rectangular wooden crate sat inside the door. Its short end reached Torr's hip, and each long side was as big as a door. "Come on, it's not too heavy," Jasper said.

They dragged and pushed the crate out into the sunlight. Painted on the box's sides were off-world runes. Jasper levered the lid open with a crowbar and set it aside. The crate was filled with clothing and a collection of small wooden boxes.

"What's all this?" Torr asked.

"Bought the whole crate off a Delosian ship a few days ago. I need to find something for a friend of mine." Jasper went inside the shipping container and emerged with two large empty plastic bins. He started sorting through the contents of the crate, putting the clothing in one bin and the boxes in the other.

Torr set his rucksack on the ground and unfolded some of the clothing. It was the style of garb worn by the men standing near the spiked, cube-shaped ship, though these articles were in pristine condition: white ruffled shirts, leather jerkins and arm guards, leather pants and boots, and heavily embroidered, knee-length velvet coats.

"So that boxy ship with the spikes was from Delos?" Torr asked.

"Yeah," Jasper said, glancing up from the collection of small boxes. "You saw it?"

Torr nodded. "There was one at Gandoop, too," he said.

Jasper stopped with a box half-open. "What do you mean, Gandoop?"

"We flew into Gandoop, then got a ride to Peary."

Jasper frowned. "Why'd you go to Gandoop?"

"That was the only option we had," Torr said.

Jasper turned back to the crate, pushing clothing aside distractedly.

Torr looked inside the crate and lifted out a pair of leather arm guards. They were beautifully tooled with various twining patterns that reminded him of Celtic knots. "Are Delosians archers?" Torr asked.

"The best," Jasper said. "Antler Kralj, the ruling house of Delos, spend all their free time hunting. They maintain large forested estates filled with game. Those are nice, aren't they?"

Torr loosened the laces on one of the bracers and pulled it on, reminded of the scars on Ming-Long's forearms. "How did Ming-Long get so many knife scars?"

"They're laser scars. He was a guerilla fighter in the Shanghai resistance. They held the Tegs back for several months in a ground battle for the city. When the Tegs finally won, he fled to Wenchang, where he had a bunch of relatives. One of his uncles was a guard at the spaceport and smuggled him out."

Jasper leaned against the large crate, opening a small wooden box. "Khaled was a rebel in Jordan before it fell to the Tegs. He escaped Amman with all his father's gold. His father had joined the Tegs but left the gold hidden for Khaled with a photo of the two of them together. He thinks his father wanted him to escape to freedom. He left from Beersheba Spaceport, which was still free at the time."

Torr's eyes inexplicably filled with tears. He held his face stiff, having learned long ago to keep his tears from flowing when he had to. He felt a bond with these men, though he'd not said two words to them. "What about the twins?" he asked.

"Ah. Frick and Frack. Trained at the Berlin Conservatory of Music, they left to join the Germanic ground forces when Tegea's forces invaded northern Europe. Their whole unit deserted when the Germanic League surrendered. The twins escaped to their dairy farm where they found their family and cows butchered. They walked to the coast and got a boat to the Great Isles, and flew out of Glamorgan."

Torr's pulse quickened. Men like himself. They would understand him. "And Faisal?"

"That arrogant billionaire has a Ph.D. in Astrophysics. I don't know if he's ever fought. He doesn't talk much. But he loves his daggers." Jasper grinned and opened another box. "And he wins all the knife-throwing contests."

Knife-throwing contests. Torr had found the right camp. He set aside the arm guards and lifted a leather jerkin from the box. It was a dark chocolate brown, soft and buttery, with short sleeves. "Do you think it's too hot here to wear a leather shirt?" Torr asked, removing his vest and peeling off his sweaty t-shirt.

"Yes." Jasper's mouth twisted to one side as Torr pulled on the jerkin. It fell to his hips, with lacing up the front. He tied the lacing and stretched his arms across his chest. The shoulders had just the right amount of give.

"The temperature here actually feels perfect," Torr observed. "As long as you're not running laps around the perimeter."

"Air Control keeps it a balmy seventy-eight degrees Fahrenheit," Jasper said. "But it feels a bit cooler. They keep it dry on purpose."

"Right," Torr said, tying the lacing below the notch at his collarbone.

Jasper regarded him, eyebrows cocked. "Don't you want a ruffled shirt, Your Highness? Or perhaps this maroon doublet?" Jasper reached into the crate and showed him a long wine-red waistcoat with gold piping around the seams, and gold buttons.

"Nah," Torr said. "I don't want to look like a girl." Jasper held up a long purple velvet gown covered with tiny gold studs in an intricate scroll and floral pattern. "Uh-oh. Don't show that to Cassidy."

"Don't show what to Cassidy?" Cassidy appeared behind him. "Ooh." She went to Jasper and pulled the gown from his hands. "Where'd you get this?" She held it up, admiring it, and pressed it to her chest while trying to keep the hem from dragging on the ground.

"It's from Delos. Totally impractical for the moon."

Cassidy looked disappointed and handed the gown to Jasper, then started pawing through the bracers, leather jerkins, and pants.

"Those I can sell here," Jasper told her. "And for a handsome price." He turned his eyes to Torr. "Don't think I'm giving you that jerkin for free, pretty boy."

Torr gave him a smirk and admired the leather shirt. Cassidy held up an arm guard.

"These are kind of like the ones those Scrid dwarf guys wore," she said.

"Kinda," Jasper agreed. "They probably got them from Delosian traders. Delosians are the best leatherworkers."

"So Berkeley told you those hairy Scrids knew we carried crystals?" Torr asked.

Jasper's eyes lit up. "Hermes' wings, yes. Why do you think I came looking for you? Only I didn't know it was you. Hell of a surprise. But yes, we will be discussing those crystals." Jasper turned a gold coin in his fingers as he watched Cassidy admire a leather jerkin.

Jasper didn't know they carried Solidi and were unimpressed by Jasper's one measly gold coin. But let him think they were destitute. Torr could negotiate a lower price for the Delosian shirt that way. If he wanted it. It would hold up better than a cotton t-shirt, he rationalized, fingering the fine leather and knowing he shouldn't spend his coin frivolously.

Cassidy disappeared into the shadows of the container with the jerkin, and Jasper continued looking through the small boxes. Torr pulled up a plastic crate and sat on it. "What are you looking for?"

Jasper sighed. "My friend Gabira loves gold, but she's very picky. I need to find her just the right thing." He lifted a gold necklace from one of the boxes, then replaced it. "She has a crystal I want. I'm paying for it bit by bit. The rest of this jewelry will go to Muria. They love gold but don't have much on their planet."

Cassidy emerged from the container wearing a short-sleeved jerkin of soft beige leather that hugged her breasts and flared out at the hips. She twirled around.

"Cute," Jasper said, his cheeks flushed. So much for blending in, Torr thought dully, though with the shapeless field vest over it she shouldn't draw too much attention.

"What's all this?" Cassidy asked, peeking into a box of gold jewelry Jasper was looking through. She examined the pieces, lifting a plain gold chain.

Jasper laughed. "Wanna buy that?"

"How much?" She smiled.

"Its weight in gold. Quadrupled for the Delos factor. You know, exotic planet, frightfully far away."

Cassidy frowned and set it on the lip of the crate. "What's this one?" she asked, opening a small square of forest-green velvet to reveal a gold chain with a large gold pendant that glimmered in the sunlight.

"Ah, there it is. You have good taste. You just found the most expensive piece in this whole collection. Worth more than the rest combined. Most of the other pieces are Delosian. That one is Ilian."

"Oh," she said, examining the pendant. "I suppose anything from Iliad is priceless."

"That's an understatement. Over a thousand years old? From a warring planet that's been thoroughly ransacked by the Cephs? It's irreplaceable."

"What is it?" she asked, rubbing the large round medallion, which had several tiny gems laid out in an asymmetrical pattern.

"It's the Pleiades constellation," Jasper said. "The Seven Sisters. Gabira will love this."

Torr peered more closely at the pendant, taking it from Cassidy. It was heavy, and the flat circle of gold was etched with circles and glyphs around the good-sized gems. Torr counted more than seven, some clustered in pairs or triples. Binary or trinary stars. Some gems were clear, others were gold, red, or blue. Many tiny black diamonds were set around the larger gems. He assumed they depicted planets. Muria was in the Pleiades, and he wondered which of the black diamonds it was.

"Strange that Antler Kralj should have a pendant of the Pleiades, don't you think?" Jasper asked. "The Delosians and Murians hate each other."

Torr shrugged. "How would I know?"

"This is Ilian," Cassidy said, pulling the gold medallion from beneath her jerkin. She lifted the chain over her head and handed it to Jasper.

He gazed at the obverse side, a nude woman pouring water from an urn. "Algol's hell," he said. "That is one of the legendary Star Children. The sister, obviously." His dumbstruck expression faded, replaced by his pirate's smile. "That's you, Cassandra," he quipped, eyeing her breasts lasciviously. She frowned, ignoring his ogling jest, and gazed at the pendant.

"Where'd you get it?" Jasper asked, dropping his leer.

"Great-Aunt Sophie," Cassidy muttered, looking up through the dome at the stars that glowed like eyes watching them.

"Of course," Jasper said. "On Delos they call the sister *Golden Falcon*. And the brother they call *Bringer of Death.*" He threw Torr a pointed look.

Torr's skin prickled. "That's not what they call him," he said acidly.

"Yes it is," Jasper said. "I heard the Ilians made coins of him, too."

"They did. I saw it in a book," Cassidy said. "He was on one knee shooting a bow and arrow."

Torr swallowed.

"I'd love to get my hands on one of those," Jasper said, his eyes narrowing.

"And there was a third coin," Cassidy said. "It was a man holding a glowing orb and a wand."

Jasper met her eyes, one corner of his mouth curling down in a sick grimace and the other side turning up in a grin. His cockeyed expression faded slowly, and he said, "The Ilians and Delosians have similar legends and prophecies. The Murians, too. Each race calls the children something different and has different stories about them, but they're fundamentally the same. Twin brother and sister appear every millennium to find the Star People and save our asses. Maybe you guys are them. If so, you'd better find those bloody Star People before it's too late."

Shivers ran up and down Torr's arms. "That's a load of Star Seeker bunk," he said, trying to laugh it off.

"You think? Wait a second. Check this out." Jasper was examining the back of Cassidy's medallion. "These are the eyes of the Star People, who are watching us," he claimed, his green eyes glowing. He showed Torr the medallion, stamped with a triangle with three eyes in it. Jasper and Cassidy locked gazes with a mixture of superstition and infatuation.

"That same symbol is on the cover of my book." Cassidy said, reaching into her daypack and pulling out the blue, gilt-edged book. The triangle with the eyes stared up at them.

Torr shook off an eerie tingling at the nape of his neck. It was an odd coincidence, but he was more intrigued by the design. The symbol would make a great tattoo, he mused.

Jasper inspected the book's cover. "You'll see that three-eyed symbol all over Delos. They call it Heaven's Window. The eyes of the Star People. In fact, I have some Heaven's Window pendants somewhere in this crate. You could get a lot of money for that Star Girl pendant." He gave the book and necklace back to Cassidy, and continued opening small wooden boxes and stacking them neatly in the plastic crate.

"I tried to sell it on Earth," she said, pulling the chain over her head. "But nobody had enough gold. Then the Tegs came."

Torr rubbed the Pleiades pendant with his thumb, his eyes drawn to the glistening jewels. Suddenly, Torr desperately wanted to believe in the Star People and the salvation awaiting them somewhere out in the galaxy. Maybe if he and Cassidy could find the mythical golden angels, then all would be well.

He chuckled out loud. Was he getting sucked into this destiny bullshit so easily? Torr snorted, and Jasper eyed him curiously. Fleeing the Tegs had made Torr as desperate and crazy as everyone else. But what if it were true, and it was up to him and Cassidy to rescue all of humanity from destruction? He examined Cassidy's face. She was smart. Strong. Idealistic. Stubborn as all hell. Beautiful. Kind. Honest. Cunning. Brave. Everything a true leader needed to be.

"How much for the Pleiades necklace?" Cassidy asked, taking it from Torr and dangling it in the light, the gems glittering and casting little shards of light across her face.

Torr watched as Jasper assumed the same pose as when they used to play cards as teenagers, sitting around their kitchen table. Jasper pressed his left index finger to his bearded chin and puckered his lips like he was thinking deep thoughts. "I'll trade it for the Golden Falcon necklace."

Cassidy's face got pouty. "I need both, Jasper Manann."

Jasper guffawed. "Really, Cassafrass?"

She pursed her lips. "If I'm Golden Falcon, I should have both."

"I don't quite follow your reasoning, but if you want the Pleiades pendant so badly, what else you got to trade for it?" Cassidy's brow furrowed. "You've got crystals," Jasper said, licking his lips.

"Not a chance," she said.

"Give it back, Cassidy," Torr said. He shook his head at her, knowing she was thinking of her pocket full of gold. She frowned as she carefully folded the green velvet around the gemladen pendant and handed it to Jasper.

Jasper tucked it into his pocket and continued searching, dipping his head and arms into the wooden crate as he rummaged around. He popped up with a wooden box in hand.

"Found them," he announced. He opened the box to reveal three flat triangles of solid gold. Each side of the triangles measured an inch long. Three eye-shaped gems were set into each pendant in a triangular pattern, one gem above the other two, with a gold loop at the top of the triangle to hold a chain.

"Ooh," Cassidy cooed. She took the box from Jasper and handled each of the triangles, holding them up to let the light shine through the semi-translucent gems. "Can I have one?"

"Cassidy," Jasper said, sighing, "I need to sell all this stuff, or I'll go broke."

"Are they Ilian?"

"I don't know. They're extremely old, I know that much. Or so I was told."

"If these three eyes are the eyes of the Star People, and if we're the Star Children looking for them, then don't you think we need these? Torr and I?"

Jasper and Torr exchanged glances. Cassidy continued, her eyes distant, speaking in that way she had when she was connecting dots to make sense of the world. "Yes," she said softly. "If they can watch us through these pendants, they'll be able to help us find them. Right?" Her eyes focused on Torr, suddenly bright and determined. "We need these, Torr. And you need the third," she said, turning her insistent gaze on Jasper. "You're the friend the passage speaks of. You'll need their help, too."

"What passage?"

Cassidy turned to a page in the book and pointed to it. Jasper read it to himself and frowned. "Sounds like superstition to me."

Cassidy laughed. "Yeah. And?" Jasper shook his head helplessly, his lip curling to one side as he regarded her blue eyes and contagious smile. "You were just telling us we needed to save everybody," she said. Her smile grew smug. "I'll buy them," she said. "One for each of us. Look, this one's gems are goblin green to match your eyes," she told Jasper with an impish grin, handing it to him. "And these are storm gray, for you," she said, handing one to Torr. "And ocean blue for me."

"I don't need this," Jasper said, rubbing it with his thumb and turning it over.

"Me neither," Torr said. "Besides, they're for women," he complained as his eyes were drawn to the gems.

"They are not," Cassidy argued. "Just string it with a leather cord and it will look masculine enough. How much?" she asked Jasper, her eyes sparkling.

Jasper shrugged, meeting her gaze with a sideways smile. "Four Eagles each, I guess."

Torr cringed at the price, and noted Jasper wasn't bothering to negotiate hard because he didn't think Cassidy had enough gold. Torr watched Jasper's face as Cassidy pulled out her coins and started counting out Eagles. At least she hadn't revealed the Tetras and Solidi.

"Where'd you get all that?" Jasper asked, his smile dropping with surprise.

"No, Cassidy," Torr interrupted. "We'll need that money later. Besides, each pendant is less than an ounce. Four Eagles is too much." He kept his emotions detached and his expression uninterested. He wondered if Cassidy might be right about the pendants.

"Yeah, okay. I'd better save my gold," Cassidy relented, disappointment heavy in her voice. Their father had done his best to instill frugality in them, but restraint had always been harder for Cassidy than for Torr. She closed the box and handed it to Jasper.

Jasper was eyeing the coins cupped in her palm. Cassidy was a buyer, gold in hand. Jasper was probably trying to determine when he might find another buyer willing to part with twelve

Eagles for pendants of unknown worth. Jasper spoke noncha-
lantly, as though he was doing her a favor. "All right, then, what
else have you got to trade?" He poked inside Cassidy's pack,
which sat on the ground next to her.

"Get out of there, Jasper," she said, pushing him away and
laughing as he held her wrist. "Here," she said, shouldering
him aside. "What about some herbs? How much are herbs
worth here?"

"Depends." Jasper leaned on the edge of the wooden crate
and folded his arms. "What've you got?"

"Well." She hesitated. "They're not like normal herbs."

"What do you mean?"

"They've got... special qualities. You know."

Understanding lit Jasper's face, and his forefinger went to his
chin. "Oh, you mean *magic.*"

Cassidy winced. "Sort of. Kind of. Not completely. I mean,
they can cure a simple headache, heal infections, treat insomnia,
stomachaches, you know, like regular herbs."

Torr shook his head at Jasper's guile. Jasper had lived with
them. He knew the deal. He was acting stupid to make a
better trade.

"Well, that's important, but maybe not worth the price of
those pendants." Jasper's finger was still pressed to his chin.

"I'll tell you what," she said, pulling out four notebooks of
different colors: black, yellow, green, and the red notebook of
their mother's. The most magical of Brianna's notebooks, the
one even she could not read until plant spirit medicine was
called for. "See what you can find of interest in here," Cassidy
said slyly as she passed the red notebook to Jasper, who flipped
slowly through the pages.

He stopped, his eyes intent. He was reading. He had
found something.

Cassidy watched him carefully. "What does it say?" she asked. Jasper's face darkened.

"What? Read it," Cassidy said.

Jasper read, his voice wavering, *"Douleia – Take two drops when the stranglehold of obsession tightens at your throat. Fling the serpent of addiction to the demons where it originated before you become hopelessly enslaved."*

Cassidy's mouth drew down, and Torr furrowed his brow. Most people could not read the book. That must mean either Jasper was making it up, which didn't look to be the case judging from his crimson complexion, or he had stronger shaman talents than Torr had given him credit for. He'd never been able to read the red notebook before, though he'd tried several times when Brianna had insisted he take some herb or another.

"Let me see," Torr said, taking the notebook. The script flowed like snakes, then solidified. He read it out loud.

"Douleia – Administer two drops to those abusing strong substances that they don't understand. Force feed if necessary." Torr laughed and glanced at Jasper who looked like a child caught stealing.

"What else you got?" Jasper asked sourly.

Cassidy took the red notebook and looked through the pages. "Looks like you might be able to use a couple others. Gordsel soothes hunger and heartache. Horehound treats sore throats and homesickness." She looked up at him. "Do you want either of those? I think I have an extra bottle of each."

"Okay," Jasper said, trying to sound like he wasn't still shaken by the message of the Douleia. "I'll take all three."

Cassidy's face brightened. "Really? You will? For all three pendants? And the leather shirts? And I need a chain." She plucked the plain gold chain from where she had set it on the crate's edge and strung it through her Heaven's Window pendant. She smiled, her eyes the same blue as the gems.

Jasper softened when he looked at her. "One herb per pendant, plus three gold Eagles each, and I'll throw in the chain and jerkins as a welcome gift."

"Two Eagles apiece," Torr countered.

Jasper sneered, but tilted his head in acquiescence.

Cassidy smiled and handed him six gold coins, and Jasper handed her the box holding the green-jeweled triangle.

"No," she said, pushing his hand away. "That one's for you. You'll need it. Remember? You have to wear it, not sell it. You, too, Torrance," she said, pointing at the triangle in his hand.

"Thanks," Torr said. "Wait. You paid Jasper for his own pendant?"

They ignored him as they each stared down at their Heaven's Windows.

Torr turned to his, and three gray eyes stared up at him. They frightened him a bit, as though the Star People really could see him through the gems. He kind of liked the creepy feeling, and cut a length of black leather cord from a spool Jasper found in the craft tent. Torr slipped it through the pendant's gold loop and tied it around his neck, and Jasper tied on his own. Cassidy smiled happily at them.

Jasper continued sorting through his goods, while Cassidy sat on a plastic crate and watched him dreamily.

"Don't you have any guns?" Torr asked.

"I told you, no guns allowed past the spaceport. Sorry."

Torr sighed. "Bows and arrows? Swords? Anything else useful?"

"No bows and arrows, spears, or swords allowed in the dome, Your Royal Deathness."

Torr scowled at the nickname. "A dagger or a club, then. What's the line between a knife and a sword?"

"You've already got a knife," Cassidy said, but Torr ignored her.

Jasper answered, "A knife can't be longer than fingertip to elbow, blade and hilt combined."

"Whose fingertip to elbow?"

"Eighteen inches," Jasper said. "That's the rule."

"You got anything like that?" He was secretly glad no swords were allowed. That required a whole other skill he did not have.

"Hmm," Jasper said, looking through the remaining items in the wooden crate. He surfaced with a rectangular wooden box. "Just this," he said, opening it. "Of course, it's the only other Ilian antique of the lot. You two have a nose for the good stuff."

Torr reached for the box. Inside was a long knife, sheathed in a black leather scabbard. The handle was missing, exposing the bare metal tang. The tang was etched with two intertwining serpents, with two metal wings forming the guard. The pommel was a large disc of multi-colored metal.

He slid the long blade from its sheath and placed the knife alongside his arm. It stretched from his fingertips to just shy of his elbow crease. He held it up to admire it, noticing that Hiroshi's eyes followed the blade from across the yard. Torr had forgotten about the little men, the buzz of the tattoo gun having faded to a comforting drone.

The blade was forged with folded steel, the flat surface shimmering with water-like ripples that led to a single cutting edge of white crystalline steel. He held the blade up towards the glass dome, its edge disappearing in razor sharpness. Even without a proper handle, the balance felt good. He turned it over, looking at it from all angles, his eyes resting on the pommel, which was made of swirling metals of black, bronze, gold, and silver. On one side, the metals of the pommel formed an image of a wolf sitting and facing forward, looking at him. On the other side was a spiraling petal design.

He looked at Jasper, stunned. "It's beautiful."

"It's Ilian steel."

"Ilian steel," Torr repeated. "I suppose that's good?"

Jasper looked towards the sky like Torr was an idiot. "Look," Jasper said, taking the knife. "Here, Cassidy, get me one of those lengths of silk from the crate."

Cassidy produced a long Delosian scarf that shimmered a deep sapphire blue. "You're not going to hurt this, are you?" she said, hugging the scarf to her chest.

"It's just silk," he said. "Made from worm shit."

"Worm cocoons," she corrected.

Jasper took the long scarf and tossed it into the air, letting it fall onto the upturned edge of the knife, where it sliced cleanly in two with the faintest of whispers. "But of course you've seen that trick before. Only it's the rare blade that actually does that, and this apparently passes the test." He bent to retrieve the two pieces of silk and handed one to Cassidy. "Here. You keep half. It matches your eyes." He winked at her, then tied the other half around his forehead with the long tail hanging down the side of his head, Delosian style.

She blushed and tied hers around her head. Torr rolled his eyes. They were sickening.

Torr returned his attention to the knife. It was more museum piece than weapon. He turned it over in his hand, his eyes drawn to the wolf. Torr froze. The wolf seemed to have moved. He could have sworn it had been facing forward before, its proud chest puffed out, its two front legs strong and stiff as it had stared at him. But now it showed its profile and craned its neck in a mournful pose, howling at a golden moon. He hadn't recalled a moon there before. Goosebumps prickled his flesh. "I'll take it," Torr said, his voice shaking.

"You'll take it," Jasper drawled, bringing his finger to his chin.

Torr had blown it, violated the first rule of negotiating. "It doesn't have a handle," Torr said, trying to recover.

Jasper shrugged. "Which crystal you giving me for it?" His sideways grin crept across his face.

"Go to hell."

Jasper held out his hand. "Give me the knife back, or give me a crystal. Your choice." He smiled evilly at Torr. "I haven't even seen the crystals," Jasper said in a conciliatory tone. "I'm offering the trade sight unseen."

"You are so full of shit, *Jaz*. You've seen them all before."

"I forget what they look like," Jasper said, innocently.

"Lying horse thief," Torr growled. Rather than waste time arguing, Torr sheathed the knife, set it on the edge of the wooden crate, and fished the crystals out of his rucksack, lining them up on a plastic crate from largest to smallest: the fat crystal the Scrids had detected, the dagger crystal, the fluorite octahedron, and finally the garnet.

"This one," Jasper said, lifting the fat one.

Torr realized he shouldn't have even put that one out there. He wasn't about to part with it. Or the dagger crystal. He was doing horribly at bartering today. His concentration was shot. He looked at Cassidy. She shook her head. Not the fat one. They agreed on that. He wrenched it from Jasper's grip and placed it in his vest pouch, then quickly scooped up the dagger crystal that Jasper was reaching for and slipped it into the large cargo pocket at the side of his thigh.

Jasper sneered, and Cassidy gave Torr a little shrug and a tug at her lip that said either of the others was okay with her. Torr looked between the garnet and the fluorite. His eye kept returning to the pale green fluorite, intrigued by the triangular facets of the double pyramid. "It's the red one or nothing," Torr told Jasper. "I don't know what it does, but if it's from Great-Aunt Sophie, it does something. If you're talented enough to discover what. You seem to think you're something special. Prove it."

Jasper smiled at him crookedly. "I only use my talents when necessary, not for show." He pointed his long nose in the air.

Torr waited.

Jasper's gaze slowly made its way back to the garnet. He held it up to the light, the many facets of the dark gem alternating between black and red as they caught the light. "Deal," he said, resignedly. "The wolf knife suits you."

Torr's heart quickened as he picked up the round-pommeled knife. The wolf was facing forward again, and its golden eyes locked onto his.

27

LAND CLAIM

That evening Jasper returned to the yard with his father. Torr's heart swelled at the sight of the man who'd helped raise him. Kai hurried across the yard with the usual rolling hitch to his gait and engulfed Cassidy and Torr in big bear hugs like they were still children. Torr felt comforted, as though he'd returned home to Shasta.

He looked fondly into Kai's eyes. The man looked older than Torr remembered, his face longer, his skin more weathered and creased. His dark hair was graying, and his hairline was receding. But his eyes were the same. Small and brown and set deep in his bony head, giving him a look that had always reminded Torr of a scarecrow. He was tall with long limbs, and his wiry frame was strong under his navy blue flightsuit. A round patch on his left breast pocket was embroidered with a dark blue speedster set against silver mountains and a golden sun. The patch read, PEARY PILOTS. On his other pocket was a name patch embroidered with KUJO.

Fragments of childhood memories flashed through Torr's mind. It was summertime and Torr had fallen from his bicycle and badly scraped his elbow and leg. Torr sat in Jasper's kitchen where Kai gently cleaned his road rash and fed him cookies until Torr's mother picked him up.

Another time, the families had been camping at Lake Siskiyou, and their mothers had been bragging around the campfire about how they were such strong shamans that they could control their husbands. Caden and Kai had retorted that they had some talents of their own, and the women shouldn't get too cocky. Caden had proven it by calling a deer to him from the forest, which he fed with an apple from his hand at the edge of the halo of light cast by the fire.

Kai had proven his powers by going into a trance and channeling Torr's Grandpa Leo, who had died before Torr was born. Torr could still see Kai's sunken, vacant eyes flickering in the firelight. His expression had transformed from his normally rigid frown to a broad smiling face Torr barely recognized. Kai's normally sharp, tenor voice had boomed out in a baritone, filling the campsite and making Torr clutch Grandma Leann's hand.

"Torrance," Kai's voice had bellowed. "You have Grandpa Robert's eyes. Has anyone ever told you that?" Grandma Leann's fingernails dug into Torr's hand as Kai laughed deeply. "I'm so glad to get a chance to talk to you. I've been wanting to tell you and your sister that your timing could not be better. The planets are aligning in just a few years. You two will need to stay alert as forces converge to send you on your way. Don't miss any of the signs."

"What signs?" Cassidy asked in a squeaky voice.

"Way to what?" Torr asked, shaking with fear and wonder as his dead Grandpa Leo spoke to them through Kai's body.

"Why, signposts to the path you both volunteered to follow. The path to the golden stars. Don't you remember?" Grandpa

Leo laughed heartily. "Don't fret, I'll be watching over you, as I promised I would."

Afterwards, Kai had remembered nothing from his trance, and had no idea who Torr's great-great-grandfather Robert was. Grandma Leann had found a picture a few days later, and Torr had his eyes. Brianna and Melanie didn't tease their husbands after that, and the kids treated them with newfound respect and wariness. Now, sitting in the Fen, the memory of Grandpa Leo's words made Torr's spine tingle.

Kai sat with the three of them and Berkeley around the rectangular Delosian crate. It had been completely emptied and its top replaced, and made a decent table. Upturned plastic crates served as chairs. Torr liked this little courtyard, hidden away from the larger Fen camp.

Kai had brought six bottles of beer. They were chilled and sharp with carbonation. Jasper produced strips of something resembling beef jerky, except they were green and smelled of seaweed. Jasper handed one to each of them, then wrapped the remainder in a soft green cloth and tucked them away in his black leather daypack. Torr bit into his strip. It was chewy like jerky, both salty and sweet, and its savory flavor satisfied something he never knew he was missing. It was the perfect complement to the beer, and he gnawed on his happily.

"Gish," Kai said of the food. "Jaz's specialty."

"What is it?" Cassidy asked.

Berkeley answered for Jasper, who was busy chewing. "A plant from Muria. Jaz has cornered the gish market on the moon. His is the best quality available anywhere. He refuses to divulge his secret."

Jasper smiled knowingly. "It's a staple food on Muria," he said, swallowing a mouthful. "Here it's considered a delicacy."

"And is very expensive," Berkeley added. "Keeps Jaz flush with gold. That, and his other Murian specialty."

Jasper responded with a cold glare that made Berkeley close his lips and become suddenly fascinated with the label on his beer bottle. Torr and Cassidy exchanged glances but did not press the topic. Pushing would only make Jasper clamp down tighter on his little secret.

Kai listened attentively as Torr and Cassidy told him about their parents, the Shaman's Shield, and their escape. "Do you think my parents will be able to make it to the mountains and get through the Shaman's Shield to Shasta?" Cassidy asked, her eyes begging him to say yes.

"Well ..." Kai paused, then said slowly, "They both know how to survive in the forest. And if anyone can make it through the Shaman's Shield, your mother can."

Cassidy nodded, and Kai tried to smile encouragingly, but Torr could tell he didn't think the odds were good.

"Dad," Jasper said. "These guys flew into Gandoop."

Kai's brow furrowed. "Really? Why?" He turned to Torr.

"Ships from Moffett Field aren't coming here anymore, they're all being routed through Ridge Gandoop."

"How do you know that?"

"The Tegs at Moffett told us. They actually helped us get out. We showed them the deeds."

"What deeds?" Kai asked. "Tegs helped you?"

"It was Cassidy's idea," Torr said. "Brilliant, actually. A crazy gamble, but it worked." He spread out his arms, then patted his chest. "See? We're here."

"When they saw Metolius's personal seal on them," Cassidy said, "they let us through. They were very courteous. Must have thought we were some Teg general's kids or something. They helped us get a ship and everything."

Jasper and Berkeley gaped, while Kai glared impatiently.

"What deeds?" Kai repeated.

Torr continued, "But they were only flying to Gandoop, so when we got there we managed to get a ride over here. That was the scariest part, actually. Well, to be honest, it was all terrifying. I thought we were bound for a work camp for sure. Anyway, we think the Tegs at Gandoop didn't want us to leave, but we slipped out with the help of some guy with a metal hand."

"Tegs?" Jasper asked.

"Metal hand?" Berkeley asked.

"Yeah," Cassidy said. "Some little scared-looking guy named Murphy, and a pilot named Hunter. Some guy who looked like he was in charge told them to take us here. Ali, I think his name was."

"Ali?" Berkeley echoed.

Torr described their brief stay at Gandoop.

"Are you sure they were Tegs?" Kai asked skeptically. "I would think they'd be in uniform."

Torr shrugged. "Not if they're special forces. Undercover. You know, infiltrators into enemy territory." Kai had been an airman in the Early Wars and a prisoner of war to boot. Torr didn't need to tell him that. Kai's brow creased with worry.

"If they're at Ridge Gandoop, they're probably here, too," Torr said ominously.

"No," Kai said. "Peary is a neutral zone."

"Why would Tegea care about respecting a neutral zone?" Torr asked bitterly.

"Well, mostly because not all races in the galaxy will trade with the Global Alliance directly. The Alliance has to work through the Traders Guild to get access to them. They wouldn't want to mess that up."

"The Nommos already trade directly with the Global Alliance," Berkeley pointed out.

Jasper said, "That's because the Nommos have no morals. I heard they are trying to broker a deal between the Delosians and the Cephean Federation."

Berkeley's expression soured. "That would be the end of Delos. But the Antler Kralj would never be so stupid. Or maybe they would," he said with concern. "At least Muria and Lingri-La will never be charmed by the Cephean Federation."

"Those planets don't produce anything of value, anyway," Kai said.

Berkeley stared at him, his eyes popping. "Are you kidding me?"

"Lingri-La only exports glassware, and Muria is not industrialized," Kai explained. "And they both have a very small humanoid population. The Cephean Federation wouldn't waste their time and resources on them."

"Muria is the source of the most powerful magic," Berkeley said impatiently. "And the Lingris are perfecting its use."

"Cephs don't believe in magic," Kai said.

"They do now," Torr said, despair suddenly clouding his mood. "The Shaman's Shield proved magic to be a potent weapon. And if there's one thing Cephs respect, it's weapons."

The small yard resounded with a gloomy silence.

"Well," Jasper said, clearing his throat. "Murian and Lingri ships rarely come through Peary. Lingris are all women and they hate men, and the Murians only have two ships. Most of their trade is done through the Delosians and the Scrids."

"I thought you said the Murians and Delosians hated each other," Cassidy said.

Jasper shrugged. "They do. But when it comes to hard-to-find goods, and gold, feuds get set aside, I guess."

"What he's trying to say," Berkeley said, "is that traders are an unscrupulous bunch."

"Very funny," Jasper said, not smiling.

"So," Torr broke in, "there's no reason Tegea wouldn't take over Peary."

"I think you're dreaming up nightmare scenarios, Torr," Kai said. "You always had a vivid imagination. This isn't Earth. It's a galactic hub. Things are fine here."

Torr was not convinced, but what did he know? He had just arrived.

"Let's see your deeds," Jasper said. "Dad, they're the deeds their Aunt Sophie gave them. Remember?"

Kai frowned. "Yes, now that you mention it. Where are the parcels? Are they on the near side?"

"Yes," Torr said. "Just barely." He retrieved his deed and map from his rucksack and handed them to Kai. Jasper took Cassidy's, and they plotted the coordinates.

Kai's face slowly hardened. "Bloody hell."

"What?" Torr asked, feeling Kai's anxiety through the air.

Kai pressed his thin lips together. "These deeds are for crater Anaximenes," he said flatly.

"We have three craters," Cassidy said.

"What's wrong?" Torr asked, not liking the way his own hands had started shaking.

"They're all called Anaximenes," Kai said, his eyes hollow and dark.

"The biggest one is just plain Anaximenes," Jasper explained. "The others are called Anaximenes G and H, for Giant and Huge." His lips curled down, despite his attempt at a joke.

Berkeley looked over Kai's shoulder and let out a long, low whistle.

Torr stood up. "What is going on?"

Kai met his eyes. "Gandoop is in Anaximenes."

At first, Torr did not comprehend Kai's words. Then they sank in, the way a knife tip breaks through the rind of a watermelon and thrusts slowly into the pink flesh.

Torr and Cassidy locked gazes.

Berkeley's voice bubbled with excitement. "Anaximenes is a gold mine. Not literally. What I mean is, it's worth a fortune. The Gandoops are filthy rich. The younger son, Ridge, he's a genius. He invented half the technology we use on the moon: oxygen and hydrogen capture from moon dust, core sample fittings for the tankers we use to mine ice, waste recyclers, lots of stuff. Plus, Anaximenes has the highest concentration of rare-earths anyone's found on the moon. We buy tanks of oxygen from them, for space walks, and ships. And that Ali you met, he's Ridge's older brother."

Torr turned to Berkeley. "Ali owns the mine?"

"Ali, Ridge, and their father, Ishmar," Berkeley said. "I worked there. It's a hell-hole. They work you like a dog, and the living conditions are horrendous. They had us stuffed down in one of their big black cubes in tiny barracks. More like a prison. They act like you're lucky to be there, and they have strict security.

"They don't like their workers to leave," Berkeley continued. "They make you sign some sort of bullshit contract that they actually expect you to keep. They keep a tight watch on all shipments in and out, so you can't just hop any old freighter to get out of there. Plus, they keep a stranglehold on the black market traffic, so I couldn't get anything done there. They only accept payment for their elements in gold, and you can't steal the elements or the gold without them finding out. Actually, you can't steal anything. They'll chop off your hand if they catch you. More than one guy at the mine has only one hand." Berkeley arched his eyebrows. "Murphy was the first to lose his."

Torr cringed, and Cassidy's face took on a greenish pallor.

Encouraged that he had Torr's and Cassidy's attention, Berkeley kept talking. "But they produce the best elements and metals, all the expensive ones. They found a huge rare-earths deposit in Anaximenes H, and Ridge invented some new way to isolate and store helium-3. They even have huge industrial-scale furnaces and smelters, and a fluid bed reactor."

"Can you please shut up?" Kai snapped.

Berkeley's lips clamped shut and he stared at Kai.

Torr's head was swimming. He had sheltered the hope of settling their land. Creating a homestead. Saving his parents. Starting a new life. But now the only thing he could think of was the look on that Teg officer's face who'd stomped off looking for his superior, and how the soldiers with the assault rifles had watched Torr and Cassidy run after Hunter, wondering if they were supposed to stop them.

Cassidy was watching and listening, absorbing everything around her like she always did. Withholding judgment until some mysterious connection process inside her head completed. Apparently there were too many dots to connect just yet, because she sat silently with a pained look on her face. Jasper pressed his hands together, his long fingers meeting each other in a steeple. Torr recognized the calculating look that was normally followed by Jasper getting into trouble.

"The Gandoops are rich," Jasper said slowly. "I bet they'd pay you for the deeds. Right, Dad?" Jasper's eyes glinted, and Torr scowled.

Torr knew he should be happy. Isn't that what he really wanted? Get more gold and leave the moon? Then why did the idea of selling the deeds to the Gandoops give him the shivers? The bad, warning kind of shivers.

"You shouldn't tell anyone else you have them," Jasper said. "Berk, can you make these guys document belts? Something they can wear to hide the deeds under their shirts?" Jasper's gaze darted between Cassidy and Torr. "You can't just leave those lying around. They could be worth millions." A sideways smile stretched Jasper's mouth, and knots of anxiety tightened across Torr's shoulders.

———————)———————

Kai left, and Torr and Cassidy sat around a picnic table with Jasper and Berkeley. They stayed up late, talking and drinking tea. Torr brought out two protein bars, the last of their food from Earth, and portioned them out as though they were gold. He chewed on the nutty, chocolaty bar, and was brought back to the Miramar commissary. The crush of bodies. The smell of panic. The brush of Reina's hand. Bobby's sure but frightened gaze. Tears stung his eyes and he blinked them back. Cassidy was watching him and smiled sadly.

Midnight was approaching when a rhythmic thudding resonated through the dome, so deep that Torr could feel it in his bones as much as hear it with his ears. It was a bass drum, soon joined by several higher-pitched drums, sweeping Torr away in their interweaving patterns and feeling like a language Torr should understand.

"Scrids," Berkeley said. "They're talking to the stars."

Torr turned to Cassidy. She nodded slowly, blood rising to her cheeks in a reddish glow. "Yes," she said faintly, listening. "It sounds ... familiar."

Torr's pulse quickened. He wanted to chase the sound and find its origin.

"They're calling their wizard," Jasper said, his eyes glinting mischievously.

"Really?" Torr asked, intrigued.

"Yep. They must want their wizard to meet you. You'd better stay alert." Jasper winked at Cassidy, and Torr couldn't tell if Jasper was kidding or not.

"Ha, ha," Cassidy said, then shushed Jasper as he began speaking again. "Quiet, I'm listening." Her eyes grew distant.

Torr stepped out from under the tarp and looked up at the star-speckled sky, then closed his eyes and let the drumbeat carry him away.

28

JİDNA GANDİ

Ridge left Gandoop Spaceport and headed southeast towards Last Chance. Anaximenes had finally turned away from the sun, but Earth was almost full and cast a radiant Earthshine. Shadows cast by crater rims reared then fell away as he sped over the ghostlike moonscape towards Mare Frigoris, the "Cold Sea," an inlet at the upper reaches of the Black Maria whose shores Last Chance sat upon.

Ridge gripped the throttle and went into high gear, then exhaled as the acceleration subsided. Earth glistened with gem-like blues and greens as he flew towards the desolate stone sea. After a relaxing journey of silence, he decelerated and descended towards his outpost. It was a harsh life on the moon, and even harsher at the outer rim, the lifeless edges of the Black Maria where the regolith thinned and miners made a living by extracting titanium and iron from the vast expanses of basalt.

After receiving this stretch of land in exchange for storing a freighter, Ridge had decided to build out the Last Chance facility for a few reasons. Primarily, it served as cover for his identity as Jidna Gandi, outer rim mining lord. To maintain his deception, he always went to Peary via Last Chance. Secondly, there was a market for the elements available in abundance in the basalt. But most importantly, it was a place for him to escape to when he could no longer tolerate Balty.

He hovered above the facility, regarding with satisfaction the shiny new white titanium roof on the residential facility. The crew had finally made it airtight and got the air control and electrical systems up and running. Ridge had walked around inside without a spacesuit for the first time a week ago. The large square building was attached to the western wall of the four-ship hangar that had been completed last year. It had one pair of compression chambers large enough to accommodate a local moon freighter, and a small gravity bar whose gravitational field covered the residential facility as well as a perimeter around the compound.

Half a mile to the east sat a lone white dome. It had been the only structure when the Gandoops had acquired the land, a self-contained unit made from a kit, with a solid roof and two small round portholes recessed into the sides. Ridge had taken over the dome for his private lab. One half of the building served as a compression chamber/hangar combo that was just big enough for one moon freighter and his speedster. He navigated to the lab and floated into the compression bay, navigating precisely into the tight parking spot with the speedster's nose tucked under the freighter's stubby wing.

When the chamber filled with air and the pressure light flashed, he climbed out of the speedster, removed his knee-high, shiny black boots that he kept polished with a cream he had formulated to repel moon dust, and passed through the man-sized airlock into the living quarters. He peeled off his clothes and threw them into the laundrobot, pressing the button to start the automated dry-cleaning, pressing, and folding process. Then he showered and changed into a clean flightsuit and his slippers. He rubbed his palms slowly down his chest, enjoying the smooth fabric, and then settled onto the stool at his workbench.

"Good afternoon," he said, waving his fingers in greeting at three glass canisters sitting on the shelf in front of him. Three gnarled claws gestured back at him. He idly regarded the skeletal hands perched inside. Murphy's, Bocci's, and Pinto's. Casualties of Balty's crackdown on theft. Ridge had taken the freshly severed hands to Yen to see if the physician could reattach them, but Yen didn't have that kind of skill or equipment, so Ridge had frozen them in hopes of figuring it out himself. After a time he'd given up. He was an engineer, not a surgeon. He'd considered 3D printing new hands with living cells, but he didn't know where to get the right printer or the source bio-materials, and the pilot he used to rely on for special medical supply orders from Earth had died. Ridge had given himself over to the task of designing a mechanical hand that was just as good as the natural one, or better.

Secured in a clamp on his workbench was Murphy's half-finished, five-finger prosthesis. Ridge had stripped the real hands down to the bone layer by layer, meticulously modeling the skin layers, muscles, ligaments, and tendons. The metal prosthesis now mirrored the bony structure of Murphy's hand in the jar. He planned to enable the hands to grip and release with pressure sensitivity, and he'd mapped the nerves as best he could, hoping to replicate the subtleties of sensation.

Still, he dreamed of making a hand that looked and felt real, so he had set out in search of the right material to mimic muscle fiber. He thought he'd finally discovered something that would do the trick. He'd stumbled upon the idea for the material by chance, as was often the case with his discoveries. The material was called fisorial, and was from a life form found in the seas of

Delos. It was not clear if fisorial was plant or animal, but seemed a combination of the two. Something between squishy seaweed and fleshy squid. It had an elasticity that retained its flexibility and strength over time, and its fibers had a perfect blend of friction and fluidity. Janjabar, the wigmaker, had extolled its properties and used it as the base for his wigs. The fisorial adhered securely to the scalp, stretching to fit, and hugged it gently but firmly. It had struck Ridge one day that this would make perfect muscle fiber, and maybe skin, for the prostheses. Now all he needed was to find time to get to Delos and procure a supply of the stuff.

Ridge left the half-finished hand and turned to his other project: a spherical cryogenic canister he called Silox, a porous silicon and liquid oxygen explosive device that fit comfortably into a cupped hand. He had already successfully deployed two of them out on the basalt with a remote-controlled detonator. Now he was fashioning a pin release mechanism to use as a hand-thrown grenade. That was a little trickier, since he had to be more precise about the timing and blast radius.

He didn't really know what he intended to do with the Silox grenades. He fantasized about tossing one into Balty's bedroom while the creep was fucking one of his girls, but that would kill the girl, too, and damage the house. Ridge shook off his dreams of vengeance and turned his attention to the timing mechanism.

———————)———————

Ridge spent the night at the lab. The next morning he decided to visit Peary Dome. It had been a couple weeks since he'd last been there, and he missed the open air of the spacious glass enclosure. He folded the single bed up into the wall and regarded the efficiently designed unit, complete with kitchenette, a narrow table with built-in benches, a tiny bathroom, and a small closet. It was all he needed, really. He took a hot shower and shaved his scalp and face, then toweled himself dry.

Next, he set about transforming himself from Ridge Gandoop, owner of the most powerful mine on the moon, to Jidna Gandi, outer rim mining lord. He didn't know why the outer rim mining lords had such a bad reputation. He supposed it was because the two or three most notorious gang leaders who'd fled during the Peary uprising had ended up working mining claims at the edge of the basalt sea. He shrugged. It suited him just fine to have a reputation as a scummy outer rim mining lord. Better that people were a bit wary of him than to think they could take advantage of him.

He had taken the name Jidna from his given name, Rjidna. It sounded close enough that it rang true to his ears, but different enough from Ridge that people did not connect the two. And Gandi was close to Gandoop, but reminded people of the old Indian prophet, Gandhi. It didn't hurt for people to subconsciously believe that he possessed a high moral character.

Ridge stood in front of the full-length mirror on the bathroom door and began by carefully adhering bushy eyebrows over his own, neatly groomed ones. Jidna's eyebrows were dark brown with long hairs sprouting every which way, and filled in the gap above his nose to form one long brow. Janjabar had delighted over this detail of his disguise. He had wanted Ridge to use a prosthetic nose, but Ridge had thought it would be too easy to detect. Besides, his nose was so unremarkable—straight and pudgy like half the men he'd ever met—that he deemed a fake nose an unnecessary nuisance.

He'd decided he needed a disguise after getting harassed in Peary Dome. He had expected to be bullied for being a half-breed, like he had back on Earth. But Peary Dome was a galactic community, and although he drew his share of curious glances and an occasional sneer or rude comment, by and large, people accepted him. The real problems came as a result of his power and wealth. People were constantly pestering Ridge for business deals or threatening him. Two men who'd worked the mine had spit at him on a Peary road, and it had really bothered him. The Gandoops intentionally ran a strict operation, but he hadn't realized the workers resented it so much. The Gandoops insisted their workers fulfill their three-year labor contracts, but some still managed to escape early. Then after Balty's hand-chopping incidents, Ridge had been attacked on the Peary perimeter road by a group of former mine workers. He'd managed to crawl to the infirmary, and the medics had radioed his brother to come get him.

He'd stayed away from Peary for a full year after that. But he loved it there. It was the closest thing to Earth on the moon, and he couldn't take the two-week flight to Delos every time he wanted to experience open sky and walk around freely. It was on one of those infrequent trips to Delos that he'd come upon the idea for his disguise.

On Delos it was fashionable for the women of the ruling Antler Kralj House to wear enormous, ornate wigs, with half of the hair piled high on top of their heads in a nest of curls, and the remainder cascading down their backs to their waists. He had been standing outside a wigmaker's shop, gawking at the ostentatious wigs on the stands in the window, when the wigmaker, Janjabar, had started chatting him up. Ridge learned Janjabar also made wigs and costumes for the theater, and the idea for Jidna Gandi had been born.

Janjabar had approached the task with relish. He loved nothing better than to create characters, and the idea of crafting a true disguise instead of one for the stage made him laugh like a child. Ridge spent the entire day in the back of the shop.

Janjabar chose a wig with hair that was nearly as dark as Ridge's own, but a deep, dark brown instead of pure black, and of a slightly finer texture. They decided Jidna would be an unkempt slob of a man, in stark contrast to Ridge's austere, clean-cut self. After all, Janjabar stressed, Ridge was creating an illusion—a deception—and the mind was more easily tricked by emotional response than by physical appearance. If Ridge was prim and proper, let Jidna be dirty and vulgar.

Janjabar fitted the wig to Ridge's head, showing him the stretchy fisorial base, then gave the wig a long, ragged cut. The thick hair hung down over his eyes and past his shoulders. Janjabar turned the luxurious, silky curls into a mass of greasy strands with a pomade, and Ridge assured him the moon dust would make it even worse. Janjabar gave him a couple jars of the pomade, and several hair extensions that he could clip up into the thick mane of hair to make it longer. "You can't always look the same," Janjabar told him. "Hair grows." That sent Janjabar off in a flurry to provide him with a second wig that was shorter and a bit more groomed. It still hung over his eyebrows and ears in a scruffy mess, but ended just below his collar. "For when you need a haircut," Janjabar said.

Next, Janjabar prepared him two beards. One was as greasy and wild as the first wig, with the moustache hanging distastefully over his lips, the bushy sideburns and beard covering his jowls and neck, and the whole thing trailing down over his chest like a rat's nest. The second beard was shorter and a bit more tidy, but not overly so. They decided Ridge had enough chest and arm hair to match Jidna's scruffiness. At least the body hair that had always disgusted Ridge was good for something. Janjabar finished his hairy masterpiece with the addition of the eyebrows, which tangled nicely with the overgrown bangs.

Next, Janjabar gave Ridge a cream that turned his normally pale olive skin into a subtle bronze, swarthy tone reminiscent of the traders of Delos Monger House, who frequented the moon in their boxy, spiked ships. The skin creams were theater quality, with a fine powder Ridge needed to pat on to set it, and required a special solution to easily remove, which Janjabar provided Ridge in a large jug. The final touches were the eye lenses that turned his emerald-green irises a dark, chocolaty brown.

Once back on the moon, Ridge had lightly stuffed a couple pillowcases with foam and sewed them inside a t-shirt front and back to make himself look paunchy all the way around. Then he rummaged through the clothing left over from workers who had died at the mine and found army-green cargo pants, a few dingy t-shirts, and a green camouflage field jacket that fit in a loose, slobby way that suited Jidna. The outfit was the opposite of the sleek black flight suit Ridge always wore. The clothing was well broken-in, and Ridge followed Janjabar's advice of dousing the clothing in beer and letting it sour so that he gave off an unpleasant odor.

Ridge returned his attention to the mirror, stretching the long, unruly wig over his bare scalp. Next he attached the beard with a special adhesive. He gave his head a shake. The hair, eyebrows, and beard were as secure as if they were his own. He popped the lenses into his eyes, smoothed the skin cream over his face, neck, and arms, set the whole thing with powder, then donned the stinky clothing. He found a beer in the refrigerator and downed most of it, letting the rest spill over his beard and chest where it soaked into his shirt and added fresh alcohol to his acrid stench. He darkened his teeth with a yellow Delosian spice that would fade with a good brushing, then smiled at himself in the mirror.

"Hello, Jidna," he greeted himself, and belched loudly. He donned his final accessory: a pair of gray, mirrored, Teg officer's sunglasses he had traded with one of Balty's men for a 25-year-old Scotch. He had found mirrored sunglasses to be the best way to distract people from examining his face—everyone loved to look at themselves. Ridge went into the hangar and pulled on Jidna's scuffed brown boots. As a last touch, he wiped moon dust from the ship's hull and rubbed it into his hair, beard, and clothing.

He had purchased an old, beat-up moon freighter for Jidna that he kept at the lab. It was a Korova—a utilitarian Russian model that had been supplied out of Baikonur for the past three decades. He had hand-painted Last Chance on its gray side in big black letters. The ship looked as ratty as Jidna did. He threw a few sacks of titanium powder into the back for trade, climbed into the pilot's seat, and headed for Peary.

———————)———————

Jidna had some good qualities that Ridge lacked. A sense of humor, for example. Jidna loved to laugh, and Ridge delighted in the carefree ways of his alter ego. Jidna always felt relaxed and comfortable in his old clothing, which hung loosely around his body and was butter-soft to the touch. He was unconcerned about what others thought of him, and allowed himself to slouch and burp and fart whenever he wanted to. Ridge entertained himself in this manner as he traveled at high speed towards Peary Dome and reflected on his double life.

The primary disadvantage of his disguise was sex, or the lack of it. Except for Danny, but she almost didn't count. He was afraid that any new bed partners would tug off his wig or beard in the throes of passion, or find his partial tan odd. It was probably a needless worry. After all, he would be paying the women well. But the possibility of discovery made him uncomfortable. He longed for the wild days before the Peary uprising, when the prostitutes had been young and plentiful, out for wealth and adventures of their own in the new frontier. Now, they were sedately organized into two brothels, under the watchful eyes of their keepers. A third group of women lived underground. Not prostitutes, but a reclusive sect of women who followed Gabira Ben Najam, a tempestuous shaman whom he'd never bothered to meet personally. He had no use for snotty, arrogant women.

During the period when he'd kept away from Peary Dome for his safety, two of his three favorite girls from the wild years had left the moon. The one who remained was the woman he'd given his virginity to: Danny Rodriguez. He still went to her bed sometimes, but the years that had passed between them had mellowed his lust-filled passion into the calm comfort of familiarity. She was a prostitute, after all. A madam, now. How much of his heart could he give to someone who shared her body with so many men?

Still, he had succumbed to her even in his disguise, and when she'd taken Jidna into her bed the first time, she'd recognized him. "I like it," she said, stroking his long hair and gazing into his brown eyes as he bent over her, naked and erect. "I almost didn't recognize you." She kissed his lips tenderly and drew him to her.

"It's a secret," he said hoarsely as he let his arousal find her succulent flesh.

"I won't tell," she whispered breathlessly into his ear as they moved together. "Discretion is my business."

He'd believed her, and trusted her still.

The only other person in the dome who recognized him happened to be the pimp of the second brothel. Schlitzer knew him not because they shared a bed but because it was Schlitzer's business to know things, and he did so with an uncanny perception that rendered Ridge's disguise useless. Schlitzer worked with energy, and had vast talent in that domain. Ridge suspected that Schlitzer could only sense, but not see, the energy lines. Ridge alone had that freakish gift.

Ridge always wondered if his mother had seen energy as he did, but he would never know. Ishmar had met Ridge's mother, Zerrin, at a job site where he was managing the construction of a hovercraft corridor. She was a Cephean engineer and helped him design sensors that kept the vehicles inside the lanes. It was revolutionary. Of course, the Cephean rulers took credit for it, taking her designs and patenting the technology for themselves. But it got Ishmar several more hovercraft corridor contracts.

Zerrin stole Ishmar's heart, and Ishmar divorced Ali's mother when Ali was three years old. Ishmar won full custody of Ali and took the boy with him when he moved onto the next job in a different country, leaving Ali's mother in a city that was taken over by the Tegs a couple years later. She was not heard from again. Zerrin had died giving birth to Ridge, leaving both half-brothers without a mother. Most of the child-rearing had been done by Ishmar's mother, who did not show much love for Ridge. He always thought her cold treatment was because his mother had been a Ceph. Or maybe it was because Zerrin had driven off Ali's mother, who was the daughter of a friend of hers. Or maybe she was just a mean person. Or maybe Ridge was simply too quiet and strange, though he was sure his mother would have loved him if she had lived.

Ridge had yet to test a full-blooded Ceph to see if his heritage was to blame for his sight, and he hoped he would never interact with one enough to find out. If full-blooded Cephs could see energy lines, then they surely would be masters at controlling them, and Ridge would be helpless under their power.

Ridge surmised that most Earthlanders perceived the energy connections as warmth and attraction, or fear and revulsion. The rare ones were somewhat conscious of the energy tendrils, even if they couldn't see them, and used the connections to charm or manipulate others.

When Ridge had first gone to Schlitzer's brothel as Jidna, Schlitzer had looked at him with that unseeing way he had when he felt the energy of another, then focused on Jidna's brown eyes, and with a quirk of his lips said, "That's good. Very good." He'd clapped Ridge on the back and nodded appreciatively as he led him to his private consultation tent. "Masterful."

"I want to be unnoticed," Ridge said.

"And unnoticed you shall be. Who are you now?"

"Jidna Gandi, outer rim mining lord. I want to join the Traders Guild."

"Right. Excellent. I'll sponsor you. You've got the Solidi, I assume?" he asked with a wry grin. "Or would you like to apprentice under me for two years?"

"I'll pay the Solidi."

"I thought you might. You're new to the moon, right? I haven't seen you around before. How'd you get the outer rim mine?"

Ridge had already fabricated his tale and appreciated Schlitzer giving him a chance to rehearse it. He told him with a straight face, "Bought it from the Gandoops. Our families knew each other back in the old country, and they promised to help set me up."

Schlitzer nodded approvingly. "It's always helpful to have powerful friends."

"Indeed," Ridge agreed. And that had been the last they'd spoken of it.

The only others who knew of his deception were his father and brother. They thought it a good thing that he could freely roam Peary Dome undercover and were pleased with his Traders Guild status. He had never bothered joining the Guild before, since Ishmar and Ali were already members and normally took care of the trading. Ridge had been glad to let them deal with that side of the business while he sought the pleasures of the dome or spent his time inventing and expanding the mining operation. And so, for the past couple years he had frequented the dome as Jidna Gandi, Traders Guild member, and had come to love his other self.

———————)———————

Jidna arrived at Peary Spaceport, submitted to the weapons search, showed his Traders Guild patch, and went into the Traders pen to see what new sorts of oddities had found their way across the galaxy. He strolled slowly up and down the aisles between open containers.

It was the usual stuff. From Earth, there was an assortment of jewelry, watches, clothing, tools, knives, eating utensils, batteries, solar panels, and scavenged electronics of all kinds. From Lingri-La, there were delicate glass sculptures and dishes. From the Cephean Federation were books of law and star maps. All dull stuff. One container held something interesting. Clothing and jewelry from Delos.

Jidna recognized the trader: Jaz was his name. A tall youth with auburn hair and green aviators. The man seemed to be more sensitive than most, his abundant energy filaments exploring the air around him and retracting quickly when he detected danger. Jidna allowed Jaz to gently probe him, so as not to alarm him. Jaz's filaments were not the malevolent, dark sort like Balty's, but the fine golden threads of a normal person seeking to connect with another. Finding no purchase in Jidna's subtly shielded energy body, Jaz withdrew his filaments, not out of fear but because there was no reciprocated interest and nothing to be learned.

"Jidna, right?" Jaz greeted him, holding out his hand.

Jidna smiled brightly and laughed his coarse laugh. "That's right, good memory. Jaz, isn't it?" Jidna shook his hand heartily as Jaz returned his gregarious smile. Jaz seemed a warm soul, and smart, but a bit suspicious, as all good traders were.

"What have you got here?" Jidna asked, picking up a pair of leather arm guards ornately embossed with a complex knot motif.

"Got a haul from Antler Kralj. Came in a few days ago."

Jidna whistled. "Antler Kralj. Lucky you."

Jaz nodded and sat casually on a stool while Jidna sorted through the goods. There were some fine articles of clothing but nothing he couldn't get on Delos, which was the only place he wore such garb. The jewelry was a bit more interesting, but nothing caught his fancy until he opened a small square wooden box. He tried to mask his surprise, but Jaz was too aware, and surreptitiously eyed Jidna as he drew the caged orb from its velvet nest. A small, round blue crystal was impaled on the gold axis of a spherical enclosure made of longitudinal gold bars like a tiny globe-shaped birdcage. The whole thing was no bigger than a large marble and hung on a gold chain. Jidna feared to hold it for long lest Jaz divine its purpose and charge him an inordinate amount of gold, or decline to part with it at all.

He glanced up at Jaz. "What's this?" Jidna asked, letting it drop gently onto the forest-green velvet that lined the box.

Jaz shrugged his shoulders. "I don't really know. Never seen one like it before."

Jidna did know what it was. He had seen one years ago, during his first trip to Delos. It had been on display at the Antler Kralj Royal Museum as part of a special showing of items associated

with the Royal Tellers, those of the Teller House who served the
Antler Kralj. Members of the Teller House worked as diviners:
counselors, seers, advisors, or, more commonly, scribes, historians, librarians, and the like. The Antler Kralj royalty and all
the families of the various Houses were descended from Iliad
and kept their ancient bloodlines and traditions alive on Delos.
The exhibit was part of the millennial anniversary of the fall
of Iliad, and the Royal Museum was paying tribute to the Star
Children who had died when the Cephs invaded Iliad. Or so
the story went.

Jidna didn't pay much heed to the Star Seeker legends, but
most everyone else seemed caught up in them. Even the Cephs.
Balty had told him one drunken night that the Cephs had conquered Earth because their maps showed it was a planet with
potential to receive the Star People, now that the portal on Iliad
had been destroyed. Balty thought it was a load of crap, but the
Cephean leaders were taking no chances. They were grooming
the planet for the Star People's arrival, so that the Cephs could
properly welcome the divine beings and lead them to Thunder
Walker, the Cephean seat of power.

"I'll give you a gold Eagle for it," Jidna told Jaz, digging into
his pocket and fishing out a gold coin. "Or a Springbok," he
said, glancing down at the golden antelope on the coin he had
randomly selected. Springboks were rare and prized over Eagles
among the traders.

Jaz raised a finger to his chin, his eyes glinting. "It's not every
day you see Antler Kralj goods," he said.

Jidna wagged his bushy eyebrows. "It's not every day you see
a Springbok."

Jaz laughed disdainfully and took a handful of coins from
a vest pocket, then, after searching for a moment, flipped a
Springbok to Jidna, who tossed it back good-naturedly. "Okay,

you got me there. Two Eagles, then," he said, using the common name for one-ounce gold coins, though many were other than the ubiquitous Eagles. "One Springbok, and one, let me see ..." He sorted through his coins and came up with a Delosian Stag. "Got one of these?" He tossed the coin to Jaz.

Jaz inspected it and shook his head. "No. I had one once when I was on Delos, but I spent it." Jaz regarded Jidna with mild curiosity.

They finally settled on four Eagles, and Jidna took the golden amulet into his possession. If he had been Ridge, he would have been circumspect and stashed it away in his pocket, waiting for the privacy of his own quarters before investigating it further. But Jidna was outgoing and a bit of a braggart, and so he lifted the globe by its chain while Jaz followed it with his eyes.

"If this is what I think it is," Jidna said, concentrating on the blue crystal, "it should ... aha!" The blue orb started spinning and emitted a soft blue glow. He heard Jaz's intake of breath, and grinned, knowing Jaz regretted his deal already. Too late. A trader should always learn the value of his goods before parting with them. It was the key to wealth. That's why he was so rich, he thought smugly, as the orb spun faster and the glow expanded and brightened, bathing them in its subtle blue aura.

"What is it?" Jaz asked.

"It's a Truthsayer. The Priests on Iliad used them to counsel the kings."

Jaz wheezed with dismay, causing Jidna to laugh and break his concentration. The light flickered and died.

"Let me see," Jaz said.

Jidna passed it to him and watched as Jaz held it aloft. Slowly, the orb spun and glowed, albeit feebly. Even so, Jaz demonstrated some level of extrasensory awareness and control. Jidna regarded Jaz carefully. He'd met few who could harness their power at all, never mind wield it intentionally. To cause an Ilian Priest's Truthsayer to light up, no matter how dimly, won his respect.

The orb faded, and Jaz handed the amulet back to him. There was no undoing the trade now, and Jaz slouched with resignation. "How did you know what it was? How does it work?"

Jidna liked this man. Jaz was a kindred spirit, and he had met few of them in his lifetime. "I saw one at the Royal Museum on Delos. I couldn't hold it, but the guide described it for me. It's just a pendulum, really. And I know how they work from my grandmother." His grandmother had used a simple plumb line to divine answers to her questions. She would hold the string, and the metal weight would hang at its end and slowly swing in a circle.

Jidna held up the globe again, causing it to light up. He stilled his vagrant thoughts and focused on a simple question. "Did this amulet originate from Delos?" Jidna asked aloud. The whole cage started to swing in a slow, clockwise circle.

Jidna looked up at Jaz, who was staring with fascination at the circling pendulum. "Clockwise means no," Jidna told him.

Jaz's face flushed, and he said stiffly, "I thought it came from Delos. I didn't lie."

"I know," Jidna said. He returned his attention to the amulet, which had stopped its swinging and rested motionless at the end of the gold chain. "Did it, or rather, did you come from Iliad?"

The amulet circled slowly counterclockwise. "Aha!" Jidna chortled. "I thought so."

"Hermes' balls," Jaz cursed. "I should have known."

Jidna felt Jaz's frustration and shrugged apologetically. "Sorry. It was a legitimate trade between Guild members."

"I know," Jaz said. "It's just that there were other Ilian artifacts with this lot. I should have wondered about this one, seeing as it's so unusual."

Jidna nodded kindly and smiled. "Glad I caught you when I did. This could come in handy." He laughed and stroked his untidy beard. "Thanks."

"Yeah, you're welcome," Jaz muttered gloomily.

Jidna felt a bit guilty. Jaz seemed truly upset about losing such a treasure, whereas Jidna thought a pendulum simply read the energy of its bearer: that is, if he believed a thing to be true, then the pendulum would read that and reflect it back to him. But others put true stock in these devices, so he held out the possibility that there could be some merit to them. His grandmother was no fool; neither were Ilian Priests, he imagined. It would make a fun toy, regardless.

"What's the blue glowy thing?" Jaz asked, still intrigued.

"That, I don't know," Jidna answered honestly. "The museum guide said nothing about that, only that the amulet divined the truth." He settled the orb into its velvet cocoon, closed the box, and slid it into his vest pocket. "Nice doing business with you," he told Jaz sincerely, shook his hand, and left the Traders pen.

Balty was in the game room shooting pool, and Ridge joined him. They had an ongoing rivalry. Closely matched, it was the one thing they enjoyed together. They played while exchanging few words. Ridge won one game, then Balty the next. As Ridge neatly put away three balls in a row and then scratched, he admitted to himself that with forty new Teg soldiers living at Gandoop and taking over the spaceport operations, Ridge's opportunity to easily dispose of Balty had passed. Everyone knew you needed to kill vermin before they multiplied. He should have suffocated them all in the tunnels when he'd had the chance. He was an idiot.

His mounting despair shot his game to hell, and Balty won

three in a row. Ridge always had to let Balty win the last game anyhow, so he took the opportunity to retreat to his private chambers and tumbled into bed, staring up through the glass ceiling at a brilliant roof of stars.

He couldn't sleep and finally switched on the light, found the box with the pendulum, and lay back against his pillows, examining the device. It was beautiful. The small blue crystal glimmered knowingly, illuminating from within to cast a warm glow. The golden cage held it like a precious jewel. He turned out the light so that only the blue orb hung above his abdomen in the darkness, waiting.

He asked, "Will Balty kick us out and control Gandoop completely?" The orb slowly circled in a counterclockwise direction. He glared at it disdainfully. "I knew that already."

He stilled the amulet with his free hand and tried to think of a question he didn't already know the answer to. "Do the Star People really exist?" Without hesitation, the amulet circled counterclockwise. Ridge watched it go around and around. "Maybe I knew that already," he said sullenly. He felt for the velvet-lined box on his bedside table and settled the amulet into it, closing the box to extinguish it. He stared up at the stars. Maybe they really were out there and would save him, too.

29

RUNE BELT

Torr stood outside his tent and glanced at his new next-door neighbor, Prince Faisal, who was sitting in a lawn chair facing south, gazing at Earth. Torr followed his gaze to the planet, and his heart caught in his throat. There was Europe, green and brown, with swirls of clouds obscuring the center of the continent. He pulled his binoculars from the case at his belt and focused on where the Great Isles should be: England, Scotland, Wales, Ireland. The Isle of Man, where Jasper's ancestors were from. But all he could see was a patch of white clouds. The Druid's Mist. Great-Aunt Sophie was behind those clouds somewhere. If she was still alive.

The Americas would be beyond the cusp of light at this hour, facing away from the moon. His heart pounded as he thought of his mother and father. They would be sleeping now. Or using the cover of night to make their way north. It had been nearly two weeks since Torr and Cassidy had left Earth, the longest two weeks of his life. Under the best of conditions, on foot it would take his parents ten days to reach the border of the Shaman's Shield south of Shasta. Trying to avoid Tegs, it could take much longer. He wondered about the fate of his friends—those he'd fled with, those who'd turned Teg. They were down there, and he had escaped. He almost wished he were there still, helping his parents reach Shasta, or hiding in the forest with Bobby, or even making his way through the sprawl of LA with the others, though they would have arrived at their homes long ago, or been carted off by the Tegs. He could not think of that. Reina ... The pain was too much. He ground his teeth. He had made a choice, and he had to live with it.

At least he still had his sister, and Jasper. Torr lowered the binoculars and glanced over at Cassidy and Jasper, who were seated at the picnic table studying a large map. Cassidy knew Torr better than anyone. She even knew he had killed people, without him telling her. The herb, Pine Flower, must have told her. His mother's red notebook told the healer what was wrong with the person who needed the herb, and it told the person what they needed to hear to take it. He could still see the magical ink—it was emblazoned in his mind and would be until he no longer needed its medicine. *Pine Flower – Take two drops to douse the flames of grief and guilt that threaten to consume you and those you love. The universe has need of you yet. The fight has just begun. Take heart and soldier on.*

Torr took a deep, shaking breath, and reached for the small bottle of Pine Flower in his chest pocket, raised the dropper over his mouth, and let two drops fall onto his tongue. The herb was bitter. He liked it that way. Its sharp bite roused him from his depression. He still ached inside, but he no longer felt like stabbing himself in the gut.

He did not have the luxury of mourning. He had responsibilities. Maybe even more than before. The unfathomable task of the male Star Child. Maybe he had come to the moon for a reason. Maybe this was the first step along his destined path. A hidden path, to be sure, but it was his duty to discover where it led.

It still felt strange that he had killed people. Numbing. As though a stranger was walking around in his dead husk of a body. But it had been war, after all. He had been defending freedom. Or at least he had tried. Regardless, it was done, and he had to move on.

He lifted his gaze to the tapestry of stars. Jupiter stood out like a diamond stud. He found Orion the hunter with his sword and shield, two hunting dogs at his side, and the rabbit at his feet. Torr raised the binoculars to his eyes and tried to locate the star Delos orbited, but was too lazy to dig out his star map and figure out exactly which one it was.

Talking and laughter floated through the Fen, followed by the strum of a guitar. Fritz was sitting on a plastic crate, tuning an acoustic guitar of pale golden wood. His brother joined him, holding a guitar of dark reddish wood. They sat across from each other, tuning to the same pitch.

Torr felt Faisal watching him. He offered the binoculars to the solemn man, who took them silently, eyes hidden by blue mirrored sunglasses. Faisal perched the sunglasses on his head, thanking Torr with deep brown eyes, then raised the binoculars towards Earth.

Next to Faisal's tent, Sky and Thunder were walking in and out of theirs, arranging their things that were stacked outside in the dust. Roanoke and Raleigh stood outside the next tent, talking through the open door flaps to their father and Hawk.

Berkeley appeared from behind the water wagon. His long dreadlocks were loose and hung in dusty clumps. Jasper and Cassidy motioned for Torr to join them. Torr retrieved his binoculars and retreated to the small, private yard, and sat with his friends around the wooden Delosian crate.

"Here," Berkeley said to Torr and Cassidy, handing them each a long rectangle of new khaki-colored tent canvas. "For your deeds."

They were flat pouches with button closures, attached to green web army belts with black buckles that snapped together. A red rune was embroidered on each pouch, in a shape that reminded Torr of the writing on the cover of the blue and gold book.

"What'd you do, Berk?" Jasper asked, running his fingertips over the rune on Torr's belt pouch.

"Oh, just a bit of a spell I learned from Eridanus. I can't make a very strong one, but it should help a little."

Torr inspected Berkeley. The eccentric man was full of surprises.

"It says *fold into shadow*," Jasper said.

Berkeley frowned. "How do you know that?"

Jasper grinned smartly. "It says so."

"What are you talking about?" Cassidy asked. "What spell? Who's Eridanus?"

"It's just a basic glamour spell," Berkeley said. "Hides the pouch, in a way. Makes it difficult to detect. Advanced spells could hide it completely, but I'm only a novice. This one hides it from sight and touch as long as the belt is clasped around bare skin, and as long as the observers do not touch it directly. That means if you keep it under your clothing and are frisked, they won't feel it. And if it is against your skin but your clothes aren't covering it, they won't see it. But as soon as they touch it directly, they will feel it, and unclasping it will make it visible again. Like I said, it's a basic spell."

"Really? A spell?" Cassidy asked, intrigued.

Torr furrowed his brow. The Shasta Shamans frowned upon witchcraft and spells, saying they were used to manip-ulate others and were not a fair use of power. Torr didn't understand how hiding a deed in a canvas pouch was any less fair than hiding the Western Free States behind a cloud of ash. The shamans had even complained about his mother's herbal practice. That was one of the things that had caused Brianna to leave the sect. Their leader, Remo, had claimed she used magic ink, which made her herbs magic potions instead of plant spirit medicine; the former being witchcraft and the latter being a legitimate shamanistic practice. His mother had insisted the ink was from a plant spirit and therefore was shamanism. Remo had given her an ultimatum: stop using the ink or leave the sect. She had chosen the ink. As far as Torr could tell, the Shasta Shamans thought they were smarter than everybody else, and their rules were the only rules. Shamanism, witchcraft, what was the difference, really? None, as far as Torr was concerned.

Torr watched with interest as Cassidy took her deed and map from her daypack, folded the parchments neatly, then slipped them inside the canvas pouch. She clasped it around her waist under the jerkin, then raised the leather shirt and exposed her bare belly. The belt was not there.

Torr rose and pressed his hand to her waist. The belt was solid under his fingers but was still invisible. He felt around her side for the clasp and pinched it open, and the belt appeared in his hands. He snapped it closed again, and it disappeared. Excitement coursed through his blood.

"Hermes' wings, Berkeley. You're a genius!" Jasper cried.

Torr stared at Berkeley with wonder as Jasper clapped and praised Berkeley for his handiwork. Torr touched Cassidy's waist again, the fabric materializing under his fingers. When she pulled her jerkin down over it, he could not feel it through the leather. Jasper took a turn, stroking Cassidy's bare skin a bit more enthusiastically than was necessary, Torr judged, but

Cassidy stepped in closer and rested her hand lightly on Jasper's chest as he clasped and unclasped her belt. Torr took his own belt and strapped it to his waist, testing its invisibility properties over and over.

"Can you teach me how to make such a spell?" Torr asked, trying to memorize the rune.

"I don't think so," Berkeley said. "It's not so simple. It has to do with weaving intention in with the thread as you place the stitches, by hand, of course. But there's more to it than that. Something I can't explain in words. It requires a basic under-standing of intentionality that I can't teach. You need a Master like Eridanus, or Ramesh, to teach you. And believe me, the lessons aren't always fun."

"Who's Eridanus?" asked Torr.

"Who's Ramesh?" asked Cassidy at the same time.

"Eridanus is a wizard on Delos. Lives in the mountains. A hermit, really, but he takes apprentices occasionally. Usually stupid foreign novices like myself, who agree to work as not much more than indentured servants for two years in exchange for small bits of knowledge. Mostly I fetched water and gathered food and herbs for him. Cooked and sewed. Copied texts. Chopped firewood. Cleaned latrines. Stuff like that." He settled onto a seat, and they all sat with him, eyeing him curiously.

"So, you apprenticed as a wizard?" Cassidy asked with open admiration. Torr examined the man, the strange beard and wild locks suddenly seeming appropriate. "What else did you learn?" Cassidy asked.

Berkeley shrugged. "Stuff." He smiled mischievously, his gracefully curved eyelashes lowering, accentuating the exotic slant of his eyes that was normally masked by his bug-eyes.

"Who's Ramesh?" Torr asked, then turned to Jasper abruptly. *"Doctor Ramesh?"*

"Doctor Ramesh?" Cassidy repeated.

Jasper nodded with a smug grin. "Yep, the very same."

"A wizard?" Torr asked. "No…" Ramesh was a soft-spoken doctor in Shasta. He was no wizard.

"Yep. Not only that, but he led the Peary uprising before he left for Muria."

"Ramesh?" Torr asked, finding it hard to believe that the gentle, erudite man had led any uprising.

"Yep. True fact. Then he left to seek the Star People. A total convert. Can you believe it?"

"No, not really." Torr shook his head. Ramesh had always debated with their mother and grandmother about magic, claiming there was a rational, scientific explanation for everything. He had been the first of their circle to criticize the Star Seekers and the Shasta Shamans for their fanaticism. If Ramesh had converted like that, anything was possible. Perhaps it was even true that the Star People really existed. If that were so, then it could also be true that twin Star Children were born every millennium to complete some legendary hero's journey. The weight of Torr and Cassidy's mysterious task grew heavier, and Torr squared his shoulders.

"I went to visit Ramesh on Muria," Jasper said. "Stayed with him a couple times, for several months each time. He taught me some of what he's been learning there. Berkeley studied with him, too."

"Then, you know how to arrange passage to Muria and find Ramesh," Torr said.

Jasper shrugged. "I do. More or less."

"You?" Cassidy asked, squinting at Jasper. "A wizard?" She burst out laughing. Jasper's proud expression wavered, then settled into a playful sneer. Torr inspected Jasper, wondering how far he had advanced in his studies and what he would choose to do with his powers.

"You be careful who you laugh at, Miss Plant Spirit Medicine Woman." Jasper came around the table and loomed over Cassidy with hands raised like claws, then descended on her in a swooping motion, grabbing her shoulders. She gave a small, startled squawk, then giggled and pushed him away.

"Do you like wizards?" Jasper asked, as he pulled up his crate and sat beside her.

"Only good wizards."

"I'm good," Jasper said, his voice sultry.

"Hmm," Cassidy replied skeptically.

Jasper didn't argue but smoothed Cassidy's hair, then leaned over and kissed her gently on the cheek. Torr looked away, and when he glanced back, they were kissing on the lips.

"Knock it off, you two," Torr mumbled. The two of them shared a bond that by its nature excluded him. He got to his feet and caught Berkeley's eye. They traded a look of patient disgust, then stepped away and gazed up at the stars.

The two lovebirds parted as Hiroshi and Tatsuya came in from the main yard. Tatsuya carried a small metal teapot, and Hiroshi had a handful of small metal cups. They gathered around the table, and Tatsuya served them a pale, yellowish tea. Torr lifted his cup to his mouth, breathing in the fragrant steam and touching the hot, grassy-tasting liquid to his lips. It smelled like Earth.

Tatsuya sat to Torr's right, and his eyes kept dropping to Torr's side. Torr removed the wolf knife from its scabbard and placed it on the table in front of him. The small, wiry man examined the knife curiously, holding it by the tang and turning it this way and that, then holding the blade up to the light and squinting at it. The folded steel shimmered with water-like ripples.

"Fine blade," Tatsuya said in an awed voice. "Where on Earth did you get this?" He passed it to his son, Hiroshi.

"Not Earth," Jasper said. "Iliad."

"Ilian steel," Tatsuya said. "I'd never thought to see any myself. Where did you get it?"

"Jasper," Torr said.

"I got a whole crate of Antler Kralj goods from Delos," Jasper said. "I happened to be at the port when the ship landed and got first dibs on their load. Never seen a crate full of Antler Kralj stuff before. Someone must have died or something. Cleared out their castle. Or some thieves made off with a fine haul." Jasper shrugged and smiled crookedly.

"Must've cost a lot," Berkeley said, as he took a turn inspecting the blade.

"Yeah, pretty much cleaned me out."

"You gave the knife to him?" Berkeley asked Jasper. "You never gave me nothin'."

"You're not my long-lost brother," Jasper said.

"He didn't give it to him," Cassidy said. "He traded it for a crystal."

Berkeley looked up curiously and passed the knife back to Tatsuya.

"Not the big one," Jasper said.

He took the red garnet from his pocket and handed it to Berkeley, who rubbed it between his fingers, looking into each facet.

"What do you think it does?" Jasper asked.

"Don't know," Berkeley said. "Never seen one like this before. I don't think it's from Muria."

"Nuh-uh," Jasper said. "Delos, maybe?"

Berkeley shrugged. "Possibly somewhere in the mountains? I don't know."

"It's just a garnet. Could be from Earth," Torr said. "Not everything is a big mystery."

Jasper narrowed his eyes at him. "You saying you ripped me off?"

"No. Who says Earth's not magical?"

Jasper glared at him.

"This tang, the snakes," Tatsuya said, drawing Torr's attention back to the knife. "Etched into the metal tang itself. Very unusual."

"It's a herald's staff," Torr said. "A caduceus."

"The ancient snake god," Berkeley said. "Or Hermes, messenger of the gods. A serpent-slayer."

Torr stiffened. *The brother who dreams, slays the beasts.*

"I can make you a hilt," Hiroshi offered. "I'll need some wood, and leather." He looked up at Jasper.

"You've got wood right here," Torr said, tapping the table with his knuckles. "And leather." He pulled at the hem of his jerkin.

"No. The blade is too fine for that. That wood is soft. And the leather ... well, it's just leather. I need shagreen. Ray skin. And a hardwood. Magnolia, or cocobolo."

Jasper frowned. "What, does it look like I live on Earth? Like I've got an ocean and an old-growth forest in my backyard?"

"You're the closest link we have to it, being in the Traders Guild and all," Hiroshi said, bobbing his head and shoulders in short, jerky bows. He smiled at Jasper, then asked Torr to unsheathe his combat knife. He examined Torr's grip, then traced his hand on a piece of tent fabric.

"This round pommel is the most unusual part," Tatsuya observed.

"It's a wolf," Torr said. "Is it looking at you? Is it sitting down and facing forward?"

"No, it's not looking at me. Yes, it's sitting and facing forward."

"Do you see a moon?"

Tatsuya shook his head. "No. Why?"

Cassidy pointed to the reverse side of the pommel. "That side makes me dizzy," she said. "It's like a whirlpool made of flowing metal. See it moving?"

Tatsuya shook his head. "No."

Torr took the knife. The wolf was howling at the moon again, showing its profile, making Torr's spine shiver. On the reverse were metal inlays of overlapping petals that spiraled inward. It was not moving as far as he could tell. "A handle would be great. I'd appreciate that very much."

Hiroshi smiled and bobbed his head again. "While we wait for Jaz to get us proper materials, I will polish the blade for you."

Torr removed the sheath from his belt, slid the blade into it, and set it on Hiroshi's open palms.

30

TEST FLIGHT

"You kids want to take a little tour? Cassafrass? Torrance?" Jasper asked cheerily. "They got some new speedsters. My dad said he'd take us out on a test flight. Take a ride out to, you know ... see some craters," he said, eyeing Hawk, who looked up curiously from the picnic table where he was helping Cassidy decipher the blue and gold book.

"Hell, yeah," Torr said, suddenly appreciating what it meant that Kai was a Peary pilot. A stifling sense of claustrophobia he hadn't realized he'd been holding at bay came rushing in. He hopped over the bench and bounced on his heels, waiting anxiously for Cassidy to show Hawk what she'd been working on. She left the book and loose papers in his care and joined them.

They cut over to Spoke Road Nine and headed up the long, wide road as a small transport rumbled by, towing a trailer with two empty water tanks. Jasper walked between the two of them, reminding Torr of when they were little and still living in Shasta. He and Cassidy had been barely five, attending their first year of school. It had been Jasper's duty to walk them home from school every day, though it was only three blocks away. He would hold

420

each of their hands as they crossed the streets. Torr could still see Jasper hunched between them one day when they had been let out of school early. A blizzard howled in from the north, and snow fell in a thick blanket around them, stinging Torr's cheeks with its icy claws. Jasper had carried all three of their school backpacks and dragged each of them along by the arms as they'd tripped and struggled through the blinding storm.

He looked over at Jasper, who must have recently turned twenty-five this past June. His baby fat was long gone, replaced by strong, angular features, and deep, solemn eyes that hid behind a playful exterior. He met Torr's eyes, and the two men smiled at one another.

Another memory came. More snow on the side of the mountain where they had been playing on the hill behind the school. They had lingered after school had finished, sliding down the long slope on the big plastic saucers and beat-up sleds the neighborhood families stashed under the trees for everyone to share. Night came early that time of year, and they were supposed to be home before darkness fell. The sun had already dipped below the cloud-masked horizon, and the hillside stood grayish white below the dark forest in the deepening twilight.

Snow was falling, coating the slope in muffled silence. The hill they'd been sliding down ended at the back of the school's ball field. Torr crawled under the chain-link fencing, where they'd dug a little trench in the snow, and walked ahead as they started towards home. He stopped, tilting his head to the sky, catching snowflakes on his tongue.

Cassidy did not follow, and he walked back to the fence where she was wriggling underneath. He saw in one frozen instant that her hood string had somehow gotten tangled in the jagged fencing and was wrapped around her neck. Her face was dark and her eyes protruded as she stared up at him, a faint rasping coming from her throat. He pulled at her head, but it was wedged firmly between the metal and the ice, and the string only pulled tighter.

"Jasper!" he yelled. Jasper was far behind them, throwing snowballs at some other kids. "Jasper!" Panic amplified his voice to a roar that bellowed through the falling snow. *"Jasper!!"* His heart pounded in his ears as he pulled frantically at Cassidy's hood, trying to pull it over her head as her eyes stared dully up at him. Footsteps trampled towards them. "Jasper!" Torr screamed. "Her hood, she can't breathe!"

Jasper fell to his knees on the other side of the fence and put a shining blade to Cassidy's throat, wedging it under the strangling string and slicing through it, drawing a bead of blood. Jasper pulled Cassidy from under the fence as she gasped and rolled onto her side, choking and coughing as Jasper pounded on her back, terror burning in his eyes as they met Torr's. They both knew, without any doubt, that they had nearly lost her.

Sounds and smells of the tent city pulled Torr back to the present. The sun was to their left, almost touching the jagged peaks on the far side of the moon beyond Peary Crater. Torr matched Jasper's strides, resting his hand on his friend's shoulder, on their way to the spaceport.

The men working security at the spaceport door recognized Torr and Cassidy, greeting them and trading a few words with Jasper.

"We found him," Cassidy said to the guards.

"Oh. You were looking for Jaz?"

"Yeah, and Kujo," Torr said.

"Oh." The guards laughed and smiled sheepishly. "Sorry."

Torr put his sunglasses in his chest pocket and let his eyes adjust to the filtered light. He followed Jasper's gaze to his father's tall frame. Kai stood among a group of men surrounding two red speedsters in the middle of the hangar. Kai's bearing was stiff and confident, and he displayed his disturbing habit of looking over his shoulder in quick, furtive glances, as though he expected to be attacked at any moment. Torr figured Kai's quirk was no more annoying than his cheek's twitch, which was quiet today, thankfully.

One of Kai's glances caught them approaching, and his face lit up. He limped over and clapped Torr on the back, then bent and kissed Cassidy's cheek and gave her a hug. "I still can't believe you're here," Kai said warmly. Torr felt the tension in his muscles unwind a notch. Kai rested his hand on Torr's shoulder as they walked to the speedsters.

"Check these out," Jasper said. The new craft were long and sleek, like hovercraft, and painted a glossy red. The color popped like starbursts in the dreary hangar. Four men in mechanic's coveralls were examining every inch, running their hands over the glassy surfaces and crawling underneath, and stepping in and out of the cockpits with sensors in their hands.

The small crowd parted as another group of men approached, two of whom walked up to the craft and spoke with the mechanics. Kai left Torr's side and joined them. One man was striking in his stature and bearing. He stood taller than Kai's six feet, and was broad-shouldered with thick, muscular arms, and legs that bulged under tight, green cargo pants. His skin was dark brown, and his hair hung in a mass of black braids that lined his scalp in neat cornrows and fell to his shoulders. Red beads hung at the end of each braid. His face was stern, and he wore a neatly manicured beard over strong chin and jaws.

The other man was short by comparison, and portly, with a loose white tunic covering a large belly over skinny legs. His hair was short and wavy, jet black with streaks of gray. His skin was a dark olive, and he wore a long, bushy salt-and-pepper beard.

He surveyed the hangar while nodding to the mechanics as they briefed him. His gaze rested on Torr and Cassidy for a moment, then moved on.

"That's Ramzy," Jasper murmured under his breath. "He's in charge. Rodney, the big guy, is his second."

"Who are the other guys?" Torr asked, eyeing the four muscle-bound black men who stood to the side.

"Rodney's Rangers. They run spaceport security."

The name Rodney's Rangers sounded familiar. "Like Chicago's Rodney's Rangers?" Torr asked.

"One and the same," Jasper said, chuckling at Torr's surprise.

The Chicago rebellion against the invading Teg forces had been led by hundreds of escaped convicts. Their leader, Rodney, apparently now stood before them in Peary Spaceport. Torr surreptitiously examined Rodney and the four guards. They all had indigo tattoos covering their arms, the details difficult to make out against their dark skin in the dim hangar light. Torr noted scars on Rodney's arm and face. The four guards wore tight black t-shirts and black tactical vests. Each wore a handgun and radio at his belt along with an assortment of knives and clubs. One had a rifle slung across his back. It looked like an old TAR-21 bullpup. The man noticed Torr looking at him, and Torr turned away.

"Ramzy's a pilot, too," Jasper said. "He and my father flew together in Alexandria. He's the one who brought my dad here."

Torr watched Ramzy climb into a cockpit and play with the controls, a studious look on his bearded face. Kai climbed into the co-pilot's seat and the two men pulled down the wing-like hatch doors, sealing them inside the airtight ship. Torr could see them talking and glancing their way.

Torr was reminded of the stories Kai told of when he'd been squadron commander in Alexandria during the Early

Wars, when the Cephs had started coming to Earth in greater numbers. Earthlanders were freaking out that an alien humanoid race was immigrating to Earth, interbreeding, and building settlements. The Holy Landers, however, had welcomed Cephs into Jerusalem, thinking they were the awaited Messiah People. The conflict escalated and resulted in a bloody massacre of the Cephs who had fled to Jerusalem for safety. During all this, Kai's plane had been shot down, and he had ended up in a prisoner of war camp. He was released after three months when the Jerusalem Massacre ended the war, but not before suffering a bullet in the foot from a prison guard.

The speedster doors opened, Kai climbed out, and Rodney took his spot in the co-pilot's seat.

Kai walked over and motioned to the second speedster. "Ready?" he asked.

Torr hesitated. Did he even want to go near Gandoop Spaceport again? "Is it safe, at the, uh ... craters?" he asked.

Kai glanced over his shoulder. "We've always had friendly ties with Gandoop," he said, sounding almost relaxed. "We trade with them all the time. I doubt they'll shoot us out of the sky." Kai gave him a wan smile, and Torr frowned. "We'll just do a flyover. But we don't need to go there if you don't want. We can go in the other direction."

"No," Torr said, curiosity getting the better of him. He glanced at Cassidy, whose eyes had that look she got when she was sensing the air for danger, her nostrils flaring slightly.

She lifted one shoulder in a half-shrug and nodded. "I didn't get much of a look last time," she said. "I was too busy staring at Earth. And I hadn't realized that it was our ..." Her voice trailed off, and her eyes darted to the guards standing nearby.

Torr nodded in agreement. Torr and Cassidy climbed in,

folded down the small rear jump seats, and fastened their harnesses. Jasper took the co-pilot's seat.

Kai sealed the doors, and his long fingers clasped the throttle. They entered the decompression bay. Ramzy's speedster joined them on their flank, and they passed together through the dual chambers, then sped silently through the tunnel and out into the open.

The mountainous Peary Rim cast long, jagged shadows across the land. The high plateau that Peary Dome sat upon quickly fell away, and the flat floor of Peary Crater spread out below them, reflecting sunlight off the gunmetal gray surface. It was deathly still. The speedster did not make any sound, but Torr could feel the power and movement beneath him as the craft sailed along. They crossed over Peary's eastern rim and curved south in a wide arc to head west. Soon they approached the border of light and darkness, a distinct line dividing the landscape into gray and black. Unlike Earth, where the atmosphere dispersed the light, here the transition from day to night was instant. They crossed the terminator line with a slight bump and entered the shroud of darkness. Torr's eyes adjusted to the glow of Earth, which hung like a blue lantern above the southern horizon and bathed the dusky terrain with soft Earthshine.

Torr gazed across the eerie wasteland riddled with craters on top of craters as though a hailstorm of meteorites had all converged on this one place. A massive crater gaped below them like the yawning mouth of a giant troll, black and forbidding. "What crater is that?" Torr asked.

"Erlanger," Kai said, as they flew over it. "There's an ice lake down in the shadows. Some of the mines get water there."

"Does Peary, too?" Cassidy asked.

"No, we have exclusive rights to Peary Lake, the largest ice lake in the north."

Erlanger fell behind as they sped along. Kai raised the nose of the craft and they slowly climbed.

"How does it handle?" Jasper asked.

"Sweet," Kai said, and zigzagged the craft. Ramzy appeared on their right flank, imitating the maneuvers. "Hold on," Kai said, and dropped sharply into a roll that made Torr's stomach do flip-flops.

"Ugh," Cassidy moaned.

Torr held his stomach. "Is this the first time you've taken her out?" he asked, taking a deep breath.

"No," Kai said. "We've had them for over two weeks now. A couple more test flights and they'll get put into rotation. Here, you take it," Kai said, and transferred control to Jasper.

Jasper flew in smooth curves, banking to the right and left. Torr wondered with envy if Kai would give him flying lessons, too. Ramzy did more rolls and loops off to their right, but, thankfully, Jasper kept to simpler maneuvers. Ramzy's voice blasted into the cockpit, making them all jump.

"Hey, you jelly brains, ready for high gear?"

"On your tail, old man," Kai said. Ramzy's craft blurred into a streak of red light and disappeared. "Hold your breath," Kai commanded, taking over the controls. He looked back at Torr and Cassidy. "Tighten your abdomens to push the blood up to your heads, okay? I don't want you guys passing out on me."

Torr and Cassidy nodded and inhaled.

"Ready?" Kai asked.

The craft surged forward, throwing Torr back against his seat. The panorama flitted by at a rapid rate, then became a gray blur as his face flattened against his bones and his skull pressed into the cushioned headrest. He closed his eyes, tears streaming across his temples.

"Exhale," Kai commanded as the air pressure lessened

suddenly. Torr let his breath out and sucked it back in. "You guys still with me?" Kai and Jasper glanced back at them.

Torr nodded, his muscles relaxing down into the seat. Cassidy looked dazed, and Jasper shook her knee gently. Torr breathed deeply and thought of the massive facility on their land. *Their land.* He couldn't help thinking of it that way, even though all he held was a piece of parchment. So what if Metolius's seal was on it? Possession was nine-tenths of the law, or something like that. Besides, the wealth and power demonstrated in the few minutes he'd spent in Ridge Gandoop Spaceport proved that he and Cassidy had no hope of ever claiming their land. But he couldn't help but imagine. After all, legally it was still theirs, if they could only figure out how to claim it without getting killed. A sudden resentment flared inside him. He hated feeling so powerless. Why should he have to abandon his own property just because some thieves had managed to build on it? It felt like a personal invasion.

If the mine and spaceport were worth as much as Berkeley claimed, and if they could gain control of them, then he and Cassidy would suddenly be rich. The mine alone, with its rare-earth minerals and oxygen production, would be lucrative enough. But with the spaceport under their control, the value went far beyond money. It would open up the galaxy to them.

His body grew hot as he thought of the possibilities, fueled by the scale of the facility. He imagined running a large mining operation and hosting ships from other planets. They could build a moonside militia and mount attacks on Teg bases on Earth. He would command a contingent that struck from the sky, pummeling the Tegs and preventing them from piercing the Shaman's Shield and capturing Shasta. He'd mount surprise attacks from the rear. The Teg forces would be thrown into disarray. Teg troops who realized their allegiance had been to the wrong side would join the unbeatable moon forces, swelling their ranks, creating a tidal wave that would drown Tegea's armies across the world. Torr and his army would scour the countryside and throw open the gates of the work camps. They would cut off trade with the Cephs and send the colonizers back to where they had come from. Torr and Cassidy would find their parents and their friends, and the reign of Metolius and Tegea would go down in history as a dark period when Earthlanders had nearly lost their souls.

Torr spoke suddenly to Kai. *Lieutenant Manann.* "If Ramzy was in the airforce, and Rodney led the Rangers, why haven't you all formed a militia? There are thousands of men in Peary Dome, doing nothing."

Kai's brow furrowed. "What would we do? Who would we attack?"

"We could do spot raids against the Tegs on Earth, attack them from above. Hit the forces surrounding the Shaman's Shield."

Kai did not answer. He was quiet that way. Even Jasper kept his mouth shut.

Torr sat in silence, the fever of his dream cooling as he considered the realities of their situation. They were on a lonely, rocky satellite, more than two hundred thousand miles from Earth. Ships were easy to detect with radar. They would be picked off like migrating ducks. Torr hadn't seen anything that looked like a battleship in Peary Spaceport. He had seen only freighters, tankers, and speedsters. Maybe a freighter could drop a bomb, but even so, he doubted they had access to any bombs here.

"At minimum we could build a force to defend Peary Dome," Torr said into the quiet cockpit.

Kai pulled back on the throttle, and they slowed gradually, flying in silence. Torr wondered morosely if the leaders of Peary

were washed-up cowards. Maybe they needed Ramesh back on
the moon, if what they said about him was true.

They descended and passed over a low ridge that bordered
a wide, dark crater. "This is Anaximenes G," Kai told them,
breaking into Torr's thoughts.

The crater was a massive pit of shadowed dunes that stretched
for miles. Torr's heart thudded in his chest. This was his land.
He pressed his nose against the window and peered down into
the deep crater. Ramzy's red lights blinked ahead of them, then
extinguished. Kai followed suit and extinguished their exterior and interior lights. The pale ground stood in contrast to
the dense black shadows that blanketed the southern half of
the crater.

"It's huge," Cassidy said breathlessly.

Torr's eyes were drawn to a formation of red dots of light
that looked like glowing insects crawling slowly across the ashen
land. Torr got out his binoculars and zoomed in on them.

"Soil harvesters," Jasper said.

Indeed, they could have been farm equipment plowing or
harvesting a field. They looked like tractors, each pulling some
sort of tiller followed by a long enclosed trailer.

They left the soil harvesters and Anaximenes G behind. Not
long after, they came upon Anaximenes H—the second crater
in Torr's parcel. At the center of the immense pit, the Earthshine
revealed a dark, perfectly round crater that Torr would have considered enormous had they not been inside a crater that dwarfed
it by comparison. A shadowy, man-made gash was cut into the
rim of the crater-inside-a-crater, neat terraces marking it as a
mine. Tall cranes stood like long-necked storks. Earthmoving
equipment was active on the terraces, which descended like
giant steps into the dark side of the crater. Two large sections

were illuminated by floodlights. A backhoe shoveled moon soil into a transport, dust rising and sparkling in the light.

"That's their rare-earth mine," Kai said.

Torr's two craters, G and H, did not have the spaceport, but they were both being actively mined. The squatters would not part with the land willingly. The speedsters passed over the far ridge, leaving Anaximenes H behind, and curved south. Another ridge loomed and passed below them, exposing the deep expanse of an even larger crater.

"Anaximenes," Kai announced. "The largest of the three."

Torr had not comprehended its massive scale when he'd climbed out of it the first time. It was truly monstrous. Like the Grand Canyon, only round. "How big is this?" Torr asked.

"Fifty miles across. Mile and a half deep," Kai answered.

Torr whistled. "Bloody hell."

Red lights glowed in the distance, outlining the black cubes and white spaceport. Torr lifted his binoculars and zoomed in on the buildings that sat on the flat, pitted land. *Their land.* Strange how the simple piece of parchment he carried against his belly changed his perspective of the moon completely. He owned a part of it. He *was* a part of it. He *belonged* here.

31

FLYꙨVER

Cassidy liked to imagine their land with a glass dome. A smaller version of Peary, but filled with a forest of trees instead of tents, with birds and insects, streams and grassy glades. Wild flowers springing up from clumps of brown earth and moss. Butterflies and hummingbirds, dragonflies and bees circling in the sunshine.

But what appeared below them as the speedster approached Ridge Gandoop was the opposite of her vision. A grid of red lights outlined massive black cubes and towers, desolate and forbidding. The white spaceport was austere, but its curved lines were graceful compared to the other buildings.

She glanced at her brother, who was gazing intently out his little window. His cheek was twitching. "What's wrong, Sundance?" she asked.

"I don't like the feeling of this place," he said, not taking his eyes off the scene below.

"Me neither," she said.

Kai dropped vertically in altitude and glided slowly towards the industrial complex, the dark shape of Ramzy's craft shadowing them to their right. The air crackled and a sharp voice sounded from the control panel, making Cassidy jump.

"Gandoop Control. Identify yourselves."

Ramzy's voice responded through the console, deep and clear in the small cockpit. *"Peary 77268. Just passing over. Destination Carpenter. Over."*

Kai repeated the same. *"Peary 77269. Destination Carpenter. Over."*

"You're in Gandoop airspace."

Ramzy spoke, *"Climbing into common airspace. Out."*

Kai's craft rose vertically as though rising swiftly in a column. Cassidy's head swam for a moment until the craft settled. They were above ground level, the rim visible in the distance and the crater plunging far below. Kai glided slowly away from the interior towards the ridge.

"Go around." The voice was not friendly. *"And put on your lamps, or else I'll shoot you down for violating regulation."*

"What regulation?" Kai muttered, and flicked on the red exterior lights, the dull glow permeating the cabin.

"They're getting awfully cocky," Jasper said.

Cassidy shuddered. They were more than cocky. They were downright threatening. A rush of indignation came over her. How dare they chase them off their own land? The Gandoops were trespassers. They had no rights to this crater. It belonged to her, Cassandra Cethlejan Dagda, officially transferred with the Salmon Seal of Metolius. She wanted to tell Kai to turn around and demand entry to the spaceport so that she could wave her deed in Ali's face and demand that the Gandoops leave.

Wrangling the binoculars away from Torr, she zoomed in on the buildings far below. Cassidy counted four large, cube-shaped buildings of similar size, flanked by towers and tanks. The spaceport was large and shaped like a clamshell, topped with a sloped roof, with several igloo-shaped landing bays protruding from the curved side. Torr took the binoculars back, and she slipped her hands into her vest pockets, her left hand cupping the crystal ball and her right hand finding the crystal shaft.

"Here," Kai said. He lit a panel on the console, displaying a green radar screen with gridlines over a topographical map. He pressed a button and texture filled in the green patterns with shades of gray. The crater was a circular depression with a vast, level floor, with many small craters and boulders scattered randomly. The cube-shaped buildings were clearly visible, the radar offering much more detail than the eye could detect in the dim light. Narrow rectangular shapes connected the buildings, which Cassidy guessed were passageways. "Torr," she said. "Look." He lowered the binoculars and watched the radar screen.

Kai zoomed in. Several round solar collectors stood beyond the buildings, useless in the darkness.

"Uh-oh," she and Jasper said in unison. Two green dots exited the spaceport, rose in one smooth movement, and headed their way. The craft appeared swiftly at their sides to escort them from the crater. Kai and Ramzy accelerated, shooting over the ridge and away from Anaximenes.

Jasper zoomed the radar screen onto the two craft that followed at a fair distance. They were not the finned bullet shapes of the Peary speedsters, but wider and flatter, and fluid, the edges undulating like rays swimming through the ocean.

"Those are not Earth craft," Jasper said.

"Those are Ceph speedsters," Torr said darkly. "Mantas."

"Mantas?" Kai repeated curiously.

"They started showing up on Earth after you left," Torr said. "I saw some close up, flying over Miramar after the Shaman's Shield fell. Came from Teg territory. Ceph technology. You ever seen anything like that before?"

"No," Kai said, studying the waving shapes on the radar screen. "Wouldn't mind getting in the cockpit of one of those."

Cassidy could feel Torr's anxiety mount. She met his eyes. "Those aren't interstellar craft," Torr said, his voice tense. "They're local cruisers. They're here to stay. What the hell?"

A cold chill passed through her, and an even darker fear awoke in the pit of her stomach. She and Torr were carrying deeds to Ceph-controlled land.

Kai said, "I've never had a reception like that before. Normally Gandoop Control is friendly, or bored. I'm on a first-name basis with most of their controllers. But I didn't recognize that voice."

After a few minutes the Cephean craft turned around, and another massive crater appeared ahead of them.

"Carpenter," Jasper said.

They passed over the rim and dipped inside, cruising above the shadowy panorama. The crater was just as deep as Anaximenes, and several miles across. Near the center of the crater, the radar revealed two small dome structures on a flat area next to two pointy hills. Nearby, a backhoe stood idle next to a large mound of moon soil. She looked out the window as the little settlement passed underneath, the two white domes reflecting Earthshine in a soft glow. This was more what she'd expected when she'd imagined mines squatting illegally on their land, not a small city with an interstellar spaceport guarded by Tegs and Cephean craft.

Jasper zoomed the screen out and located the two Mantas, which were hovering far behind, over the flatlands between Carpenter and Anaximenes. They were graceful creatures. Or machines. Their wings undulated in perfect time with each other. Cassidy watched the lifelike 3D images on the radar screen turn and slowly head back towards Gandoop.

Cassidy fidgeted with her crystals, wishing the entire Ceph invasion was only a bad dream. Jasper peered over his shoulder at her, reached his arm around the side of his seat, and touched her knee. She squeezed his hand, feeling the electricity of his touch. Kai and Ramzy started back towards Peary, charting a wide curve to avoid Anaximenes. She and Jasper dropped hands, and she folded her hands in her lap. Leaning her forehead against the cold window, she stared out over the desolate moonscape.

— ♪ —

The mechanics and Rodney's guards were right where they'd left them, standing in the center of Peary's massive hangar. Cassidy and Torr climbed out and waited while Kai and Ramzy debriefed the mechanics. Jasper stepped away to speak with Rodney.

Cassidy examined the imposing black man. His eyes were large and serious, with thick, black lashes that curled up at the tips. Underscoring his right cheekbone was a clean line of a scar that added to his ferocious beauty.

Rodney felt her looking at him, and his eyes locked onto hers. He seemed like a man who was accustomed to intimidating people with his looks. Cassidy wasn't going to play that game. She'd seen men more fearsome-looking than Rodney break down and cry like a baby when her mother had read their diagnosis from the red herb notebook. She clenched her jaw and held his gaze until he turned back to Jasper.

Jasper walked over and spoke in a hushed voice. "My dad told them about your deeds. He wants you to talk to them."

"What'd he do that for?" Torr whispered.

"He thinks they can help you."

"Help us with what?" Torr asked. "Get our land back?"

"Against the Tegs?" Cassidy asked.

"Maybe. Ramzy knows Ishmar Gandoop, the father."

Cassidy and Torr traded skeptical glances. Why did Jasper have to go and open his big mouth? She pressed her lips together and tried to stay calm. This was his territory; maybe he knew what he was doing. They followed Kai, Ramzy, and Rodney across the floor. The four guards flanked the three men. The guards were all dark-skinned like Rodney, though none as tall, and had their own assortment of indigo tattoos, braids, close-cropped beards, and weapon belts. They walked proudly, with straight postures and an easy confidence.

At the far corner of the hangar were two rows of shipping containers. They passed through a door that led to a gap between the rows, guarded by two more of Rodney's men, and entered the corridor. The walls were painted a dull gray to match the dust that coated the cement floor. Ramzy opened a door, and they squeezed into a small half-container, the four guards remaining out in the hallway as the door closed.

The walls were lined with metal shelves and filing cabinets. A rectangular folding table stood in the center, covered with a brown and red floral tablecloth that reminded Cassidy of Grandma Leann's house.

Ramzy turned to face Cassidy and Torr, and Kai formally introduced them. Ramzy was not much taller than Cassidy, his big, barrel chest balancing over stick legs. Large, brown eyes looked at her wearily. His manner was gruff but his handshake was gentle. She turned and shook Rodney's large hand, and he squeezed hers painfully. They locked eyes and frowned at one another until he released his hold with a quirk of his lips and looked away.

Ramzy sat heavily in a folding chair and motioned for them to take chairs that were leaning, folded, against a shelf. He pulled a pair of black-rimmed eyeglasses from the breast pocket of his white tunic and slid them onto his oily nose, and set his gaze on Torr.

"How is it down there? On Earth?"

"Not good," Torr said, unfolding a chair for Cassidy and getting one for himself. Cassidy sat between Torr and Jasper, facing the two Peary leaders, while Kai sat at the short end of the table by the door.

"The Shaman's Shield pulled back to Shasta," Torr said. "Gaia United surrendered Los Angeles and San Francisco, including LAX and Moffett Field."

A scowl passed over Ramzy's face. "That's very bad news. How'd you get out?"

Torr and Cassidy exchanged glances, then looked at Kai.

"You can trust them," Kai said. "Show them your deeds."

Torr sighed and stood up, then turned his back and went under his shirt to remove his deed and map from the rune belt. He turned and handed them across the table to Ramzy, then sat down. Cassidy stayed put, watching the man's face as he scanned the documents. Rodney looked over Ramzy's shoulder, his stony glower replaced by surprise. He raised his eyes and examined Torr with curiosity.

"Where'd you get this?" Ramzy asked, his eyes fixed on Torr.

"From a relative," Torr said.

"Cassidy, show them yours," Jasper said.

She threw Jasper a pointed look, then stood up and turned away to delve into her belt, not liking that they were revealing their hiding places. She reluctantly handed the parchments to Ramzy.

Ramzy and Rodney crouched over her deed, then examined the map and plotted the coordinates. Their expressions were unreadable.

"They've got Metolius's seal on them," Rodney said, his bass voice resonating in the small room.

"True," Cassidy said. "That's what got us off the planet. We think."

Rodney nodded thoughtfully. "Lucky."

"They flew into Gandoop," Kai said.

"Gandoop," Ramzy said darkly. "Moffett always sent their ships here. Until the Shaman's Shield halted traffic, that is. We've been waiting for their food shipments to resume."

"The Global Alliance controls Moffett now," Kai said.

"So? All the other ships coming in from Earth are controlled by the Global Alliance. Except Glamorgan."

"They said all traffic from Moffett Field is being routed through Gandoop," Cassidy told them.

"Who said?" Ramzy asked.

"A Teg at Moffett. The officer who helped get us a flight. He didn't know when the next ship to Peary would be. As if there might not be any."

The lines in Ramzy's forehead deepened.

"We rely on food shipments from Earth," Kai said. "Ever since the Gandoop port opened, Peary traffic has slowed way down. Our food shipments have dropped off. Gandoop is paying gold for food, and we can't compete with that."

"Gandoop will suck us dry," Rodney muttered. "Their thirst for gold is unquenchable."

Cassidy thought there was more to it than that. Ali hadn't asked for gold when he'd sent her and Torr to Peary; Murphy had told Torr that Ali had more gold than he knew what to do with. That didn't speak of bottomless greed to her.

"What if the Global Alliance cuts off food shipments to Peary completely?" Cassidy asked.

The men stared at her.

"No." Ramzy faltered. "Gandoop just wants to corner the food market and charge exorbitant prices for it. Ishmar is a businessman, after all, but not cold-hearted enough to let us starve. I don't think the Global Alliance is behind it."

"I do," Torr said. "We'd starve to death. All of us."

Ramzy stared at him coldly.

"The food shortage is actually good for the Traders Guild," Jasper said with an edge of guilt. "Any food I get, I make a killing on." He wilted under the glares of the men. "We have the soy," he added, half-heartedly. "And the kale and spinach."

The men looked at one another, concern growing in their eyes. "We tried that before," Ramzy said. "Only giving people bread. It wasn't pretty. People stole each other's rations. Fights broke out every day. Gangs raided the canteens and bakery and the storage containers. People got sick and died. Even at that time, with a smaller population, we supplemented the bread with grain from Earth; the soy was not enough. No, we couldn't survive."

"Why don't you build more greenhouses?" Cassidy asked.

"We should," Jasper said.

"It's water intensive," Kai said.

"I thought all the water gets recycled anyway," she said. "There's plenty of vertical space. The entire place could be one big greenhouse."

"So you get food from Glamorgan?" Torr asked.

"Some," Jasper said. "Not enough. They don't have many ships, and the Global Alliance monitors their airspace. It's risky for Glamorgan to penetrate their mist shield. They're reluctant to support us more than they already do."

"What about food from other planets?" Cassidy asked.

"Too far," Kai said. "Too expensive. We go through food too fast. That wouldn't be sustainable. But, maybe ..." Kai's voice trailed off. "Anyway, not your problem. I doubt the Global Alliance is behind the weird behavior at Gandoop. We're a benefit to the Global Alliance. A neutral port for interstellar trade."

"The kids said they saw soldiers at Gandoop Spaceport. Looked like Tegs," Jasper said, looking between Ramzy and Rodney.

"So what?" Ramzy snapped. "Tegs pass through the moon all the time. We're a waystation."

"They weren't passing through," Torr said. "They seemed to be in charge. Or trying to be."

"And what about Gandoop Control?" Kai added. "That was not normal. I've never heard that guy's voice before. Why do they suddenly care if we do a flyover? And escorting us out? What in Algol's hell was that about? Those were Cephean craft, you know. Something is wrong. What about the missing speedsters?"

"What missing speedsters?" Torr asked.

Cassidy thought for a moment that Ramzy was not going to answer. His eyes bulged and his complexion turned a disturbing shade of purple, making Cassidy wonder if he was having a heart attack. But then he spoke. "We were expecting six of the red speedsters. We only got two. The ship carrying the other four disappeared when they were on the far side during their approach orbit, beyond the range of our radar towers."

The room grew heavy with silence again.

"Maybe they crashed," Torr said.

Ramzy took a deep breath and folded his hands over his belly. "Hate to say it, but I wish that were so. We searched the path of their trajectory. Still searching, actually. Nothing so far. Right, Kujo?"

Kai shook his head. "Of course, the moon is large. We'd hoped to find something after the sun lit the far side. But nothing so far."

"It could have blown up on impact," Torr said.

"Maybe," Kai said, "but not likely."

"Maybe the pilots stole them," Cassidy suggested. "Went to another mine, or left for another planet."

Kai looked at Cassidy. "That's possible. But why would they come all the way here just to leave? They could have headed for a different destination directly from Earth. As for going to a mine, there aren't many large mines on the far side. Granted, some are run by unsavory characters. Worse than the outer rim mining lords, some of them. But there aren't any spaceports big enough for a cargo ship carrying four craft, other than Peary and Gandoop."

"They could have landed on the ground and flew the speedsters out from the cargo bay," Torr said.

Ramzy ran his hand over his beard. "That's possible, though the freighter would still need to go somewhere."

"Maybe they abandoned it in a crater," Jasper said. "Or left the moon already."

"Maybe," Kai said. "I think the most likely culprit is Gandoop."

"We radioed Gandoop," Ramzy said. "I talked to Ishmar myself. He claims they don't know anything about it. I respect Ishmar. He may be a ruthless businessman, but I don't think he would lie to me. If he wanted more speedsters, he's rich enough to buy them himself. He wouldn't need to steal them from us."

Cassidy looked at Jasper, who was looking at Torr with a cocked eyebrow. She followed his gaze. Torr looked like he had indigestion. "What?" she asked, nudging her brother's arm with her elbow.

Torr cleared his throat. "Are red speedsters common? I mean, does Gandoop have any?"

Ramzy lowered his brows. "No. It was a custom order. I requested that color. Candy Apple Red."

Cassidy thought the man was actually embarrassed.

"Why?" Jasper asked Torr.

"Did you notice the ships under the tarps?" Torr asked Cassidy. "At the back of the small hangar at Gandoop?"

She tried to remember. She seemed to recall mounds of something under tarps. "I think so. I was kind of preoccupied at the time. There was something under canvas. Could have been ships. Small, like speedsters."

Torr nodded. "I'm positive there were ships under those tarps. Four of them. Anyway, one's wingtip was exposed. It was bright red."

The air crackled with tension. Ramzy got to his feet and turned to the wall. He poured water from a ration jug into a teakettle and turned on an electric hotplate. Torr's revelation had brought the conversation to a halt.

Finally, Kai mumbled, "That explains why they want to keep us out of there. They don't want us to see the stolen craft."

"They can't hide them forever," Rodney said.

The heating water roiled loudly. Ramzy still had his back turned and brought down an assortment of glass jars from a shelf above the hotplate.

"Murphy said there's a new administration at Gandoop," Torr said.

"Berkeley said Murphy got his hand chopped off when a new guy from Earth came to Gandoop," Jasper said.

Ramzy cleared his throat and clattered jars together.

"Must be some kind of vicious bully," Rodney said. "I know the type. They'll cut your eye out if you look at them the wrong way."

Cassidy glanced at the scar below his eye.

Ramzy shook loose leaf tea into a teapot and poured the steaming water in after it.

"What are you going to do about it?" Torr asked.

Ramzy brought the teapot over with a bowl of sugar, then set an empty jar in front of each person and waited for the tea to brew. The smell reminded Cassidy of home.

"Can't you mount an attack?" Torr asked. The men were quiet and somber. Torr's face was getting red.

Cassidy tried to fend off a growing sense of unease. If Tegs were settling on the moon, the prime target would be Peary Dome. And forget about ever claiming their land. They could end up slaves at the mine on their own property. At least if she were a slave on Earth, she'd have the comfort of plants around her. She clutched the crystal ball with one hand and found Jasper's hand with the other. Jasper's fingers squeezed hers, and his eyes rested on her face.

She avoided his gaze. Fear and anger fought within her. She took a deep breath to quiet her heart and interlaced her fingers with Jasper's, feeling his strong, steady pulse.

Ramzy poured tea into each jar, steam rising into the air. He slowly stirred sugar into his tea and finally spoke. "First of all, I would not mount an attack on a neighbor without solid proof."

Torr glared at him.

"I'm not doubting you believe what you saw," Ramzy said. "But there could be a reasonable explanation. Perhaps the pilots betrayed us and sold the speedsters to Ishmar without him knowing they were ours. Or some other scenario. But he would have told me when I asked." His brow furrowed.

"Even so," Kai said. "Let's suppose for a moment that our worst fears are true. There is no atmosphere on the moon. We cannot field a ground assault of any significance. We can only enter Gandoop through the compression chambers. Even if we could get inside, we would be trapped. It's the same reason we're safe in Peary. With Rodney's armed guards, it's impossible to attack the dome other than by destroying it."

"Not impossible," Cassidy said. All eyes turned to her. "Just saying," she said, dropping Jasper's hand. "If they could get inside, by sneaking in or whatever, there are no real defenses inside the tent city, are there?"

The only people of any authority she'd seen outside Peary Spaceport were the ration guards, who were armed only with knives and clubs, and the men in the PCA tents who were administrators. Groups of men rode around on transports delivering water and food, and crews who cleaned out the composting toilets and groomed the roads carried shovels and rakes but did not appear to be soldiers.

Jasper seemed to be considering her point, but Ramzy's face reflected a foul temper. Rodney passed the sugar to Kai and noisily sipped his tea.

"You should build up a force inside the camp," Torr said. "You've got enough people." He looked directly at Rodney this time, who held his gaze.

"Are you a young general, then?" Ramzy asked Torr.

Cassidy couldn't tell if he was being respectful or taunting. She decided it was the latter, and felt a growing dislike for the man.

"I'm just saying," Torr said.

"I'm saying we have everything under control," Ramzy said, his eyes blazing.

Cassidy deemed that if he really felt everything was under control, he would not be losing his temper so easily.

Jasper turned to her and Torr. "Montana maintains order inside the dome. Distributes the food and tents. Anything violent gets escalated to Rodney, and then to Ramzy."

"But nobody in the dome is armed," Torr said.

"They're right," Kai said to Ramzy in a conciliatory tone. "What harm would it do to train a small force inside the dome?"

"No," Ramzy said, slamming down his jar, the golden liquid sloshing onto the tablecloth and narrowly missing Cassidy's deed, which she pulled back hastily. "This is a neutral zone. We are not building a militia. We discussed this a million times." He glared at Kai. "You weren't here during the uprising. After we won, we specifically outlawed firearms, and demilitarized the camp. I have maintained the peace ..."

"But the Tegs are militarized," Torr broke in. "They don't care about your rules."

Ramzy cut him off with a swipe of his hand through the air. "When you are in charge, young man, then you can make the decisions. Things are complicated here. I have the welfare of ten thousand people to think about. I am not starting a civil war on the moon." He pushed Torr's deed across the table, signaling an end to the conversation. "Who knows you have these?" he demanded.

"The officers at Moffett," Torr said. "And you guys."

"And Berkeley," Cassidy said.

"Berkeley?!" Ramzy demanded. He glared angrily at Jasper, whose head sank into his shoulders. "Are you still hanging around with that moat scum? He's not to be trusted."

"He's okay," Jasper said, lifting his chin.

Ramzy snorted, his face purple again.

Kai ignored the outburst and said to Ramzy, "Maybe you should hang onto the deeds. Lock them up." Kai glanced at Torr, who frowned. Cassidy did not like the idea, either.

Ramzy shook his head. "I will not have those in my possession. If Ishmar were to find out about it, he'd think I was plotting to take his land, and all hell would break loose. No, keep them close, keep them hidden. And tell that Berkeley Barnswallow to keep his filthy mouth shut." His voice was shaking.

Cassidy and Torr stashed the deeds away and sipped the hot tea in silence.

"And what are you planning on doing with your sister?" Ramzy asked Torr abruptly, as though Cassidy were not there. She straightened in her chair and glared at the man, who pointedly ignored her.

"What do you mean?" Torr asked, his eyes darting between Cassidy and Jasper.

"Peary Dome is no place for a young woman."

"We'll take care of her," Jasper said firmly.

Ramzy harrumphed and took a sip of tea. "I'll ask Gabira if she'll take her, if you'd like," he said.

Cassidy's face flushed with anger. "I'm right here," she said. "You can address me directly, if you please."

Ramzy glanced at her with dour eyes, then turned to Kai. "Gabira says she's full, but she'll make an exception if I ask."

"What is he talking about?" she demanded, turning to Jasper.

"My friend, Gabira," he replied. "She leads a community of women who live hidden underground." He stomped his foot on the floor. "Down below us there's a system of caves."

A strong feeling of apprehension rose inside her. "I do not want to live hidden in a cave." She pushed the chair back noisily and got to her feet. This was all too much. This dismal refugee camp. Tegs and Cephs on their land. And now this arrogant man was trying to stuff her away in a dungeon. "There are plenty of women around," she said, though not as many as she would like. "I'm not a little girl."

Ramzy's voice was low as he addressed her. "It's too tempting to be flaunting yourself about with so many hungry men."

"Too tempting? For who?!" It took all her self-control not to scream at the man. Her voice was shaking. "Flaunting myself? I'm just living. If those men can't control themselves, that's not my problem." She looked down at her dusty, oversized pants and vest. She could not make herself any more unattractive than she already had. And why should she?

Ramzy snorted and started clearing empty jars off the table as if hinting for them to leave. She didn't need any more encouragement. She'd had enough of this blustering fool.

They took leave of Ramzy and Rodney with awkwardly formal handshakes. Once outside the block of containers, Kai left to find the mechanics, and Jasper led them through spaceport security and out onto the perimeter road.

"That guy is horrible," Cassidy said with a shudder.

Jasper laid his hand soothingly on her back. "He's not so bad. He's just old-fashioned, that's all."

"You mean stuck in the dark ages."

"Why does Ramzy hate Berkeley so much?" Torr asked.

Jasper's mouth turned up in a sardonic smile. "Berk was sleeping with Ramzy's daughter, Carmen, and the old man found out about it."

"Ah," Torr said.

"Ramzy said they should have been married first, and Berkeley should have asked his permission. Worse than that, my dad says Ramzy had already arranged a marriage for Carmen to a cousin he was going to bring to Peary, but since she was no longer a virgin, he had to back out. Dad said their family was dishonored and Ramzy was shamed. Ramzy took Carmen and hid her away with Gabira's women."

Cassidy was horrified. "That's so ... so ... nineteenth century!"

Jasper nodded. "It is." He shrugged. "Those times are still alive and well on the moon, I guess."

"Didn't Carmen have a choice? What about poor Berkeley?" Cassidy asked.

"Berkeley's heartbroken, still, even though it happened more than two years ago. Don't mention it to him, he gets really upset."

"Oh," Cassidy said softly. "That's so sad. He must hate Ramzy."

Jasper shrugged. "I don't know."

"What about Carmen? Can't she get out? Doesn't Berkeley get to visit her? Can't he just go get her?"

"Gabira cloisters the women away. She keeps men out except in her receiving room, to protect the women. Berkeley's visited Gabira a bunch of times. He always goes with the intention of finding Carmen, but always leaves without doing so. It's a little strange."

It sounded creepy to Cassidy. It reminded her of her mother's warnings about shamans whose power went to their heads and how dangerous they could be.

"You can meet Gabira if you want," Jasper said to her as they headed down Spoke Road Nine. "I need to go down there to get my crystal. Want to come? Maybe you can find out something about Carmen."

"Sorry, but no. That Gabira woman sounds like a witch."

Jasper gave her a sideways smile. "A shaman, maybe. She has some interesting stories. Gabira is cunning, but not evil. You'll see."

Cassidy shook her head. "No, thanks."

Jasper looked at her, shrugging his shoulders. "Maybe you could learn something from her."

"Like what?" she asked skeptically.

"I don't know," Jasper said as though he didn't care a bit, which told her he cared a great deal. "She's very powerful, and I hear she teaches the women things. How else are you going to protect yourself against the Tegs, if not through magic?"

She stared at the ground, unable to think of a smart retort. He had a point. Her mother was depending on magic to get through the Shaman's Shield. California had relied on the magical barrier to hold back General Tegea. Her grandmother had encouraged her to seek help from others to regain her abilities. She longed to be able to access her second sight the way she used to, when she could just think about something and see it clearly, and navigate the world from her bed.

"Maybe," she said grudgingly, "so long as you don't lock me away down there."

He gave her a sidelong look. "Why would I ever do that?" He reached out and took her hand, and held it as they walked along the dusty road.

32

———————)———————

THE PROMISE

Torr walked with Cassidy and Jasper to a vacant stretch of land at the southern end of Spoke Road Twelve near the edge of the glass dome. A breathtaking view spread out below their vantage point high atop Peary Rim. Earth shone above the southern horizon, casting a bright Earthshine on an otherwise dark land. He glanced behind him where the sun perched directly atop the row of peaks beyond Peary Crater. The sun's oblique light blazed through the camp, making Torr shield his eyes with his hand.

He turned back to the dusty patch where they stood. At its center stood a sundial, a raised bronze disc, big as a table and hip-high with a long, thin rod jutting up from the center. The rod was taller than a man and cast a long shadow on the notched face to track time. The sundial seemed like an artifact from a life Torr had left behind, but it gave him a strange comfort nonetheless. They all checked their wristwatches against it, counting the larger hour slashes within the day segment, and then the smaller, ten-minute interval slashes. Twenty-one-ten. Spot on.

Earth showed the landmasses of North and South America centered between the Atlantic and Pacific oceans. He could be there right now, with his parents, or with Bobby, exploring the Pacific on *Moon Star,* avoiding this whole mess. What difference was there really between floating out at sea and floating out here? In either case, it would be only a matter of time before the Tegs snared him in their net.

The only truly safe course was to leave the moon. Head out to Muria and try to build a new life. But it felt wrong, somehow. He could feel his parents. They were right there, on that big, beautiful globe. They would want them to go find Ramesh on Muria. To be safe. To live. His father had told him that he and Cassidy must survive.

Torr hated Tegea. He hated Metolius. He hated the Gaia United generals who had surrendered California. He hated his squadmates who had turned Teg. He hated that the male Star Child was a slayer of beasts.

"We have to fight," he blurted out, making Cassidy and Jasper turn to him in surprise. "I'm not running away this time. Those fucking cowards, Ramzy and Rodney, they don't know what they're doing."

Jasper raised an eyebrow but said nothing.

Cassidy looked at Torr, listening.

"You don't know what it's like," Torr said to Jasper. "You didn't have to run away from the Tegs." But Jasper's campmates had. And the Boyers. They would understand. They would want to fight, too.

Cassidy nodded. "We should take our land back before it's too late. Before the Tegs take over the whole moon."

"How are you going to do that?" Jasper asked. "You don't have any weapons or ships."

"Ramzy does," Torr said.

"You heard what he said. He'll never go for it, and his men won't defy him."

"You mean like your dad?" Cassidy asked.

Jasper threw Cassidy a flat look. "Him, and others. They're a tight-knit group. Loyal."

"Loyal to a braying ass," Torr said. "If we lose the moon to the Tegs it will be the end of everything. Earth's lifeline to the free galaxy will be severed." The thought of such a future pushed Torr's mood to a new low. Earth's people would have no hope, completely defeated by a conquering race. When they looked up at the moon for comfort, all they would see would be another Teg base.

"Look," Jasper said, putting his hand on Torr's shoulder and his other arm around Cassidy. "If you want to make a difference, then be the Star Children. Learn magic."

Torr put his hand on Cassidy's shoulder, closing the circle. He looked into his friend's eyes, then met the gaze of his sister. If she truly was Golden Falcon, then maybe she could find the Star People and save Earth. He would sacrifice himself. Do whatever it was the Bringer of Death did. Wreak destruction, then bury himself in misery.

Take heart and soldier on. The prescription of Pine Flower echoed in his head. "If we are the Star Children, then we'll need each other more than ever. The three of us," Torr said, lifting his chin. "Promise we'll stick together, no matter what."

"I promise," Cassidy said.

They both turned to Jasper, whose startled gaze darted between the two of them. "Me?" His voice was a squeak.

"You," Torr insisted. "You're the Friend. We can't do it without you. You in?"

Jasper looked panicked for a moment, then his eyes narrowed. "That could be cool, to help the Star Children save the galaxy."

Torr rolled his eyes. "First, just help us get our land."

"That sounds dangerous, but ... okay," Jasper said, a pained smile turning up one side of his mouth.

"Promise," Cassidy said, poking Jasper in the ribs.

"I promise," Jasper said weakly. They looked at one another, not sure what they had just agreed to.

Even so, Torr felt a bond strengthen between the three of them. They could do this, together. A silent buzz filled the air, and the stars grew brighter. Earth glimmered on the horizon, and the moon stood solid under their feet.

33

EMBARGO⊙

Ridge stood in Gandoop warehouse surrounded by crates and barrels of rotting food. It was a crime, letting fresh Earth food go bad. It was Balty's latest initiative. Scare the fuck out of Peary Dome. Balty talked about it as though it were merely malicious fun, but Ridge knew Balty always did things for a reason. Ridge suspected it was tied to the build-up of Teg troops at Gandoop. It seemed to Ridge that Balty intended to put Peary Dome under siege, and take over the spaceport and dome.

He wondered how long it would take Balty to go from constricting the flow of food to blocking traffic in and out of Peary altogether. But that would be all out war, and Balty couldn't be sure whose side the other mines would take. If they sided with Peary, Balty would most likely lose. He didn't have enough craft or firepower to defeat Peary and the dozens of mines if they banded together. And why would the mines side with Gandoop? Most mines considered Gandoop a threat to their own livelihoods. It had been a careful balancing act to keep good relations with them as Gandoop grew. Ever since Gandoop Spaceport had been completed, everyone watched them warily, wondering what their next move would be. Some refused to do business with them, particularly the outer rim and far side mining lords who were suspicious of everyone. But more significantly, everyone hated the Tegs.

Perhaps that was why Balty was playing with limiting food shipments. It was within the realm of possibility to divert most or all Earth food shipments to Gandoop and starve the moon rats out of their nests, even the smaller mines, who relied on the Peary and Gandoop ports. Many of the moon inhabitants would flee before they died of starvation. Maybe that was Balty's plan. Decimate the moon population and force Ramzy to surrender the dome. Only, Balty didn't know how stubborn Ramzy was. Worst case, everyone in the dome would starve to death. He wondered how many people those greenhouses could feed. Probably only a few hundred, if that.

If the siege did work, once Balty had control of Peary Dome, what would they do with so many dead bodies? Ridge's invention, the corpse shredder, took only one body at a time. It'd be easier to dump them all out into space, but littering space with so many corpses felt like dumping raw sewage in their own backyard. Most would fall back to the moon eventually, unless Balty wanted to pay interstellar freighters to go beyond the moon's gravitational field and open their cargo bay airlocks. Ridge shook his head, determined not to let it come to that.

In retrospect, Ridge could see that Balty was a patient man and was playing a long game. Soon after his arrival, Balty had convinced Ishmar to double what he paid ship captains for food, and to always pay in gold. This resulted in weakening the Peary market and increasing the traffic through Gandoop. In the years since, more and more ships came to Gandoop to unload their food, receiving gold from Ishmar instead of the simple trade for docking fees, which was the deal at Peary.

The practice at Peary had been for captains to bring enough staple foods to pay their fees. The rest of their cargo was generally hard goods, or alcohol and choice foodstuffs, which they sold for gold to the Peary Traders Guild or interplanetary traders whose ships were berthed at the hangar. Interplanetary craft were in the habit of parking at Peary for a month or more. They would trade with other alien ships, wait for Earth craft to arrive with something interesting, or place an order with a moon mine for certain minerals and wait for their order to be fulfilled.

Gandoop, although not nearly as large as Peary and unable to hold interstellar craft for any length of time, still maintained a steady flow of traffic and conducted a brisk trading business. The large warehouse was now filled with off-world goods, storehouses of minerals, and tanks of gases. There was often no need for Earth freighters to go to Peary at all anymore, and many of them didn't. But Ridge had assumed this whole time that staple foods like rice, beans, and perishables had been making their way to Peary, by far the largest food market on the moon. Recently, however, he'd noticed the warehouse shelves and aisles were jammed with sacks of grains and beans, cases of canned goods, barrels of olive oil, and crates of produce. When he asked around, one of the old workers told him the Tegs had instructed that no food was to be sold to moon rats; it was only to be sold to off-world traders. Ridge realized he should be paying more attention.

A forklift operated by one of Balty's soldiers entered the warehouse and slid its forks under a pallet of cases marked Canned Albacore Tuna, Carnarvon. Ridge followed the forklift back out into the hangar and watched the workers load the Australian tuna onto a Cephean freighter. Ridge went back into the warehouse. Several dozen cases of chicken eggs were stacked in a corner. He pulled his hand screen from his pocket and scanned a case. It had arrived at Gandoop over two weeks ago. The eggs should have been taken to a cold storage room, not left out here.

"What are you going to do with these eggs?" Ridge asked the forklift operator when he returned for another pallet of tuna.

The man shrugged. "I don't know. Nobody told me."

"Well, if the eggs have been washed, they'll go rotten sitting out here," Ridge said, irritation ringing in his voice.

"Last week we dumped some in the refuse recycler," the man said, and backed away with his tuna. He did not seem at all concerned that precious, fresh Earth food was being shamelessly wasted. Ridge was sure Balty was behind it, happy to let food rot rather than send it to Peary.

Ridge tore open a crate and was trying to determine if the eggs were still good when the operator returned for the last pallet of tuna. The man looked at him with a hint of amusement. "Another load of eggs just came in from Beersheba, if you're hungry."

Ridge left the egg problem for later and walked out into the hangar, ignoring the curious glances of the workers. He rarely inspected freight anymore, but Balty's soldiers knew who he was and let him pass without question. Crates, sacks, and barrels from the Beersheba ship were being unloaded and stacked beside it. There were cucumbers, eggplants, and tomatoes; onions, fresh garlic, and potatoes; rice, wheat, and millet; raisins, dried apricots, dates, and figs; almonds, peanuts, and sunflower seeds; vinegar, olive oil, and olives; salt and sugar; tea leaf and wine.

He walked over to Flanders, one of Balty's men who had taken over Murphy's role of inventorying all the goods passing in and out of the spaceport. Flanders was a tall, soft-spoken soldier, and was busily scanning and marking items on his screen. "Do you have a buyer for the food?" Ridge asked.

"No, not yet," Flanders said, not looking up from his screen. "I'll take it," Ridge said impulsively. "Mark it as transferred to me."

Flanders glanced up, his eyes darting quickly over Ridge's crisp and clean black flightsuit and resting on his Cephean-green eyes. Ridge held Flanders's gaze, not about to be challenged by this newcomer. "Have them load all the food in the old cow," Ridge said, pointing to one of the Gandoops' moon freighters, another Russian Korova.

Ridge stood back and watched the workmen load the ship. When the cargo hold was full, Ridge piloted the old cow through the decompression chambers and slowly ascended out of the crater. Compared to his speedster, the Korova was like a lumbering elephant. He flew to Last Chance's main hangar, unloaded some of the food for the grateful workers there, then tried to figure out his next move. There was no one to stop him from taking the food to Peary. He dwelled on his scheme for a minute and decided to do it. Fuck Balty.

Now he only had to manage his disguise and transfer the load from the Gandoop Korova to his Last Chance Korova. Jidna couldn't very well pilot a craft with Gandoop's insignia on it. The Last Chance freighter was in the lab's port, which could not accommodate two freighters, and his speedster was at Gandoop. This whole second identity thing was becoming a hassle. Rather than ask a worker to ferry him over, he decided to don a spacesuit and walk the half-mile to the lab building.

Once outside, he stood for a moment to enjoy the profound silence and peaceful vista of the rolling regolith dunes to the north. He liked it like this, during the two-week periods when the muted surface was bathed in soft Earthshine instead of the glaring reflection of the sun. He turned south to face the Black Mare, which extended in a dark sea to where black basalt met blacker sky, a sprinkling of stars marking the horizon. Being out of doors on the lunar surface was relaxing and frightening at the same time.

The gravitational fields created by the Scrid gravity bar in the main compound and the smaller one in his dome didn't quite overlap, so two-thirds of the way there he found himself taking long, bounding leaps in slow motion. He did a couple forward flips just because he could. The freedom of low gravity made him wonder for a moment why he even bothered installing gravity bars at all. When he reached the gravitational field outside the lab and could walk normally again, he dismissed his frivolous thoughts. He entered the building through the "front door," a man-sized airlock that opened directly into the living area.

He removed his spacesuit, piloted the Last Chance freighter to the main facility, had the workers transfer the cargo from one freighter to the other, ferried the ship back to the lab, transformed into Jidna, then took off for Peary. What a pain in the ass. Perhaps he should just grow out his own hair and beard and become Jidna for good.

A Peary guard glanced at Jidna's Traders Guild chest patch when he stepped out of the cargo ship. As a member of Peary Dome Traders Guild, a guild open only to moon residents, he would either pay five percent of his trades to Peary for a docking fee or one ounce of gold, whichever was less. He flipped a gold Eagle to the guard, not wanting them to inventory his goods or track his trades.

"You got food," the guard observed as Jidna lowered the cargo bay ramp. "Ramzy will want to buy it."

"Can't," Jidna said. "This is Guild business."

"Where did you get it?"

"Gandoop." Obviously. Where else would an outer rim mining lord find a cargo-hold full of Earth food? Earth freighters didn't like to deal directly with the small mines. The Gandoops were respected for running a legitimate trading business. But most mining lords were not so scrupulous. More than one Earth pilot and his cargo had gone missing while trading with outer rim and far side mines.

The guard turned and stalked away in the direction of Ramzy's office. Things were unfolding just as Jidna had anticipated. In the meantime, he was attracting attention from other Guild members. A small group gathered around, peering into the hold. Jidna recognized two as Schlitzer's agents, and another was the tall, lanky Jaz, whose rust-colored hair made him easy to spot.

"Hey, Jidna," Jaz greeted him. "Where'd you get all that?" His hazel eyes scanned the contents of the hold.

"Gandoop."

"How much did you pay?"

"Three times the going rate."

Jaz's mouth fell open in dismay. "No shit. In gold?"

Jidna nodded smugly and leaned against the side of the freighter, folding his arms across his chest while being careful not to tug at his beard. Ramzy was laboring across the wide floor, carrying his portly body on short, skinny legs. It had been several years since Jidna last caught sight of the Peary Dome leader, and the years had not been kind. Ramzy came huffing over to the ship, and the men surrounding the freighter parted to let him pass. Despite his ragged appearance, Jidna found Ramzy to be more charismatic than he remembered, exuding a sense of gravitas as if responsibility for ten thousand lives had worn him down on the surface but strengthened his core.

Jidna held his breath, hoping Ramzy wouldn't see through his disguise. It had been many years since they'd last spoken, and he had been Ridge then. Ramzy's eyes passed over him in annoyance, with no hint of recognition. Jidna released his breath and shamelessly picked at the dust crust that was clogging one nostril.

"This isn't an Earth freighter," Ramzy said, stating the obvious. "Where did you get this food?"

"Gandoop."

Ramzy's complexion darkened. "Did they have more?"

"A whole storehouse full," Jidna said, flicking snot from his fingernail.

"What are they doing with it?" Ramzy demanded, shooting Jidna an angry look, as though an outer rim mining lord would know the answer.

Jidna shrugged and took out a small knife and began scraping away moon dust that had embedded itself under his fingernails.

"What mine are you from?" Ramzy asked, inspecting Jidna with distaste.

Jidna continued scraping at his nails. "Last Chance."

"Where's that?"

"Near Timmy's crater."

Ramzy gave him a blank look.

"North of Plato," he said, citing a major landmark.

"How'd you afford all this food?" Ramzy examined him the way a bird examines a worm, his eyes lingering on the stains and patches that dotted his pants and jacket.

"Guild business," Jidna said, tired of being interrogated. He tapped his Traders Guild patch.

"How much you selling it for?" Ramzy asked, as if Jidna hadn't spoken.

"It's Guild business," Jidna repeated, meaning it was none of Ramzy's business. Ramzy couldn't very well object. It was Ramzy himself who had set up Peary Dome Traders Guild to be independent from Peary operations. Ramzy hadn't wanted to manage all the goods coming in and out of the dome. He only wanted to deal with camp operations, which had grown to include water and food rations. The rest of the economy was left to the Traders Guild to take care of, including any food outside the ration system. Jidna smiled at him, and Ramzy frowned.

"What are you going to do with all those eggs?" Ramzy asked tensely.

Jidna sighed. "I'm not allowed to sell anything to Peary directly. That was part of the deal I made with Gandoop." He had just made that up, and tried not to smirk as Ramzy's face looked like a balloon about to burst. "Now, if something should make its way into your hands after I sell it to another trader, there's nothing I can do about that. Of course, that might get expensive." He smiled again, eyeing the growing group of traders who surrounded them. They were all Peary moon rats, the regular traders who trolled the shipping floor to intercept ships as soon as they landed. He wondered with a twinge of panic if Balty had planted any spies among the traders. Maybe Ridge had taken things too far. Well, it was too late now. He snapped his pocket knife closed, turned his back to Ramzy, and climbed into the hold.

Jidna asked the Guild members for help unloading. The men stepped forward eagerly, and trading began. Security guards entered the bay, running sensing rods over the sacks and crates and tearing some open for inspection. He suffered the intrusion. He would suspect Jidna of smuggling black market goods, too, if he were them. Next time he looked, Ramzy was gone.

He sold his entire load within an hour, at four times the normal rate. The moon rats were hungry, there was no doubt about that. The eggs went to one of Schlitzer's men. Jaz bought an assortment of things, haggling with Jidna and the other Guild members. The redhead even threw in a rare gold coin from Delos to get all the nuts and dried fruit. Jidna had never seen the coin before—on the front was a castle, and the reverse depicted a bird of prey perched on a gauntleted fist. Antler Kralj.

Jidna anticipated that word of the transactions would spread, and soon Gandoop would be called on by mining lords from the outer rim and far side wanting to buy food to sell at Peary for a nice profit. They would get turned away, but Jidna's true identity might get discovered. Then he would have to deal with Balty.

Jangling his pocketful of gold, Jidna left the hangar and stepped out into the sunshine of Peary Dome. He put on his mirrored shades and headed straight for Danny's. He went with her into her tent where they shared their bodies in a familiar, habitual way. Afterwards, he let himself doze off next to her for a time.

Temporarily satiated and relaxed, he gave her a few gold Eagles, then went to Schlitzer's bar. Not finding the pimp there, he quickly drank a beer, ignoring the girls at the bar who wanted his money, and left. He wandered the dome aimlessly, stopping briefly to press his nose against the window of a greenhouse where the soy plants were flowering. He should build a greenhouse. It was next on his list, though it had been next on his list since they'd finished the spaceport, but he always seemed to find something more urgent to do.

He headed east across the dome to the spaceport. It was dim inside, but he kept his sunglasses on, not interested in people studying his face. Eyes followed him across the hangar floor, wondering who this scruffy mining lord was showing up with a freighter full of Earth food.

Jidna climbed the two steel rungs and settled into the Korova's cab, backed it out of its parking spot, and decompressed through Bay Four. He flew out into the Earthshine and relaxed into the seat, feeling fat with his foam-padded gut hanging over his belt. He pulled off the wig, peeling the fisorial from his shaved scalp, and tossed the mass of hair onto the empty passenger seat. He scratched at his beard, wishing he had brought the solution with him to remove it. It was hot and itched like hell.

"Jidna," he said aloud as the ground sped by underneath him. "Being you is fucking exhausting."

Ridge tightened his harness and leaned his head back against the headrest, then curved Earthside towards Last Chance and started planning his next food shipment.

The next day, Ridge walked the Gandoop warehouse, picking out goods that one of his workers loaded onto a small transport. Ridge chose a couple dozen sacks each of various grains and dried legumes. From the next aisle he took sacks of nuts and dried fruits. From the aisle stuffed with pallets of canned goods, he chose an assortment of vegetables and fruit. He finished off with cases of dried milk, spices, sacks of sugar, a few barrels of olive oil, and several casks of red wine. That should restock Peary's non-perishable food supplies for a little while. Ramzy would never know Ridge Gandoop was personally helping them out, but Ridge did not need recognition for doing the right thing.

Out on the shipping floor, Flanders was marking the items on his screen. He looked up at Ridge. "More food?"

"Sure," Ridge said. "Hot market for food on the moon right now. Might as well get some profit while I can. Besides," he said, adopting a scolding tone, "the warehouse is packed floor to ceiling. If we don't move some inventory, we won't be able to buy anything else."

"We've been recycling the food," Flanders said into his screen, avoiding Ridge's eyes.

"I know," Ridge said coldly. "And that's a crime."

Flanders did not respond. Ridge wondered how long before Balty would hear of his escapades, if he didn't know already. He would be pissed. Ridge inhaled a long breath of metallic moon air, whistling through his left, stuffed-up nostril. He stood by the old cow's loading ramp, in a spot he had intentionally chosen behind a large interstellar freighter that blocked the view from Balty's office. He didn't know if the sadistic control freak was in there or not, and he didn't care to find out. Ridge hadn't taken his ten percent in months. He could do whatever he wanted with his own goddamned food.

He watched silently as the loading crew expertly arranged and secured the cargo. When they were done, there was more space available, so Ridge sent them to the warehouse for pallets of canned tuna and sardines, and cases of eggs, until the hold was filled.

He made a last tour of the warehouse, looking for items to squeeze into the cockpit with him, things that would really send the Guild traders into a frenzy: tea and coffee, chocolate and chewing tobacco, fresh oranges and mangoes, cases of hard alcohol. He stopped there, afraid he wouldn't have room to sit. It was crazy how much food had piled up in the facility. Balty was a lunatic. Ridge left the warehouse and instructed the workers to load the goods into the cockpit, filling the stowage compartments built into the back panel, the space behind the seats, and the co-pilot's chair and floor space.

He went to Last Chance and let his crew transfer the cargo from one Korova to the other. They knew he was up to something, but it was none of their business. They had been trained well at Gandoop not to ask questions. Besides, Ridge kept the workers' food supplies at Last Chance well stocked and was not stingy with the liquor and other desirable items. He flew the Korova out over the Black Mare, looped back to the small lab building, changed into Jidna, and left for Peary.

Inside the spaceport a group of Guild traders were waiting as he climbed out of the cockpit. Three of Schlitzer's men were among them, as were Jaz and several other traders he recognized. He waved his hand at the group. "I already sold it all," he called out.

Moans and complaints tumbled over one another. "We didn't even get a chance to bid on it." "You promised me olives." "Do you have any cheese?" "Who'd you sell it to?"

"Schlitzer's getting it all," Jidna lied, stepping back as the cargo bay door lowered, serving as the ramp. He had promised Schlitzer's men their fair share, but he hadn't specified how much that would be. This tactic would squeeze the most gold from the other traders.

"Schlitzer! That's not fair, we're all in the Guild. We can each bid on any cargo."

Jidna shrugged. Regardless of who bought it, most of it would make its way into the camp food supply one way or the other. One of Schlitzer's men drove a forklift up the ramp, grabbed a pallet of canned fish, and slowly backed out. A security guard stood by, passing a sensing wand over the freight as it came down the ramp. Other traders climbed into the hold and began passing goods down the line of men that had formed by custom. It was the Guild way, to help each other load and unload, even if they were not in on the deal. Usually by the time the cargo was unloaded everyone had a small piece of the action, or at least the promise of a future trade.

This time was no different. While the cargo hold was being emptied, he relented and sold each of the men something or other. Jaz got all the eggs, which he would most likely sell to Ramzy for a good price. At about two hundred eggs per crate, there was enough for a serving of protein to each of the camp inhabitants. It felt good to contribute to the cause, and he smiled at Jaz as they carefully stacked the crates on the hangar floor. One of Jaz's friends guarded the eggs while Jaz started in the direction of Ramzy's office.

"Hang on a sec," Jidna called to the redhead. "The best stuff is in here."

The traders gathered around as he opened the co-pilot's door. Fierce haggling ensued over the alcohol, coffee, and tobacco, and within minutes the entire stash was gone. The traders hung out by his door and followed him around to the pilot's side, thanking him repeatedly and making friendly chitchat to get on his good side. He locked the cockpit and took a satisfied breath. He hadn't had this much fun in years.

Several traders trailed him as he sauntered across the hangar floor towards the perimeter road exit. He waved them away as he stepped outdoors, and walked by himself to Danny's.

34

————) ————

THE WATER WAGON

Cassidy lay in her sleeping bag, staring at the yellowed tent wall and listening to the sounds of the camp as it settled down for night curfew. Torr was three doors down at the Boyers' tent. She and Torr had imitated the others in the Fen, and thrown a tarp over their roof, casting the tent into welcome shadow for sleeping.

They'd spent the evening sharing a late dinner of rice and beans that Fritz and Frank had prepared. Everyone had been invited: the original Fen inhabitants, plus Durham and his sons, and Sky and Thunder. No one mentioned the added numbers, but supplying extra food for so many would get expensive, and she wondered who had paid for all the food in the Fen's storage tent.

Maybe they had all chipped in. They all seemed to have some sort of business. Fritz and Frank played music, touring around to the different ration trailers with their hats out, collecting coppers. Jasper was a trader. Berkeley made clothes. Tatsuya was a tattoo artist. Hiroshi was a craftsman, sharpening knives and repairing tools and leather. Jasper told her Ming-Long and Khaled hired themselves out as bodyguards to the Delosian traders when they wanted to wander the dome. Faisal was independently wealthy, and apparently had mounds of gold hidden away somewhere.

Perhaps she could start a little business dispensing her herbal medicine, although once the herbs ran out they'd be gone for good. Maybe she could import dried herbs from Earth using Jasper's trading license and make extracts. But it wouldn't be the same as harvesting the plants herself. Much of the power of the herbs came from the herbalist's connection with the plants while they were harvested.

She didn't really need to work. She still had all the gold Torr had given her: two Solidi and six Tetras, along with a handful of gold Eagles, gold bits, and tenth-gold bits, plus her own silver and copper coins. That much treasure could last her many years if she was careful.

She checked the rune belt that was secured around her waist. She'd stashed the Solidi and Tetras inside it, but couldn't feel their bulk or weight unless she touched the fabric. She tucked her hands under her head and thought back on the evening. After dinner, they'd all sat around talking, while Fritz and Frank played their guitars in the background. Then they'd all played cards. Jasper had gotten hailed on his radio halfway through a hand. He'd folded and left the camp, and still had not returned by the time night gong struck.

She wondered where he was. They had made out in his tent a couple of times over the past few days, but had been interrupted each time. There were always people wanting their attention. She'd been too shy to go to his tent at night, and he hadn't invited her.

She rose on one elbow and reached for her herb pack. She found Waning Moon and placed two drops on her tongue. It was one of her mother's most popular herbs, reliably preventing pregnancy if taken consistently. Her mother had left her with several bottles of it.

She dug into her pack and found the small strip of two photos from the photo booth on the boardwalk. Her and Jasper's teen-aged faces peered back at her, bringing a smile to her lips. She set it gently on her pile of folded clothing and lay back down.

She curled up again and thought of times back on Earth when she and Jasper had been close. It had started in Shasta when they were very young, playing kissing games. She liked to grab him by the hand and announce that they were going to get married. The adults laughed and thought it was cute. Jasper had not objected until he got a little older and started pushing her away.

A few years later they had been alone, standing in the kitchen and wrestling playfully. Up between them had sprung his teenaged manhood, pushing up his pajama bottoms like some strange animal struggling against a cocoon. They'd both frozen and stared at it in muted shock. After a long moment, they both snickered, their faces turning red. Cassidy had given him a playful tap on the cheek and scampered away. After that they'd kept a wide berth, edging round each other whenever they crossed paths in the hallway or kitchen.

When they got older, some weekends Cassidy, Jasper, and Torr would backpack overnight in the redwood forest above the valley. They would sit around the campfire late into the night, telling ghost stories. Then the three of them would squeeze into their two-man tent, Cassidy in the middle. She would fall asleep near Jasper's solid body, matching his breathing.

One time she was awakened by moonlight streaming in through the mesh window of the tent, crickets chanting loudly in the forest. She rolled over in her sleeping bag to find Jasper

looking at her. Lulled by sleep and the enchanted night, she
leaned over and kissed him. His lips met hers with surprise.

"No," he whispered, breaking their kiss and firmly turning
her away.

She lay with her back to him, holding her breath, listening as
his breathing slowly settled into an even rhythm. At first light,
she awoke to find his heavy arm flung across her torso, her back
snuggled against his chest. His knees were tucked into the curve
of her knees and their hips were nested together, their sleeping
bags layered between them. She kept still, luxuriating in the feel
of him and the comfort of his breathing, until he stirred and
pulled away, the morning birds trilling from the treetops.

After that she had been more conscious of his body. His
strong hand catching hers as she hopped over a stream. Helping
her up a steep rocky path. Nudging her aside as they stood at the
kitchen counter making sandwiches, their knives fighting for the
peanut butter jar. She would sit on the driveway pavement next
to him and hand him tools as he worked on his motorcycle, his
hands covered with grease. Then they would ride together over
the winding mountain passes and coastal highway, her arms
wrapped around his waist, her knees gripping his hips, her chin
resting on his shoulder. They explored hidden beaches and fern
grottos carved into the bluffs by the waves, and strolled along
the boardwalk, eating cotton candy. At home, he'd help her in
the garden. Digging. Turning the soil. Planting seedlings. Tying
up vines. Picking ripe tomatoes.

The months had gone by. He had started to leave for weeks at
a time to live elsewhere. Couches of friends. Garage apartments.
Vehicles. None of those lasted very long. When he returned
they would fall into their routine of staying up late and watching movies of the old Wild West or the new space frontier, or
playing cards and board games in the kitchen. Her parents liked

to retire early, and Torr would disappear to read, stealing time for himself in the room he shared with Jasper.

One time they had been alone on the couch watching a movie about gunslingers and bank robbers in the desert. It was a good movie, but they were both sleepy. They were seated next to each other, their shoulders touching. As they dozed off, their heads leaned against one another, her head slipping to his shoulder. His cheek rested against her head. His nose nuzzled hers. Their lips found each other in the cloaking darkness. They slowly stretched out onto the cushions, the quivering whisper of lips upon skin like butterflies fluttering from flower to flower. Blood rushed in Cassidy's ears, drowning out the muted gunfire and horses galloping on the screen. They stayed together until dawn, exploring each other's bodies, going a little too far but not far enough.

A few days later he invited her to go motorcycle riding along the coast. At a sheltered beach hemmed in by cliffs, he led her away from the crashing waves to the sand, where they lay down together and made out with none of the shyness of the night on the couch. If there hadn't been a family picnicking on the beach, Cassidy thought they might have gone all the way. But as it was, they just felt and rubbed each other, and got sand in their mouths.

The next afternoon they found an excuse to climb up to the Crow's Nest, just the two of them alone in the shelter of the swaying branches. But they just stared at one another. It was too real. Too possible. They climbed back down and did not speak of it.

A few days later he'd moved out to live with some buddies from the university. Then next thing she knew he was leaving for the moon, and she had been left with an aching belly and a heart that would not stop breaking.

———————)————————

Cassidy awoke to the deep gonging that flowed through the camp from different directions, creating a chorus that resounded in her bones. She pulled on her dragon t-shirt, dusty pants, vest, and shoes, and stepped out into the light. After a breakfast of stale bread dunked in tea with honey, she went to the Fen's water tank to fill her canteen.

The tank sat on a wagon tucked away between the kitchen and the small cluster of tents where Berkeley, Hiroshi, and Tatsuya stayed. A tarp was stretched above it to shade the water. The sounds of the tent city droned in the background.

Jasper appeared and came around the wagon. "Hey, Cassafrass," he said with a cocky grin.

"Hey, *Jaz,*" she said, as she screwed the top onto her canteen and clipped it to her belt. She stepped aside so he could get at the spigot, but he shook his head.

"I don't need water. I just came to say hi."

"I just saw you two minutes ago," she said.

"Yeah, with everybody else." He held her gaze, then leaned over and gave her a gentle kiss on the lips. "I miss you."

"I miss you too." She returned his short kiss with a long one and leaned her hands against his chest. "Where did you go last night?" she asked.

He brushed back a strand of her hair that had fallen across her cheek, then rested one hand on her shoulder and the other around the curve of her back in a loose embrace. "There's a bar across the camp where I conduct business sometimes. I had to jump on the deal right away or I would have lost out."

"Sounds, um, a bit sketchy," she said, raising one eyebrow.

"Yeah, well, it is the moon, and a guy has to make a living." He cracked a crooked smile.

"I didn't hear you come back. Do you have a girlfriend or something?" she asked, trying to keep her voice nonchalant.

"No. Do you have a boyfriend?"

"No."

Jasper studied her. His strong jaws and chin were covered with a freshly trimmed beard, and his ever-present sunglasses were missing, revealing his dark hazel eyes rimmed by short russet eyelashes.

"You've grown up to be incredibly beautiful, Cassandra Dagda," he said, his voice low.

She felt herself blush, but lifted her chin and held his eyes. "Why, thank you, Jasper Manann. You've grown up to be quite fine yourself."

"Really?" he drawled, his wide mouth twisting into a sideways grin. He drew her in closer.

She relaxed against him and rested her head on his shoulder, and traced the Heaven's Window pendant that hung at his throat. She went to pull away, but he held her tighter and pressed his warm lips to her temple. Her breath caught in her throat, and she moved her hand to his pocket, where the shooting star was pinned. "You're wearing this," she said, running her fingers over the polished stones. She lifted her head.

"I always wear it," he said, meeting her gaze. She had forgotten how beautiful his eyes were. Mottled green like dew-covered moss.

"And did you think of me whenever you looked at Earth?" she asked, feeling the pressure of his arm around her waist and the firmness of his chest under her hand.

His mouth softened. "I did."

"Every time?"

He chuckled, the soft rolling laughter feeling good against her body. "Well," he said, nodding in the direction of Earth that was hidden behind the tarp. "As you've noticed, Earth is always out. So I would be lying if I said I thought of you every single time I looked at it." She could not argue with that. "And did you think of me when you looked at the moon?" His voice was teasing, but his eyes were not.

She looked sideways at him and pursed her lips playfully. "Sometimes."

He feigned a pout and wove his fingers through the hair at the back of her neck, making her spine tingle.

"I was so sad when the Shaman's Shield was up," she said. "I couldn't see the moon for a whole three years, but every night I still said, 'Good night sweet Jasper, may the stars shine down upon you.'"

Suddenly his lips were on hers, and she was breathing him in. His mouth was salty and sweet, from bread and honey. Their lips parted, and their eyes met, sweat breaking on her brow. His chest was rising with short breaths, and her heart was pounding.

They both looked up. Tatsuya was standing there with a teakettle in his hands. He backed away, repeating something in Japanese while bobbing his shoulders up and down in short little bows.

"It's okay, Tatsuya," Jasper said, as he and Cassidy pulled apart, but the man backed out of sight.

Jasper and Cassidy grinned at one another. She reached into her vest pocket and pulled out the photo booth pictures from the boardwalk, and showed them to him.

"Look what I found," she said.

"Oh, Cassie," he said, chuckling. "Look how young we were." Their teenaged faces were silly and bright with joy.

She leaned against him and they laughed together.

"We always had so much fun," he said. "Remember gardening? And camping?" He looked at her slyly. "Do you remember kissing me that time in the tent?" She blushed and nodded. "You don't know how badly I wanted to be with you that night," he said.

"Or the Crow's Nest," she said, looking up at him from beneath her lashes.

"Oh my god, that almost killed me," he said, sending them into another fit of laughter.

He reached into the inside pocket of his vest and pulled out a small, stiff paper. He unfolded it to reveal his half of the photo strip, protected these five years from the dust of the moon in the little paper sleeve.

"Aww, you kept it," she said. His gaze was tender, sending a rush of emotion through her body. She handed him her strip of photos and took his. "Let's trade. My turn to carry this one."

He went to fold hers in his paper wrapper when he stopped. On the back of the photos was a heart with an arrow through it, in faded blue ink. JM was printed above it, and CD below. He shot her a pointed look.

She made a face and shrugged. "I drew that after you left. I had a mad crush. I was a silly teenager."

His mouth curved into a lopsided smile. "Me too. Why do you think I moved out of your house?"

"What do you mean? For the moon?"

"No, to move in with my friends. I couldn't stay in your house any longer."

"Why not?" she asked, incredulous. "You left because of *me?*"

"Partly. Mostly." His eyes were dancing. "I didn't know if I could withstand another night on the couch with you, without risking your honor."

"My honor?"

"Or mine. You were barely fifteen and I was going on twenty. Your parents would have killed me." He narrowed his eyes and traced the curve of her jaw with his finger. "Can you imagine if I'd planted a baby in your belly?"

"No, that would not have been good," she agreed, chuckling.

He pulled her into a hug. "I was a flood of crazy hormones, Cassie. I couldn't trust myself. Or you, for that matter. I'm not sure who was worse."

She pressed her cheek against his neck. "You're right," she said. "It would have been fun, though."

"Oh, holy stars, it would have been." He squeezed her, and his mouth moved to her ear. "Come to my tent tonight," he whispered. "After night gong. Come stay with me."

"Okay," she said breathlessly.

The rising and falling of his chest matched hers as he kissed her neck, and her body melted into his.

35

THE SCRİDS

Cassidy and Jasper left the shelter of the water wagon, and Cassidy stood at the picnic tables while Jasper stepped away, talking into his radio. She regarded his taut body and the serious look on his face as he tended to his Guild business. His playful demeanor was replaced by that of a businessman making a deal. One hand held the hand-sized radio to his ear, while the other set on his hip as he paced back and forth. He was the same Jasper she remembered on Earth, yet he had changed.

Cassidy stepped out from under the tarp that shaded the tables and glanced over at the sun. She still found it strange that it did not brighten the sky outside the dome, leaving the heavens perpetually black and studded with stars.

Peary Rim was also referred to as the Peaks of Eternal Light. Here at the north pole of the moon, the sun scooted slowly across the horizon in a circle, making a low arc across the southern sky then skipping along the jagged peaks to the north, which is where it was today. Tomorrow the sun would be a few degrees to the east, inching along the mountainous ridge.

Cassidy did not know if she would ever become accustomed to the surreal nature of time here, where the sun neither rose nor set. She glanced at her watch to try and ground herself. It was eight in the morning.

Berkeley swaggered into the courtyard from the back area. He wore a calf-length vest-cloak that hung loosely over his tan cargo shorts and vest. The cloak was of a fine, shimmery, dark brown fabric nearly the color of his dreadlocks and forked beard. The sleeveless garment was embroidered with an intricate, interlocking knot pattern of golden thread, which ran down the front edges and around the armholes. Leg slits that reached up to the thigh on each side of the cloak were also trimmed with the golden embroidery, as was the hem. Cassidy looked him up and down and shook her head with amusement.

"What?" he asked, grinning widely. "You don't like my cloak?"

"You just look odd, that's all."

"Why, thank you," he said, beaming at her.

"Where did you get that?" Jasper asked, clipping the radio to his belt and joining them. "It looks Delosian."

"I made it myself. Just finished it. From that Delosian fabric I got from you a few months ago, remember? Do you like my embroidery? I modeled it after a cloak Eridanus wore."

Jasper nodded with approval. "Good job."

"Thank you," Berkeley said, looking pleased.

"Did you sew a spell into it?" Cassidy asked.

Berkeley shrugged noncommittally and turned to greet Torr.

The four of them went to Center Ring and joined the ration line. Cassidy pulled her bandana from a vest pocket and tied it across her face. A faint haze hung at shoe-level across the entire circular yard, making it look like people were walking on a cloud. Those who wore shorts had a film of gray dust coating their lower legs. The ration queue was long, a snaking line of scruffy men.

A subtle disturbance spread across Center Ring like a ripple in a pond. Cassidy identified the source to be a band of women who emerged from Spoke Road Three and cut through the sparse crowd, leaving men staring in their wake. There were at least thirty of them of various ages, all wearing desert military attire and walking confidently, some with dust masks, some without. "Look," Cassidy said, elbowing Jasper.

"Ahh, the Smith gang," he said, following them with his eyes. The sight of so many women together made Cassidy consider how few women she'd seen in the dome. "You might like to get to know them," Jasper suggested. "They're led by four sisters, the Smiths, as you could guess. They're always looking for new recruits to join their gang. Not a bad option for you. Not too friendly to men, though, so we keep our distance."

The women wore knives and clubs at their sides or strapped across their chests, and their eyes scanned the yard. A few noticed Cassidy and nodded. Cassidy smiled back. They looked strong and independent. Suddenly a weight she had not realized she'd been carrying lifted. It had made her uncomfortable that there were so few females here. One in twenty, if that. The fact that a gang of them could survive here cheered her up. Many were young, like her, and they were taking care of themselves.

"We'll go see Gabira later on," Jasper said, looking at her sidewise. "That shaman woman I told you about."

Her eyebrows lowered. "Yeah, hidden underground," she said. "Why would women want to live down there?" She glanced at Berkeley. His face was rigid, and his bug eyes stared straight ahead.

Jasper answered, "They retreat down there for safety, or simply to follow Gabira. She supposedly is running some sort of shaman school, but no one knows for sure. Nobody down there will talk about it." Cassidy knit her brows together. "But Gabira is interesting," he continued. "She has a bunch of her own crystals, and she knows how to use them." Jasper's eyebrows rose, as though trying to tempt Cassidy.

Her hands went into her pockets, cradling the crystal ball in her left hand and the shaft in her right. It would be good if she could learn how to use them. They must do something, if she could only discover what.

Jasper went on, "Men aren't allowed past Gabira's receiving room, though I've tried more than once." He scowled.

Cassidy wondered if his pained look was from the sting of rejection or simply because he was obsessed with mysteries, a trait he shared with his mother.

"The women stay down there like cloistered nuns," he said, "and don't come out. It drives me crazy with curiosity. They worship her, supposedly, and are learning all sorts of secret powers." The more Jasper talked, the stonier Berkeley's face became. "Maybe you could find out what they're up to down there," Jasper ventured hopefully.

"No, thank you," Cassidy said.

Jasper gave her a disappointed frown, then his gaze darted away. Cassidy knew that look all too well. He was already plotting another approach to get her to help him. When he wanted something, he didn't give up.

But Cassidy was having none of it. Gabira sounded like a cult leader to her. A charismatic individual with devotees who wouldn't, or couldn't, leave—like Lawrence Remo of the Shasta Shamans. That was one reason her parents had tired of Shasta—the shamans had become too fanatical. Remo warned that anyone who left the Star Seeker community would be unable to connect with the Star People when they came, and would be doomed to an eternity of darkness. Some people actually believed him and were too scared to leave.

Cassidy regarded the assortment of men who crisscrossed the yard. Many walked in groups of four or five, but a few groups were as large as eight or ten. At the moment, they were all stealing glances over their shoulders as the Smiths disappeared up Spoke Road Twelve.

Cassidy couldn't find any other females in the yard aside from an old woman vending sewing needles and thread. That left Cassidy the lone young woman surrounded by a couple hundred young males. She noticed that some men slowed to look at her as they walked past the ration line, as though the sight of the Smiths had aroused everyone's senses and they were now on the lookout for young flesh. A couple of men caught her eye and smiled, others looked away awkwardly when they realized they were staring. She pulled the bandana higher up across her nose and edged closer to Torr's shoulder. Jasper flanked her on the other side and bristled when anyone's glance lingered too long. Torr simply glared at them, forcing eyes to look away. Cassidy shifted on her feet, wishing the line would move faster.

"I want a hat," she said through her bandana, suddenly wanting a brim to hide under.

"I'll get you one, Cassafrass," Jasper said, and tugged gently on her braid. She nudged his shoulder with hers, and he dropped his hand to her waist.

After twenty long minutes, they entered the canteen. The day's rations consisted of four sardines in oil, a clump of sticky rice, six leaves of raw spinach, and six cherry tomatoes. She clamped the lid down over the dish, filled her water jug, and stepped out into the light of the yard with Torr and Jasper, and waited for Berkeley to exit the trailer.

A faint tinkling of bells turned her head. Striding fiercely across the dirt were the two Scrids from the other day, their boot fringes and bells waving and jangling as they walked, and their wild red hair and curly beards spilling over broad shoulders and barrel chests. Cassidy backed away as Jasper stepped forward to intercept them. Berkeley hurried to join Jasper. The four men talked, waving their arms and talking loudly, Jasper and Berkeley speaking Globalish with a few Scrid words thrown in, and the Scrids doing the opposite. Torr stood at Cassidy's side, his hand grasping her shoulder. The Scrids finally backed away a few paces, their thick arms folded across their chests.

"What do they want?" Torr asked.

Jasper looked warily at the Scrids. "Come on." He motioned to the PCA tents. "Let's go in there, where it's private." Jasper gestured for them and the Scrids to follow.

They crossed the yard after Jasper, the Scrids keeping their distance behind Berkeley, who walked behind Torr and Cassidy. Jasper greeted two men standing at the entrance of the closest PCA tent, both wearing the khaki shirts and shorts Cassidy had come to recognize as Peary staff uniforms. One was the guard with the buzz-cut who was always standing there. His jaw was set like he was clamping his teeth. The second man was older and taller, wearing a floppy green hat with wisps of gray hair peeking out from under the brim. He leaned lazily against a support pole, chewing on a wooden toothpick, his hairy calves showing above black, lace-up army boots.

"Yo, Bratislav," Jasper greeted the younger guard, who glared at the Scrids. "Hey, Montana," Jasper said to the older man. "This here's Torr and Cassidy. Friends of mine from home."

Montana tipped his hat with a friendly smile and held the wide tent flap open for Cassidy, Torr, and Berkeley. Jasper followed a few moments later with Montana and the Scrids, and Bratislav trailed behind.

Cassidy turned to face them. She stepped back a pace, not liking the sour smell of the squat, hairy men. Their amber eyes examined her and Torr as though they were naked. She felt goosebumps on her skin and stepped behind Berkeley, peering over his shoulder. Jasper listened and nodded as the Scrids spoke quickly, and Cassidy could see that curiosity was getting the better of him.

"Jorimar and Helug want to see your crystals," Jasper told them.

Cassidy shifted warily, clutching the crystal ball in her pocket, but the Scrids weren't looking at her anymore. Their eyes were locked onto Torr's abdomen.

"They want to see the big crystal Torr is carrying. They're calling it the Bear crystal."

"Since when are you fluent in Scridnu?" Montana asked, rolling the toothpick over his tongue.

"I don't know," Jasper said, looking a bit bewildered. "I'm not, really. I mean I trade with them sometimes. I've picked up a few words here and there."

"Bear, like the animal?" Berkeley asked, showing his teeth and crooking his fingers like claws. "Grrrhhh," he growled playfully at the Scrids.

The one named Jorimar pounded his fists to his chest and pulled the vest lapels out from under his red mane of a beard for Berkeley to see. The vest was made of a tan suede, but each front edge was folded back showing a wide strip of glossy black fur with small bells and copper medallions sewn into it. Bear hide.

"*Asbjorn Skr,*" Jorimar said, pointing with his clutched fist at the canvas pouch that hung from the front of Torr's vest.

"Spirit Bear crystal," Jasper translated.

The Scrid's eyes were boring into Torr's pouch. Torr glanced over his shoulder, looking for Cassidy. She stepped forward to join him.

"I might as well show them," Torr said to her under his breath. "If they can sense it and have a name for it, maybe they can tell us what it's good for. Maybe even teach us how to use it."

His gray eyes looked into hers, and she nodded. Torr unclasped the pouch and pulled out the large, chunky crystal.

"Dje, dje, *Asbjorn Skr,*" the Scrids sputtered excitedly, reaching for the crystal.

Torr pulled it out of their reach, and Bratislav stepped forward threateningly.

"What do they want with it? What does it do?" Torr asked Jasper.

Jasper shrugged as the Scrids jabbered at him. "I can't speak Scridnu well enough to ask them, I can only understand it. They're saying they need to show the crystal to their wise man. They want you to go with them." He shook his head. "Don't do it."

"Why not?" Torr asked.

"It's not a good idea," Jasper said with a frown of caution. "You shouldn't go into their camp."

"Why not?"

"The Murians who live here say the Scrids have some sort of portal. That would explain why there's a bunch of them here, even though no one remembers so many coming in on ships. I wouldn't go in there if I were you."

"Sounds intriguing," Torr said, eyeing the Scrids curiously.

Fear prickled across Cassidy's arms. She wanted nothing to do with a portal. Grandma Leann had spoken of such things with Jasper's mother, Melanie. Cassidy remembered the fanatical, glazed looks in their eyes.

"The problem with portals," Brianna had told the two women curtly, "is getting back."

Grandma Leann and Melanie had stared at Brianna, as though the wonder of such a phenomenon, were it really to exist, would outweigh all considerations of sense and safety.

"But think of it," Melanie had said breathlessly. "A passage to another world."

"Yeah," Brianna retorted. "Just like death. A one-way ticket to who knows where."

Cassidy nudged Torr's arm. "What good will it do to learn about the crystal if you disappear in the process?"

He glanced at her, the downward curve of his lips reminding her for a moment of Grandma Leann and her disappointed frown. He sighed. "You're right. They can teach me how to use it right here," Torr said, pointing to the ground and meeting Jorimar's gaze.

Jorimar rattled off a long line of syllables that Jasper translated. "Must come with them. The stars depend on it. They have been looking for you. And your sister. They call her *Golden Cloud.*"

The Scrids looked at Cassidy with what she interpreted as adoration, their smiles revealing an overabundance of yellowed teeth behind long red moustaches. Shivers ran up her spine, and she stepped behind Torr's shoulder. He slipped the Bear crystal into his pouch. Jorimar and Helug looked after it longingly, then returned their gazes to Cassidy.

"Some other time," Torr said. He motioned with his head to Bratislav. The guard and Montana took the Scrids' thick arms and firmly led them from the tent. Cassidy let out a long breath as the wild-haired men reluctantly left. The air swirled behind them as the canvas doors billowed in their wake.

"What in Perseus's name do you make of that?" Torr asked as the door flaps settled.

"Aunt Sophie had access to some good shit, that's what," Jasper mumbled.

Cassidy burst out in a giggle. The men started laughing with her. What else could they do with such an outrageous claim by the hairy ox-men, going so far as to name the crystal and call her Golden Cloud? Except that the Scrids' crystal-sensing ability was uncanny. And Golden Cloud was eerily close to Golden Falcon. The laughter trailed off as Berkeley looked at her and Torr, and then settled his gaze on Jasper as if he'd have an explanation.

"Don't ask me," Jasper said.

Cassidy shook off the strange shivers that tickled her spine. Everyone seemed to think she and Torr were the Star Children, but she didn't feel any different than she always had. She didn't even know what it really meant to be a Star Child. She had no idea where the Star People were or how to find them. She shrugged off the idea, as she had for years. She didn't like people staring at her, expecting her to perform miracles.

"Murians live here?" Torr asked.

"Yeah, a few," Jasper said. "I'll introduce you sometime. Maybe they know something more about your crystals. And they won't steal you away to their planet through a portal."

"Would be a fast way to get there," Torr quipped.

"Haha, true," Jasper said. "Come on. Let's go out back."

Cassidy looked around the large PCA tent and removed her bandana, tucking it into her pocket as she followed Jasper. Along the outer wall were a ping-pong table and a star shooters table. Running down the center of the tent, three white plastic picnic tables were lined up end-to-end in front of a wall of stacked plastic crates. They walked around the tall barrier. Behind the crates were two makeshift offices filled with tall metal cabinets and shelves. It was necessary to pass through the first office to get to the second one.

They stopped in the first office, which had a round table, bare shelves, and nothing else. They set their ration dishes and water jugs on the table. The office in the back was cluttered, with books and plastic boxes filling the shelves, a desk littered with books and tools, and long scrolls sticking out of tall cardboard boxes.

Montana joined them and exited a door at the far corner of the empty office. They followed him into a small enclosed courtyard, hemmed in by the PCA administration tent where they had registered, and several large shipping containers, plus an assortment of smaller metal sheds. The base of the gravity bar was hidden behind a blue plastic porta-potty and an unpainted aluminum shed.

Cassidy was drawn to the glimmering white pillar. She stepped behind the shed and found a clear circle of packed dirt surrounding the solid stone. The pillar was wide as an ancient redwood tree. She laid her palms flat against its surface, and a sudden warmth spread throughout her body. Her eyes followed the length of the gravity bar as it thrust upward. Craning her neck, she gazed past the blunt end of the pillar that stopped halfway to the dome's peak and scanned the star-filled sky. Her pulse throbbed rhythmically in her hands as they pressed against the stone. There was something about the pillar that filled her with longing, as though it were part of a place she knew and loved.

Torr came up beside her and pressed his hands to the pillar, and leaned his cheek against it, closing his eyes. His face was tired and strained, but grew relaxed as he rested against the glittering white stone.

After a long moment of peace, she left the pillar to follow

Montana and Berkeley up a ladder to the top of a red shipping container. A telescope stood on a tripod and was trained on Earth, which was still nearly full, though waning. Jasper and Torr climbed up behind her.

The rooftop offered them a good view of the city, with the twelve spoke roads radiating out from Center Ring. The gravity bar cast a long, straight shadow along Spoke Road One, turning the city into a giant sundial. She calculated that the sun was about two and a half days into its twenty-nine day journey around Peary Dome.

They took turns looking at Earth through the telescope, pointing out countries and islands, mountain chains and seas. Eurasia was facing them, the Free States turned away from the moon. She sent out a silent prayer for her parents, calling on the stars to cast their light and guide them to safety. She closed her eyes and felt for her mother's heartbeat. In the span of two breaths she found it. It was slow and steady. She followed the link to her father. His was slow and steady as well. Comforted that her parents had found somewhere safe to sleep, Cassidy opened her eyes.

Jasper turned the telescope to Jupiter and stepped aside so she could have a turn. Cassidy put her eye to the scope. She could clearly see the planet's stripes. Next, Jasper found the Pleiades. Cassidy could make out more than seven bright blue stars and wondered which were the seven sisters.

"The planet Muria orbits the Alts, a binary star system on the left edge of the Pleiades cluster," Jasper told her. She wondered how Ramesh could really be so far away, and how Jasper had made it all the way there and back. Twice.

Torr opened a black document pouch that hung from his vest and unfolded two large star maps. They compared the maps to the sky and found the portion of the heavens that arched overhead. Torr took a turn at the telescope.

"Where'd you get those maps?" Jasper asked.

"Stole them," Torr said stiffly, looking through the scope, his amber aviators perched on top of his head.

Cassidy exchanged glances with Jasper, but Torr's tone discouraged any further inquiry.

She took another look through the telescope and scanned the horizon, swiveling the telescope slowly on its stand and adjusting the focus. The star music crept into her awareness, the celestial chorus of intertwining melodies dancing just beyond her ear's physical perception. "I can hear it," she muttered under her breath.

"Hear what?" Jasper asked.

"The music," she said softly, looking up and meeting Torr's eyes. "It's louder on the horizon."

"What music?" Jasper asked.

"Star music," Torr said. "I heard it once, in a dream."

"What does it sound like?" Berkeley asked, examining her face intently, as if by looking at her he'd be able to hear it himself.

"I can't describe it," she said, and turned her eye back to the scope. It was as if she heard the music with her whole body. Sensed it. Felt the undulating, flowing modulations that went beyond anything she perceived in normal life. She could not give words to the sensations.

"It sounds like angels singing," Torr said, his voice far away.

"Maybe you hear it on the horizon," Jasper said, "because its source is below us. In the southern sky."

Cassidy looked up from the telescope and settled her attention on Jasper. "That's the most intelligent thing you've said all day."

"All week," Torr added.

"All month," Berkeley said, grinning at Jasper.

Jasper gave them a long-suffering look.

"There's no air out there to carry any sound," Montana said, stepping up to the telescope to take a turn.

"I know it doesn't make any sense," she said. "But I feel something."

"Could be cosmic rays," Berkeley said.

"Solar wind," Jasper said.

"Star People," Torr offered.

Cassidy met Torr's eyes again. His irises were steely gray.

"The center of the galaxy is in the southern sky," Montana said.

They gathered around Torr's star maps and located the center of the galaxy, which lay near the Sagittarius and Scorpius constellations.

"It's far away, that's all I know," Berkeley said, rubbing his bearded chin. "Maybe the Star People came from that direction. They always showed up at Iliad first. Then they went to Delos and Muria. The three planets form a triangle. The Delosians and Murians say the Cephs blew up Iliad's Star Globe portal, so now there's no portal trine. No Star Globe trine, no Star People," Berkeley said matter-of-factly.

"That's how they travel across the galaxy," Jasper explained. "Through huge crystal globes. Except now one is gone."

Cassidy's hand went to the Heaven's Window pendant at her throat, and she felt for the three points and the three gems. Torr and Jasper followed suit, touching the pendants that hung from their necks. They each looked slightly pale.

"How are the Star Children supposed to find the Star People if the portal trine is broken?" Torr asked.

Cassidy suddenly felt sick to her stomach. If Iliad's portal was gone, the help of the Star People could be beyond their reach forever. Was the prophecy of Star Children arriving in the twenty-ninth age an ancient myth from many millennia ago, back when the pathway across the galaxy was intact? She and Torr might spend their lives on a fruitless journey, wandering the star systems, seeking an avenue that no longer existed.

"You'll need to find a new corner point," Jasper said.

Cassidy's blood surged. "You mean, *we'll* need to," she said, straightening her spine and meeting Jasper's gaze. Maybe they really were the Star Children, and it really was possible to find the Star People and save Earth. What did they have to lose by trying? They were never going back to Earth, the way things were looking, and the moon was not the sanctuary she'd hoped for. Better to believe anything was possible and search for a way out of this mess, rather than admit defeat before even trying. "We need to," she repeated insistently, propping her hands on her hips.

"Look at her," Torr said to Jasper with a cocked eyebrow. "She's acting like it was her idea."

"She's downright bossy," Jasper said with a wry chuckle.

Berkeley and Montana exchanged curious looks.

Another wave of doubt drowned Cassidy's enthusiasm. More than likely the prophecy was complete foolishness. She dropped her hands from her hips. "Whatever," she muttered.

"Let me see that," Berkeley said, taking the map and studying it with Torr and Montana.

Cassidy took a deep breath and stepped to the edge of the container where she looked down over Center Ring. She thought of their brave and heroic promise of the day before, to claim their land and protect the moon from the Tegs, and start their journey as the Star Children. It had seemed reasonable last night. Today it felt silly and impossible.

Jasper came up beside her. "You okay?" he asked. "You look kind of ... spooked."

She shrugged. "It's nothing. It's just that this Star Children thing is getting to me. I start thinking it really might be us. Then I get overwhelmed with it all. Next I think I'm going crazy. Then I think I have to be brave and try something. But what? What are we supposed to do? We're just kidding ourselves that we can do anything at all."

He gazed at her sympathetically. "I don't know, Cass. We need a miracle, that's what."

She frowned at him.

"You want to live here the rest of your life?" he asked, gesturing to the drab tent city and the colorless landscape that stretched beyond the dome walls.

"A miracle," she scoffed. "Maybe we should go to Muria like Torr says. Maybe Ramesh will know what to do. You've been there twice, right?"

"Yes. And to Delos once. I'd love to go to Delos again. It's like Earth, with towns and forests and oceans."

"What's Muria like?"

"Strange. Interesting. With glowing jungles and crystal caves. Long days and long nights. Incredible animals. You'd like it there."

"How did you get there?"

"By ship. I've made friends over the years, trading."

"How long does it take?"

"Only a couple of Earth weeks. They slip into Galaxy Time and cross into a Focus Sphere. It feels weird, like falling in a dream. That part takes no time at all. What takes time is navigating, and targeting the proper coordinates, and focusing the energy to cross dimensions."

She nodded, not needing to understand how it worked, only that it was possible for her and Torr to leave this place if they wanted to. If they had to. "What about our land? Seems silly to stay here for that. I don't know how we would ever claim it. Torr's idea of going in with guns sounds like suicide."

Jasper put his arm around her. "Magic. It's the only way."

"Yeah," she said weakly. "Unfortunately, we don't know any magic. A rune belt is one thing. Defeating Tegs is another." She felt under her shirt. The rune belt materialized in her hand and she could feel the stiffness of the parchment through the fabric. "This belt is amazing," she said.

"Berkeley's full of surprises," he said proudly of his friend. Jasper squeezed her shoulder and she relaxed against him.

"How can I learn magic here?" she asked. "My mother couldn't even teach me anything, other than plant spirit medicine."

"Maybe you could learn something from Gabira," he said.

She sighed. He was persistent. "She sounds wicked. I want to learn from someone good."

"Beggars can't be choosers."

"What about the Scrids?" she asked. "They could sense our crystals."

"Yeah. They might look primitive, but they're very powerful. Dangerous and unpredictable. You should stay away from them."

"Who can I learn from, then? You? Berkeley?"

Jasper shook his head reluctantly. "I don't think so. We're both still apprentices. You need a master."

"What about the Murians?"

"They might be able to teach you something. I'll introduce you, but they're not masters. Besides, it's really the planet Muria itself that does the teaching. You have to be there."

"What do you mean by that?"

"The planet has a sort of presence. I don't know how to explain it. I guess it's all the crystals. The cave walls are covered with them. They grow there, in colonies."

"Oh. Cool." She sighed. "But we can't go to Muria and get our land back at the same time." Her gaze wandered across the yard at the groups of men who meandered here and there, when her eyes locked with Jorimar's. She backed away from the edge, pulling Jasper with her. "They're looking at us," she said, catching Torr's attention. "The Scrids."

"Really?" Torr asked. He stepped over to the edge of the container and looked out over Center Ring.

"Come on, let's get out of here," Jasper said.

Montana was already descending the ladder.

They climbed down to the courtyard and into the big tent, retrieved their ration containers, and left Montana and Bratislav at the main entrance with a parting wave. The two Scrids were across the yard, smiling at them. She and her companions took off at a brisk walk towards Spoke Road Eight where they could cut over to the Fen.

"I've looked inside the Scrid camp before," Jasper said as they passed out of view of the two dwarfish men and slowed to a comfortable walk. "They have a ring of light crystals around a chunk of gravity bar that's short like a table, with a crystal similar to your Bear crystal sitting on it."

Torr raised one eyebrow with interest. "I want to see it. Let's go look after we eat."

"You need to be careful," Berkeley said.

"We can't go inside," Jasper warned, glancing at Cassidy as though pleading with her to talk some sense into Torr, even though Jasper had known his comment would spark Torr's curiosity.

"We'll look from a distance. With my binoculars," Torr said.

She was curious about the Scrid camp as well. What harm could there be in viewing it through binoculars? After all, she and Torr had finally made their way to the moon, the doorway to the rest of the galaxy. They might as well explore a bit. The Scrids were the first off-worlders they'd met.

They sat around the Fen tables and ate their rations. Cassidy soaked her dry bread in the sardine oil. Never had she found sardines and rice so delicious before. And cherry tomatoes. They didn't have much flavor, but they had juice inside, and she savored them. What if food shipments stopped coming to Peary?

She needed to somehow tear off Grandma Leann's shield, reclaim her second sight, and learn the ways of magic. Become powerful in her own right. Stand up to the Tegs with something they couldn't defend against.

When her food was gone, she watched Jasper's animated expression as he talked about court politics on Delos. His eyes were glittering and flashed between her and Torr. Her attention rested on his lips, and she remembered his kisses and her promise to go to his tent that night. She was tempted to grab his hand and take him there now, but she let him prattle on, his words fading to a pleasant drone as she imagined his body on hers.

———————)———————

Hawk pouted when she told him he couldn't come with them, and Raleigh and Roanoke frowned unhappily at Torr.

"We've got to take care of some business," Jasper said apologetically to the brothers. "You can come along next time." The brothers glared resentfully at Jasper and Berkeley, who had swooped in and come between them and their new friends. Cassidy felt bad, but she'd known Jasper forever. And Berkeley was Jasper's best friend.

"We'll play cards after dinner, okay?" she said to Hawk, gently shaking his shoulder. His eyes brightened a little.

"Okay," he said, kicking at the ground.

They left the Fen and headed towards Center Ring. She walked next to Berkeley, his long vest-cloak drawing curious looks. "The Scrid camp has taken over the whole block between Ring Roads K and L and Spoke Roads One and Two," Berkeley said.

They cut across Center Ring and headed down Spoke Road Twelve, towards Earth. A small group of a half-dozen women holding small children by the hands walked past, surrounded by a gang of men with large knives prominently displayed. The men looked at Torr, Jasper, and Berkeley threateningly, warning them with hard faces to stay away. Their eyes lingered on Cassidy, as did the women's.

"Maybe we should go back and get the brothers, after all," Torr said, looking with concern at Cassidy. "And Sky and Thunder, or some of your friends," he said to Jasper. "Young women seem to be a prized commodity out here."

Jasper grunted and watched another small group of men pass by, their eyes resting on Cassidy as well. "We should be okay," he said, lacing his fingers together and cracking his knuckles. "We've got a few tricks up our sleeves if anyone tries to mess with us, right, Berk?" He looked at Berkeley smugly. Berkeley pulled one corner of his mouth to the side, not looking nearly as confident as Jasper.

Cassidy wondered what kinds of tricks Jasper was talking about. Seeing as Berkeley had made the rune belts, she couldn't discount Jasper's boasting completely. "Like what?" she asked.

"Oh, secrets," Jasper said, grinning at her.

"Yeah, secrets you're going to show me later."

"I'll show you some secrets later," he assured her, his eyes sliding up and down her body.

She gave him a teasing smirk, and Torr broke in. "Maybe we should go back."

"I'll be fine," Cassidy said, raising her chin. "I can take care of myself." She was strong and fit, and was a fast runner, if it came to that.

"Where's your scarf?" Jasper asked, pulling his length of blue Delosian silk from a vest pocket and tying it around his head, the tail hanging down the side of his head to his shoulder.

"Oh, yeah," she said, laughing, and took hers from her daypack, letting Jasper tie it around the crown of her head.

"You look ridiculous," Torr muttered.

"You're just jealous you don't look as cool as us," Jasper said. "We're official Light Fighters," he said, playfully poking at Torr's tattoo. "This is our uniform. You'd better get yourself a blue headband like us." He tugged at Cassidy's scarf tail, letting his hand rest on her back as they strode along.

After walking for several minutes, they passed Ring Road K and followed Jasper into an alleyway on the right, formed by two lines of tents whose windowless backs faced each other. They stepped over guy wires and trod silently over the dust. Jasper stopped several tents away from Spoke Road One and crouched. "This should be good. Get down."

Torr and Cassidy imitated Jasper and Berkeley, dropping onto all fours then lying on their bellies on the ground. She propped herself on her elbows, and Torr pulled out his binoculars and pointed them through the gap between the tents and across the spoke road, which was about fifty yards away. Torr crawled up between Jasper and Berkeley, and Cassidy squeezed between Torr and Jasper.

"You smell good," Jasper said, pressing his nose to her shoulder.

"I need a real shower," she mumbled. She was due for her second sauna tomorrow. The first one had been awkward, sharing the shack with Torr, Sky, and Thunder. They'd all had to keep towels wrapped around themselves, when the custom was to use the sauna with your own gender, naked. But no one in their group knew any other women.

She leaned against Jasper, liking his solidness and warmth, and regarded the Scrid camp.

Torr scanned the area with the binoculars. "Pretty cool tent they made," he said, and passed the binoculars to her.

"It's a closed circle with a courtyard in the middle," Jasper said. "Like a donut."

Cassidy found the gap and focused in on a tight group of tarp-covered tents, then froze as a red beard crossed into her field of view. She zoomed out and inspected the Scrid guard who paced on stocky legs back and forth in front of the wide canvas barrier. Cassidy couldn't make out the entire camp because of the alleyway tents that blocked her view, but she could see enough to determine the Scrids had made a large structure by placing tents edge to edge, with the backs facing out and tarps spanning the roofs to create a single edifice.

"That's smart," she said.

"How many Scrids live in there?" Torr asked.

Berkeley answered, "Got to be thirty or forty by now. They like it here, I guess."

"Or they're looking for something. Or some*one*," Jasper said.

"I think they found them," Berkeley said.

"What do they call the male twin?" Torr asked.

"I don't know," Jasper replied. "I'll ask later. There's an entry-way in the center of their tent. See it?"

Cassidy slowly panned the binoculars across the canvas structure and found the tent with its door flaps facing out. "They cut a door on the other side of the tent to make a passageway?" she asked.

"Yep," Jasper said. "Leads to a big circular courtyard inside."

She focused on the closed entrance and waited. A minute later the flap opened and a red bearded face looked out. It was the one called Helug, with his tangled reddish-gold hair and beard. Helug held the flap open as he spoke to the guard.

Cassidy peered past Helug's squat body through the open passageway, seeing daylight through the entry tent. She adjusted the lenses to view the inside of the ring. She could only see a small segment, but the sliver showed a white stone slab with a crystal sitting upright on top of it. She focused onto the crystal. It was similar to Torr's chunky crystal, but its facets were more uniform. She zoomed out a little, and her eyes were drawn to the base of the white cylindrical slab. Embedded in the dirt and pointing upward were smaller crystal shafts, pulsating with a yellowish glow. She held her breath to still the wavering lenses, trying to understand how the crystals were glowing and why they were arranged in such a fashion, when a hairy chest blocked her vision.

She zoomed out to see a Scrid standing with Helug. It was the one called Jorimar. She examined him up close. His torso was bare, covered only with the bear-hide vest, showing a stocky chest, bulging belly, and shoulders covered with red curly hair. Short, thick legs were covered with tan animal-hide pants, and he wore his leather boots with fringes and bells. Cassidy focused in on the bearded face. Wide, heavy cheekbones and dark auburn facial hair were punctuated by a fat burl of a nose covered in purple veins and little hairs. His long red hair hung loose down his chest and intertwined with his beard. Cassidy froze as she focused on his eyes. They were a deep golden amber and were directed straight at her, as though the Scrid was looking into her eyes through the binoculars.

"Jorimar's looking at me," Cassidy said.

"They're coming this way," Torr said.

"Come on, we'd better go," Jasper said.

"More of them are coming out of the tent," Torr said, taking the binoculars and rising to his knees.

The four of them jumped to their feet and trotted away through the alleyway, hopping over wires and jogging up Spoke Road Twelve. Cassidy's heart pounded, and she looked over her shoulder. The Scrids were entering the spoke road, running on their short, stubby legs.

"Let's lose them," Berkeley said, and took off at a loping run.

Cassidy strained to match Berkeley's long strides as he turned into another alleyway and zigzagged between tents. They darted across spoke roads and through large blocks of clustered communities. Adrenaline surged through Cassidy's veins.

They ended up on the perimeter road in front of the spaceport, panting and wiping sweat and dust from their faces. At the main spaceport entrance, Jasper pounded on the metal door. A guard opened it, and they pushed their way inside. Cassidy peeked through the crack as Jasper pulled the door closed. The Scrids were nowhere in sight.

36

THE GİLDED CAVE

Cassidy walked with the guys across the hangar, adjusting her blue silk headband, which was damp with sweat. They drank some water, and then Jasper led them on a tour down the shipping lanes. There was not much activity. No off-world ships were present. One Earth freighter bore the red Teg insignia, visible through a layer of dust.

"What is that?" Cassidy asked Jasper.

"Oh, that. Yeah. It's a Teg freighter. It's broken down. It's been here for two months, waiting for parts. The pilots have a tent out in the city somewhere. One of them told my dad their commander has more important things to worry about than rescuing them. I've seen them getting very drunk at the bar a few times."

"What bar?" Torr asked.

"Schlitzer's. I'll take you there sometime," he said, as they strolled along, looking at the various ships.

There were two other large Earth freighters, a few smaller moon freighters, some dusty speedsters, and a tanker. Jasper pointed at one of the moon freighters, which was a worn wreck with little dents all over it. He explained that it belonged to a far side mining lord, and that the far side of the moon was more exposed to meteorite showers than the near side, in addition to the constant barrage of space dust and solar rays. Some settlers parked their vehicles outside; not everybody had pressure chambers big enough for vehicles. The smart ones built roof structures. This guy must have parked his out in the open, or he was flying during a particularly bad meteorite event. Cassidy examined the pilot, who leaned against its hull and gave a slight nod to Jasper as they walked by.

He was the first far side mining lord she had seen. He did not look very lordly. His skin was wrinkled and he wore the same faded khaki pants most people wore, along with a matching khaki field vest with bulging pockets, and an old baseball cap from Earth that said Baltimore Orioles. All manner of knives, flashlights, wrenches, and other tools weighed down his belt.

Jasper pointed towards a back door. "I'm going to Gabira's. You coming?"

"I'm coming," Berkeley said.

Torr glanced at her.

She could tell he wanted to go. "I don't really want to," she said. She didn't want to keep Torr from exploring, but something did not feel right. "You guys can't leave me here alone. The Scrids might show up. Where's Kai?"

"I'll stay with you," Torr said.

Jasper scratched at his beard and regarded Cassidy and Torr. "Come on, you guys. Don't you want to get to know the camp? Not everyone has a personal guide who can get you in anywhere. People beg me to take them to visit Gabira, a plea I regularly refuse. She doesn't let just anybody in." Jasper cocked an eyebrow at Cassidy, as though she were refusing a fine gift.

"I don't need to meet another witch. I was raised by one. A *good* one. I'm not interested in meeting a reclusive cult leader."

Jasper relaxed his stance, folding his arms across his chest. "We talked about this. I thought we agreed the only way to beat the Tegs was with magic."

She crossed her arms over her chest in response. "So?"

"You need teachers. If you want to learn fast, that is."

She glanced uncomfortably at Torr, trying to catch his eye, but he was staring into the shadows. She exhaled loudly and met Jasper's eyes again.

"Come with me to visit Gabira. See if you can sense how she works her magic. Maybe ask her to teach you."

"I don't want to live down there," she said, holding his gaze.

"I don't want you to live down there, either. Maybe you can learn from her some other way."

"You need to be careful," Berkeley cut in. "A sorceress like Gabira will not easily part with her secrets."

"Yeah," Cassidy said. "She's a sorceress."

Jasper sucked his teeth with annoyance. "Don't scare her, Berkeley. Gabira's harmless."

Berkeley snorted. "Yeah, right."

Jasper rolled his eyes. "All we ever do down there is talk and trade. But she's interesting, and so are her daughters."

"Daughters?" Cassidy asked.

"Two of them. They're our age. You'd like them."

"I don't know," she said hesitantly, though she felt her resolve weakening. Torr was staying out of it, scanning the hangar. "What do you think, Berkeley?" she asked. "Do you think I could learn anything from Gabira?"

He tugged at one of his beard points, considering. "Well, Eridanus told me this once. The path to power is cloaked in shadows, so if you avoid all the shadows you'll never learn anything."

That sounded like something her mother would say. She felt herself relenting, curiosity getting the better of her. "Okay," she said, her skin breaking out in a cold sweat. "I'll go."

Jasper grinned brightly, and Torr started paying attention again.

They stepped out onto a vacant strip of land that ran between the spaceport's back wall and the foot of the dome, next to the long landing tunnel. Lined up against the base of the dome stood tall water troughs. The "moats." Cassidy went up to one, lifted the clear lid, and held her breath. The green moat water glistened and stank of salt and rotten fish. There were supposedly krill living in there, but she couldn't see any; the water was too cloudy. Torr came up next to her.

"Don't mess with the water," Jasper said.

"I won't," she said, dropping the lid. "I miss the bay. I miss the ocean." She suddenly wanted to cry, but glared angrily at the dusty ground instead. "It sucks here."

"I know," Jasper said. "But at least we're together." He tugged at her hair.

"Yeah, I guess."

They walked to the northeast corner of the spaceport building, turned left, and entered a narrow alleyway that ran between the spaceport and a collection of shacks and trailers that Jasper explained housed solar inverters and banks of batteries. No one was around. A thin slice of the perimeter road was visible at the end of the spaceport's long northern wall.

A single door broke the high metal wall on their left. The door was steel with a peephole in it. Jasper knocked and the door opened.

Two guards toting assault rifles greeted Jasper and Berkeley by name and opened the door wider, letting them file into a bare metal room, a converted half-container—the building material of choice, apparently. The young men leaned lazily against an inner airlock door, cradling their rifles and blocking further passage. Cassidy wondered if the guards were keeping people out, or the women in. Chills ran up her spine.

"What kind of fancy robe are you wearing?" one of them asked Berkeley.

"I made it myself," Berkeley said proudly. "Do you like it?" He held the embroidered lapels in his long fingers.

"You look like a wizard," the guard replied.

"Why, thank you very much." Berkeley grinned, looking pleased.

Jasper introduced Cassidy and Torr. They engaged in idle chit-chat, and she realized the guards were delaying simply because they were bored and hungry for company. Finally, the guards did a cursory search for weapons. The guard's hand passed lightly over her sides and patted around her torso where her rune belt was. She held her breath, but he continued down her legs, then moved on to Torr. The guard did not detect his rune belt either, and Torr and Cassidy exchanged a brief glance as the guard patted down his legs. Berkeley looked on with smug satisfaction.

The other guard pressed a buzzer next to the inner door. After a minute, the hiss of the pressure lock being released echoed through the chamber. The heavy door creaked open. An even more bored guard appeared from the other side and motioned them through. Cassidy stepped over the threshold into refreshingly cool air. The guard sealed the door and stood with them, the five of them squeezed together inside a small airlock.

"Who are they?" the small, wiry man asked Jasper and Berkeley, his eyes glancing at Torr and Cassidy.

"Friends of mine," Jasper said. "I've got gish for Gabira." He took a strip of green gish from his side leg pocket and handed it to the guard.

The guard sniffed it and took a bite. "What else you got?" he asked with a grin.

Jasper gave him an exasperated look.

"Come on," the guard said, holding out his palm. "You said."

"Oh, all right," Jasper said, and dug in his black leather bag. He pulled out a small metal vial and gave it to the guard.

The guard's grin widened, and he stashed the vial in a vest pocket. "Don't cause any trouble." He opened the second airlock door, which led to a short corridor.

Berkeley wiped his hands nervously on his brown robe and asked, "You seen Carmen?"

The guard rolled his eyes. "No, Berk. I told you I'd tell you if I did."

Berkeley slouched dejectedly. "Just asking," he said under his breath as he passed through the doorway.

The guard sealed the door behind them and perched on a stool, gnawing on his gish. They stood for a moment in the eerie silence, then left the guard and trod quietly to the end of the corridor, where a long set of stairs carved into the moon rock plunged down into the shadows. Cassidy had a sinking feeling in the pit of her stomach. She steeled her nerves and followed Berkeley down the steps.

Berkeley glanced over his shoulder at her. "A friend of mine's down here. I haven't seen her in so long, I'm afraid she's forgotten me by now."

"Carmen?" she asked.

He nodded and swiped at his nose with the back of his hand.

"Maybe we'll see her," she said. "You can ask about her."

He nodded again, sniffing loudly.

The stairs ended at the opening of a long stone tunnel that was dimly lit by a nest of solar filaments hanging from the ceiling in the distance.

"What's down here?" she asked, controlling an urge to race back up the stairs.

"Just the women," Jasper said. "And some emergency rations."

"Why is there an airlock?" Cassidy asked.

"The first colony was down here. There's a bunch of rooms that still store food and stuff in case there's a breach in the dome. Other than that, the only thing down here now is the women. They took it over."

"When?"

"During the uprising. Berkeley was here, he'll tell you," Jasper said.

"What happened?" she asked.

Berkeley wiped at his nose. "After the big dome was built, the mining lords turned these tunnels into a big whorehouse."

That seemed to be as much as Berkeley cared to share. He clamped his lips shut and retreated into his own world.

"They say it was crazy in the dome back then," Jasper prompted. "Gangs. Killings and thievery."

Berkeley shrugged. "Yeah. They were dangerous times," he admitted, brushing dust from his robe and arranging his dreadlocks. He took a deep breath and continued. "When the Free Men won the dome, they came to flush out the last of the mining lords who were hiding down here in the tunnels. The Free Men were trying to bust through the airlock, when the mining lords came running out, chased by Gabira and a bunch of women with pickaxes and hammers. Gabira was screaming bloody murder and holding a glowing crystal that sent those mining lords straight into the arms of the Free Men. Gabira turned around with the women and sealed the airlock, and hasn't come out since."

Cassidy was pleased that the women had driven off their male captors, but there was something about the tunnel that made her uncomfortable, like a charge in the air, or like they were in a tomb and spirits were watching them. "I don't like it down here," she said, shivering.

"Come on," Jasper said reassuringly. "Gabira's receiving room isn't far."

They walked fifty yards along the tunnel and came to a door on their right made from a blond-colored wood with a dark brown grain running through it. The wood was polished to a lustrous gleam. Seeing the wood, Cassidy was reminded of Earth. Her fear dropped away, and she could almost smell sunbaked soil and the tangy scent of the chaparral back home. Jasper grabbed a large bronze doorknocker molded in the shape of a leaping dog and rapped loudly.

A matching bronze dog door handle turned down and the door swung open, sending a puff of air and the scent of patchouli into the hallway. A large, purple-robed woman stood there, with masses of gold chains hanging heavily around her neck, and a large crystal shaft pendant pointing down between protruding breasts.

"Jaz," the middle-aged woman crooned, her voice like honey. Shiny black hair was piled on top of her head over wide cheekbones and coppery skin. Her brown eyes were large and overly made up with thick black eyeliner and mascara. Large gold hoop earrings almost touched her shoulders. "Where have you been, darling?" She smiled at Jasper, showing a line of straight, green-stained teeth behind full, brown lips. Her Globalish was thick with an accent Cassidy did not recognize.

"I've missed you, Gabira," Jasper said charmingly, and kissed her loudly on each cheek. "Here's your gish." He handed her two bundles wrapped in canvas, which she stuffed into the deep side pockets of her robe. Stacks of gold bangles clinked on her forearms.

"Darling," Gabira said, grabbing his head with two gold-ringed hands and kissing him on the forehead. "Thank you, thank you. Now, who have we here?"

Cassidy found herself smiling. Gabira's hearty voice brought comfort to Cassidy's core. A motherly, woman's voice. Jasper introduced them, smiling proudly, as though he had brought Gabira a great treasure.

"Come here, darling," the large woman said, motioning to Cassidy. "Come right over here. My, what a lovely girl you are." She encircled Cassidy with gold-laden arms and pulled her against her plump body. "Have these boys been good to you?" she asked, releasing Cassidy and casting stern glances at Jasper and Berkeley.

"Yes, yes," the men chorused. "Yes, Gabira."

She looked at Cassidy with one eyebrow raised, and Cassidy nodded.

"Good. And who have we here?" Gabira drew Torr over to her, clutching him with a talon grip on each upper arm. She looked him up and down and then settled on his eyes. Her dark brown lips smacked with approval. "Well, you are something," she said. "What a handsome young man." She smiled at Torr, and his stern demeanor melted away. He looked almost like himself again. *Happy.* He disappeared behind Gabira's flowing purple sleeves as she hugged him.

"Come in, come in," she said. "I've been rude."

She led them into a man-made cave carved into the moon rock. The room was lit by coils of luminous solar filaments suspended from the ceiling like trailing vines. The walls were painted a burnished gold, with a mural of green trees blossoming with white flowers and laden with small, purple fruit. The ceiling was the cerulean blue of an August sky, and the floor was covered with multi-colored, geometrically patterned rugs. The scent of spiced oils hung heavily in the air.

Gabira motioned for them to sit on piles of smaller rugs set against the stone walls like couches and backed with large, bright silk pillows. Cassidy removed her daypack and sat on a stack of rugs, running her fingers along the scratchy wool. Jasper sat next to her as she settled back into the soothing embrace of the pillows.

Torr and Berkeley sat against the next wall, facing the door, and Gabira sat across from Cassidy and Jasper. Filling the center of the room was a low, round, ornately engraved brass table.

Gabira clapped loudly and tugged on a tasseled gold rope that hung against the wall by her head, and soon three young women appeared, bearing polished brass goblets. The women were stiff and aloof, avoiding eye contact, and didn't say a word. Each wore a solid, brightly colored robe, similar to Gabira's but in blue, green, and gold. They appeared to Cassidy like exotic birds, flitting around a gilded cage and ignoring their owners. The women handed each guest a goblet. Cassidy accepted hers, examining the delicate face of the server, and cupped the chilled metal in her hands. The coolness calmed her hot, dry palms, and she breathed a sigh of relief.

Thirst tugged at her, bidding her hands to lift the goblet to her lips, but she refrained from drinking until the others did. Jasper was holding his cup politely. After each guest had a goblet, the three serving women left silently. The eyes of everyone in the room followed them until the door closed behind them.

"They're lovely, aren't they?" Gabira purred.

The men grunted with approval. Torr looked drunk. Cassidy wondered why the women hadn't talked or made eye contact, but she didn't ask. She looked down into her goblet. It looked like clear, pure water. She smelled it.

"It's water," Jasper said to her softly from where he was lounging against a collection of pillows.

Gabira's voice bellowed as she held up her goblet. "To the ices of the lake!"

"To the ices of the lake!" the men repeated, lifting their cups and putting them to their lips.

Cassidy lifted her goblet and sipped slowly. The cool liquid bathed her tongue and settled in the bottom of her mouth where she swished it around and swallowed.

"They have a well," Jasper whispered to her.

"A well?" she asked. She hadn't known there were wells on the moon.

"A well?" Torr echoed.

"Shhhh!" Jasper hissed.

Deep rolling laughter flowed from Gabira. "Jaz, you know everything can be heard in this chamber. There are no secrets. It's not really a well, darling, it's an ice mine."

Well or no well, Cassidy's skin was beginning to crawl with uneasiness at the sugary tone of Gabira's voice. Cassidy watched Jasper as he sipped his water with no ill effects. She looked down at hers, thirst pulling her lips towards the goblet for another mouthful.

"Gabira," Jasper said coyly.

"What, darling?"

"I have something you might be interested in."

"Really? Don't tease me. What have you got?"

"A gold pendant from Iliad."

"Iliad?" Gabira asked with a twist of her mouth. "You're not a very good liar, Jaz." Cassidy could see excitement burning in Gabira's eyes through her disdain.

Jasper pulled a small wooden box from his daypack and opened it on the brass table, the gold Pleiades pendant gleaming on its bed of green velvet, its tiny colored gems and black diamonds catching the light. Cassidy tensed with jealousy. She wanted the pendant for herself. She could not very well argue for it now, and held her tongue, wishing she'd bought it when she'd had the chance. Gabira reached for the box and held the pendant in her open palm.

"What do you want to swindle me out of for this piece, Jaz?"

"Only the crystal you've been saving for me," he said simply. "It's Ilian."

"It is not," Gabira scoffed. She reached to the side of the stack of rugs and lifted a small scale and placed it on the table. Jasper and Berkeley did not blink, as though it were normal to keep a scale in a sitting room. She placed the necklace on the scale. "Three ounces," she said. "I'll give you three gold Eagles."

Jasper got a pained look on his face. "The gems are priceless, Gabira. You know that. Ilian gems? Don't insult me."

She laughed a deep, rolling laugh. "You are such a thief, Jaz. They are glass."

Jasper's brow furrowed. "Nice try." He smiled.

Gabira smiled back, but not so merrily this time as her eyes darted quickly to the pendant, then to Jasper again. "Keep it, then," she said, dangling it over the box.

"Okay, no matter," Jasper said calmly. Gabira cupped the pendant in her palm.

Jasper sighed as though the pendant negotiation had ended, and said, "In exchange for the gish, then, there are a couple items I need. Maybe you can help."

A smile crept across Gabira's face.

"I'm looking for a piece of wood to make a knife hilt. Magnolia. And a bit of ray skin."

Ripples of Gabira's melodic laughter reverberated in the small room. "Magnolia? Jaz, darling, you must be joking. Ray skin?" She laughed. "This is the *moon.*"

"I know," Jasper said. "That's why I came to you. You are a collector of Earth treasures, are you not?"

"Of course I am. The best. However, I do not deal in wood or skins. I have finer tastes."

Jasper's eyes narrowed, and Cassidy felt him uncoil next to her as he leaned back against the pillows. His voice was calm. "You have olivewood."

Gabira's face froze, as if she had been confronted with news of a death. "I do not trade my olivewood."

Cassidy eyed the pendant as Gabira set it gently in the box.

"The size of a knife hilt, you say?" Gabira asked softly.

"Yes," Jasper said. "Wood from an old tree is best."

"All I have is wood from old trees. An ancient species of olivewood. They live for hundreds of years. They are in the souls of my people. In *my* soul."

Cassidy felt a sudden kinship with the woman, who loved plants as Cassidy did. She could understand Gabira not wanting to trade away her precious wood from a planet she might never return to.

Gabira sighed. "Let me take a look. Wait here." Her voice was gruff as she got to her feet and lumbered out the door.

Jasper looked at Torr proudly. "Who's looking out for you?"

Torr grumbled, "What will I owe you for this?"

Jasper shrugged. "I'll put it on your tab."

"It should be part of the knife trade," Cassidy said. "Who sells a knife with no handle?"

"Yeah," Torr said.

Jasper looked pleased with himself and sipped at his water.

Gabira returned after a time with a short length of a large tree branch or small trunk. "This is my favorite," she said glumly. "But it wanted to go with you." Jasper looked at her oddly, but Cassidy knew exactly what she meant. "And I found this," Gabira said, lifting a black purse. It was small, and of black leather textured with little bumps that shimmered in the light.

"Ray skin?" Torr asked.

"Close. Sharkskin," Gabira said. "What do I need with an evening bag on the moon? Still, it's invaluable. That and the wood should suffice as trade for the pendant." Her coppery face gleamed in the reflected light cast from the gold-painted walls.

Jasper guffawed. "These are perfect, thanks. But for the gish only. They're not worth the pendant by any stretch. The pendant should pay off the crystal, though."

Now it was Gabira's turn to laugh. She lifted her double chin and chortled at the blue ceiling like it was open sky.

After endless haggling and insults, Gabira agreed to accept the gish and Pleiades pendant in exchange for the olivewood, sharkskin bag, and the crystal. After they both complained bitterly that they had been cheated, Gabira fastened the necklace around her corpulent neck, the pendant lying on her bosom next to the crystal shaft. Cassidy glared possessively at the glittering pendant, while Torr happily wedged the olivewood into one cargo pants pocket and the sharkskin bag in the other.

"Where's the crystal?" Cassidy asked.

"I'll get someone to bring it before you go," Gabira assured Jasper, who still appeared grouchy about the trade, though Cassidy could see he was actually gloating inside.

Cassidy was ready to go. The trade was done, and she was feeling a bit unwell. Gabira's large brown eyes met hers, and Cassidy's wooziness intensified.

The men did not seem ready to leave, however. They were lounging comfortably against the cushions and chatting with

Gabira about Earth. Cassidy wondered if she should find her way back to the surface by herself and wait for them there. She tried to calm her mind and looked at Jasper, struggling to remember why else they had come here. Hadn't Berkeley wanted something? Wasn't Cassidy supposed to be paying attention to something? She rubbed her temple, trying to clear her head.

"Why do you stay down here?" Cassidy asked. The oddness of finding silken-robed women in a hidden cave right below the spaceport made her head hurt. She raised her chilled hand to her forehead. Her skin was burning hot.

"It's a long story, my darling," Gabira said.

"A long story," Jasper echoed.

Cassidy gripped her goblet tightly and tried to catch Torr's attention. His nose was covered by the goblet that was tipped to his mouth, and his eyes were closed contentedly. Berkeley wore a dopey smile, enraptured by Gabira.

"Who should tell it?" Gabira asked, touching the rim of the goblet to her large brown lips.

"Giselle," Jasper declared.

"You love Giselle, I know." She smiled, and laughter rippled from her throat. A needle of jealously pricked Cassidy. Gabira leaned forward and set her goblet on the brass table, her cleavage gaping and the new pendant and sparkling crystal swinging on their gold chains. The dark planets of the Pleiades winked at Cassidy.

"Giselle!" Gabira called out, her voice strong and melodious. She tugged sharply on the gold tasseled rope.

Cassidy looked around the gilded room filled with rugs of many colors. This was so incongruous with her experience on the bleak and dreary moon that she felt as though she were in a dream. Torr looked stupefied and grinned at her like a child surrounded by mountains of candy. The three serving women had seemed so strange. *Did they want to be here? Were they slaves?* The whole thing felt wrong, somehow. She lifted her hand to her forehead as a stab of pain lanced through it.

Her attention was drawn back to the cool liquid in her goblet and she sipped slowly, savoring the pure, fresh water. Lightheadedness made her see double, and she leaned back against the pillows, blinking hard to clear her vision. Was the shaman woman trying to put a spell on her? Or perhaps the water was drugged? She sniffed it and reached out to it with her senses, feeling for any toxic plant essences, but could not detect any.

Cassidy instinctively constructed a mental shield in the form of a dust cloud, fashioning it after the Shaman's Shield, and placed it between her and Gabira. The pressure in her head eased somewhat. Gabira cast her a sharp glance, as though she could sense the shield. She did not look pleased. Cassidy's dizziness passed, and she held Gabira's eyes. *You do not know who you're dealing with,* Cassidy told the woman silently. *I am the daughter of a Shasta Shaman.* Gabira's lips tightened in a thin line, and she looked away.

Cassidy wrapped her hand around the smooth crystal ball that lay in the bottom of her vest pocket, thinking it might help her stay grounded and resist the woman's powerful energy. The crystal shaft resting on Gabira's bosom glinted at Cassidy from across the room, and Cassidy gripped the crystal ball tighter.

A pretty young woman came through the doorway, holding a goblet. She sauntered casually to a stack of rugs next to Gabira and sat down against the pillows, smiling at the guests.

"Hello," the young woman said, acknowledging each of them in turn. The men smiled in response, taken in by her heart-shaped face framed with large dangling earrings that glittered in tiers of golden droplets.

"Giselle," Jasper and Berkeley murmured in greeting.

Giselle was a younger version of Gabira, strong and regal in her bearing but at the same time curvy and womanly, exuding calmness and radiance. Long black hair was piled on her head, like her mother's, and her robe was an emerald green. Her long, graceful neck was encircled by an assortment of gaudy, gold necklaces. Her brown eyes were large and slanted up at the outer corners, accentuated by dark eyeliner that made them look even larger.

"How are you, Jaz?" Giselle asked.

He smiled dumbly, the blue scarf tied rakishly around his head. Cassidy watched him with disgust. Could he gape any more openly? Perhaps he could drool. But it was not just him. Torr and Berkeley were also ogling her like they'd never seen a woman before.

"Our lovely young guest, Cassidy, wonders how we came to be here," Gabira said to Giselle, avoiding Cassidy's eyes. "Will you tell her? I'm much too tired to tell her myself."

"Ah," Giselle said, sipping at her water. "I'd be happy to." She nodded at Cassidy, giving her the knowing look of another young woman. Cassidy couldn't help but smile back, fascinated by Giselle's glamorous eyes. Women were so different from men, flamboyant and colorful, making men seem drab by comparison.

"Well, it went like this," Giselle began. "Before I was born, times were peaceful. My mother," she nodded to the large woman who was perched primly on her pile of rugs, "was raised in the countryside among the olive groves. She was married off to a cousin from the city who was a wealthy merchant, my father. Mother quickly bore six children, all of them girls. I was the youngest of the six. Her seventh, thankfully, was a boy, and she vowed to stop there. However, one more child, a girl,

Daleelah, was born a year later, as accustomed as mother and father were to making babies."

The men laughed knowingly, while Cassidy shifted uncomfortably. She glanced at Torr, who was enthralled by Giselle. The dark beauty continued in her lilting voice.

"Her only son, my brother, Hasan, was killed by a landmine when he was playing out in a field. Mother didn't speak for weeks. The next year, the Near East Flu struck. Father died, as did my five older sisters, and all of Mother's aunts and uncles. Of all the children and cousins, only myself and Daleelah survived. All the gold of my father and my uncles went to Mother. Not long after, General Tegea and his army swept through the countryside, raping and pillaging as they went."

"Tell them about the olive trees," Gabira said.

"I'm getting to that," Giselle said with a hint of irritation, taking a sip from her goblet. Her toes were bare, and her nails were polished a gleaming ruby red. She wore leather sandals, and the straps framed the delicate arches of her feet. Cassidy looked at her own feet, covered in dust-caked hiking shoes.

"Mother had always loved the olive groves. So when word came that the Tegs were headed towards our town, we fled in the night with donkey carts piled high with food and crates of gold, our carpets and fine clothing. We headed out to the land of the olive groves where she had grown up, and hid the carts in the quartz caverns that dotted the hillsides. We camped out amidst her beloved olive trees, under their soft green leaves and dark black fruit."

Cassidy sipped at her water, imagining she was looking up at the sun filtering through the olive branches and pale green leaves, and breathing fresh, fragrant air. She looked at the painted walls and realized the mural was of an olive grove.

"A few days later, the Tegs came through the land and cut down all the trees for firewood while we hid deep in the quartz mines. The saddest part was that the newly felled timber wouldn't even burn, so when the Tegs moved on, we were left with bare, amputated tree limbs littering the fields. My mother was heartbroken and sobbed for days. We hid in the quartz mines with the gold and escaped detection for weeks. We almost died of dehydration, but Mother learned how to find water in caves. And we found crystals."

Gabira fingered the long crystal hanging from her neck.

"That spring, we traveled across the lands to the spaceport at Beersheba. It took us many weeks on foot, with our donkeys pulling the carts. We traveled only at night, and hid in the hills during the day. We were once approached by thieves, but Mother was able to scare them off with the strange crystals."

"With my charm and cunning," Gabira interjected, as if correcting her.

"Yes, yes," Giselle said. "She was able to scare them off with her charm and cunning. Mother bribed passage for us and her gold on a spacecraft bound for the moon. She wanted to bring the donkeys, but they would not allow it."

Jasper chuckled. "I love that part. You should have brought the donkeys, Gabira, we need donkeys on the moon."

Gabira bellowed a loud, rolling laugh. "I sure do miss those donkeys," she said.

"What happened next?" Torr asked.

"We ended up here," Gabira said in her rich voice, taking up the tale. "My daughters and I were tricked by a group of no-good men, some of whom are now in charge of mines on the outer rim. They brought us down here with our gold and belongings, saying it was a safe place, but when we got here we found they were using women for their pleasure." Cassidy held her breath and gripped the goblet. Gabira eyed Cassidy meaningfully. "I could not let my daughters suffer such a fate."

Cassidy silently agreed and held Gabira's fierce gaze.

"Yes, yes," Giselle said, a bit exasperated. "I'm telling the story. Mother could not let us suffer such a fate," Giselle continued, "so she banded the women together, and we rebelled, driving out those horrid men and securing the caverns and gold for ourselves. The men thought they had us trapped down here, with no access to water, and that we would give up quickly. They were wrong. They didn't realize Mother knew how to find water in caves.

"We blockaded ourselves in the tunnels and searched for water. We survived on the food supplies the men had left behind until we finally found a water source in the ice buried in the caverns below. That water sustained us for a few more weeks. By the time we came out of the caves, at the risk of starving to death, those men were gone."

"Where did they go?" Cassidy asked.

"When we came to the surface looking for food, all we found were the Free Men who had won control of the dome. Mother and the men entered into an agreement. Mother shelters and cares for the girls and women, and the men provide us with food and security."

"But the guys who captured you aren't in the dome anymore," Cassidy said. "There are women up top. So why do the women still need to stay down here?"

"Ah, but the camp population is mostly men, as I'm sure you've noticed," Gabira said. "Miners, construction workers, soldiers, adventurers, war refugees, gangsters, and criminals. Men who are brave or crazy enough to venture to the moon.

Beautiful women are a rare sight and a temptation to the lustful. They drive even good men insane, and bring a high price on the black market—which thrives in Peary Dome." Her thick eyebrows perched meaningfully on her forehead.

"Don't ask me why they can't keep women safe up there," Gabira said, turning her eyes to Jasper, who fidgeted on the stack of rugs. "In order to protect the women down here, men are not allowed in, and women are not allowed out. The only contact with the women is through the Ambassadors, those being myself, my daughters Giselle and Daleelah, and whomever the serving girls might be for any visit such as this."

"So the women are prisoners," Cassidy said, panic gripping her. She knew there had been something odd about the serving women. They were probably tricked into thinking it was dangerous above ground, when in reality there were women living safely up top. Gabira was spinning a web of fear for her own purposes. A paranoid delusion that she was imposing on others. Perhaps she was even trapping women with her magic.

"Torr, let's go," Cassidy said, strengthening her cloud shield and trying to feign calmness. She eyed the door, wondering if she should make a run for it. She looked stealthily at Torr, trying to catch his eye.

"Now, darling, don't be afraid," Gabira said soothingly, rubbing the crystal that hung between her breasts. It was beautiful, glinting with specks of gold that caught the light of the solar filaments. "Women who join us can leave whenever they want. Most women choose to stay. It's a decent life, a good alternative to slavery on Earth or being kidnapped from Peary and exported to another planet. It's very dangerous for women right now. Things will get better in the future, then we can return to normal life." The crystal in Gabira's fingers shimmered.

"Why didn't the serving women speak to us?" Cassidy

asked, her indignation starting to melt away. She certainly did not want to be kidnapped and exported. She relaxed against the soft pillows. It was so comfortable here. She curled both hands around the goblet and took more of the cool water into her mouth.

"They're afraid of men," Giselle answered simply. She had the most beautiful eyes. Cassidy felt warm inside; it was such a relief to be with other women. Giselle glanced playfully at Jasper, who grinned lopsidedly. Cassidy sneered at Giselle, who caught her look and twittered with a laugh that reminded Cassidy of birdsong. She couldn't help but laugh with her—two girls sharing a secret.

Cassidy pulled her eyes away from Giselle and sat up stiffly, her hands clenching the goblet, and felt for her pack with her foot. She felt disoriented, shaking her head to settle the peculiar dizziness. Giselle caught Cassidy's eyes again and smiled, reminding Cassidy of her girlfriends back home. Suddenly, Cassidy wished she and Giselle could sneak off and whisper together.

Giselle narrowed her eyes, as if she had read her mind and was scheming with her. The wind flapped gently through the tent, brushing Cassidy's hair in front of her face. She pushed a loose strand behind her ear. The breeze felt so good on such a hot day. The sun beat down onto the roof of the golden tent, and a gust of wind was accompanied by the patter of leaves. The smell of dry earth and spicy wood made Cassidy's nose scrunch up.

She looked around at the large, square tent. It was made from heavy gold brocade silk and billowed gently in the wind. The sides were rolled up halfway, letting in the breeze and a partial view of the olive grove, but kept out the worst of the afternoon sun. They lounged against colorful rugs and pillows scattered on the ground, the men entranced by Gabira's recounting of how she had found dozens of women tucked away in small rooms underground.

Giselle motioned for Cassidy to follow her, and she rose willingly from the pillows. She grabbed her pack and looped one strap over her shoulder, placed her goblet on the low brass table, and ducked under the tent wall into the green shade of the fluttering olive leaves. The sound of Gabira's voice faded away, replaced by the rustling of the wind in the trees. Cassidy breathed deeply, the air feeling good in her nose and lungs.

"Come on," Giselle whispered, taking Cassidy's hand and leading her through the trees, ducking underneath low-hanging branches. Cassidy pushed aside a twig and trotted beside Giselle, who was giggling gaily. "This is so much fun," Giselle said airily, catching Cassidy's eyes with her sparkling ones that were big and brown and shining from within.

Cassidy pulled her arm through the pack's other shoulder strap.

"You can just leave that here," Giselle said. "We'll get it later."

Cassidy placed her backpack on a tuft of parched grass, leaning it against a short, gnarled tree trunk. The olive tree had bent gray branches with dry knobs, like the knuckles of an old woman's hands, with withered fruit hanging from her fingertips. Cassidy tried to think if she needed anything from her pack, but thought not. She adjusted the blue silk scarf around her head, pushing the hair away from her face.

It was so strange; the orchard felt so familiar, yet so odd. She couldn't quite put her finger on what was wrong, but had no time to figure it out. Giselle grabbed her hand with slender fingers and tugged her along, gold bangles clinking together, and the green silk robe shimmering in the sunlight.

"Come on," Giselle said, her voice ringing through the air.

"Aren't the trees beautiful? Oh, Daleelah!" she called, "Daleelah!" Her voice sang across the treetops.

Giselle ran up to a younger woman robed in turquoise-blue silk who was gathering olives in a large basket resting on her wide hip. Daleelah's hair was gathered in a pink scarf wrapped around her head, with loose strands falling over her flushed cheeks and smooth neck. A simple gold necklace, a few gold bangle bracelets, and small gold hoop earrings were all the jewelry she wore. She had the same wide brown eyes as Giselle, only softer and quieter, and without any makeup. She stooped to put the basket on the ground and wiped her palms on her skirt, her long eyelashes lowering shyly.

"I'm Daleelah," she said, so softly that Cassidy had to strain to hear her over the clatter of dry leaves rattling on a dead branch.

"I'm Cassidy." She did not attempt to shake Daleelah's hand, for fear of startling her.

Giselle smiled brightly. "Do you want to see the well?" she asked, her eyes alight with excitement.

"Sure," Cassidy said, her mood brightening. Perhaps she'd be able to drink as much ice-cold water as she wanted, whenever she wanted.

"Daleelah, be a love and show Cassidy the ice mine, won't you?"

Daleelah's eyes met Cassidy's for a moment, then dropped to the basket of olives.

"Oh, here. Let me help you with that," Cassidy said. The basket was as big as a laundry basket and half filled with black, glistening olives. She took one handle, and Daleelah grabbed the other. Cassidy glanced over her shoulder at Giselle, who was prancing back the way they had come, waving cheerily at Cassidy.

Daleelah and Cassidy carried the basket of olives through the dry grass until they left the shelter of the trees and came upon a squat hill. Chalky banks rose nakedly above clumps of brush. The sky was a pale blue and rippled in the heat. They placed the basket on the ground, and Cassidy wiped sweat from her brow. She looked back from where they had come. A nagging feeling tugged at her, making her eyes squint.

"What's the matter?" Daleelah asked gently.

Cassidy hesitated. "I'm not sure. I think I've forgotten something, but I'm not sure what."

She had forgotten something. Someone. Where was she? She did not know, but hurried to follow Daleelah as she headed towards the base of the hill, stepping around low, dry shrubs and leaving the olive basket behind.

"Come on," Daleelah said, a hint of a smile touching her dark pink lips. The graceful young woman led Cassidy to the side of the hill where there was a dark fissure in the rock. Daleelah held out a small olive branch that had one dried leaf and a shriveled olive still clinging to it. "Hang onto this," Daleelah said. Cassidy took it, and Daleelah's intense brown eyes studied hers. "Keep it in your pocket."

Cassidy tucked it into her vest's side pocket and followed her into the cold breath of the cave entrance. She looked around, her eyes adjusting to the dimness. The cave widened out and disappeared into darkness. Daleelah lit a match, holding the flame to the stub of a white taper candle that she produced from her pocket. They walked along, misshapen shadows of themselves following as they descended into the silent rock. Cassidy held the back of her hand to her forehead. She felt hot and dizzy despite the cool tunnel, and struggled to keep up with Daleelah.

A heavy weight pulled at Cassidy's belly and she swallowed, trying to ease the disquiet. Was she hungry? Yes, but there was something else. She felt queasy and her head hurt. The shadow of Daleelah crossed in front of her as they turned a corner and headed down another long tunnel. Soon the tunnel expanded into a low-ceilinged chamber that formed a large room. At the far wall, several women huddled around a sobbing woman sitting on the ground. Scattered around the women were hammers and pickaxes they had evidently been using to widen a narrow tunnel that led away from the chamber. Rock that had been chipped away sat in small piles at the base of the wall.

Daleelah hurried to the weeping woman. She was dark-haired, like Daleelah, but her hair was long and loose, its ends lying curled on the stone floor where she was hunched over, her face in her hands. She lifted her head to reveal pale, olive skin and brown eyes that looked beseechingly up at Daleelah.

Daleelah knelt down and hugged her. "Now, now, Carmen, it's okay, it's okay." She made soothing sounds and rocked the woman back and forth.

Cassidy waited, feeling awkward, and rested her hands in the side pockets of her vest, her fingers curled around her crystals. She stepped back into the shadows of the tunnel they had just exited, wanting to give privacy to the woman who probably would not want a stranger witnessing her sorrow, whatever the cause might be.

Cassidy pulled the crystal ball from her pocket and gazed into it. Streaks of color glowed in its center. The rounded surface reflected the cave walls that flickered from several candles placed on the floor. *What had she forgotten? Something was niggling at her mind, but what was it?*

The view in the crystal ball expanded, showing her the long tunnel she and Daleelah had walked down. A long, bright cavern that Cassidy did not recall passing through was strung with garlands of solar filaments hanging from dead branches.

The cavern narrowed into another tunnel and continued with a couple of turns, and ended at a doorway into another passageway lined with several more doors. The crystal showed her the rooms behind the doors—some were storerooms, and two were bedchambers. Further down the tunnel was a small room with three brightly robed women sitting on a stone bench and talking quietly. Across the tunnel from the small room was a larger room painted gold and blue with brightly colored rugs. Three men sat across from Gabira and Giselle, laughing with the women and holding golden chalices.

Cassidy stiffened. It all came rushing back to her like a dam had opened. She backed further into the shadow and gaped into the crystal. *None of it was real. The olive grove. The air. The trees. The sun and the wind. It was all an illusion. A bewitchment.*

Cassidy turned and crept quietly over the bare rock, entering the long tunnel that was smothered in darkness. She stopped to let her eyes adjust, putting the crystal ball in her pocket and feeling for the cold wall with trembling hands. She followed slowly by touch, trying to remember the way. She should have taken a candle. The darkness was complete. She prayed to the stars that she could find her way out and closed her eyes, shaking with fear. Holding her breath, she shuffled as quickly as she dared into the blackness, running one hand along the wall, and reaching the other out in front of her.

She thought the tunnel should have taken a turn by now and she slowed down, afraid of losing her way. Panic coiled around her. The wall curved and she gratefully followed it, climbing up a sharp incline. A hint of light allowed her to discern the tunnel opening in front of her, and she inhaled a small breath of relief. She moved faster.

The tunnel opened up into a long, high-ceilinged cavern. It was not like the caves on Earth, which were moist with water dripping from shining stalactites. Instead, it was a dry vault of severe gray rock. Silver and gold speckles in the stone caught the light cast by strands of solar filaments, which hung over a lattice of branches draped over the long path.

Cassidy took out the crystal ball and peered into it, but it was cloudy and revealed nothing, not even a reflection. She clutched the crystal and trotted across the cavern floor and into another tunnel. The tunnel turned this way and that, and ended at a door that creaked open under her trembling hand. A long stone hallway stretched out before her: the same hallway she had entered from the airlock up above, the stairway faintly visible at the end. Several wooden doors stood closed on either side. She inspected the doors as she passed by, listening and searching for a large one with a brass dog doorknocker.

One door stood ajar, and leaning against the doorjamb was her backpack. A rush of anger flooded through her. That trickster, Giselle, had made her believe she was leaning her pack on a tree, when in fact she had been inside a cold, dark tunnel. Fury burned in her blood. She breathed heavily, trying to control her temper.

She grabbed her pack and pulled it onto her shoulders, and continued towards a cluster of solar filaments up ahead. The faint sound of muffled laughter reached her ears, and she ran towards a great wooden door. She pushed down the brass dog door handle and burst into the room.

Shock stopped Gabira mid-sentence, her mouth dropping open. Giselle flinched, as though a balloon had burst and startled her. Gabira's gaze was drawn to the crystal ball in Cassidy's hand, her large brown eyes widening with indignation.

Cassidy slid the crystal into her pocket and marched over to Torr, grabbed him by his vest, and dragged him to his feet, his goblet falling from his hand. It bounced on the carpet and splashed drops of water onto the red wool, leaving dark splotches. He stared at her with a dull, stunned expression. Jasper regarded her with a drunken frown. She could feel Gabira and Giselle staring intently at her back, wanting her to look at them. *Fat chance of that, you vile witches.* Instead, she met Berkeley's wide brown eyes. *Run,* he said with his eyes. No words had passed his lips, but she heard him as if he had spoken.

She dragged Torr behind her and made for the door, nearly tripping over Jasper's long legs that were stretched out in front of him.

Jasper looked confused, as though he did not recognize her. "Come on, you," she said, hoisting his pack over her shoulder. She grabbed his wrist and yanked him to his feet. "Come, Berkeley," she commanded, pushing Torr through the open doorway and pulling Jasper with her as she entered the hallway.

"Hey!" Jasper said. Then, "Cass? Cassidy? What're you doing?" He sounded as if he had just awoken from a deep slumber. Berkeley staggered to his feet and followed them, tugging at his robe.

Cassidy tuned out Gabira's voice as she screeched, "It's not safe for her up there. Jaz, bring her back here!"

Cassidy gritted her teeth and rushed down the hallway, dragging the two men with her. "Hurry, Berkeley," she called as she headed towards the stairway. Berkeley's eyes were round and glassy. He stumbled into a run and the four of them reached the foot of the stairway. Cassidy stole a glance over her shoulder as Gabira and Giselle emerged from the room, glowering after them darkly.

At the top of the long stairs, the guard jumped up from his stool. She elbowed past Torr and fumbled with the pressure lock, not sure how to open it.

"Here, let me help you with that," the guard said, reaching

his arm past her. He threw back a large red lever, then turned a metal wheel. "Didn't want to stay, huh?" he asked Cassidy, peering at her from slitted eyes. "I don't blame you. They never come out."

They entered the airlock, and there was a sucking sound when the guard broke the seal to the second door. He swung open the heavy door.

She held Jasper's cold hand and pushed Torr through the antechamber, past the two surprised guards, and out into the sun. She took in gulps of air and released the men, then trotted to the front corner of the spaceport, a confused Torr shuffling behind her. She stopped at the edge of the wide perimeter road, panting, and looked up and down the road, remembering the Scrids. The road was vacant.

Earth hung in the sky, blue and peaceful, as though it had not even noticed that she had almost disappeared from its view forever. She wished with every drop of her blood that she could go home. She set Jasper's bag on the ground and bent over, resting her hands on her knees with her head hanging, trying to dispel the fog that was lingering around the edges of her consciousness. Gabira and her daughters had nearly succeeded in keeping her hopelessly spellbound. She shivered with apprehension and looked up at Torr, who was scratching his head, distracted and perplexed, as though trying to recall a dream.

Jasper and Berkeley appeared from around the corner. "What in Hermes' name was that all about?" Jasper asked peevishly, picking his bag up. "Why did you drag us out of there so fast?" His eyes were sleepy and glazed over. So much for the protection of the wizard's apprentices. They were powerless against a little magic.

Berkeley was studying her face curiously, as though he wanted to ask her a question but couldn't remember what it was. He seemed to be the only one of the men who hadn't been completely hypnotized. She looked at him quizzically. Had he warned her to run?

"Why'd you tear out of there like the place was on fire?" Jasper insisted.

"Gabira's a witch, that's why," Cassidy snapped. "And so are her daughters."

"You knew that already," Jasper said, confronting her with his bleary eyes.

"No. I mean, she's *really* a witch," Cassidy said. She put her hands on her hips and returned Jasper's glare. "She had you guys wrapped around her fat little finger, with her sugary voice and batting eyelashes. It was sickening." She pursed her lips at Jasper and threw Berkeley an angry glance.

"What'd I do?" Berkeley asked innocently.

"And you call yourself a *wizard,*" she said scathingly to Jasper. "Didn't you see what she was doing?"

Jasper looked at her blankly.

She sucked her teeth in disgust. "Some wizard. You were defenseless against her."

"Against what?" he asked, throwing his hands up in frustration. "We were trading. Visiting. Giselle was telling us stories. You could have stayed and been polite."

She lowered her eyebrows. "I might have stayed if they had been normal. Instead, they cast a magic spell and bewitched me with olive trees and wind and sky."

Cassidy started trembling. It had felt so real. So right. She missed Earth so much, would it be so horrible to think she was back home?

Jasper scowled, and Berkeley looked at her oddly. Torr's face was blank, as though she were speaking another language.

"What's wrong?" Torr asked, turning his sleepy gray eyes to her.

"I told you. Giselle took me into an enchanted olive grove, and I met her sister, Daleelah. She took me into a cave and I nearly got lost." The men looked at one another. She went on, her voice steely, "Gabira had you guys under a spell. Her eyes, and that crystal hanging from her neck. Weren't you getting dizzy?"

"No," Torr said, shaking his head. "I thought Gabira and Giselle were nice."

Cassidy exhaled loudly. She would tell them again when they had their wits about them. Getting through to them now was like trying to saw through a board with a hammer. "Let's go back to the Fen. I'm tired." Exhausted, really, from the effort to create the cloud shield, then getting sucked into the spell regardless, like a helpless swimmer pulled by a sneaking undertow. But, she realized with a spark of excitement, she had created a shield that had helped a little bit. All on her own, with no one to help her. And the crystal ball. It had shown her the tunnels. It had cut through Grandma Leann's blanketing shield, giving her back her vision, if only for a moment. *It had broken the spell.* She curled her fingers around the smooth sphere in her pocket, and a smile cracked her lips.

"What's so funny?" Jasper asked as they headed north on the perimeter road.

"Nothing," she said, pleased with herself, and turned to Berkeley who was padding silently beside her. "Why didn't you ask about your friend Carmen?"

Berkeley's clouded face fell in confusion. "Oh. Carmen? Oh…" His mouth got round. "I don't know. I meant to ask, but I forgot. I always seem to forget." He pulled at his beard distractedly.

Cassidy searched her memory for something she was forgetting. A wave of lightheadedness made her steps falter. She let the wisps of memory go and planted her feet firmly on the ground.

"Next time," Berkeley said, rubbing his forehead.

Jasper stopped walking, and she turned to see what was the matter. "My crystal," he said, digging into his bag. "You made me leave before she could get me my crystal."

"Well, you're not getting it now," Cassidy said curtly, and pulled him by his vest to walk next to her.

————————) ————————

They cut across Spoke Road Eight, heading back to the Fen. Cassidy lengthened her strides to keep pace with the long-legged men. A man was sitting in his open tent doorway playing a flute, the breathy tune filling the air. The sound soothed her and reminded her of home. She started singing something they used to sing when they went on family trips. *"Eight for the eight bold rangers, seven for the seven stars in the sky…"*

The men joined in. Jasper's voice was deep and melodic. Torr's was also deep, and Berkeley sang in a fine, high falsetto. They strutted along as Cassidy shook off the remnants of vertigo from Gabira's enchantment. She noted that her companions' faces were still slightly flushed as though they were drunk, and their singing was a bit too boisterous.

They passed a ration station, and the men in line followed them with their eyes. Some had identified her as a female. Gabira's warnings rushed forward. Cassidy hunched her shoulders and lowered her gaze, and stopped singing. Torr and the others stopped singing as well. They left the ration station behind.

Other men on the road glanced at her but continued on their way, minding their own business. She exhaled, twinges creeping up the back of her neck.

Jasper and Berkeley traded glances, and Torr's hand went to the hilt of his combat knife. Their eyes were still glassy from Gabira's spell, and she could see them struggling to stay alert. She stole a glance over her shoulder to see if anyone was following them. No one was. They put another long block behind them. The stretch of road was quiet and empty of people.

Cassidy scanned the sides of the road as they walked, looking for any signs of trouble. Torr glanced over his shoulder and set his jaw, his cheek twitching. She forced herself forward, trying to keep her attention on the road in front of her.

A large pack of men turned onto the spoke road. Two women were cocooned in the center of the group. One woman held an infant in her arms. The other held a toddler by the hand. They were both wearing long, traditional robes, like they came from another century.

As they passed, the men followed Cassidy with their eyes, and the women looked down. The pack of men exchanged glances among themselves while Jasper grabbed her arm protectively, and Torr and Berkeley fell behind to guard the rear. Cassidy watched over her shoulder as four of the men pulled the women and children away while the others turned, and with the eyes of hunters sprang towards them.

Before she knew what was happening, she was being jostled by men who pulled Jasper away and grabbed roughly at her arms. The thud of fists on skin and grunts surrounded her as the mob swarmed Torr, Jasper, and Berkeley. They were no match against so many. Her brother and Berkeley were trying to fight them off and Jasper was thrown to the ground under flying fists and feet as she was dragged across the dust.

She struggled and screamed, but her cries went unnoticed as the clamor of fighting and yells rang through the air. Her wrists were quickly tied behind her back, and hard hands held her arms as she fought to get free. She yelled as Torr went down under a flurry of swinging clubs. Men broke away from the fight and encircled Cassidy in a larger group. Hands lowered her blue silk scarf across her eyes, while another scarf was stretched across her cheeks and shoved between her teeth. The fabric tightened across her face, tearing at the sides of her mouth, and was knotted at the back of her head. Her pulse pounded in her neck and chest, raging in her ears, her lungs straining for air. The sounds of more men surrounded her as she was hauled away, grunts and groans of the dying fight fading into the distance.

GL⊙SSARY
AND CHARACTERS

6 Creed – Short for 6mm Creedmoor.

6mm Creedmoor – A rifle cartridge. See Browning.

Algol – A trinary star system in the constellation of Perseus in which two of the stars regularly eclipse one another. Also known as Head of the Ghoul, or Demon Star.

Ali Gandoop – Brother of Ridge Gandoop. The family owns the Ridge Gandoop mine and spaceport.

Alissa – Friend of Brianna and Caden. A Shasta Shaman.

Anaximenes crater – (an-ax-IM-en-ees) A large crater in the northwest quadrant of the near side of the moon. Cassidy Dagda holds legal title to the land encompassing this crater. Forty-eight miles in diameter, one and one half miles deep.

Anaximenes G crater – (an-ax-IM-en-ees) A large crater to the northeast of Anaximenes. Torr Dagda holds legal title to the land encompassing this crater. Thirty-three miles in diameter. Approximately one mile deep.

Anaximenes H crater – (an-ax-IM-en-ees) A large crater to the north of Anaximenes. Torr Dagda holds legal title to the land encompassing this crater. Twenty-five miles in diameter. Approximately one mile deep.

Antler Kralj – The royal ruling class of planet Delos. Of Ilian origin.

Aunt Sophie – See Great-Aunt Sophie.

Baikonur – A Russian spaceport in Kazakhstan.

Balor – Friend of Brianna and Caden. A Shasta Shaman.

Balthazar, General – A former two-star Teg general. An Earthlander-Ceph half-breed.

Balty – See Balthazar, General.

Bates – A squadmate of Torr's at Miramar.

Beersheba – A spaceport in Israel.

Berkeley – A friend of Jasper's; campmate at the Fen. A seamster. Has some magical skill. Boyfriend of Carmen.

Bernie – A neighbor of the Dagdas who worked at Moffett Field.

Beth – A friend of Cassidy's on Earth.

Black Guya ink – (goiə) Magical ink from the Black Guya tree that renders plant spirit medicine diagnosis and treatment illegible until it is needed. Diagnosis and treatment, when it is revealed, varies based on the reader.

Black Guya tree – (goiə) Tree in Africa whose sap is used to make Black Guya ink.

Black Guya warrior – (goiə) The spiritual embodiment of the Black Guya tree.

Black Mare – (Singular of Black Maria.) See Black Maria.

Black Maria – (Plural of Black Mare.) The vast basalt plains on the moon formed by pooled lava. See Maria.

Blessed Fire – Star orbited by Thunder Walker and Tree Nut; primary star of the Gamma Cephei binary star system. Aka Errai.

Blue and gold book – A book of prophecies written in Ilian. Brought back from Delos by Great-Aunt Sophie. In Cassidy's possession.

Bobby – A squadmate of Torr's at Miramar.

Bone spinner woman – The spiritual embodiment of the Sweet Alyssum plant.

Boyer – Surname of family in Peary Dome; friends of Cassidy's and Torr's. Durham is the father, and Raleigh, Roanoke, and Hawk are his sons.

Boyers – (Plural of Boyer.) See Boyer.

Brent – Teg officer at Moffett Field Spaceport.

Brianna Cethlejan Dagda – Mother of Cassidy and

Torr. A shaman in her own right. A plant spirit medicine woman. Former member of the Shasta Shamans.

Browning – Long-range rifle Torr used for competitive shooting. Also referred to by its cartridge: 6mm Creedmoor (6 Creed).

Brujo – A Spanish word meaning a male sorcerer or witch doctor.

Caden Dagda – Father of Cassidy and Torr. A trader in fresh produce and other goods. An animal whisperer.

Calico Jack – Freighter that takes Cassidy and Torr to the moon.

Carmen – Ramzy's daughter. Berkeley's girlfriend.

Carnarvon – A spaceport in Western Australia.

Carpenter crater – A large crater southwest of Anaximenes.

Cassidy (Cassandra/Cassie) Cethlejan Dagda – Female Star Child. Torr's twin. A clairsentient. A clairvoyant whose sight is blocked. An apprentice plant spirit medicine woman. A history student. Daughter of Brianna and Caden.

Center Ring – A circular yard with a diameter of 300 yards, at the center of Peary Dome. The PCA and the gravity bar stand at the center of Center Ring.

Ceph – Natives of two planets in the Gamma Cephei star system (Thunder Walker and Tree Nut). Alien humanoid race very similar to people on Earth. Descendants of the

Star People. An aggressive race that has invaded Earth and is intent on turning it into a Cephean colony.

Cephean – (Noun) Language of the Cephs. (Adjective) Of the Cephs.

Cephean Federation – A federation of planets including Thunder Walker, Tree Nut, and several colonized planets in neighboring star systems. The Cephs are trying to expand their empire to other planets, including Earth.

Cephei – See Gamma Cephei.

Cethlejan – Brianna's maiden name.

Clark – Teg officer at Moffett Field Spaceport.

Concha Scrolls – Sacred texts on Turya.

Copper bit – See Global credit.

Cyclops – A Cephean terrestrial and airborne craft/weapon with a large laser dish that looks like a single eye; commonly used to raze buildings, leaving behind bare dirt.

Dagda – The family name of Cassidy and Torr.

Daleelah – Gabira's youngest daughter. A sorceress.

Dana Point – A small city on the California coast north of San Diego, known for its large marina.

Dana Point Marina – The marina where *Moon Star* was berthed.

Danny – (Danielita) Madam of a brothel in Peary Dome. Ridge Gandoop's lover.

Dashiel – Torr's Gaia United bolt-action sniper rifle. Effective range of one mile, but capable of hitting a target at up to two miles in the proper conditions.

Delos – Planet populated by humanoids very similar to those on Earth, also descendants of the Star People. Closest populated planet friendly to Earthlanders. Primary planet visited by Earth diplomats, scholars, Star Seekers, and wealthy tourists. Source of much of the knowledge of the Turyan diaspora and Star People legends and prophecies. Long ago it was a vacation spot for Ilians; Ilians fled to Delos to escape the Cephean invasion, and now control the government and economy of Delos.

Delosian – (Noun) Citizen of Delos; language of Delos. (Adjective) Of Delos.

Diaspora – The population of Turyan descendants who have settled on various planets across the Milky Way galaxy. All humanoids are part of this diaspora.

Diego – A Peary Dome ration guard. Pablo's brother.

Donald – A squadmate of Torr's at Miramar.

Douleia – A plant spirit.

Dreamcatcher – A hoop with a web of plant fiber, horsehair, or sinew, and decorated with beads and feathers. Believed to ward off bad dreams, letting only good dreams through, when hung over the bed.

Dreamwalking – An advanced form of lucid dreaming in which a dreamer enters the dream or conscious reality of another person and observes or interacts with them, or visits a remote physical location for exploration.

Skilled dreamwalkers can enter these alternate realities at will.

Druid's Mist – A magical cloud barrier protecting the Great Isles from the Tegs. See Great Isles.

Durham Boyer – Father of the Boyer family. A veteran who lost his leg in the Early Wars. Has a small family radio business in Peary Dome. See Boyer.

Eagle – A common gold coin currency worth one thousand global credits. See Global credit.

Early Wars – A series of battles in the Middle East and North Africa during 2061-2063, between those who accepted and supported the Cephean immigrants and those who did not. A global war that ended with the Jerusalem Massacre. See Jerusalem Massacre.

Earthan – (Adjective) Of Earth.

Earthlander – Native citizen of Earth.

Edgemont – A Teg whom Torr kills and later dreams about.

Errai – Star orbited by Thunder Walker and Tree Nut; primary star of the Gamma Cephei binary star system. Aka Blessed Fire.

Erlanger crater – A large, deep crater near Peary crater.

Faisal, Prince – A friend of Jasper's; campmate at the Fen.

Far side – The half of the moon that faces away from Earth.

Far side mining lords – Miners on the far side of the moon with the reputation of being unsavory characters at best, or outright criminals.

Father-Heart-of-Sky – Star Globe portal on Turya.

Fen – A compound in Peary Dome where Jasper and his friends live.

Fisorial – A stretchy, organic material from Delos used for wig making.

Free States of North America – The united territories of the North American continent comprising the former Canada, United States, and Mexico.

Fowler – A Teg officer working for Balty at Gandoop.

Frank – A friend of Jasper's; campmate at the Fen. A guitarist. Identical twin brother of Fritz.

Frick and Frack – Nicknames for Fritz and Frank.

Fritz – A friend of Jasper's; campmate at the Fen. A guitarist. Identical twin brother of Frank.

Gabira ben Najam – A sorceress who leads a women's colony in caves below Peary Spaceport. Mother of Giselle and Daleelah.

Gaia United – Rebel forces of the Free States. A collection of Free States militias that came together to resist the Teg invasion.

Gamma Cephei – A binary star system whose primary star, Errai, is orbited by planets Thunder Walker and Tree Nut. Home star system of the Cephean race.

Gandoop – Short for Ridge Gandoop mine and spaceport. Family name of Ridge, Ishmar, and Ali.

General Balthazar – See Balthazar, General.

General Tegea – See Tegea, General.

Giselle – Gabira's older daughter. A sorceress.

Glamorgan – A spaceport in southern Wales, in the Great Isles.

Global Alliance – The Earthan world government comprising countries that either willingly joined or were defeated by the Teg army. The Global Alliance is run by President Metolius and General Tegea, and backed by the Cephs. See Tegea, General. See Metolius, President.

Global credit (GC) – Official unit of currency on Earth and the moon. Gold-backed.

- Solidi = 1 million GC. Square-based, solid gold pyramid with etched spiral pattern.

- Tetra = 100,000 GC. Triangle-based, solid gold pyramid with etched wave pattern.

- Eagle (or other officially minted one-ounce gold coins) = 1,000 GCs.

- Gold bit coin = 100 GCs.

- Tenth-gold bit coin = 10 GCs.

- Silver bit coin = 1 GC.

- Copper bit coin = 1/100th GC.

Globalish – Official language of Earth, based on English.

Gold bit – See Global credit.

Golden Eagle – See Global credit.

Gordsel – A spirit herb.

Grandma Leann – Brianna's mother; Cassidy and Torr's grandmother. Former member of the early Shasta Shamans.

Gravity bar – A white stone slab or pillar imported from Scridland that provides Earth-like gravity in the surrounding area.

Great-Aunt Sophie – Grandma Leann's sister. Brianna's aunt. Cassidy and Torr's great-aunt. Former employee of the Free States State Department. Early member of the Shasta Shamans. Currently resides in the Great Isles.

Great Isles – The united territories of England, Scotland, Wales, and Ireland. Protected from the Tegs by a magical mist, the Druid's Mist. Where Great-Aunt Sophie resides.

Greenhouses – A group of large greenhouses in Peary Dome. Their primary crop is soy. They also grow assorted vegetables.

Grolsch – Teg officer at Moffett Field Spaceport.

Hawk Boyer – Youngest son of Durham Boyer. Aka Kitty Hawk. See Boyer.

Heaven's Window – A triangular symbol with three eyes inside. A symbol common on Delos and Iliad, signifying the eyes of the Star People.

Helug – A Scrid in Peary Dome.

Herbert – Captain of the *Calico Jack* freighter. See *Calico Jack*.

Hiroshi – A friend of Jasper's; campmate at the Fen. A craftsman. Son of Tatsuya.

Horehound – A spirit herb.

Iliad – Planet populated by humanoid descendants of the Star People. Iliad's once-advanced civilization has been ravaged by a thousand-year war started by a Cephean invasion. See Thousand-year war.

Ilian – (Noun) Citizen of Iliad; language of Iliad. (Adjective) Of Iliad.

Ishmar Gandoop – Father of Ridge Gandoop. The family owns Ridge Gandoop mine and spaceport.

Jacobsen's – An off-world antiquities shop in San Francisco.

Janjabar – A wigmaker on Delos.

Jared – See Metolius, President.

Jasper – Childhood friend of Cassidy and Torr who lived with them during his high school years. Four years older than Cassidy and Torr. Kai and Melanie's son. Grew up in Mt. Shasta with Cassidy and Torr, then went to the Peary Dome moon colony to be with his father.

Jaz – Nickname for Jasper.

Jenna – A female soldier at Miramar who escaped with Torr and his squadmates.

Jerusalem Massacre – A massacre of Ceph immigrants and half-breeds (including women, children, and babies) that ended the Early Wars. See Early Wars.

Jessica – A friend of Cassidy's on Earth.

Jessimar Jones – A squadmate of Torr's at Miramar.

Jidna Gandi – Ridge Gandoop's alter ego. A persona Ridge adopts when he visits Peary Dome, posing as an outer rim mining lord.

Jiuquan – A Chinese spaceport in Inner Mongolia.

Johnson – A squadmate of Torr's at Miramar.

Jorimar – A Scrid in Peary Dome.

Junior – Co-pilot of the *Calico Jack* freighter. See *Calico Jack*.

Kai – Jasper's father. A security pilot for the Peary Dome moon colony.

Kalpa – Turyan word for a period of time equivalent to one thousand Earth years.

Khaled – A friend of Jasper's; campmate at the Fen.

Korova – A Russian-made, local lunar freighter.

Kujo – Nickname for Kai.

Laris – Eldest Keeper of the Concha Scrolls, on planet Turya.

Last Chance – A small mining claim on the shores of Mare Frigoris, owned by Ridge Gandoop.

Lawrence Remo – See Remo, Lawrence.

Lectros – A Cephean handgun used by the Tegs that shoots ammunition called snake jaws. See Snake jaws.

Lieutenant James – Torr's lieutenant at Miramar.

Lingri – (Adjective) Of Lingri-La. (Noun) Inhabitants of Lingri-La; an all-female alien humanoid race. Language of Lingri-La.

Lingri-La – A planet with a small humanoid population. A female-dominated planet.

Manta – Cephean aircraft that moves like a manta ray.

Mare – (**mahr**-ey) (Singular of maria.) See Maria.

Mare Frigoris – "Cold sea." A basaltic sea formed by molten lava, south of Peary.

Maria – (**mah**-REE-ah) (Plural of mare.) From the Latin word "mare," meaning sea. The vast basaltic plains of the moon formed by volcanic eruption and molten lava. From Earth, they look like oceans.

Matthew – A Teg whom Torr kills and later dreams about.

Melanie – Jasper's mother. Kai's wife. Former Shasta Shaman. Left Earth and her family in search of a pathway to the Star People.

Metolius, President – President Metolius grew up in

Oregon in the Free States. He joined the Free States military, trained in the special forces, then left to form a private military company with contracts across the world for security services. His mercenary forces joined Russia in support of the president of Afghanistan and backed coups in several African nations, bringing the sub-Saharan continent under one military rule. His firm was then hired by the Russian government to bring the Baltic states, Poland, Belarus, the Ukraine, Romania, and Bulgaria under Russian control. Metolius combined forces with Tegea to wage a campaign to control the remainder of the globe. See Global Alliance. See Tegea, General.

Mike – A squadmate of Torr's at Miramar.

Ming-Long – A friend of Jasper's; campmate at the Fen.

Miramar – Gaia United base in Southern California, north of the city of San Diego.

Moats – Water troughs filled with plankton that line the lower border of the glass walls of Peary Dome and generate oxygen.

Moffett – Shortened form of Moffett Field.

Moffett Field – An interstellar spaceport located at the southernmost tip of San Francisco Bay in California.

Montana – Third ranking official in charge of Peary Dome, after Ramzy and Rodney. Manages the PCA, day-to-day camp operations, and ration stations.

Moon rat – An inhabitant of the moon, worn down by the harsh living conditions.

Moon Star – Yacht that Torr and Bobby steal to escape the Tegs.

Mt. Shasta – A small city at the base of Mount Shasta. Aka City of Mt. Shasta, Mt. Shasta City, or town of Mt. Shasta.

Mount Shasta – A volcanic mountain at the southern end of the Cascade mountain range in northern California. Seat of the Shasta Shamans' power.

Muria – Planet populated by humanoid descendants of the Star People. Located in the Pleiades star cluster.

Murian – (Noun) Citizen of Muria; language of Muria. (Adjective) Of Muria.

Murphy – Administrator at Ridge Gandoop facility.

Near side – The half of the moon that always faces Earth; it rotates on its axis at the same rate as it orbits Earth, with a slight libration (oscillation).

Nommos – An all-male alien humanoid race who live on floating islands on Delos. The "fish people."

Orbiter – Gaia United military standard issue pistol. SIG Sauer.

Outer rim – The lands bordering and surrounding the maria on the near side of the moon. See Maria.

Outer rim mining lords – Miners who settled on the shores of the lunar maria. The outer rim areas are poor locations for mining, so those who settle there are generally desperate or destitute and must rely on other means for survival, such as the black market, and therefore have bad reputations.

Oxygenator – An invention of Ridge Gandoop that extracts oxygen from moon soil.

Pablo – A Peary Dome ration guard. Diego's brother.

PCA – Peary Central Administration. A compound of administrative tents and storage containers in the Center Ring of Peary Dome.

Peaks of Eternal Light – A location on astronomical bodies that is always in sunlight, due to its location on one of the poles and its terrain of mountainous peaks.

Peary Central Administration – See PCA.

Peary crater – A deep crater at the north pole of the moon, portions of which are in perpetual shadow. One mile deep; fifty miles in diameter. Contains ice deposits. See Peary Lake.

Peary Dome – A moon colony built by a consortium of Earth nations on Peary Rim at the lunar north pole. Completed in 2070. A politically neutral zone. Galactic trading hub and waystation. A large geodesic dome with an interstellar spaceport. The dome houses a refugee camp and trading hub with inhabitants from various planets. One-and-a-half miles in diameter (1131 acres); population approximately 10,000.

Peary Dome Traders Guild – A guild of traders open only to lunar inhabitants.

Peary Lake – Large ice deposits in the depths of Peary crater, where the sun never shines.

Peary Rim – The mountainous rim of Peary crater at the north pole of the moon, which, because of its altitude and the libration (oscillation) of the moon, is in perpetual sunlight. See Peaks of Eternal Light.

Pegasus – An antiquities shop in San Francisco that specializes in off-world treasures.

Pensacola – A city in Florida, in the Eastern Free States. Ground zero for the Cephs' first attack on Free States soil. The city was destroyed with a single, devastating bomb.

Perimeter road – The outermost ring road at Peary Dome. Ring Road M. See Ring roads.

Pine Flower – A spirit plant.

Plato crater – A large lunar crater south of Mare Frigoris.

Pleiades – A cluster of stars in the Taurus constellation. Also known as the Seven Sisters. Muria is located in the Pleiades.

Pleiades pendant – A pendant from Iliad.

President Jared Michael Metolius – See Metolius, President.

Prince Faisal – See Faisal, Prince.

Raleigh Boyer – Oldest son of Durham Boyer. See Boyer.

Ramesh – A medical doctor from Mt. Shasta. Member of the early Shasta Shaman community. He left Earth for the moon colony in the early days of Peary Dome. Led the Peary uprising.

Ramzy – Top official in charge of Peary Dome.

Rashon – A squadmate of Torr's at Miramar.

Ration stations – Trailers where daily rations are served in Peary Dome. There are two ration trailers in Center Ring, and one at each spoke road intersection of Ring Road G.

Red herb notebook – A notebook of Brianna's, in Cassidy's possession, which contains magical plant spirit medicine diagnoses and prescriptions. Written with Black Guya ink.

Reina – A squadmate of Torr's at Miramar.

Remo, Lawrence – Leader of Shasta Shamans.

Ridge Gandoop – A spaceport and mine on the moon. Also the name of the inventor behind the success of the businesses; he owns the mine and spaceport along with his father, Ishmar, and brother, Ali.

Ring roads – Roads laid out in concentric circles at Peary Dome. Ring Road A is the outer border of Center Ring. Ring Road M is the outermost, perimeter ring road.

Rjidna Gandoop – Ridge Gandoop's given name. See Ridge Gandoop.

Roanoke Boyer – Middle son of Durham Boyer. See Boyer.

Rodney – Official under Ramzy; second in the leadership hierarchy of Peary Dome. Runs Peary Spaceport security.

Rodney's Rangers – Security guards under Rodney, responsible for Peary Spaceport security.

Rune belt – A magical belt wallet made by Berkeley, with semi-invisible properties.

San Jose – A city in California.

San Francisco – A city in California.

Santa Cruz Harbor – A small craft marina in the northern curve of Monterey Bay, Santa Cruz, California.

Schlitzer – A pimp in Peary Dome who runs one of the brothels and a bar.

Scrid – A humanoid race inhabiting planet Scridland. Members of the Turyan diaspora.

Scridland – The planet of the Scrids. Located in the Orion constellation.

Scridnu – Native language of the Scrids.

Scripps Ranch – A hilly region north of San Diego city, adjacent to Miramar base, where Gaia United troops are deployed along a portion of the Shaman's Shield, at the front lines.

Scripps Ranch company – A company of Gaia United rebels stationed at Scripps Ranch.

Scrying – Looking into a clear surface, typically water, for the purposes of remote viewing. A tool for clairvoyance. Can refer to any reflective surface, including crystal balls. Can also be used for foretelling the future or viewing events from the past.

Shaman's Shield – A defensive barrier created by the Shasta Shamans to protect against the Tegs. It is made from volcanic ash from the volcanic Cascade Range, and held together with magic. At its inception it protected the west coast of North America from San Diego to Alaska, and from several miles out to sea to central Nevada. Its walls reached five miles high and formed a protective roof enclosing the entire region from aerial attacks. It allowed in filtered sunlight, but did not allow any objects to pass through. It stopped all wireless communications inside the barrier. It shrank to protect a smaller territory from Mount Lassen and Mount Shasta in Northern California to Silverthrone Mountain in British Columbia.

Shasta – See Mt. Shasta. See Mount Shasta.

Shasta Shamans – A Star Seekers sect located in the City of Mt. Shasta and caves of Mount Shasta, California, which utilizes shamanic magic to defend against the Tegs. Creators of the Shaman's Shield.

Silver bit – See Global credit.

Silverthrone Mountain – A mountain in the Pacific Range in British Columbia, Western Free States, north-west of Vancouver, British Columbia.

Sky – A Peary Dome neighbor of Cassidy and Torr.

Smiley – A squadmate of Torr's at Miramar.

Smith gang – A group of women in Peary Dome.

Smitty – An antique dealer in San Jose.

Snake jaws – Ammunition for the Cephean handgun, Lectro.

Solidi – See Global credit.

Sophie Airmid Cethlejan – See Great-Aunt Sophie.

Spoke roads – Twelve roads that radiate from Center Ring in Peary Dome.

Star Children – Twins born every thousand years to reunite the Star People with their descendants who are scattered across galaxy.

Star Globe – Larger-than-human sized crystal globes used as portals to reach the Star People. A trine is required to connect with the Star People. There used to be one each on Delos, Muria, and Iliad, but the one on Iliad was destroyed by the Cephs.

Star People – Ancestors of human beings. From the planet Turya. Turyans.

Star Seekers – Religious cult that formed on Earth after the Cephs arrived and travel to other planets brought off-world legends to Earth. Combines various Earth religions, ancient legends, and off-world traditions that are based on the following beliefs: humans are literally children of gods who inhabit a planet in the center of the Milky Way galaxy; angelic visitations via shafts of light; gods impregnating virgins; giants descending from the sky or mountains to impregnate humans; alien saviors coming to Earth to save humanity, fight off oppressors, and infuse people with the holy spirit.

Sundance – Nickname for Torr.

Sweet Alyssum – A spirit plant.

TAFT – Gaia United standard-issue, semi-automatic assault rifle.

Tatsuya – A friend of Jasper's; campmate at the Fen. A tattoo artist. Father of Hiroshi.

Teg – A member of the Teg forces. See Tegs.

Tegea, General Djedefptah (Jed) – (tegiə) An Earthlander-Ceph half-breed revolutionary who joined forces with Metolius's mercenary armies to form the Global Alliance. Tegea commands the Global Alliance military, the Tegs, which he named after himself. He negotiated backing from the Cephs, gaining access to their superior weapons technology. See Global Alliance. See Metolius, President.

Tegs – Term that refers to the military under General Tegea, the fighting force of the Global Alliance, backed by Cephean technology. The Tegs are on a campaign to conquer Earth in order to transform it into a Cephean colony.

Teller House – A class of Ilian descendants living on Delos, the top ranks of whom serve the Antler Kralj. They are diviners, counselors, seers, advisors, scribes, historians, writers, and librarians.

Tenth-gold bit – See Global credit.

Tetra – See Global credit.

Thompson, Mr. – Neighbor of the Dagdas on Earth.

Thor – See Thunder.

Thousand-year war – A war ravaging Iliad, started by the Cephean invasion of Iliad and the destruction of Iliad's Star Globe a millennium ago. See Iliad. See Star Globe.

Thunder – Nickname for Thor. A Peary Dome neighbor of Cassidy's and Torr's.

Thunder Walker – Ruling planet of the Cephean Empire.

Timmy's Crater – Nickname for Timaeus crater, on the northern shore of Mare Frigoris.

Torr (Torrance) Brenon Dagda – Male Star Child. Cassidy's twin. A dreamwalker, necromancer, and clairsentient. Junior champion in long-range target shooting. Designated Marksman in the Gaia United forces, stationed at the southern border at Miramar. Son of Brianna and Caden.

Traders Guild – See Peary Dome Traders Guild.

Tree Nut – Cephean planet whose forests were all clear-cut, leaving it a desert planet good for only mining and metallurgy.

Turya – Home planet of humankind's ancestors, located somewhere in the center of the Milky Way galaxy. Orbits the star Uttapta.

Turyans – Humankind's ancestors, from the planet Turya. The Star People.

Uttapta – Turya's sun. See Turya.

Water scrying – See Scrying.

Wenchang – A Chinese spaceport on the South China Sea.

Western Free States – The western region of the Free States of North America, comprising Baja California, California, Nevada, Oregon, Washington, British Columbia, Yukon Territory, and Alaska.

Wimble, Michael and Kathy – Neighbors of the Dagdas on Earth.

Wolf knife – A knife forged from Ilian steel, with the image of a wolf embedded in the pommel.

Zerrin – Ridge Gandoop's mother, deceased. She was a full-blooded Ceph, and a brilliant engineer.

APPENDIX

)

HİSTORİCAL ART

Albrecht Dürer – "Northern hemisphere star map," 1515 [1]

Athanasius Kircher – "The Selenic Shadowdial or the Process of the Lunation," 1646 [2]

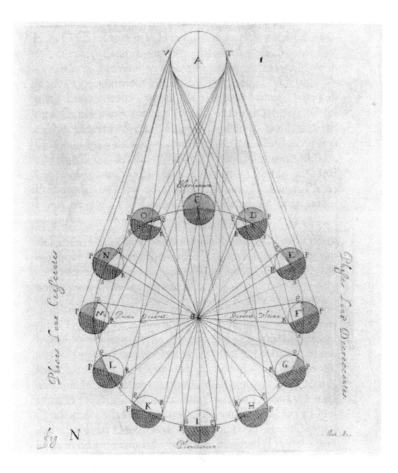

Johannis Hevelii – "Phases," 1647 [3]

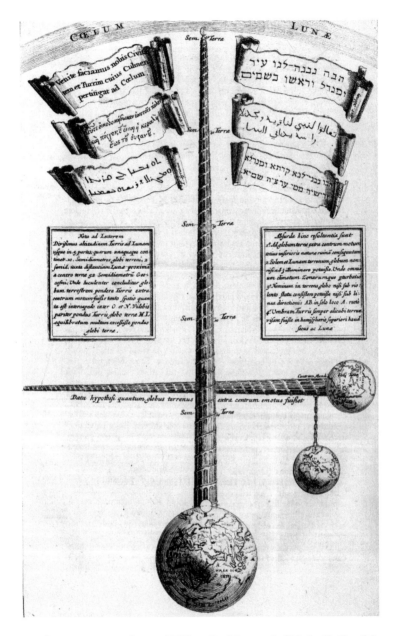

Athanasius Kircher – "Why the Tower [of Babel] Could Not Reach the Moon," 1679 [4]

Flammarion engraving, 1888

A missionary of the Middle Ages tells that he had found the point where the sky and the Earth touch ...

Sidney Hall – "Urania's Mirror – Cepheus," 1824 [5]

Johannis Hevelii – "Telescope," 1647 [3]

Thomas Stothard – "Jacob's Dream," 1791

Anne Pratt – "Gold of Pleasure, Dyer's Woad, Sweet Alyssum," 1855-1866 [6]

ATTRİBUTİ☉NS

Cover Art and Design

By J Caleb @ jcalebdesign.com

Maps

Thank you to the following Graphic Designers for their work customizing the maps in this book:

Brad Reynolds

Dennis Bolt at www.dennisbolt.com

Gretchen Dorris at www.inktobook.com

Map image sources:

"Dana Point Marina" – Dana Point Harbor Slip Map, www.danapointmarina.com

"Northwest Sector of the Near Side of the Moon" – NASA/ LRO_LROC_TEAM

"North Pole of the Moon" – NASA/GSFC/Arizona State University

"Peary Crater" – Lunar Reconnaissance Orbiter (LRO) laser altimeter data, NASA

Part One illustration

"The Earth with the Milky Way and moon," Wladyslaw Theodore Benda, 1918

Part Two illustration

"Map of the Moon," Johannis Hevelii Selenographia sive lunae descriptio, 1647. ETH-Bibliothek Zürich. RAR 8932 q

Heaven's Windows illustration

Gretchen Dorris at www.inktobook.com

APPENDIX: HISTORICAL ART ENDNOTES

1. Northern hemisphere star map by Albrecht Dürer (1515) (courtesy Art Collections of the City of Nuremberg)

2. Athanasius Kircher – Sciathericum Seleniacum Siue Lunare Expansium (The Selenic Shadowdial or the Process of the Lunation), "Ars Magna Lucis Et Umbrae" (The Great Art of Light and Darkness), 1646.

3. Johannis Hevelii Selenographia sive lunae descriptio. Hevelius, Johannes Gedani, 1647. ETH-Bibliothek Zürich. RAR 8932 q

4. Why the Tower Could Not Reach the Moon, displayed in the book *Turris Babel, Sive Archontologia Qua Primo*

Priscorum post diluvium hominum vita, mores rerumque gestarum magnitudo, Secundo Turris fabrica civitatumque exstructio, confusio linguarum, & inde gentium transmigrationis, cum principalium inde enatorum idiomatum historia, multiplici eruditione describuntur & explicantur. Amstelodami, Jansson-Waesberge 1679 by Athanasius Kircher's Principis Christiani archetypon politicum.

5. Cepheus, Reverend Richard Rouse Bloxam, 1824 By Sidney Hall – This image is available from the United States Library of Congress's Prints and Photographs division under the digital ID cph.3g10053.

6. Anne Pratt (1806-1893) from Kent, England, is one of the best known botanical illustrators of the Victorian age. This print is from the first-edition three-volume set of *The Flowering Plants of Great Britain, c. 1855-1866,* and later changed to *The Flowering Plants, Grasses and Ferns of Great Britain.*

CORRECTIONS

In the First Edition of Moon Deeds, the glossary definition for dreamwalker mistakenly used language from Llewellyn Worldwide without proper attribution. Llewellyn Worldwide has kindly granted explicit, written permission for the publication of their content in the First Edition. We apologize for this oversight. The content has since been changed. Check out www.llewellyn.com for many interesting New Age books and other cool stuff.

The Saga continues

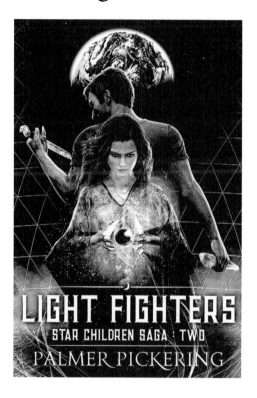

Cassidy and Torr are trying to survive in the moon colony while facing threats from all sides. The more they confront their enemies, the more they unlock their magical powers. The more power they gain, the more attractive a target they become for those who want the power for themselves.

Ridge is stuck between the sadistic Balty and the desire to control his own life. His magical gifts become entangled with those around him, pulling him between opposing forces. When his path crosses that of the Star Children, he must decide whose side he is on.

Printed in Great Britain
by Amazon

84426163R00345